W9-ATT-843

This adventure is for God,

and for everyone who remains faithful.

1

Much could have gone wrong tonight, but their escape plan had worked . . . so far. Sweet, salty air filled Philip's lungs as he pelted down a densely wooded hill so fast he feared he'd tumble on his face. Trees flashed by in the dark making him twist and turn to avoid them. The Toshinians would surely be after them, but that was fine. Philip never felt freer.

Philomena, Philip's younger sister, and Balin their uncle, followed at his heels eager to distance themselves from their captors. Twigs snapped under their boots as they ran. Fallen leaves rustled in their wake. They startled some parrots sleeping in the low branches making them squawk noisily and fly off in to the night. Philomena slipped on a slick, moss covered stone, causing Balin to nearly trip over her.

Glancing over his shoulder, Philip skidded to a stop and hurried back to help. He and Balin hefted Philomena to her feet.

"You have to wait till now to do something girly?" Philip chided breathless from running. Philomena scowled at him.

A horn cut through the night, sounding from the castle behind them with three short, startling blasts. The entire castle guard now knew they had escaped.

"Keep going," Balin said. They surged down the hill, their hearts pounding.

The stone walls surrounding the squat, clustered towers of the only castle on the small island of Tosh loomed behind them through the trees; their former prison for the past eight years. Angry shouts echoed down to them from atop the hill. The door on the northern side of the castle's wall finally banged open sending the log Balin had propped against it flying.

Guards came rushing out, their swords and armor glinting in the moonlight.

"Run them down! After them!" bellowed a guttural voice that felt like a whip at their heels urging them faster.

Philip grimaced. He recognized that angry voice. It was Nyrim, the buff captain of the guard, a man not to be trifled with. Had Nyrim spotted them racing down the hill? Philip dared not look passed his shoulder.

"Over there!" said Balin. He shoved Philip and Philomena in to the shadow of a large boulder out of the direct sight of the Toshinians. They slumped against the cool stone panting.

"Are you alright, Philomena?" asked Philip between heaving breaths.

"Fine," Philomena replied, resting her head against the boulder and closing her eyes. "Stop worrying about me. I'm just as capable as you are," she added, gripping fistfuls of her dark blue dress that was now mud stained and ripped at the hem. Her sword rested at her side, hidden in the skirts of her dress.

"I made a promise, little sister," Philip breathed, turning a grin to her. "No harm is to come to you while I'm alive and I intend to keep that promise," Philip winked.

Swallowing welling emotions, Philomena looked away to the woods that stretched before them. Scents of citrus and damp soil filled the cool night air. The trees, though thick with foliage and laden with their plump fruits, could not entirely block out the stars and moon shining bright as white gems. To any of the Toshinians, this would be a normal autumn evening, but to them it was a night to embrace. They were free.

The first time they were outside in eight years, breathing in the fresh air and hearing the chirping music of the crickets without having to strain to hear it from within the castle towers.

Philomena had always wondered what it would be like. It was all so enchanting and yet frightening, but they couldn't even savor their achieved freedom. With one step in their plan accomplished, so much more had to be done or else everything they hoped for would be lost.

Philomena listened to her brother take in one long, deep breath than another.

"We did it, Philly," Philip smiled, using her nickname.

Looking over at him Philomena could see the excitement in his steel blue eyes. No fear and no worry. It actually concerned her.

"We made it out, all thanks to you," Philip gripped Philomena's hand in his and her concern vanished. Balin was a father to her, but Philip was her rock.

"You know you can never accomplish anything without me," Philomena smirked cockily.

"Of course I know that," Philip played along.

"Quiet, before they find us," Balin hissed at them, peering around the side of the boulder to see if their enemies were near. He stepped back and turned a glare on his niece and nephew, his dark, brown eyes flashing. Even in the dark Philip and Philomena could detect the over protective, fatherly expression he wore.

"Don't worry," Philip whispered. "They can't hurt us too much. They know Salvador wants us kept alive,"

Balin snatched out a hand and gripped a fistful of the front of Philip's tunic, yanking him forward around Philomena.

"Don't underestimate Salvador like I did," Balin snapped, his voice low and his expression dark making Philip's pulse quicken. "He is a demon without a heart, without empathy, without care except for himself and his own wicked desires. Promise me you won't waste my sacrifice," Balin said.

Guilt stabbed Philip as he stared in to Balin's wild expression, remembering his uncle's selfless sacrifice.

Balin had allowed himself to be taken in to house arrest to raise Philip and Philomena and train them for this moment and for what they had to accomplish in the future. But in doing so, Balin had given up raising his own child. He didn't even know if his wife and child were well or not.

"I promise, uncle," Philip assured, covering Balin's hand that still gripped his tunic with his own. "I promise we will do everything in our strength to succeed,"

Balin's expression softened and his grip slackened from Philip's tunic. "Sometimes your reckless thoughts frighten me, Philip," he said, placing a hand on the side of Philip's face.

Philip gave him a lopsided grin. "They frighten me sometimes, too," he said.

Shaking his head, Balin lowered his hand and looked away his jaw set in a tight line. His own burden of guilt weighed heavily on his slumped shoulders. Philip stepped back next to Philomena and leaned against the boulder.

"What now?" asked Philomena, glancing between Philip and Balin eager to redirect their attention.

"We do as we planned," Balin whispered. "We make for the docks. The mainland is only a day's worth of sailing away,"

"Then what?" asked Philomena.

"One step at a time," said Balin, turning one of his rare reassuring smiles to her. "Let's just worry about getting off of Tosh first,"

"And not getting recaptured by the grumpy Toshinians," Philip put in.

"Or killed," Philomena added glumly. Philip corked his mouth upsettingly.

Suddenly, everything felt so terrifyingly real. If they did not succeed in reaching Castle Caelum on time to throw Salvador Corea off of his throne of power and free their parents, the rightful rulers of Alamia, then everything they loved would be lost.

Yes it was true; Philip and Philomena were the children of King Paul and Queen Catherine, the lost prince and princess. Sometimes it was hard for Philip to grasp this fact. He was a *prince*. A prince whose family and country were depending on him to end the depression and brewing war that Salvador had created.

These coursing thoughts made Philip clench his teeth and grip the hilt of the sword sheathed at his side. They would succeed. They had too.

"I think it's clear," Balin's voice started Philip out of his thoughts.

Balin looked to them with a readying nod. "Let's try for the docks," He shouldered the plump leather satchel filled with the food and pouches of coins they had managed to steal from the castle. Philip carried a matching satchel that was stuffed with changes of clothes that were ideal for hard travel and colder temperatures for each of them. Stealing was wrong they knew, but their situation was too dire to fret over such sins. They would remember to pay back the Toshinians after their mission was complete.

A loud shout from above made them jump and a Toshinian guard dropped before them from atop the boulder. He twisted around to face them and whipped out his sword. With a murderous battle cry he charged giving them no spare time to react. He raised his sword for an overhead blow aimed for Philomena, his eyes sparking dangerously beneath the visor of his helmet.

Philip snatched his sword from its sheath and jumped in front of Philomena, raising his blade to block the guard's blow. Their swords met with a ringing clash. The guard pushed against Philip's blade, pressing him against Philomena.

Growling, Philip shoved back. The guard's sword sliced upward as he stumbled, slashing the boulder above their heads and sending sparks flying. Philip rushed at him and attacked. The guard retreated further under the rain of Philip's blows.

Balin grabbed Philomena by the arm and pulled her closer to him far out of harm's way. Thudding footfalls reached Balin's ears drawing his attention around the boulder. His eyes widened at the sight of five more guards racing down the hill towards them with their swords drawn and flashing in the moonlight.

"Stay here," Balin ordered Philomena, unsheathing his sword.

"I can help," Philomena insisted, gripping her own sword hilt.

"No!" Balin snapped, his brows coming down like thunder clouds. He turned abruptly away before Philomena could argue and stepped out from the boulder's shadow to meet the five men. More sounds of clashing swords filled the night air.

Philomena growled in frustration and stomped her foot. Why had her uncle listened to Philip in the first place about training her to fight if he wasn't going to let her use the skills he had taught her?

Movement caught Philomena's eye and she snapped her gaze to her left as two of the guards rushed by prepared to overwhelm Philip. Slipping her sword out, Philomena surged forward and slashed her blade in a downward arc. She caught the one guard on the front of his foot and flipped him on his back where he lay bleeding and moaning. Swinging her sword around, Philomena pointed it at the second guard who slid to a stop and hesitated. Philomena detected shock and amazement in his eyes beyond his visor.

"You're a girl," he noted with disbelief, his sword arm slack at his side.

"Glad you noticed," Philomena smirked pleasurably, and then she charged.

After having regained his composure, their first attacker seemed evenly matched with Philip. They jabbed, blocked, slashed, and parried, never seeming to find an opening in the other's defense. Philip's pulse pounded urgently in his head. He could hear the clanging of the other swords in the background. He had to end the fight or else even more guards would come and they would be over run.

Spinning off of his opponent's blade, Philip faked a cut to the shoulder and in the last second redirected his sword for a jab at the guard's foot. The blade pierced through the leather of the boot and then Philip felt it bite in to flesh.

Howling in pain the guard slashed out blindly. Philip reeled back his sword pulling free of the man's foot as he did. The guard's blade swooshed an inch from his chest stirring his tunic only to knick the inside of his upper arm. Philip winced, clenching his teeth from the sudden sting on his bicep, but he did not look down. He knew it was nothing compared to the wound he inflicted on guard who now sat on the ground clutching his throbbing foot, his ruined boot covered with blood.

Pity pulled at Philip. He wouldn't kill the man as he was certain many others would. Philip didn't wish to kill anyone if he could help it. The guard was no longer a threat to them with his wounded foot anyway.

"I told you to stay out of the fighting," came Balin's very upset voice. Philip glanced over his shoulder and saw Philomena and Balin standing there, the five guards sprawled unconscious on the ground around them. Balin's glare bore in to Philomena who shrugged.

"You couldn't fight them all," she replied, sheathing her sword. Her dress had a new tear in it that split the once flawless blue gown from the thigh to the hem on the one side.

"Wow, Philly. You are as good a fighter as me or Balin in a real brawl," Philip beamed happily at his warrior sister. Philomena smiled in return.

"Don't encourage her," Balin grumbled, striding forward and glaring accusingly at Philip. "She shouldn't be holding a sword let alone slashing one around,"

Philomena huffed and rolled her eyes. Philip spread his hands innocently under his uncle's accusing stare.

"What do you hope to accomplish, boy," spat the wounded guard, regaining Philip's attention. The man still clutched his bleeding foot, and his breath was sharp from the pain as he glowered up at Philip.

"Do you think you can stop him? I've guarded you for eight

years. I know the limits of your abilities,"

"The limited abilities we just used to defeat you," Philomena snarled, storming toward the guard. Philip held up a hand and she immediately froze, but her nose still crinkled haughtily.

"You think you are a prince?" the guard laughed. "You are nothing. Those who don't know the truth of Salvador believe you are dead and your father mad with grief. They won't listen to you, they're too angry. They believe Salvador holds the key to their relief of the depression they are suffering through on the main land. They may even enjoy killing you if they find out your identities,"

"Salvador caused the depression not our father, and we're going to enlighten the people of the truth," Philip said.

"Why would they believe you? Why would they even *listen* to you? Salvador has had eight years to brainwash the entire country in to thinking he is their savior even though he is the reason they need saving in the first place and has pinned the blame on your family," said the guard. His words made Philip's hope sink, but he fought down the sudden feeling.

"What of you? What do you believe in?" Philip asked.

The guard snorted with laughter. "Tosh supports Salvador even though we know the truth of his wickedness. We have a deal. We keep his secret and help him on the throne and he gives us what your father never did: our independence."

"You had freedom under my father's reign," Philip said, his jaw tightening.

"Controlled freedom, but we want our isolation from Alamia. We need no superior king to report to," said the guard.

"You believe Salvador will give you want you want?" Philip demanded, feeling his temper rising. "Why would he allow you freedom when he wishes to take over Alamia? He won't risk you opposing him in the future,"

The guard snarled.

"Philip, that's enough," Balin said, moving forward and taking

Philip by the arm.

"If you continue to help Salvador you are only going to your deaths and sealing Alamia's fate," Philip shouted as Balin pulled him away.

"We don't care about Alamia!" the guard shouted in reply. A strip of shimmery blue fabric fell in his lap and he frowned up to see Philomena standing over him.

"Bind your foot before you die of blood loss. My brother will have nightmares if you die on his account," Philomena said, and then she turned away lengthening her stride to catch up with Philip and Balin.

*****

An hour or so later after the wounded guard had indeed removed his ruined boot and wrapped his bloody foot with the cloth Philomena had given him and his comrades had woken, they trudged back up the hill to the castle. They plucked up enough courage to report to their grumpy captain Nyrim who had bellowed in rage, threw some cups and a water jug at them, and upturned a table, his face flushing red. He had then stormed out the door, still cursing in fury, to personally bring the word to Lord Mursean.

Lord Mursean was no king. He didn't have a drop of noble blood in his veins. The lord of Tosh was merely the overseer of the island who was elected by the Toshinians, approved by the king of Alamia and expected to report to the king.

But not Mursean, a corrupt and dishonest man. He had overthrown the kind Lord Siriam by order of Salvador Corea and secured Tosh under Salvador's rule. Salvador in turn wished to take over Alamia for his own revenge due to an unfilled promise made to his grandfather by the royal family that would have elevated the name of Corea to their standards through marriage. Mursean in turn was Salvador's strong arm in Tosh and had kept his largest threat contained for him until now: Prince Philip the rightful heir to the throne he was prepared to steal.

Captain Nyrim strode down a stone-roofed bridge that connected two of the castle's towers. The bridge had arched openings on either side offering views of the stretching forest of fruit trees below and the ocean beyond that sparkled brilliantly with the gradually rising sun.

Nyrim didn't care for the beautiful scenery, and he detested the pleasant smell of the fruit trees. The aroma irritated him, especially in spring when the trees were full of blossoms. He reached the end of the bridge and entered the connecting tower where the shadows and dampness of the cool stone masked part of the constant wafting smell from the forest, which Nyrim greeted gratefully. He climbed some stone steps that danced with the light of the many torches on the wall. A few more minutes navigating through a couple corridors and stairways, Nyrim reached the door of Mursean's chambers. Paying no mind to Mursean's personal guards standing on either side of the door, Nyrim rapped his fist on the wood. A gruff voice permitted him entry.

"I'll tell you straight out, lord, that I bring a troubling report," Nyrim said as he closed the door behind him not even bothering to bow to his superior. Nyrim didn't like to bow.

Lord Mursean, sitting in his tall backed chair behind his desk, looked up from his paperwork at his captain. His light colored eyes shone with calm anticipation. The morning sunlight pouring through the arched windows to the side set the lusciously furnished chamber aglow.

"Prince Philip escaped, along with his sister and uncle," Nyrim said.

Mursean broke out laughing, making Nyrim frown and shift uncertainly.

"I don't believe this is a laughing matter," Nyrim said meanly.

"Oh, I suppose not," said Mursean, composing himself. He set down his quill and leaned back in his chair, his eyes still shining amusedly. "Have you sent word to Lord Salvador?"

"A hawk has been dispatched to Castle Caelum. My men are organizing to go after the prince as we speak," said Nyrim.

"You can call off the search," said Mursean. He stood from his chair and walked around his desk, draping his long, green cloak about his shoulders.

"Why? Are you saying that you just want to let them go?" asked Nyrim, his voice enraged. He wondered why Mursean needed to wear a cloak when his rooms were always kept comfortably warm.

"Yes," said Mursean, walking by Nyrim to a well polished narrow table. He poured himself a glass of fruit juice and gazed out the window at the lush forest.

Nyrim grunted and sniffed in disagreement as he turned to face his careless lord. "Salvador will give us our own personal hanging platforms," he said, making Mursean chuckle again.

"He just might, but that won't be anytime soon. He'll be too busy chasing his prince," said Mursean, turning around and taking a sip of his juice.

"Our purpose here is to keep Salvador's most threatening enemy from causing him grief," Nyrim pointed out, his voice tight with reluctance.

"If Salvador yearns to be king of Alamia, he should prove his worth for that position," said Mursean with a shrug.

"What if he comes to wipe us out as our punishment?" Nyrim asked, folding his well muscled arms across his chest.

"Let him come. By then we will be prepared, but concerning his most feared threat, let him decide the painful way the prince will die and save us the headache," said Mursean, saluting his captain with his glass.

Shaking his head with disgust, Nyrim unfolded his arms and stomped out of Musrean's chambers and slammed the door behind him making the guards on watch flinch.

2

Balin had managed to find them a fisherman willing to sail them to the mainland. The fisherman was an old man with wispy grey hair that reached his wrinkly arms. He had lived on Tosh his whole life and didn't give a damn who they were or why they wanted to leave the island. All he cared about was the generous fee of passage promised to him and his only other crewmember. Their boat was small with a single triangular sail that had been patched many times over. The boat itself was old and battered, but as her loving pair of fishermen assured them, had years of life left to sail.

As the old fisherman stood at the tiller directing the boat northward across the Shimmer Ocean and his friend handled the sail, Balin, Philip, and Philomena kept out of their way. They had changed their clothes before approaching the fishermen so they appeared to be normal Toshinians only they didn't bear the light colored hair and eyes and tanned skin that were the usual markers of a Toshinian.

The old fisherman probably thought they were immigrants and living on Tosh hadn't suited them, Philip thought considering the old man from where he sat on a barrel of water kept in the bow of the little boat. He watched the fisherman gulp down some rum and smack his lips happily.

Philip cocked his head and raised an eyebrow. Drinking alcohol in Tosh was frowned upon and seldom entertained especially when one was working. Maybe the old man just didn't care about anything.

A burning sensation on his bicep made Philip flinch.

"Hold still," Balin told him, who stood over him and squinted at the cut on the inside of Philip's bicep. He kept a firm hold of Philip's arm to keep him steady. Philip wasn't surprised at how strong a grip his uncle had. The man was strong in more ways than one.

Balin poured more of the clear liquid onto the cut from a small glass bottle, a tincture to clean the wound and prevent infection. The burning sensation came again, but this time Philip didn't budge.

"It's not bad, but you've earned your first battle scar," Balin murmured, wiping the excess tincture off Philip's arm with a clean rag.

"I hear girls like to admire battle scars," Philomena smirked and nudged Philip's bare shoulder teasingly. Philip flashed a grin at her, and was for the third time stunned by her new outfit. The leather overcoat that dropped nearly to her knees and was split on the sides with gold buttons gleaming on the front seemed to confirm her capability as a female warrior. She had even tied back her long, dark hair and wrapped the braid in leather to protect it. With such an enormous journey ahead, Philomena reckoned she wouldn't have much spare time to sit and idly comb her hair.

Of course Balin had disapproved as he always did when it involved his niece behaving more like a boy.

"You'll be too busy in the present time to worry about girls squealing over your scar," Balin said, rummaging through one of their satchels and producing a clean cloth from it. He used it to wrap Philip's arm to cover the scratch. "We'll need to keep this clean," he added.

"You know, it *is* just a scratch," Philip protested, but still lifted his arm so Balin could pass the cloth under it.

"Do you want to die of an infection?" Balin grumbled as he tied the bandage in place, glancing at Philip as he did.

"Fine, fine, I surrender, *mom*," Philip laughed, emphasizing the last word jokingly. It made the corners of Balin's mouth twitch, the faintest hint of a grin.

Gazing out at the vast ocean rolling with waves rocking their little vessel closer to the mainland, Philip savored the salty scent the ocean offered. The sight of the wide open sky was magnificent with white clouds skidding across. No walls, no guards, no one to stop them from marching all the way to Castle Caelum to toss Salvador in to his well earned prison cell.

"So," Balin's voice started Philip out of his thoughts. "Since we accomplished our escape, what are your plans when we reach the mainland?" Balin casually leaned against the railing of the boat and crossed his arms fixing a quiet, expectant look on Philip.

Accepting his white under tunic back from Philomena, Philip considered the most logical strategy. "Salvador will soon learn of our escape," he mused, slipping off the water barrel and pulling his tunic on over his head.

Balin nodded. "He'll send out a posse to bring you to Caelum," he said.

"So we need to reach Caelum on our terms," Philip said determinedly, tying the neck of his tunic closed. A fist punched him hard on the arm making him stagger. He swung an irritable frown on Philomena.

"Maybe you two loudmouths should keep it down about our *plans*," Philomena glared at them and then flicked her eyes to the fishermen controlling the boat.

"Oh, they don't care, Philomena," Philip grumbled, rubbing his arm. He was just glad she hadn't punched the arm that had been cut.

"He's right, they don't care. That's why I chose them. Even if they did care, word of our escape will travel fast enough and I don't believe either of you are hiding from your fate," Balin assured. Philomena looked to him, her expression reluctant. Balin held her gaze steadily, the light of the sun shining in his brown eyes and on his handsome face, the breeze blowing his dark hair about his jaw line.

"You could keep it down a bit though," Philomena argued. The boat suddenly reared on a more aggressive wave and then tipped downward, slicing in to the trough. The old fisherman hooted joyfully by the sensational movement of the wave. His friend laughed heartily as well and Philip joined in with their delight. But for Philomena the rising and falling sensation made her stomach heave and her face turn a light shade of green. She reached out a hand to steady herself and Balin offered his arm. She gripped it gratefully, fighting the urge to vomit.

"As we were saying," Balin continued their discussion. "We need to have a plan for when we reach the mainland. Time is critical and we need to be organized. Now is as good a time as any to be sure we know what we're doing," he said.

"The fishermen are dropping us off at a port called Seshrik?" Philip asked and Balin nodded. Musing, Philip slipped into his leather jerkin. He knew their disadvantage would be inexperience and lack of knowledge of geography. Balin would be their anchor for the mission, but being the lord of Woodrid Realm and first brother to the king, even he wouldn't know how to navigate entirely.

"Let's see the map," Philip said, tugging the laces on the front of his jerkin snuggly before tying them secure at the neck.

Balin brought out the map from one of their satchels and they flattened it out on the top of the water barrel Philip had been sitting on. They leaned over the yellowed map, a hand on either side to keep it from being snatched by the breeze.

"Here's Seshrik," Philip murmured, tapping the name scribbled over a dot that marked the port on the edge of the smooth coast. Philip chewed his nail thoughtfully as he studied the map.

"From Seshrik we should travel to the nearest town from there which would be this one here," Balin pointed to another dot on the map a little bit above Seshrik. "Which is Niche. It's a small traveler's town. From there we can go to the city of Ezleon which is just before the Staleveerian and Lacemorian border," he said.

"Shouldn't we avoid the towns and cities?" Philomena put in having regained her composure.

"If we can yes, but we'll need supplies. From Ezleon we'll be crossing the Twin Peak Mountains," said Balin, tracing his finger from the city of Ezleon across the Ember River, to the forests and mountains of Twin Peak till his finger hit the edge of the map.

"And there we run out of map," Philip noted.

"Salvador possibly made it where maps sold and used amongst the locals have little knowledge of the north," Balin said, his voice low.

"Maybe we can find a larger map, one that shows the north," Philip suggested, glancing at Balin.

"Maybe," Balin shrugged doubtfully.

"On a smaller note, I believe we should use Seshrik to prepare for our journey," Philip said with a sigh. He straightened and folded the map, stowing it away.

"Logical," Balin agreed.

"We'll need more food, and horses," Philip said. He caught Philomena's brow pinch at the thought of riding horses. They hadn't ridden a horse in years. Philomena wondered if they'd fall off a couple times before getting use to it again.

"And another thing, I think we should keep our identities to ourselves," Philip added. Balin and Philomena offered no protests.

When the morning had passed and the evening slowly crept towards them with a rich orange and pink sunset that set the Shimmer Ocean on fire, the coast line of Alamia on the northern horizon appeared as a grey-green line.

"There she be, boys," said the old fishermen, gripping the tiller.

"And lady," his friend added with a sweeping bow to Philomena.

Balin, Philip, and Philomena all stared entranced at the line of land that was slowly growing larger, the land that was their home.

"Wow," Philip beamed his face lighting up. "It's amazing!" he exclaimed wrapping an arm around Philomena's shoulders. Philomena was speechless and she blinked rapidly to fight back tears.

Balin seemed just as thrilled but he was silent. A stone of bitter sweetness had set in his eyes and he gripped the boat's railing as though his legs were weak.

"Port Seshrik is just ahead about an hour away. Our little journey will soon be over," said the old fisherman. He gulped down more rum and handed the bottle to his friend to share.

Maybe the journey was over for the fishermen, but it was far from finished for them, Philip thought to himself.

"I'll get the passage fee together," said Balin. He bent down to their satchels, pulled out a pouch of coins and started to count out the agreed amount.

"It's so much bigger than it is on the map," Philip wondered aloud, gazing out at Alamia.

Philomena couldn't help but laugh, yet her shoulders shook under Philip's arm and a tear streaked down her cheek. Philip brushed it way with his thumb.

"We'll be with them again, Philly." Philip whispered.

He didn't have to explain. Philomena knew what he was talking about. A desperate longing tugged at her making her heart ache. She hoped he was right. She hoped that against all the odds that months from now they'd be in Caelum reunited with their parents, laughing together and sharing old memories.

Her hopes were so strong, Philip could nearly feel them vibrating under his arm he had wrapped around her. He shared her hopes. There was nothing more he wanted then to see their parents again, but he also wanted to see Balin back with his family too. Their uncle had sacrificed so much, Philip was willing to put aside his own happiness if it meant that Balin could be with his family and meet the child he had never gotten the chance to even see before.

With a deep sigh, Philip assured himself he'd set things right no matter the cost for himself, and this was something he vowed never to tell Philomena while on their journey. He gripped the wooden cross that hung about his neck, the last thing his father had given him. He didn't want her to worry, or argue against him.

Port Seshrik was loud and boisterous, full of movement and color. They could see the stream of people flowing along the roads near the water. Differing ships were tied at the many docks that stretched out to the Shimmer Ocean, creating a forest of masts. Houses and shops, inns and taverns built of stone and wood rose beyond the docks. Dark blue pennants flapped on their poles on the docks, and a larger square flag with a white wolf and cross crest waved on a higher pole.

"It seems so . . . unaffected by the depression," Philip commented.

"Nah, it has been affected, boy," the old fisherman chuckled. "This place is hardly a quarter busy of what it used to be. Ships had to lay anchor for hours out here to wait for a dock to open so they could unload their cargo. Where have you been for the past eight years?"

"Living on Tosh," Balin said dryly, gazing sidelong at Philip.

The little fishing boat bobbed along towards the port city. As they came closer to the docks they noticed that the majority of the ships were fast, sleek vessels from Tosh. Their crews unloaded crates of fruit, bottles of fruit juice, and sacks of coffee beans. Only a few of the ships were foreign, the strange structures and decorative designs of the hulls alien but beautiful. They finally came to a stop at an open dock, the boat suddenly creaking as if letting out a sigh of relief to be able to rest. Grabbing a rope, Philip jumped to the dock to help the old fisherman, tying the boat secure. The other fisherman laid down a plank connecting the boat to the dock. Philip walked carefully across it to help with their satchels.

"Twenty gold pieces as promised," said Balin, handing the pouch of coins to the old fisherman. The old man snatched it away and quickly loosened the drawstring to peer inside, his eyes widening greedily.

"Do you need to count it?" Balin prompted after a moment. The fisherman jerked out of his trance and looked around at Balin. "No, no, it looks good to me," he said.

Corking his mouth, Balin narrowed his eyes on the old fisherman, disappointed to see the greed there. "Thank you for your help," Balin hefted the satchel slung over his shoulder.

"Yes, yes, you're welcome," the old fisherman murmured, peeking in at the coins again. But Balin had already turned away and was walking across the plank to the dock with Philip and Philomena following.

Entering the wide paths of the streets of Seshrik, Balin, Philip, and Philomena were able to procure directions to the stables where they hoped they could buy their horses. As they wound their way through the bustling crowds of the chaotic streets, Philip and Philomena were in awe at the sights they soaked in. To their right, the street was lined with market stalls and shacks selling an array of goods. Jewelry sparkled in the evening sun, bright clothes flapped on their wracks in the breeze, and the inviting smell of fresh bread filled the air. The vendors and merchants called out to the people in hopes to draw their attention.

On the docks, a crewmember tripped and the crate of fruit he was carrying fell and burst open with a crack. The plump orange fruit, which looked like apricots splattered or rolled across the dock. Several screeches sounded out in response to the clatter and a whoosh of wings passed over head. Philip and Philomena gawked as a flock of what looked like bright blue and yellow splattered four legged birds attacked the fruit.

The crewmember shouted at the bird like creatures and waved

his arms to shoo them away. The creatures screeched and jumped off the dock, plunging in to the water with several splashes. But they had already eaten all the fruit, making the crewmember curse angrily.

On the street they were traveling there was a trio of young men dancing to rapid drum beats on a small three tiered podium. The bells on their bright, red colored outfits jingled with their movements. The dancer on the top pier called out enthusiastically to the passersby.

"Come on people! You don't see moves like these at home! Throw us a coin! We need to eat too!" he called his accented voice cheerful.

A man did throw them a coin which one of them caught with a joyful bark of laughter and went on dancing. The man's wife though slapped his hand and scowled at him.

"Hey friend! Is that your wife? Don't let her treat you like that! She made you wear that outfit too huh? She made you so the other ladies won't stare at you!" shouted out the head dancer and all three of them burst out laughing, but didn't miss a beat. The man laughed too, but his wife huffed angrily and pulled him away.

The head dancer continued his hilarious addressing of the crowd. "Beautiful lady! I hope that young man next to you is not your husband!" he cried out when he spotted Philip and Philomena. Philip laughed and shook his head while Philomena frowned at the dancers. They kept going following Balin as he navigated their way to the stables.

"Wait! Come back! I love you! I can be house trained!" the head dancer called after Philomena.

It irritated Philomena and she pressed her lips together to suppress a smart remark. Next to her Philip chuckled some more but quieted when she elbowed him in the ribs. They turned right onto a side street.

Not all of the sights that held them in awe were good. Beggars slouched in corners, filthy and starving and pleading for alms. A poor man was chased away from a food cart by some soldiers having tried to bargain for some food but with no luck. A poor family was desperately trying to patch the roof of their home with some canvas that tore when one of them slipped on the shingles. Seeing these things filled them with longing to help the poor people and hatred for Salvador, the tyrant who had caused it all.

"These people need help, uncle," Philomena whispered, coming alongside Balin. She watched a group of children garbed in dirty rags, their innocent faces smeared with dirt, racing from one person to another for money.

"Yes they do," Balin agreed sadly. He looked down to Philomena as they shouldered passed some robed merchants. "And we'll help them by setting things right again,"

The children ran up to them then and the one in front, a boy no more than seven with a mass of dark curly hair and large pleading brown eyes, held out his hands to Balin.

Smiling, Balin untied the coin pouch on his belt. Placing a hand on the top of the boy's head, Balin gave him eight coins, one for each of the eight children that were there. The boy's eyes widened and he thanked Balin. The children raced off once more, their voices excited.

Tying the coin pouch back to his belt, Balin looked to Philip and Philomena who both wore approving smiles towards him.

"I think it's this way," said Balin, pointing to another road that branched off to their right.

They went down it weaving around hurrying travelers and townsmen alike. More than a few taverns and three storied inns lined both sides of this road. A few groups of people stood before the buildings chatting with one another. Laughter, arguing, and general conversation whirled around them. A rattling cart filled with barrels pulled by a pair of draft horses parted the crowds. Balin, Philip, and Philomena stepped to the side as the cart rolled by. They passed a group of girls dressed in flowing, colorful pants and tops that didn't cover their slim stomachs.

"Hello handsome," one of them said in a velvety voice, catching Philip by the arm.

"Ugh, hi," Philip stuttered uncertainly. The other girls circled around him, giggling excitedly.

"Balin," Philomena spoke tapping Balin on the arm when she noticed what was going on. Balin looked back and shook his head in disgust.

"You look awfully lonely," cooed one of the girls stroking Philip's arm. Their touch made him jumpy.

"I'm not lonely," Philip assured his voice rising in pitch. He wanted very much to break away from the girls but did not want to be rude.

"Perhaps you don't realize how lonely you really are," said one of them at his shoulder, stroking a finger along his jaw line. Philip lifted his eyebrows, his eyes widening.

"Maybe one of us could provide you company," purred another on his opposite side.

"No, no, I'm fine. Besides I need to leave and I wouldn't want to keep you from . . . whatever it is you do," Philip said, his voice tight with nerves. The girls exploded with laughter and pressed even closer to him.

"You're adorable!" one of them squealed.

"You just have to pick one of us, handsome, and give us a fair price," said another.

"Price? For what?" Philip frowned, glancing to either side.

"Get away from him!" Philomena snarled, shoving through some of the girls making them stumble. Relief poured over Philip at the sight of her storming towards him.

"Jealous girlfriend?" questioned the girl clutching Philip's arm, looking Philomena up and down. But Philip couldn't find his voice to respond.

"I'm his sister, now back off," Philomena demanded her eyes flashing in warning. Some of the girls flinched away but most lingered.

"Alright, ladies, get out of here. Get lost," Balin said, marching over. His muscular, commanding stature made the girls break away from Philip and cluster back to their spot on the side of the road. They chatted like a flock of upset parrots.

"Thanks," Philip breathed, his eyes wide. He brushed himself off and straightened his jerkin. "What was that all about?" he asked, glancing over at the group of girls.

"Prostitutes," Balin replied in a disgusted tone. He turned on his heel to continue to the stables.

Philip raised his eyebrows and exchanged shocked looks with Philomena. Eagerly they hurried after their uncle.

Mud puddles and oozy smells that made them think of the color brown greeted them when they finally found the stables. It was a small stable with peeling paint and loose siding. A breezeway cut through the center between the twenty stalls, though it did little to help the smell and they wrinkled their noses as they entered.

A short skinny man with dark matted hair wearing a coat two sizes too large reluctantly came over to assist them.

"What can I do for you?" the man asked with a bored sigh.

"Um, well, we're looking to buy three horses," Balin replied instantly sensing the man's lack of willingness to help.

"Sorry, all out," the man said dully. He sauntered off with a careless air. Chewing at his lip, Balin frowned after him. Philip came beside him and Balin looked to him.

"I don't know about you but I'm not walking all the way to Niche," Philip said in a matter of fact tone. Balin flashed a grin at him.

"Why don't you two go get the supplies we need. I'll wear this guy down," said Balin his gaze resting at the skinny stable master. Philip nodded and started to leave. "And stay together,"

Balin called after Philip as an afterthought.

Philip casted a smirk over his shoulder. "No worries," he assured. He and Philomena left the stables, sliding to the far side to avoid the many mud puddles.

Sighing, and suppressing a small rising agitation to have let Philip and Philomena leave his side for the first time in eight years, Balin focused in on the rude stable master and strode over to him.

By the time Philip and Philomena returned with parcels of food, supplies, and a winter coat for each of them, Balin had purchased the horses, three stallions which were the only horses available. It had taken Balin some very good negotiating to convince the stable master to sell them the horses with full sets of tack. It was uncovered that the stable master's reluctance was due to the fact that the stallions were his own and he had wished to start a breeding operation since there was a lack of horses in Seshrik. Only when Balin had offered more than a fair price did the stable master give in.

Balin had signed the three deeds of sale with the name Bazin Stone, remembering Philip's insistence that they travel incognito. A stable hand helped them saddle the stallions and pack their things into the saddlebags behind the saddles. The stable master watched them, his mouth tight lipped and a glimmer of regret in his eyes. He stroked each stallion good-bye and told them their names and to take care of them. The black stallion was Nimbius, who Philip decided to ride. Philomena paired herself to the dappled grey named Coursio, and Balin took the chestnut the stable master called Laefin.

By the time they were on their way, riding through the streets on their new steeds, it was night and the dark sky glittered with stars. Philomena was thankful they didn't fall off the horses at all as they grew accustomed to the saddle again. Really, riding was a familiar feeling.

They galloped across the grassy fields that stretched beyond

Seshrik, and stopped a moment for Balin to use their new compass to be sure they were headed north.

"It will be a near ten day journey to Niche," Balin said, squinting at the dial on the compass in his palm. He pocketed the little device.

A thrill of excitement filled them as they gave the city one last look before urging their stallions forward once more. They were headed to Caelum, and each stride of their horses brought them closer to their family, closer to Salvador and bringing his rampage of revenge to an end.

3

Salvador Corea was in the king's study room, which he had claimed as his shortly after his siege of Castle Caelum. Over the years, Salvador had enjoyed tearing away the things that King Paul cherished, right down to the tiniest of treasures. The only thing that King Paul still had was the clothes on his back and the air that filled his lungs. Salvador knew he could not kill the king, not yet.

Salvador now awaited the king's arrival in the study, the place where he had clasped his greedy hold on Caelum and Alamia. Salvador always grinned at the fond memory; yet presently he was not in the mood to reminisce. He stood behind the king's majestic desk, rummaging through the disorganized piles of documents with an agitated energy, muttering angrily under his breath. An unkempt collection of inkwells and quills added to the cluster.

The desk though was not the only thing suffering from Salvador's untidiness. The entire study had been cast into a gloomy state. Several of the old, yellowed scrolls hung half unrolled from the bookshelves, as if someone had been hurriedly searching through them and had carelessly attempted to return them to their original places. Wax dripped from the candles incased in their glass orbs along the bookshelves and gathered on the stone floor where it gradually dried. The armchairs situated close about the desk had faded in color and appeared frail. Dust was rapidly accumulating on everything. The eight years of being under Salvador's care had destroyed the great study room, leaving only a shadow of what it had been.

Though the eight year siege had not been kind to Salvador either;

his thin face was pale and sunken in, so his dark eyes gleamed menacingly beneath heavy brows. His long auburn hair had grown another three inches or so, and was tied tightly back away from his face. The area between his eyebrows above his nose was permanently pinched from constant expressions of rage. His dark and snug clothing reflected his stained and conceited spirit. Salvador suddenly cursed viciously and smacked the closest inkwell from the desk. It broke against the stone floor with a surprisingly loud smash. Black ink and glittering fragments of glass scattered across the floor.

A young man sitting in one of the armchairs with one leg propped over the arm rest looked up with little surprise at Salvador's violent outburst. He glanced at the broken inkwell and splattered ink with little care. With an intake of breath, he turned his attention back to perfecting the finer tones of his long, double-edged knife which he gripped in his hand. He could have been no more than fifteen or sixteen years old. His black glossy hair swept over his forehead and dropped to his muscular shoulders. His eyes were as dark as Salvador's, but his jaw was squarer.

Salvador rotated a disgusted sneer on the boy, his yellow teeth clenched, and his dark eyes wild.

The door just then banged open and King Paul staggered in with clinking chains dangling from his wrists and two armored guards escorting him on either side. Salvador looked up at King Paul with a wicked smirk.

"Ah, well if it is not the great King Paul come to join me in my study," Salvador said sarcastically, easing into his chair and lacing his long, pale fingers together.

Paul aimed a smoldering, hate-filled glare at Salvador, his jaw tense with anger. Just as Salvador, King Paul appeared older than what he was. His handsome face expressed his exhaustion, and the malnutrition of the past eight years. His wavy brown hair went to his shoulders and hung in his face, tangled from not being tended to. His dark brown eyes that once were filled with such warmth now reflected only pain and hatred. The beard that grew about his chin and mouth was unkempt. His clothes were filthy and torn from being in the dungeons. Yet despite his poor health and worn appearance, Paul still held himself with the strength and dignity of a leader.

"What twisted play do you have up your sleeve this time, Salvador?" Paul asked in a grinding voice.

"Trust me," Salvador said with a savoring grin. "You're going to *love* it,"

Paul narrowed his eyes viciously, a thousand fears and possibilities flying through his mind. Salvador turned a harsh stare on the two guards who were gripping Paul's arms. The two men wore the sharp black armor that bore Salvador's insignia of a coiled serpent about to engulf a white rose emblazoned on their breast plates.

"Get out," Salvador commanded them flatly.

The two guards looked uncertainly at one another, but did not hesitate any longer in obeying Salvador's order. They stepped away from Paul, bowed devotedly to Salvador, and then departed, the door thudding gently behind them.

The young man lounging in the armchair beside the desk rose to leave as well, sheathing his knife as he started forward.

"You stay, Avador," Salvador said to him.

Avador hesitated, looking uncertainly over at Salvador. "Father, I really think-"

"I SAID STAY HERE!" Salvador thundered, his hands slamming down on the armrests of his chair. Avador merely sighed and returned to his armchair.

Paul watched the interaction with a mean interest, his sharp eyes following Avador till he found his seat again. "You seem deeply perturbed, Salvador," Paul said. "I've never seen your pale countenance so colored."

Salvador scowled. "If I did not have use for your tongue I would have cut it out myself a long time ago,"

Paul glared at him with little surprise.

"Now," Salvador began flatly, leaning back in his chair and lacing his fingers together once more. "Where are your children?"

Paul stared with confusion. The unexpected question felt like a powerful gust of wind stealing his composure. His heart was beginning to thud as it always did at the mention of his children. "What do you mean?" he finally asked, nearly stumbling over his words.

"What I mean is that my commander in Tosh has reported them missing from his city. Apparently, your children as well as your brother were clever enough to escape their prison and are now nowhere to be found on the island." Salvador said irritably. "So, I want to know . . . where are they now?" Salvador questioned forcefully in a cold voice.

Paul's face pinched with overwhelming emotions he attempted to control. "I don't know where they are," he said huskily.

Salvador bared his teeth, and leaned forward in his chair. "Are you aware of the implication you are making? Do you even remember the deal I made with your brother?"

Paul's eyes narrowed in consideration. "You no longer wish to keep to the terms of our agreement, under the circumstances that have arisen," he guessed angrily, not at all surprised.

"Not entirely," Salvador said, wrinkling his nose with annoyance. "Avador still needs to prove his worth and earn his title as prince in a duel against your son, but there's still the little problem of his convenient disappearance,"

"I already told you," Paul grinded out, beginning to feel fearful. "I had no idea of their escape,"

"Whether you did or didn't, it's still a problem," Salvador grumbled irritably. "I'm sending Avador and his men out to regain them. They'll bring them here, alive, and whether your son is ready or not, he's going in the fighting ring to face his fate,"

Paul's countenance wrinkled with rage. "I suppose I should not be surprised if you make it an unfair fight,"

Salvador cackled. "It'll be as fair as I'm capable of being. I can assure you that he'll be provided with a sword," he said with a grin, exposing his yellowed teeth.

"That's comforting," Paul growled with hollow sarcasm, his fear deepening.

Salvador glowered at him. "You should be relieved by such a comfort. Prince Philip, your son, is my greatest enemy, greater even than you. You're lucky that I'm going to allow him to enter this castle alive. My son will bring your children here, and we're going to settle this,"

Paul glared at him. "You'll never catch them. And even if you do, the people of Alamia will never accept you as their king,"

Salvador laughed, and spoke with heavy arrogance. "You forget too easily don't you? Remember that we have established your insanity to the people, and the fact that I am your only heir. You've helped me greatly, Paul. To the people of Alamia, I am a saint."

Paul's face fell with dread as his tired mind remembered. He felt his entire soul begin to sink with hopelessness from Salvador's words.

Avador watched uneasily sitting at the edge of his seat. His smooth face twitched with pity as he saw Paul's spirits crumble before his eyes. Salvador looked on at Paul with a proud sense of satisfaction.

"Get him out of here!" Salvador shouted to the guards who he knew were standing just outside the door.

They entered the study obediently, and without a word lead the defeated Paul away.

Salvador let out an irritable pent up breath when the guards left with Paul. He reclined in his chair lazily.

Avador stood from his seat and looked upon his father with an uncertain and almost fearful expression as he mulled over his opening words.

"Shall I leave in the morning?" he asked.

His father turned a furious look on him, his eyes boiling.

Avador's heart hammered with terror. He fought to retain a calm demeanor.

Salvador looked away from Avador with disgust, wrinkling his nose as if he might smell his son's nervousness. "No, you'll leave now," he said.

"Now?" Avador questioned, feeling sick with anxiety. "My men and I are not ready to travel such a distance now."

"Well then get ready," Salvador said meanly. He put his index finger to his temple as though he might have a headache. "I certainly hope you can pull your sorry self together before you truly become the prince," Salvador added dryly, glancing sideways over at his son. Avador glanced about nervously, feeling his father's pressuring gaze drilling into him. He opened and shut his mouth a few times, unsure of what to say. He balled his sweaty hands into fists, determined to hold his ground.

"What is the plan after we bring back the prince and princess if we mean to bring them back alive?" Avador managed to ask steadily.

Salvador's lips curled into a cruel grin. "We'll make a sport of it," he said, his eyes widening with his pleasurable thoughts.

Avador's features twisted with obvious reluctance. "You really do mean to kill them then?"

"Of course," Salvador said in a growling voice. "The prince at least; the princess on the other hand is a bit more of a complex and delicate situation," he said musingly.

"What do you mean?" Avador frowned, confused. "Do you intend to keep her for further *sport*?"

"That's one way of putting it," Salvador said with an agreeable smile. He straightened in his chair and crossed his arms on his desk as his vile mind rolled around his horrid ideas.

"Killing the prince will be easy. Anyone would expect a death to occur during a duel between two young men. We'll easily be able to smooth over his death with the people. The princess though we will not be able to deal with as brutally. She is descended of the Stilwell's' but she also carries the blood of the Leonard's'. Her blood is of the ancient ancestry. It is golden, and should not be spilt if we can help it,"

"Do you know what to do with her then?" asked Avador somewhat baffled.

"It's coming to mind," Salvador said quietly with a pleasurable smile touching his lips. The excitement in his voice made Avador's skin crawl. "For now, let us concentrate our attention on bringing them both back here alive,"

Avador dipped his head in recognition. "I will leave to prepare my men for the journey," he said, bowing stiffly and moving towards the door to leave.

Salvador's narrowing eyes followed him, surfacing out of his malicious thoughts and remembering his intolerance for his son. "Don't forget that the prince has a scar you can identify him by, remember?"

"Yes, I remember," Avador said, stopping before the door.

"Where do you plan on searching for them?" Salvador asked testily.

"They escaped from Tosh, did they not?" Avador said without turning around. "We will first search in Niche, and then move on to Ezleon,"

Salvador crinkled his nose. "I hope that band of savages you call your men are fit for this task, because all of you will regret it if you fail me," Salvador said coolly.

"Was it not you who first used these *savages* to gain control over Caelum?" Avador said levelly. Salvador scowled menacingly at Avador.

"We will not fail, father," Avador said.

"You best not if you dare to talk back to me like that," Salvador growled lowly, sniffing disdainfully and averting his smoldering eyes away from Avador.

Avador said nothing. He opened the door and departed to gather his men.

After he left, a dark figure shifted in the shadows between the bookshelves. Salvador flicked his eyes to the figure.

"Are you sure you can depend on that boy with such an important task?" the figure drawled.

Salvador leaned back in his chair and flexed his jaw. "No, and I will not,"

The figure shifted again and materialized out of the shadows.

The man stepped before Salvador, dressed in black and blood red with a short sword sheathed across his back. His shoulder length smoky grey hair dangled before his smooth face and malevolent bright eyes. A scabby cut ran from the corner of his mouth and dropped underneath his chin, twitching as he corked his mouth curiously.

"What are you thinking?" he asked coolly.

"I need someone to trail Avador undetected to be sure that what has to be done is done if he can't accomplish it," said Salvador. The two men met each other's gazes and an understanding passed between them bringing them to the same conclusion.

"I'll leave immediately," said the man.

"I expected nothing less from you," Salvador said satisfactorily. "Everything depends on you now, Kufenti. Don't let me down,"

"You will have your success, my king," bowed Kufenti.

"And you shall be rewarded in your return," Salvador grinned icily.

*****

Tears streamed down Queen Catherine's pale cheeks as she cradled reminders of a happier past. The doll with a friendly smile, pearl button eyes and pink satin dress was her little girl's best friend, and the pale blue cloak was her little boy's most cherished possession. The toddler princess had received the doll from a friendly village woman on her third birthday. The young prince had been given his cloak by his father on the day he had ridden his first horse on his own.

Such vivid and happy memories made Catherine's heart ache with grief and emptiness. She knew now that her little girl, Philomena, was no longer a child but a young woman, and her son, Philip, a young man. It had been eight years since Catherine had last seen her children. She had missed out on almost their entire lives, and now they were both faraway on the other side of the country. Catherine's husband, King Paul, was in the dungeons. She barely ever saw him. Her family, and her country, had been torn apart all because of the evil, twisted Salvador Corea.

Disdain rippled Catherine's whole being at the thought of the villain. Salvador Corea was the core of all the evil happening today. He was the cause of all Alamia's suffering; a whole eight years of depression because Salvador wanted revenge.

Catherine's tears kept flowing steadily, splashing on Philomena's doll and Philip's cloak.

"Please don't cry, my queen," a small voice spoke. Catherine looked down and saw her companion sitting at the edge of her chair, his front paws on her knee and his beady black eyes peering worriedly up at her. The small creature was hardly bigger than a mouse, with pinecone-like scales slicked down over its slender body and a snout resembling that of a pinecone's stem.

"I'm afraid I can't help it, Ramaro," Catherine sniffed. She laid the doll and the cloak upon her lap, stroking them with a most desired longing in her touch.

Ramaro, the pinecone like creature known as a comae, looked distressed. He moved his gaze over to the cloak and the doll.

"You know I'm terrible at comforting," Ramaro said sincerely.

"I know," Catherine said, wiping away her tears. "It's just that it's been so long being in here, wondering what's happening, if Philip and Philomena really are safe. I just prayed that it would be over soon," she said with a weary sigh.

"I suppose it has been a while. I've sort of lost track," Ramaro said.

"I guess it really doesn't matter now," Catherine sniffed, looking slowly about her chamber which had served as her prison cell. Hardly anything was in the dimly lit room, but a wardrobe, a worn bed, a bear pelt sprawled on the center of the floor, and the chair that Catherine was sitting on. There was also a small hearth to the left, a dying fire smoldering within. Grey ash blanketed the wall and the floor around the hearth.

Ramaro looked up at Catherine with a troubled expression. "There is always hope, my queen. It lies with your children,"

Catherine exhaled tiredly. "That's just it, they are children. They shouldn't have to be burdened with something as heavy as this," she said, almost exasperated.

"With all due respect, my queen, but they are not just children. They are the prince and princess, and if they are anything like you and the king, then I'm sure they are capable of much more then what you give them credit for," Ramaro said determinedly.

Catherine looked at him wonderingly. The locks that bolted the door to Catherine's prison suddenly clicked open.

Ramaro quickly scuttled out of sight beneath the bed. Catherine lunged forward out of her chair and stuffed the doll and the cloak under the cover of the heavy bear pelt. The door creaked open the rest of the way. Catherine hurriedly sat on the bear pelt, and stared off into space acting as though she had been there the whole time. A maid with a dirt smeared face wearing a dull grey dress poked her head around the door, her expression apprehensive.

"Lady Catherine," the maid said hesitantly. "Your husband was summoned before Lord Salvador only moments ago,"

"Not another wicked policy of his," Catherine murmured,

remaining on the bear pelt.

"No, my lady," the maid said.

Catherine looked to her curiously. The maid glanced over her shoulder nervously, fearful of someone overhearing her next words.

"Your children escaped from Tosh along with your husband's brother. Lord Salvador is sending out his son to capture them and bring them here," said the maid.

Catherine rose to her feet, hardly daring to believe what she was hearing. "What about my children?" she asked, excitement filling her voice.

The maid shifted her gaze uneasily, unconsciously taking a step back. "All I know is that Captain Avador is leaving soon. Your children's whereabouts are unknown at the time," the maid said.

Before Catherine could question her further, the maid slipped away and closed the door behind her. The bolts on the door clicked shut. Catherine's heart drummed against her chest.

"What did I tell you, my queen?" Ramaro said excitedly, climbing atop the lumpy straw bed and scratchy blankets. "There is always hope!" he said enthusiastically.

Catherine smiled back. "Yeah, there is," she said, suddenly distracted.

"What is the matter, my queen?" Ramaro asked, peering up at her.

"Ramaro, I need a favor," Catherine said eagerly, her eyes bright.

"Anything," said Ramaro with a beaming grin.

"I need you to take a message to Sir K'smet," Catherine said.

4

It was night now, two hours after the sun had sunk behind the horizon. Queen Catherine lay on the bear pelt on the floor, gazing up at the ceiling of her prison quarters. It was eerily quiet; not a sound from within or without her room. Catherine couldn't even hear the guard standing watch outside her bolted door, or the squeaking of the mice that nested in the straw mattress she neglected to use.

It had always been quiet before, but never like this. It was as if the entire universe knew something was astir.

It didn't matter how quiet it was though, for Catherine couldn't sleep. She stared up at the ceiling where dark shadows dwelled, obscuring the sight of the smooth stone above. She could feel the familiar hardness of the stone floor beneath the bear pelt, and the cool dampness rising up from it as it always did on a chilly autumn night. No fire flickered in the hearth to scare away the cold; it wasn't allowed, not at night.

Catherine was use to the dampness now, and the hardness of the floor, and even the musty smell of the bear pelt. None of these things trifled her; not anymore.

Looking over at the round window from where she lay, Catherine could see a few winking stars through the rugged glass, shining brightly against the night sky. Catherine breathed sadly inward, feeling the dreadful ache in her heart.

Gazing at the peaceful stars, she wondered if her children were gazing at them too, and if they remembered her enough to miss her as much as she missed them.

A thud sounded from outside the door, like someone suddenly letting himself slump against the wall. Catherine quickly sat up, staring at the door through the gloomy darkness of her room and feeling suddenly alert. Something in the air felt strange.

Her heart began to pound in her chest. She curled her fingers tightly in the dense fur of her bear pelt. She discerned soft footsteps getting closer and closer.

Catherine's mind raced anxiously. She was familiar to the usual sounds of the guards and servants moving about in the halls and down the stairs, but these footsteps she was hearing sounded abnormal.

Glancing about her, Catherine sought something to defend herself with. She quietly shifted to her feet and tiptoed over to her chair, wincing when its old wood creaked beneath her grasp as she lifted it. The footsteps stopped, and a shadow leaked through the crack beneath the door. She saw the first lock on the door begin to turn.

Catherine moved silently, gripping her chair for reassurance. She pressed herself against the wall. Her breath was short and anxious as she watched the mechanisms of the bolts being worked one by one. Finally, Catherine saw the last bolt latch lift, and the door groaned open, gently swinging towards her and casting her in its dark shadow. She heard those soft footsteps again as they entered her quarters, taking their time as if the man were strolling in the gardens.

Feeling that the time was right, Catherine lightly pushed the door away, stepping along with it as it moved. She found a cloaked figure standing in the middle of her room with his back turned to her.

Catherine tightly gripped the rough wood of her chair, her eyes peeled on the cloaked figure.

There was a thud as the door closed behind her. Four simultaneous clicking sounds clipped as the bolts snapped shut on their own. The noise seemed to echo against the silence.

Catherine froze, her eyes widening. The cloaked figure suddenly went very still, and Catherine perceived a taunt alertness ripple his body. She could not make out much of him through the gloom, but whoever he was Catherine was determined to fight to her last breath.

Lifting her chair to strike, Catherine was surprised to hear the cloaked man speak first.

"I do not believe someone could beat me with an old, brittle chair, my Lady Catherine; no offense," he said in a rough yet warm voice that was filled with light smugness and much admiration.

Catherine lowered her pathetic old chair. "K'smet?" she asked, pleasantly surprised to recognize the man's voice.

"You have never been one for formality, have you, my lady?" K'smet said with amusement as he pulled down his gaping hood and turned around to face her. His countenance was strong and ruggedly handsome. His eyes were a sparkling green, and his long wavy hair was a dusty blonde. His build was solid and strong.

Catherine beamed a relieved smile at him, hardly refraining from shouting out with joy at the sight of a friend. She rushed over and embraced him. "It *is* you, K'smet! I'm so glad that you came!"

K'smet looked about the room awkwardly, unable to return his queen's embrace. He stood stiffly as she hugged him, wondering how long he'd have to remain there. Something wriggled inside K'smet's tunic. Catherine released him and stepped back.

A tiny brown head covered in pinecone-like scales peeked out of K'smet's tunic and looked up at them with annoyance gleaming in his beady black eyes.

"What is the matter with you two? You nearly squashed me!" the pinecone-like creature said chidingly, in a small, hushed voice.

"Ramaro!" Catherine exclaimed happily.

"Yes, it's me," Ramaro said. "And can't you keep your voice down, my lady," the comae hissed, as respectfully as possible.

"You got the message to K'smet then?" Catherine asked

lowering her voice and ignoring Ramaro's unpleasant and cocky mannerism. He always acted this way with other people around. "Of course I got the message to K'smet. He's here isn't it?" Ramaro said smugly, his scaly face contorting with a cocky frown.

"Enough, you annoying little beast," K'smet said irritably. He pushed Ramaro back inside his tunic.

"Hey!" Ramaro squealed angrily as K'smet's hand shoved him back down into the tunic and out of sight. K'smet grumbled under his breath.

"I did *not* appreciate that," Ramaro's muffled voice said.

"Take your own advice and pipe down in there," K'smet said. He looked back up at Catherine. "You have no idea the patience one must possess just to deal with this annoying little creature. He must be the most irritating comae I know,"

Catherine could have laughed at the intriguing relationship between K'smet and Ramaro, but the happiness she felt was suddenly replaced by guilt; for in that short moment of joy she had forgotten all of her troubles, even her family and her country. Catherine was thoroughly ashamed, and felt the familiar grieving emptiness in her heart seep back like an awful black liquid.

Seeing the queen's abrupt change of mood and guessing the reason why, K'smet changed the subject. "So, why have you summoned me here tonight? It must be important, or else you wouldn't have attempted such a risk,"

Catherine's expression hardened determinedly as she directed her gaze back to K'smet. "I need you to find my children," K'smet stared at her blankly. "Are you serious?" he asked sarcastically. "Do you know what that would cause?"

"Yes, I am fully aware. You're cover will be blown and Salvador will know that you are loyal to my husband," Catherine said impatiently. "But if Avador reaches Philip and Philomena first, we will have no hope of defeating Salvador. You *must* go to them,"

K'smet appeared conflicted. "And do what? Warn them of Avador's search for them?"

"I'm asking you to find them. Tell them all you know of the castle and Salvador. Give them as much knowledge as you can. Give them a chance to defeat this tyranny," Catherine said, her eyes pleading, her voice strong.

K'smet hesitated, wincing with confliction. "How can I possibly justify doing such a vain mission when the king wants me here?"

"You and I both know that my husband's hope is beginning to wane, K'smet," Catherine said.

"Everyone's hope is waning," K'smet argued his brow creasing.

"Then there is little to lose. This is not a vain mission I ask of you; it will keep alive our last hope. Please, they are only two children against all the evil that exists today," Catherine said quietly.

K'smet still seemed reluctant, but he considered his queen's words with growing certainty. Catherine watched him, her countenance imploring.

K'smet took in a deep intact of breath, his softened gaze meeting his queen's. "Then may our hope stay alive," he whispered, all doubt and confliction lifting the instant he decided. Catherine nodded wordlessly, relief washing over her.

Shuffling footsteps outside the door made them both jump and instinctively lower themselves to the floor. They looked at each other with a kindling terror reflecting in their eyes as they listened intently.

They could not be caught, Catherine thought fiercely; *not now when everything was hanging in the balance.*

A few seconds ticked by, and they could still hear the shuffling footsteps. K'smet tilted his head curiously so he could listen better. "The prisoners," he whispered, recognition sounding in his voice. "They're moving the prisoners into the new cells they built."

"Why are they doing that? Is there something wrong with the dungeon?" Catherine asked with a frown.

"No, nothing's wrong with it. Salvador never spilt why he built new cells," K'smet whispered back with a shrug. Catherine was pensive for a moment, but she shook her thoughts away.

"How much time do you have?" she asked worriedly. "You can't be seen near my quarters let alone in them. You have to get out of here,"

"I gave the guard a sedative that would make him think that he had merely dozed off during his shift. Its suppose to last for thirty minutes," K'smet said, staring at the door.

There were more footsteps, this time louder and seemingly closer. Catherine and K'smet stiffened and went deathly silent, their eyes peeled on the door.

"Oy! Wake up and get off the ground!" a gruff voice commanded just outside Catherine's door. A heavy thudding sound said that the patrolling guard with the gruff voice was kicking the sleeping guard. They heard a few weary words being mumbled as the guard that K'smet sedated stirred from his nap.

"On your feet, lazy," the patrolling guard ordered.

Catherine directed a frown at K'smet and mouthed 'thirty minutes'. K'smet shrugged helplessly. They shared the same mounting fear. They were cornered. There was no way K'smet could just slip out the door now and definitely no way for him to smooth talk things over with Salvador if he were caught.

Catherine glanced about desperately as the patrolling guard severely lectured his fellow guard for sleeping on his watch.

"The hearth!" Catherine whispered excitedly.

"What?" K'smet questioned with a frown, still watching the door worriedly.

"Climb up the hearth's chimney," Catherine said urgently, pulling K'smet over to the hearth that was black with soot and ash. "It should be big enough, and it will lead outside," Catherine said. K'smet peered up the dark chimney doubtfully.

"Have you checked on your prisoner?" Catherine heard the patrolling guard ask.

"Hurry!" Catherine hissed, literally shoving K'smet into the hearth. K'smet ducked inside and turned around with difficulty, getting soot on his face. It was a tight fit for a muscular knight, but there was no choice.

"Take Ramaro with you," Catherine added.

"No problem with me," they heard Ramaro's hushed voice say. The door began to rattle as the guards began work unbolting its many latches.

K'smet looked back over at his queen, knowing that there wasn't much time. "I'll find your children, and do what I can to help them, you have my word," K'smet said.

Catherine smiled and nodded, gripping K'smet's hand. "May the Creator be with you," Catherine said. The door shook and rattled dangerously.

"Blast this door!" came one of the guard's angry voices

"Now go!" Catherine said. With that, K'smet pulled himself out of the hearth and up into the chimney out of sight. Catherine brushed away their handprints in the layers of soot with the hem of her dress. Then she rushed over to collapse atop her bear pelt just as the guards unbolted the last latch and banged the door open.

Catherine bolted upright and stared frightfully at the guards, acting as though they had woken her from her sleep.

"You see," the one guard said with annoyance, gesturing towards Catherine and placing his hands on his hips. "She's still here! There's no problem!" he said, glaring angrily at his fellow guard. The other guard appeared very embarrassed. He rubbed the back of his helmet as he looked at Catherine with confusion. "I guess you're right," he said with a shrug.

The younger guard who had been watching Catherine's door shook his head. "I'm sure I'd know if something fishy were going on in here, that's why Lord Salvador entrusted me to watch over the queen," the young guard said cockily. "I have a sixth sense for things like escape plans and plots and stuff like that," he continued with a smug smirk plastered on his face. "Yeah, maybe so," the other guard said, still mortified. He glanced curiously at Catherine one last time before closing the door and bolting it securely shut once more.

"Its fine, I guess not all of us have the gift of sensing things," Catherine heard the young guard brag outside her door. "Maybe it's because I'm not as paranoid as everyone else is around here," The last bolt was latched shut and Catherine heard the patrolling guard's footsteps fading down the hall, and her cocky young guard slump back down against the wall. Catherine lay back down on her bear pelt and sighed with relief. The ache in her heart was still there, but a warm feeling, very small, was beginning to kindle next to it. She flicked her eyes up at the hearth and saw a cloud of ash billowing down from the chimney. K'smet had escaped safely. Catherine smiled and closed her eyes.

5

Early autumn morning was as crisp as an apple's flesh as Balin, Philip, and Philomena rode out of the spaced woods and came to acres of tilled fields glowing with the morning light. About a mile or so ahead lay the town where chimney smoke drifted above. No farmers worked the fields yet for it was very early, the sun just peeking on the horizon.

"Niche," Balin said his breath fogging the cool air. Laefin, his stallion, sidestepped beneath him and bowed his head, eager to keep moving.

"Oh thank God, I thought we'd never reach it," Philip sighed with relief at Balin's right.

They had been traveling the wild country for eleven days, experiencing things they had never experienced and using skills they had only ever practiced in their quarters in Tosh. Both he and Philomena agreed that practicing to hunt and actually having to catch their dinner were two entirely different things.

After all, they had never chased down a rabbit before and in the process trip face first into a mud hole, or catch fish without a hook or line and accidentally catch a toad. Learning how to catch their dinner had given them some very amusing memories.

Balin cocked a knowing look to his nephew. "We have a long ways to go," he informed making Philip grimace.

"Are we going to stay long?" Philomena asked at Balin's left, pulling her coat closer about her rather grateful they had thought of them back in Seshrik. The further north they traveled the colder it was getting.

"Maybe a few days," said Balin tapping Laefin in to a walk towards Niche. Philip and Philomena urged their horses to follow.

"That's more than enough time for a few good meals and a night's rest," Philip grinned happily.

"But do you think it's safe?" Philomena questioned worriedly. So far they hadn't seen any sign of the Toshinians coming after them, and no sign of any posse from Salvador. Still, Philomena didn't like the idea of staying in one place for too long.

"It will be fine. We need provisions to get to Ezleon, and truthfully I'd like to look for another map. As long as we use our false identities, I'm sure things will be alright." Balin said.

This was enough to satisfy Philomena. The three of them rode their stallions leisurely towards Niche, worn from the first part of their journey and looking forward to a good meal and some rest in a real bed.

Ahead in the town, the farmers and workers of Niche were now starting to leave the comforting warmth of their homes to tend to their daily chores. A few other travelers bustled about, their schedule fixing them to be early departures. Shopkeepers opened their stores and tethered their watchdogs. By the time Balin, Philip, and Philomena entered the first streets of Niche, the town was buzzing with activity.

They gazed around curiously, Philip and Philomena especially. Compared to Seshrik it was small, less colorful, poorer, and the people more glum. Not too many smiles were worn by the villagers and farmers as they headed to work.

"Cheery," Philip commented, his bottom lip sticking out in consideration as he studied the passersby. Remembering the saddening sights they had seen in Seshrik, Philip was prepared for anything.

"Let's find the stables and rent some stalls," Balin suggested. They agreed, and looked around for someone suitable to ask for directions.

To the north, one ramshackle cottage in dire need of repair sat aside from the rest of Niche's complicated maze. The muffled sounds of the occupants arguing came from within. There was a smash, like a vase had been thrown at the wall, followed by a loud yell. The door burst open scraping against the ground beneath the poor overhang. A dark haired boy with light brown skin sprinted out, hurriedly trying to shrug into a thin, patched coat. He ducked as a clay pot sailed from the open door.

A thin, pale skinned woman appeared in the doorway, her face furious. "You better not come back to this house without a job, Lark McKnight!! Do you hear me?!!" she boomed after him, her voice brittle with anger and fear.

The boy, Lark, ran as if his very life depended on it, which in a way it did. The woman, his mother, shook her head and sighed despairingly. She brushed aside a loose strand of dark hair and hurried back inside, closing the door behind her.

Feeling as though the world was caving in on him, Lark raced up the skinny dirt path that led to the streets of Niche. His breath clouded the air. The coat he had slipped on was little protection from the cold morning.

Dear lord, I'm so late! Master Finn is going to kill me! Lark thought. He pounded on to the street that the path flowed in to. He veered in to a back alley bordered by the backs and sides of shacks and cottages. He didn't have to think about which way to go. His feet had memorized this shortcut when he was nine years old. It had saved him countless times before, though he doubted it would save him from Master Finn's wrath today. He was an hour late for work!

Master Finn was the horse master of Niche. He owned and operated all three stables, and took a personal pride in running his own breeding operation. Lark had gotten a job with him shortly after his father and the other farmers were burdened with a produce policy, demanding that they surrender one third of their crops to the Alamian armies. Lark's job with Master Finn was the only thing that assured that his family had food for the winter. He couldn't afford to lose it.

Sliding by some stacked barrels and dodging someone with a sack slung over his shoulder, Lark flew down the alleyway. A gnarled hand caught him by his coat and nearly made him fall on his face.

"Alms! Please, boy, alms!" croaked the old man. He was skinny as a board, with stained rags for cloths hanging off his thin frame.

With little effort, Lark ripped away from him tearing the side of his coat in the process. The old beggar stumbled and let out a despairing wail. Lark raced away before the beggar could grab him again, feeling bad for what he had done. Sometimes Lark would slip a coin to a beggar here and there when he could afford it, but now he most definitely couldn't.

Flying down the remaining stretch of the alley, Lark shot out the other end. He found himself on the market street which was congested with travelers, villagers and merchants.

Lark started pushing passed the people clogging up the street. He rushed to press through, hurriedly apologizing to those who shouted at him or casted angry glares his way. Lark ran into a merchant and caused the crates he was carrying to topple over and burst open on the dirt ground. The merchandise of imported bottles of ale either shattered on the ground spraying their contents everywhere, or rolled away only to be snatched up by a smiling villager.

The flustered merchant threw his hands up in the air and pulled at his locks of black hair, yelling and cursing in a foreign language. Lark apologized and ran on, this time tripping over the tethers of three hounds. Pushing himself up, Lark raced onward, shoving passed some women fussing over a roll of silk at the clothes' merchant. He treaded on one of the ladies' dresses and heard a ripping sound and a scream. Lark winced but didn't look back. He got to the point where the flow of traffic thinned and raced onto a side road going westward.

Sergeants patrolling the street, wearing mismatched armor with their hands gripping their sheathed swords, shook their heads and chuckled at the ruckus Lark had just made. They were under the command of Commander Xavier who in turn was charged by Lord Leif of Stalveer to keep law and fairness in Niche. But in the past eight years, fairness had gone slack. The commanders and sergeants had lost care for peace.

Lark ran on, feeling his legs go numb but still seeing them pound on. His lungs stung with the cool air. Nearing the end of the street, three massive stables became visible their double doors gaping open to the east. Lark checked his pace and cautioned his step for riders were coming in and out of the stables.

Stable hands scurried to and from the barns, hurrying about to complete their chores. Voices could be heard shouting out commands.

Lark veered to his right to avoid a careless traveler trotting his horse towards the stables. The scrawny, snobbish man seated upon his horse shot a baleful glare at Lark over his shoulder. Lark met the cold eyes steadily as he continued to move forward. He wasn't bothered by the man's smugness. He was immune to being treated as low-born scum.

The wealthy traveler gave an amused smirk, and then looked away as he entered the traveler's stable.

Having been distracted, Lark bumped into something before him and fell backwards on his rear with a thump. Looking up, Lark's heart pounded as he met the intimidating stare of his master.

A round and short man with dusty shaded hair dressed in a striking velvet red jacket that dropped to his stubby knees, Master Finn glared down at Lark with little tolerance and much annoyance.

"You're late," Master Finn said moodily. He stood over Lark, holding the tether of a handsome bay stallion.

Lark gulped. His being shrunk under his master's heavy gaze, yet he summoned the courage to meet Finn's pale narrowed eyes.

"I know, I over slept," Lark said sheepishly. He remained on the ground where he had fallen, as if to prove his meekness to his master. Finn's eyes widened with flared fury.

"You over slept? *Over slept!*" Finn hissed belligerently. The bay stallion jerked nervously and bobbed his head with agitation. Lark's nerves felt as though they might burst from the pressure. He let his eyes drop to the dirt ground.

"Of all the rotten things a stable hand can do and you have to over sleep," Finn muttered angrily, running a hand through his hair.

"I didn't mean to do it," Lark tried weakly, attempting to meet the stable master's gaze once more.

Finn's fiery eyes snapped onto Lark, his round face growing red. "If you weren't one of my best working hands I would relieve you of your worries of rising with the dawn this very instant!" Finn boomed, stomping his foot and gesturing frustratingly. Lark held his tongue as his master fumed and muttered under his breath.

"What do I do with you now, huh? I've been doing your chores for the past hour, but I can't take away your job as I should. There are too few good stable hands as it is," Finn said, rubbing his chin as he rolled over the predicament.

Lark grimaced. "Double shifts and pay for one for a week?" he suggested.

Finn's countenance lightened as he considered the reasonable admonition. Lark watched his master with building regret squirming on his smooth features.

"Very well," Finn finally said contently with a sudden cheerful bounce to his voice. "But no more late arrivals," he added, wagging a chubby finger in Lark's face. Lark nodded, overly relieved for his miraculous save from complete disaster.

"Now," Finn said as he helped Lark to his feet with a grunt, after which he wiped his hand grudgingly against his pants, avoiding contact with his red jacket. Lark paid no mind to Finn's snobbish way, and dusted himself off, not that it mattered with his tattered and overused garment. He was considerably young, but just as tall as Master Finn.

"Take this horse to Eric. He'll be traveling a distance so he needs some fresh shoes. Be sure the varmint doesn't kick anyone," Finn said, handing the lively stud's tether to Lark who obediently obliged with a nod.

"And don't leave without the horse," Finn added, keeping Lark by the arm. "We don't need any other horses disappearing."

"Yes, Master Finn," Lark said.

"Good lad," Finn said, releasing Lark and patting him on the shoulder.

Lark set off on his mission without another word, feeling much lighter than when he had arrived. The handsome bay he led followed him willingly. Finn watched Lark go, his hands on his hips. After a moment, Finn shook his head and returned to his three very busy stables.

Lark only needed to walk a kilometer to reach the blacksmith's. The blacksmith shack was the first structure to border the road on the left before Master Finn's stables, and it was the only shack to have smoke wafting so freely from its entrance as well as its roof. Only half of the shack was boarded with walls, while the other half gaped open to the road exposing the skeletal timbering of its sides.

Lark led the stallion inside and was immediately greeted by the thick smell of burning coals, heating iron, and sweat. He tied the stallion to a railing, wrinkling his nose from the ferocity of the stench. He could hear Eric hammering in the back where the forge was. Horse hoof shavings littered the dirt ground where Lark had tied the stallion.

Glancing about him, Lark could see that nothing had changed about the place since his last visit. The long work bench centered in the shack which Eric used for various things was cluttered with all sorts of tools and bits of metal. Several heavy, rusting chains hung in disorderly loops from the rafters, and half finished armor was suspended from nails on the thick, upright posts. A variety of horseshoes could be seen in a number of places; hanging from the looped chains, a few on the nails in the posts, more draped on railings, and many more scattered about Eric's work bench. Lark could even discern Eric's stash of favored rum and ale beneath the work bench in an old crate. Lark called out to Eric as he ducked beneath the stallion's neck. "What?!" Eric's husky voice bellowed from the back of the shack with annoyance.

Lark straightened and squinted his eyes to where he could see red hot coals pulsing as a massive, shadowed form hammered on a horseshoe. Billows of smoke rose from the forge as Eric buried the horseshoe into the coals, took it out, and hammered on it some more.

Lark saw the blacksmith lift the horseshoe up with tongs to examine it in the dim light. The shoe still glowed with a burning red. With a satisfied grunt, Eric plunged the shoe into a barrel of cool water next to him. A crackling hiss erupted and steam wafted from the barrel.

A moment later, a large, muscular man treaded out from the curtains of smoke carrying the pair of tongs that still gripped the black, steaming horseshoe.

"Ah, it's just you," Eric said dully. He chucked his tongs and horseshoe onto his already clustered workbench. They landed with a loud clatter.

The blacksmith wore only a tattered, leather apron that tied about his neck and waist and dropped passed his knees, as well as a pair of filthy suede pants that had seen plenty days of patch work. Dirt and grime were smeared on his tanned arms, chest and face. His hands were especially filthy and blackened with soot. Tufts of light colored hair curled over the blacksmith's forehead and about his ears.

"Morning, Eric," Lark said, stepping forward.

"What do you want?" Eric asked displeasingly as he took the ladle from a wooden pale hanging from a nearby post. He gulped the refreshing water noisily.

"Master Finn sent me to get this horse shod," Lark said, gesturing to the stallion standing behind him.

Eric flicked his sharp eyes towards the stallion over the rim of the ladle. Lark waited uneasily for Eric to finish his drink.

Finally, Eric lowered the ladle and tossed it carelessly back into the water pale with a satisfied sigh.

"All fours?" Eric asked, wiping the drips of water from his chin. Lark nodded. "He also told me to tell you that the horse likes to kick,"

"All horses kick," Eric said flatly, brushing past Lark and making his way towards the stallion.

Lark turned. "I suppose," he said, watching Eric lift one of the stallion's front legs and peer at the bottom of the hoof.

After a moment of muttering under his breath, Eric released the hoof and straightened stiffly.

"Right," he said wincing from his sudden soreness. "I'll have him done in about an hour. You can pick him up then,"

Eric plodded passed Lark to retrieve his tools from his work bench, a hand pressed to his sore back.

"Master Finn said for me to wait here till you're done," Lark said, turning around again.

"Is that so," Eric muttered, his broad back to Lark.

"I won't get in the way," Lark said. Eric turned back around to him with his tools and a horseshoe.

"Hope not for your sake," he said gruffly, brushing passed Lark for a third time. Lark detected his annoyance and underlining threat.

Lark allowed himself a moment to drill a contemptuous glare into Eric's back before moving away to the end of the shack. He comfortably leaned against one of the shack's supporting posts. He folded his arms and sighed, looking out at the dirt road before the shack's entrance. He watched a mother hurry her young child along as they made their way down the street towards the market. Two mules pulling a rattling wagon rolled by, their white haired master steering them towards the stables. The old man was probably an out of town farmer hoping to make a profit by selling his produce here.

This street wasn't as crowded as the market street, where market stalls are crammed together offering exotic goods. Lark heard Eric begin to hammer on the first horseshoe against his anvil to make its shape match the stallion's hoof.

Lark gazed up at the crisp blue sky. He would be here for a while. During these rare times when Lark had no work to occupy himself with, he would contemplate deeply on what the future held for him. Niche was not exactly the prime place for opportunity, especially for Lark. Simple peasants were given more chances than he, but times had hardened for everyone.

Lark had seen boys before growing up in Niche, hoping to find a route to a better life only to come to the conclusion that the best thing for them was to remain where they were. So they stayed in Niche, and Lark could see them everyday working like slaves in the fields. One of them was his father. Was that really what his life was coming too?

Lark had already turned sixteen; he'd have to decide soon, whether to spend the rest of his life in the fields or remain a stable hand to the stuffy Master Finn. He had gotten the job with Master Finn the year after King Paul had lost both his children to a mysterious illness. The king had never been the same strong, kind leader Alamia knew after the loss of his children.

The people often said that their king had gone mad. Such a claim was believable. In the past eight years since the announcement of the prince and princess' deaths, the king had let everything fall apart, and had even aided the depression to worsen.

The era of peace Alamia had been experiencing had then come to an abrupt end. Taxes had been raised and placed on obscured things; forests had been cut down causing the hunters in the north to suffer; outrageous policies had been made nearly suffocating those considered as peasants; and the law for small villages like Niche was placed in the hands of bloodthirsty men. Alamia was presently seeing things that never were before. Her people, once so kind and generous, had become greedy and prejudiced.

People of a different race were now looked upon as if they were suffering from a contagious disease. Religion was no longer pure, but tainted by falsehood. The Old Religion, as it was now called, was almost gone, and the Creator forgotten. Hunger clung to the land like a thick fog, and real crime was hardly punished. Alamia's king, once so good and just to his people, had completely lost his mind.

The town of Niche though, was considered as a fortunate refuge from the direct tyranny of the twisted king. Being a traveler's town as it was, no religion had settled here, and no restrictions had been placed on those who entered. Commander Xavier and his men merely keep order in Niche, not caring to trifle in situations to keep peace.

Though, as all men of military status do, they keep watchful eyes on those who carry weapons.

Still, though thought of as a refuge, Niche's few residents suffered from the burden of the harsh taxes and policies, and had grown to bitterly hate King Paul who had destroyed an era of peace due to his grief. Like everyone now in Alamia, those in Niche spoke with excitement and earnest of their soon-to-be king, Salvador Corea.

Acting as the king's advisor, Salvador had been chosen as King Paul's heir after the deaths of Prince Philip and Princess Philomena. Salvador seemed to be a promising leader, who spoke well and raised the hopes of the people that when he became king Alamia's glorious era of peace would be restored. So everyone was in love with him, and since he already had a son, he was even more desired by the people.

Lark cared for none of it. He did not care if everyone hated King Paul and wanted him dead. He did not care if Salvador Corea was to be crowned king in the spring. He did not care if peace was to be restored. All he cared about was how he and his family were to live. This was selfish he knew, but Lark could not remember a time of peace.

It seemed like when the peace had ended, Lark's miserable life suddenly began with a roaring awakening in the form of a horse hoof to his shoulder on his fist day working in the stables. A white scar shaped like a crescent moon still remained etched forever into his skin. The scar was like a terrible mark of time. Every time Lark saw it he was reminded that he had never laughed nor cried. He had never loved anything or anyone except for his family. Half the time, Lark wondered why the Creator had given him life if he was to live a life so useless and mundane. In all his years, Lark had searched blindly for a purpose, but every time had come up dry. Was he really meant to live out his days as a stable boy?

Breathing sadly inward, Lark let his eyes fall to the ground, confused and conflicted.

A small pebble just then glanced off Lark's arm, stirring the rough sleeve of his canvas coat. Lark glanced about him, not bothering to shift his position.

A sense of dread sunk within him when he spotted three boys on the street before him. They were sneering and snickering Lark's way.

The red headed boy, who was the shortest of the three, chucked another pebble at Lark, this time hitting him on the shoulder. The little rock stung, but Lark did not move, and kept his expression impassive.

The eldest boy of the three, who seemed to possess some sort of dominance over his two friends, praised the red headed boy's good aim.

"Good morning, Trez," Lark greeted gravely.

"Lark," Trez replied none too fondly. Trez was tall for his age, and well built for a peasant. His mass of blond hair curled above his green eyes that were filled with a mischievousness that Lark did not trust. The few young girls of Niche described Trez's voice as intoxicatingly charming, but Lark heard it more as a tricky, sly fox.

"We were just out for a little target practice," Trez said with a smile. The third boy snickered.

Lark nodded. "Your aim has improved, Florez, over the past year," he said, directing his hazel eyes steadily on the red headed boy. Florez looked to Trez uncertainly, as if hoping for some guidance in how to react to Lark's compliment.

"What about you, Lark? Still working for that grumpy old Master Finn?" Trez asked.

Lark shrugged.

"We all were chosen by Commander Xavier to be trained as sergeants," Trez announced proudly, indicating the new, black velvet tunic he was wearing.

Lark couldn't help the jealousy that stabbed at him. Trez pointed to the crest emblazoned on the tunic over his chest: a serpent engulfing a white rose.

"It's the emblem of Salvador Corea, our future king," Trez said smugly.

Lark said nothing.

Trez smirked, his dark eyes moving over Lark. "I guess you'll remain a stable boy your whole life," Trez said, snickering. "It suites a mix breed like you," His two friends laughed.

Lark grinded his teeth, his features darkening.

"Maybe when Master Finn grows old, he'll give you the business, Lark," said the third boy, Horace.

"Perhaps," Lark said passively. "Though stable boy or not, at least my father taught me how to read and write," There was a turn of the tide in the atmosphere. "While you, Trez, well you wouldn't know the difference if I wrote champion or jackass on the back of that fancy tunic,"

Trez's face flushed red, whether from anger or embarrassment or both, Lark couldn't tell. Trez snatched a rock from the ground and gave great effort in aiming it at Lark's head.

Trez's aim was true, but Lark's reflex was faster. Lark ducked and the rock flew over him, only to smack the stallion behind him in the rear.

The stallion whinnied in fright and reared against his tether which snapped like a dry twig. Finding himself free, the stallion flattened his ears and charged, the single railing splintering under his superior strength. The stallion galloped down the street victoriously.

Trez and his friends burst out with laughter. Eric hollered and yelled, kicking aside the busted railing. Lark cursed Trez and went after the stallion with all speed possible.

A frightened woman screamed and hurried out of the rampaging stallion's path. Balin, Philip, and Philomena who happened to be traveling on the same road, slowed when they noticed the charging stallion.

"Might as well help," Philip shrugged, turning Nimbius around. "Now wait a minute," Balin started to protest but Philip had already shot away to intercept the loose stallion.

Lark slid to a stop when he noticed Philip galloping after the stallion.

Easily catching up with the loose stallion, Philip leaned from the seat of his saddle. He snatched what little tether remained on the stallion's halter and sat back in his saddle and eased the horses to a halt.

Noticing Philip pull the stallion to a stop, Lark felt relief beyond his mind. He hastened over to meet him.

Philip steered Nimbius back around with a triumphant grin, leading the haughty stallion back to confinement. Balin shook his head and Philomena smirked as he jogged by.

When Lark reached him, he saw that he was a young man, a little older than himself, with rich dark brown hair, fine square features, and a fit, youthful countenance. His clothes, Lark noticed, were Toshinian in design, but he was nowhere near a Toshinian. A simple wooden cross on a cord dangled about his neck, having bounced out of his shirt when he had charged after the loose horse.

When Philip perceived Lark, he grinned with a frank friendliness, taking in Lark's worn, dirty clothes and straight faced demeanor while Lark took in his laughing blue eyes that sparkled with a rare merriment he had never seen before.

"Is this yours?" Philip asked in a sociable tone.

"Not exactly," Lark said uncertainly, receiving the stallion's tether. "Thanks," he added, almost forgetting how indebted he was to this friendly traveler.

"No problem. That was a close call," Philip said, draping an arm across his saddle pommel. "You must work for the stables here," he reasoned, considering Lark's appearance again.

Lark felt a fiery defense rise within him. "That doesn't mean I like it," he said dryly, peering up at Philip.

"No offense," Philip assured raising an innocent hand and straightening his posture. "Perhaps we'll bump into each other again," he said, that benevolent smile still on his lips. He dipped his head in farewell and urged his horse onward to join his companions.

"You really don't need to attract attention to yourself," Balin chided harshly when Philip reached them.

Squaring his shoulders and lifting his eyebrows innocently, Philip reined Nimbius alongside Philomena who smiled at him approvingly.

"The boy needed some help," Philip replied.

Balin scowled at him around Philomena and shook his head once more. "No more heroics," he ordered.

"Yes sir," Philip grinned with a mocking salute. They moved

onward to the stables.

Lark watched them go feeling conflicted between a great deal of gratefulness toward Philip and a stirring suspicion that bothered him very much.

Sighing, Lark decided to forget his confusion. The young man was a traveler from faraway. He didn't have to understand him. Lark brought the almost escaped stallion back to Eric's shack. Trez and his friends were nowhere to be seen. They were most likely rolling over with laughter behind a nearby shack, Lark reasoned.

Eric was cursing and yelling and pounding his fists against his crude work bench. When he sensed Lark and the horse nearby, his angry gaze snapped onto Lark and he marched over to him, his bulky chest puffed out.

"I hope you're plannin' on fixing my shack, boy! You ruined it by spookin' this untamed beast!" Eric hollered, gesturing contemptuously at the stallion. The stallion tossed his head nervously.

Lark stood baffled. "Eric, it's just a railing, and I didn't spook-"

"I don't want to hear your excuses! You're fixing whatever's busted in here with all cost and punishment on you!" Eric yelled, jabbing a large finger into Lark's chest.

The enraged blacksmith turned on his heel and kicked out his other foot against the leg of his work bench. The leg folded under Eric's boot causing the opposite leg to snap. The work bench then collapsed on that side. Tools, horse shoes, and scraps of steel went sliding off, rolling everywhere. The nervous stallion jumped from the loud clatter.

"You can fix my work bench while you're at it!" Eric yelled. The blacksmith then stomped off to his forge, muttering and fuming as he went.

Lark sighed, deciding not to argue with the cantankerous Eric. So far, it hadn't been one of his best days. Feeling defeated and melancholy, Lark surrendered himself to his long wretched day of labor and punishment without complaint.

6

Late evening was settling over Niche. The setting sun was melting behind the trees of Staleon Wood, blazing the sky with warm, vibrant shades of orange and pink. Only a few stars were bright enough to shine high in the sky at this hour. Most of the town's occupants had retired to bed, but several of the foreign travelers remained awake. They all were in the inn's pub, drinking their favored ale and rum and gambling away whatever they had in their pockets.

Lark could hear them where he was in the blacksmith's shack, hollering and laughing as if they had forgotten about tomorrow. Lark though was very well aware of tomorrow. Master Finn had been surprisingly generous and had told him to start his double shifts the next day so he could come and mend whatever had been broken by the lose stallion from earlier.

Lark hadn't realized how extensive the damage was till he had arrived in the shack after his usual work in the stables. Several shelves on the wall had fallen, either laying broken on the ground or clinging pathetically by a single nail. Of course there was the work bench which Eric had kicked, taking out both of the table's legs on the one end. Lark had already fixed the shelves and mended the workbench. He had put everything that had fallen to the ground back in its original place. He had also restocked Eric's supply of alcohol just as he had promised. Eric had been in quite a crazed fuss when he had realized that kicking his workbench had caused most of his bottles of rum and ale to be smashed. The only way that Lark could calm him was by promising the raging blacksmith that he would buy him more rum and ale with his own money.

Eric had been very much relieved by Lark's promise. He now was slumped in the right hand corner of his shack, snoring loudly with his head lolled to the side and a bottle of ale clutched in his limp hand.

Lifting his gaze from his work, Lark glared over at the passed out drunken blacksmith. He could smell the pungent odor of the drunken man from the opposite end of the shack. Eric obviously had no family, and no home; nothing but his livelihood as a blacksmith. He lived and slept in his shack, and ate his meals alone in the pub. Lark wondered what glum and lonely path led a man to lead such a way of life.

Whirling such contemplations, Lark began to work on replacing the railing which the stallion had charged through.

He yanked off the remains of the broken railing from the two posts. They came off easily enough. He used the hammer he had borrowed from Eric's tools to remove the nails that use to hold up the railing. Clearing away all the busted timber, Lark then lifted the new railing into place to check his measurements. The new railing fit perfectly. Lark reached for the hammer he had laying at his feet and fished out a nail from his trouser's pocket.

"What are you doin'?" came a demanding voice just as Lark was about to hammer in the nail. Lark started and dropped the railing on his own foot. He winced from the sudden throbbing pain. Looking up to see a sergeant glaring at him, Lark fought back a nasty glower himself.

"I asked you, what are you doin' here?" the sergeant asked again, emphasizing his words as if he were talking to someone stupid.

Lark put a hand on the nearby post to support himself and took in a sharp breath before attempting to speak. "Just fixing this railing here. Eric told me to do it,"

"Well, step to it. Curfew is close, boy. You only got fifteen minutes," the sergeant said arrogantly.

"Right, sir," Lark said, bending over to retrieve the railing. He had to bite his lip as his throbbing foot experienced another wave of agony.

To Lark's relief, the sergeant had better things to do than stand there and watch a stable boy nail up a railing. He moved onward down the road, shaking his head, and whistling softly.

Lark retrieved the railing and placed it over the nail holes in the posts.

About to pound again, Lark felt the other end of the railing become level with the end he was holding. Glancing around, Lark was startled to see a girl holding the other end of the railing. Her beauty stole his breath and left him dumbfounded. Long dark brown hair framed her perfect complexion and was tied back in a long braid wrapped in leather. Sparkling blue eyes peered calmly at him beneath finely arched brows. She was so stunning, she didn't appear fitting to be holding a rough piece of wood.

The girl lifted her eyebrows at him, and pursed her lips uncertainly. Lark shook himself, realizing that he had been gawking at her.

"What are you doing?" he asked, finally finding his voice. He hoped the night concealed the hot blush he felt in his face. He had not the slightest idea who the girl was, for he would remember a girl as pretty as she. Something about her eyes was familiar to him. For some strange reason, he felt that he *should* know who she was.

"You'll get done faster if you have some help," the girl said rationally. "The sergeant said you only have fifteen minutes," Her voice was strong, but not unpleasant.

"I know, but . . . what do you want?" Lark questioned, quite perplexed.

"What I really want is something to drink in this village that does not consist of ale or rum," the girl said matter of factly. Lark stared at her. "Please pound in the nails," the girl said, gesturing for him to go about his work.

Lark gave her one last quizzical stare before hammering in the first nail.

"You are that boy my brother helped earlier with that loose stallion, aren't you?" the girl asked as he dug in his pocket for a second nail.

Lark stiffened for a second, realizing why the girl's eyes seemed familiar. "You are his sister?" he asked, positioning the second nail.

"Yeah," Philomena replied.

"You're brother is a strange man," Lark said, beginning to pound.

Philomena frowned at Lark's back, looking offended. "How so?"

"Nobody helps someone for nothing," Lark said between the pounds of his hammer. The nail drove in well. Lark straightened and looked over at her. "Not anymore anyways," he added, wiping his brow. He moved over to the other end of the railing which she was holding. She stepped out of his way.

"Is that why you frowned at me when I offered to help?" she asked, watching him bring out another nail.

"Like I said, people are kind when they want something, not just to be kind," Lark said evenly. He drove in the third nail with five pounds of his hammer. "That's just the way it is," he said with a shrug.

Philomena emitted a disagreeable snort of laughter. "That is ridiculous. The whole world isn't all evil, you know," she said audaciously. Lark was taken aback by her statement. Her boldness nearly breached politeness. "I don't mind helping someone out of kindness. I'm helping you aren't I?"

"You are lucky that you chose me to bestow your kindness on, instead of someone else in this town," Lark said flatly. He brought out his last nail for the railing.

"What makes you different from everyone else here then?" Philomena asked interestedly, watching Lark drive in the last nail.

"I don't know," Lark replied uncertainly. His brow creased with pensiveness as he finished hammering. "I just don't care much about what everyone else does," he said, looking up at her and leaning against the post beside him. He felt awfully tired. Lark stared at her with sudden intrigue.

"What are you wearing?" he asked confoundedly.

Now that he saw her fully, he noticed how strange she appeared even though she was so beautiful. She wasn't wearing a dress like a normal girl, but instead she wore a brown leather overcoat with gold buttons that dropped to her knees over a white swordsman's shirt and a black belt wrapped about her waist. Just as her brother, her garments were from Tosh, but she couldn't resemble a Toshinian just as much as a cat could resemble a dog. A sword hung at her side, it's perfectly honed wooden pommel gleaming dully in the dim light. The weapon was also Toshinian, Lark noted.

Philomena was stunned by Lark's ambitious remark. She suddenly tensed with defensiveness under his scrutinizing gaze. "Oh, so now I'm the strange one aside from my brother?" she asked offensively, folding her arms and shifting her weight to one side.

Lark raised his eyebrows. "You are indeed, even in this town," he said. "With your outward kindness and your strange apparel you'll stick out like corn in a wheat field. If that doesn't make Commander Xavier's sergeants watch you that sword will do it. Your brother is just as strange,"

Philomena laughed mechanically. "I can tell that you have lived here your whole life," she remarked spitefully.

Lark shrugged without care. "I am simply telling you that if you and your brother don't caution yourselves, you'll end up in the commander's dungeon, although I doubt that would pose much of a threat to *you*,"

"What's that suppose to mean?" Philomena questioned staring dubiously at Lark.

"Judging by the quality of your clothes, I'm guessing you are rich unlike several of the people. I'm sure your father would pay a fat sum to spring you and your brother out of the dungeons, and Commander Xavier would be quite pleased to receive it." Lark said, his voice beginning to smolder with an irritable annoyance that he couldn't explain.

Philomena's face burned red as a she glowered at him. "That's quite a leap to assume my family is rich," she said in a dangerously low voice.

"You are obviously rich. Even if I wasn't judging by your clothes I'd say you're rich because most girls your age are married." Lark said crossly. He didn't know why he felt a burning resent toward this girl all of a sudden. Despite how attractive Lark saw her, knowing that she was the friendly traveler's sister made her *unattractive*.

"You know what," Philomena said, trying hard to control her sudden anger. "I'm glad I'm not like you because I don't think I could live as a narrow minded, flea bitten, uneducated stable boy!" she raged, her hand gripping her sword.

Now it was Lark's face to turn red with anger. His nostrils flared as he scowled at her.

The two of them glared crossly at each other, the sociable air that was between them before vaporized as if it had never been.

"Philly! There you are!" a new voice spoke up with relief. Lark and Philomena glanced about them, distracted from their heated brawl.

A young man bounded up to them with a cross bouncing about his neck and a beaming smile on his handsome face. Lark recognized the friendly traveler who had helped him earlier with the loose stallion.

"Why'd you take off like that? You know you shouldn't go out on your own without telling us," the young man said to his sister.

"I can take care of myself," Philomena replied with heated irritation. Lark sneered at her with his new disgust for her.

The young man turned to Lark with that friendly smile of his. "I had a funny feeling we'd meet again. I'm Felix Stone, and this snooty young lady is my sister, Phyliss," Philip said, placing a hand on his sister's shoulder. It felt strange calling each other by different names. The names felt heavy and foreign on their tongues, but Philip knew it was necessary.

Philomena scowled at her brother and batted his hand away. Lark turned his head to hide smirk. He could only imagine her burning desire to draw her sword. Philip though wasn't bothered at all by her temper.

"It's a pleasure to meet you," Philip said, extending an open hand to Lark. Lark was surprised by his frank and sociable gesture. He looked down at Philip's hand, and frowned curiously when he noticed a scar shaped like a cross with two intersecting beams on the inside of Philip's forearm.

"Don't even bother with him, Felix," Philomena said, staring at Lark. "He thinks we've reached the highest level of strangeness," she added with some heat.

Lark rolled his eyes, already tired of this peculiar confliction. Philip raised his eyebrows and looked over at his sister. "I can believe that *you* are strange," he said with mocking innocence.

Philomena glared at Philip coldly, narrowing her eyes as if daring him to say something else. Philip only shrugged under her icy gaze.

"I'll see you in the room," Philomena finally said, starting to walk away.

Philip nodded with a pursed smile as she passed him. Philomena made it a point to shoot an irritable scowl over her shoulder at Lark as she strode away with an arrogant stride. Lark felt his chest swell with angry bitterness like he had never felt before as he watched the girl walk away down the street.

"Sorry about her," Philip said once he knew Philomena was out of ear shot. Lark switched his attention onto him. "She doesn't mean what she says, whatever she did say. Phyliss is just . . ."

Philip trailed off staring in the direction his sister had departed. Lark was surprised to note a heavy sadness, an invisible burden, resting in the young man's eyes, and felt a pang of sympathy for him. But the emotion vanished as soon as Philip noticed Lark watching him.

Philip shook himself and forced a smile. "So, ugh, fixing up from the damage this morning then?" he asked, gesturing at the replaced railing.

"Yeah," Lark said with a nod. "I've mended everything already,"

"That blacksmith certainly is a harsh man," Philip said, directing a curious glance over at Eric who remained slumped and snoring.

"No more harsh than anyone else in this town," Lark said as he moved to put away the hammer he had borrowed.

"Oy! I thought I told you fifteen minutes!" an upset voice hollered. Both Lark and Philip snapped their attention onto the sergeant who stood in the road before them, staring angrily at Lark.

"Yes, sir, you did. I was just finishing up," Lark said evenly, stepping forward before Eric's new railing.

"Well, you got one minute to get your worthless hide back to whatever hole you sleep in at night, so get moving," the sergeant commanded, his voice a disturbing guttural rattle. He shot a suspicious glare onto Philip before turning on his heel and walking away, patrolling the streets with all the smug air he possessed.

"Hmm, a pleasant fellow," Philip mused, staring after the cantankerous sergeant.

Lark made no reply and did not waste another second. He had to get out of Eric's shack and into his house before the sergeant came back around.

"Tell your sister I appreciated the help," Lark said to Philip as he brushed past him and walked out onto the streets.

"You speak rather educated for a stable boy, you know," Philip said, turning to face Lark.

Lark stopped and turned back to Philip. "I'm not a stable boy," he said with an edge of defense. He glanced nervously down the street hoping that the sergeant wouldn't be there.

Philip let his bottom lip protrude in consideration. "Then what are you?"

Lark opened his mouth to reply, but no words came out. His countenance pinched with an irritable confusion.

"Tell you what," Philip spoke after a moment. "I'll take your word for it. You aren't a stable boy but yet you are," he said with a grin, as if they were sharing a secret.

Lark frowned. "That makes no sense," he said, perplexed.

Philip shrugged. "Maybe, maybe not. See you later, then," he said, starting to walk away in the same direction his sister had.

Lark stood on the shadowy road uncertainly for a moment.

"Wait," Lark called to Philip, taking a few steps towards him. Philip turned and looked expectantly to Lark. "You should be more cautious of the way you act tomorrow. Kindness is not a normal thing these days, and neither is your sister's apparel. Carrying weapons is not favored either. The sergeants will be keeping a close eye on both of you," Lark said. He didn't know why he was warning Philip; he simply felt obliged to do so.

Philip smiled. "We will adjust our temperaments and be as rude and close mouthed as anyone else here." Philip said with light sarcasm. He turned away again. "Good night," he said over his shoulder with a wave good-bye. He was soon swallowed up by the shadows of the houses and shops. Night had officially fallen like a dark curtain with winking stars and a smiling crescent moon.

Lark turned away as well, going in the opposite direction Philip had so he could avoid the patrolling sergeant. It would take him about ten minutes to reach his home by this route, but he didn't mind.

As he went along, he contemplated over his meetings with

Phyliss and Felix Stone. The siblings were both strange to Lark, but he saw Phyliss as more of an oddity than her brother. She acted like a boy training to be a warrior; sort of like Trez. Lark cringed at the comparison. The last thing he needed in his life was another smug Trez Gregus. The only difference between them was that Phyliss was a girl, a very beautiful girl in fact. Felix was different; he was kind and not as cantankerous as his sister. Lark still viewed him as a strange individual though. Felix almost seemed happy despite the era of depression they were in, and that was very odd. No one was happy in these troubled times.

Lark didn't know what it was about the Stone siblings, but they seemed to share a quality that suggested they didn't belong here. Really, they didn't seem like they would belong anywhere in this day and age. Lark's smooth brow wrinkled as his thoughts only served to baffle him further. Either way, Lark was sure there would be trouble for Felix and Phyliss Stone as long as they remained in Niche.

7

Back in the bustling town of Niche, Lark McKnight made it in his best interests not to be late a second day in a row for helping feed the many horses in Master Finn's traveling stable. Fifteen or so other stable hands scurried about the breezeway as well, motivated by the scolding voice of Master Finn to attend their chores without mistake. Some of the travelers were also in the stable, most standing about well dressed for their journeys waiting for their horse to be saddled and only a handful assisting in the care of their steeds.

A pleasant autumn breeze flowed through the breezeway of the engaging stable. Master Finn was of course quite proud of his thriving business. He was always happy to collect the boarding fees from the travelers, and always put on a sour face when he paid his stable hands. Still, the blunt horse master could go over to his two personal stables next door where he amused himself with selling and breeding some of the finest horses. This helped to ease Finn's detest of paying his help.

With everyone hurrying about busily, it created an endless tune of vigorous sound: the pouring of grain, the rustle of fresh straw, the streaming of water, and the occasional whinnying from one of the horses. All this lively and energetic activity happened about Lark in a blur. He was focused on his own work. He just hoped that he could make up for his mistake from yesterday so Master Finn wouldn't think twice about relieving him of his job.

"That all looks good," Finn said distractedly as Lark dropped off the empty feed pales at the grain storage where his master leaned lazily in the door way while checking over the list of travelers currently stabled in his barn.

"Oh, almost forgot, you have some new travelers you'll be assisting," Finn said, bringing forth three more pales of grain. Lark accepted them. "They're in the last three stalls on the left, with the grey stallion in the middle," Finn said, pointing out to Lark where the new travelers' steeds were stalled. Lark followed his pointing finger and cringed when he recognized Phyliss Stone polishing tack on a trunk between the stalls Finn had indicated.

"According to this their name is Stone. What a phony name," Finn wondered aloud, peering at the scroll he held.

"Can't someone else take care of them?" Lark asked, glancing around at Finn, unable to disguise the dread in his voice.

"Afraid not," Finn grunted. "Can't say I honestly blame you for not wanting to help them; they're some odd folk. They speak almost politely, and the way that girl dresses you'd think she's a boy. It's just really weird, and I've experienced my share of weirdness," he noted with detest.

Lark considered his words while watching Phyliss Stone as she polished a saddle she balanced across her lap.

Master Finn looked up from his scroll at Lark with annoyance. "What are you doing? Don't stand there and gawk! Get to work!" he bellowed.

Lark flinched, and hurried away with the three pales of grain. Finn shook his head and went back to reviewing his check list and scolding the other stable hands whenever he saw them doing something wrong.

Lark slowed as he came nearer to Philomena, dread twisting his stomach into nervous knots. He was almost tiptoeing when he came within a few feet of her, not that it would do much good. The three horses saw his approach and pawed excitedly. Philomena lifted her gaze, and her eyes narrowed slightly when she saw him. Lark winced and stopped before her. He glanced down at the pales of grain and back to her, opening his mouth to speak only no words came to mind. Philomena arched an eyebrow. Lark swallowed nervously, feeling his palms begin to sweat.

After an awkward moment, Philomena set aside the saddle and polishing rag and stood. Lark noticed she no longer wore her sword at her side. "I believe what you are trying to say is that you are the stable hand who will be assisting us during our stay here," She took one of the pales of grain from him.

"Yeah, I am," Lark said embarrassingly, feeling his face grow hot. This was going to be even harder then what he had thought. "Right, well then in that case you can feed the black and chestnut. They've waited long enough for it," she muttered. She moved to feed the grey stallion.

There was that burning resentment firing in Lark's chest again. He had handled being ridiculed and pushed around his whole life, but there was something about this girl that made her nearly intolerable. He set his jaw haughtily, fighting to hold his tongue. He busied himself with feeding the other two horses.

After the horses were fed, Philomena returned the empty pale to Lark and considered him with curious interest. "Well, since you're here to assist us, why don't you get some water,"

"Alright," Lark said, accepting the pale from her. "What about the stalls?"

"Oh, don't bother with them. I'm sure I can clean a stall just as good as you," Philomena said with a sneering smirk. Lark grinded his teeth angrily.

"Phyliss," a voice said chidingly. Lark recognized the voice of Felix Stone.

"Watch your tongue," Philip scolded his sister as he walked over to them from down the breezeway.

"I didn't mean any harm by it. It was simply a fair statement of opinion," Philomena said innocently as she sat down on the wooden trunk once more.

Lark could have exploded. Philomena snickered as she took up her saddle and polishing rag to assume her previous work. Lark felt his blood pulsing in his head as he drilled a contemptuous stare into her.

"Sorry about her," Philip said, stepping in front of Lark, blocking his view of Philomena. "Phyliss just has sarcastic issues," Philip said lightly, grinning at Lark.

"Oh, come on," Philomena said with irritable disagreement.

"And anger issues," Philip said, lifting his eyebrows.

"It's not like I'm as stiff and cheerless as he is," said Philomena.

"You're not exactly pleasant yourself," Lark said thickly.

"At least I can smile," Philomena said with a wicked grin. Lark's nose crinkled bitterly and his eyes flashed with contempt.

"Alright, Phyliss, that's enough," Philip said sternly. Philomena made a simulating peaceful gesture and focused on cleaning her saddle.

Philip turned a sociable smile on Lark. "You seem to work well here. You've been here long then?"

Lark frowned curiously. "I've been here my whole life," he said, his voice guarded.

"Lark!!" Master Finn's voice thundered from somewhere up the breezeway.

Lark's gaze snapped nervously up the breezeway. "I'll bring the water," he said to Philomena before hurrying away. Philomena only wrinkled her nose with disdain.

"I knew you to be kind, brother," Philomena said to Philip once Lark was out of earshot. "But now you have stooped to being a total suck up. Why are you being so nice to that stable boy?"

"I told you to watch your tongue," Philip said, turning a warning look on her. "With that mouth of yours, you'll get us both in to trouble," he added in a hushed tone.

"Why are you being so nice to him?" Philomena asked again with forced levelness.

"Because," Philip said, glancing about quickly as if he feared to be overheard. "We may need him," he whispered. Philomena frowned.

"Here's your water," came Lark's voice from behind Philip. Philip turned to him. "Thanks," he said with a grin, accepting the pale of water with his usual friendliness, yet Lark still frowned curiously before walking away to attend to his other chores. Philip sighed and moved to water the chestnut stallion a stall over.

Philomena forgot the saddle she'd been cleaning and was at his heels, pestering him until he finally explained his former statement.

"Uncle is doing his best to find a map, but the commander and his guards are strict here. Well, at least strict over certain things," Philip spoke carefully as he delivered the water. "Unfortunately for us, anyone trying to procure a map seems to be suspected of anything in their eyes, especially the kind of map we need. To add to our little dilemma, maps in general are hard to come by," Something like fear tinged Philomena's fair features. "You mean *he* might have found out about our movements?"

"It's not like we escaped from some little village like this one," Philip said, putting down the now empty pale and leaning close to Philomena so no one else could hear. "We escaped from the island city of Tosh,"

Understanding dawned upon Philomena. "That is why you're being so nice to the boy. You're thinking he could guide us through the Staleon Wood to Ezleon,"

"It's a shame we didn't get the chance to study geography during our long stay in Tosh," Philip said with laughing sarcasm. He turned away to lift his saddle from its wooden rack on the wall.

"How can we possibly trust that stable boy? How can we possibly trust anyone? If someone were to find out who we are they could easily rat us out," Philomena said as she followed Philip closely, her voice hushed and sharp with a disagreeable edge.

"Would you stop worrying," Philip groaned as he lifted his saddle on the stall door of his black horse. "You're making me nervous," he added thickly.

"Oh yeah, that would be a first," Philomena scoffed, placing a hand on her hip.

Philip grinned. "Look Philly, all I know is that we have to move fast, and someone who knows their way around the Staleon Wood will save us a great deal of time. We have to be in Ezleon and through the Twin Peak Pass before winter sets in,"

"I just don't see why you've singled that boy out of all the other people here in Niche," Philomena said grudgingly, folding her arms.

"I don't know," Philip said with a shrug, reaching for his horse's bridal that hung from a nearby peg. "He seems trustworthy; different from everyone else around," Philip went on thoughtfully. He turned a scrutinizing and teasing look on Philomena. "Is there an actual reason why you detest the poor boy so much?"

Philomena tensed defensively, her brow wrinkling. "No," she said stiffly. "It's just I don't understand what it is you like about him so much,"

"I told you," Philip said, lifting the latch of his horse's stall door and going inside. "He's different from all the other people around here," he said, beginning to tack his horse.

"What's so bad about the people around here?" Philomena asked.

Philip chuckled as he placed his saddle on the stallion's back. "Haven't you noticed how it is around here? The way the people talk? They hardly have any respect or understanding,"

Philomena pursed her lips, her eyes hard. "Let's say you are right, that the people here have no respect or understanding and this boy miraculously has acquired it. Does that prove to us that he will not betray us?"

Philip shrugged. "I guess it's not solid proof, but what happens if he truly does help us and is understanding of our situation?"

Philomena rolled her eyes and shook her head.

"Don't worry, Philly," Philip smiled, reaching for his bridal and pulling the reins over his horse's head. "You're acting like the decision of having a guide instead of a map is decided. Who knows, maybe uncle will procure a map and you won't have to deal with someone who is thoroughly irritating to you,"

"I never said he was irritating," Philomena said. Philip lifted his eyebrows at her knowingly as he opened the stall door. Philomena pinched her face into a sour glare, and backed away to give Philip room. Philip smirked at her and led his horse out into the breezeway.

"That's a good boy, Nimbius," Philip said fondly to his black steed as he turned him around to check the saddle's girth.

"Where are you going?" Philomena asked, coming up behind him.

"I'm going to take a look around the village," Philip said.

"Won't that attract attention?" Philomena pointed out.

"Not if it appears that I am more interested in the market stalls or a lovely lady who happens to be standing by," Philip said with a playful grin, patting his horse's neck. "Meanwhile, you should do your best to get to know our stable friend," he added carefully, looking over at Philomena.

Philomena's jaw dropped with surprise. "What?! Why me?" she exclaimed, her voice a challenging hiss.

Philip raised his eyebrows, tilted his head, and squared his shoulders with mock sympathy. "I need *someone* to get to know him while I'm busy, and you happen to be the only one with nothing to do," Philip smiled. Philomena growled angrily, stomped her foot, and folded her arms.

"So you're up to the task then?" Philip asked. Philomena shot a smoldering glare at him, fuming with defiance. Philip laughed, and swung up into the saddle with the ease of youth.

"How am I to get to know this stable boy? I'm sure he knows of my dislike for him," Philomena said, a small hopefulness in her voice.

Philip looked down at her, his steel blue eyes sparkling with mischievousness. "Phyliss, if you were to caution your speech you wouldn't be in such a predicament. So, by your cleverness and wit I have faith that you will complete the task. Although I'll give you a hint," Philip lowered his voice and leaned an elbow on his saddle pommel. "You are probably the most gorgeous, unmarried girl this village has seen. Our friend seems to have a courteous attitude. Put one and the other together and you create conversation." Philip grinned and winked cleverly.

Philomena stared up at him like he had deeply insulted her. "And what if I get into too much trouble?" Philomena shot defensively.

"Oh, I'm sure you can handle it," Philip said without concern.

"That would make it a lot easier if you'd let me have my sword back. I don't know why you listened to the stable boy about walking around weaponless," Philomena said grudgingly.

Philip ignored her. "Don't be too harsh on the poor boy if he does come to your aide. I am certain hardly anyone can handle your temper when it arises," he said.

Philomena flexed her jaw, holding back any smart remark from passing her lips, though her eyes flashed with her frustration. Philip grinned at her, unperturbed.

"Be safe, little sister," Philip said. Philomena's hard countenance softened. "Come on, Nimbius," Philip said to his black stallion, gently urging him forward at walk. He waved to Lark who was helping a traveler to saddle his horse in the breezeway. Lark stared after him curiously, and then swung his gaze around to Philomena, who instinctively glowered at him and turned on her heel. Lark rolled his eyes and sighed.

8

Philomena walked along the market street, making her way through the bustling crowds. It was noisy and chaotic and impossible to focus on a single face.

Merchants of all kinds were lined on both sides of the street, trying to draw attention to their merchandise by passionately calling out to the passersby. It was all a blur of color and activity.

Philomena could hear more than three different languages being spoken, and see all sorts of travelers garbed in differing clothes. She had hoped to find some sort of proof against her brother's words; that the stable boy he was fond of was no different than his fellow townspeople. But the further Philomena walked, the more she discovered that Philip was right.

It seemed like a thousand situations were happening at once. On the opposite side of the street, a large, lumbering traveler dressed in poor clothing walked right into a merchant, causing him to drop the crate of rare fruit he was about to sell. The fruit merchant cursed at the clumsy traveler and smashed a broken board between his legs. The large traveler howled in pain and toppled over.

Just behind Philomena she heard loud hollering, "Hey! You thieving pickpocket! Get back here!"

A homely looking boy pushed roughly passed Philomena, racing away with his loot. An angry, gruff man nearly knocked her off her feet as he rushed to pursue the young thief.

A falconer ahead was speaking rapidly in a foreign language, despairing as a bullying traveler cut loose one of his falcons. The traveler cackled with cruel amusement as he shooed the bird away and let it fly free.

Looking about her, seeing and hearing all these things happening, Philomena felt anxious and tense. Her hands balled into fists at her sides as she noted greed and malice reflecting in several of the faces around her. She really wished she had her sword at her side.

Many of the men she walked by stared after her lustfully. Philomena felt the hairs on the back of her neck prickle as she passed a quill merchant who abruptly stopped calling out to the flowing crowds to stare at her, his mouth gaping open.

Philomena kept going through the chaotic and noisy market, avoiding eye contact with any of the people. *None of these people can be trusted*, Philomena thought regrettably. She sighed and weaved in between some ladies fussing over a selection of dresses.

A small force just then knocked into her. Startled, Philomena looked down and saw a small boy sitting on the ground before her. He met her gaze with large, watery brown eyes shining dully beneath a mass of matted black hair.

"I'm sorry, ma'm," he said pitifully. "I was in the way," the boy said, lowering his head shamefully.

Regaining her composure, Philomena softened her countenance and knelt before the poor boy. "Oh, that's ok. It's not your fault," she said, with a kind smile. The boy lifted his eyes to her, utterly surprised by her kindness.

"You mean, you won't hit me?" the boy asked meekly.

Philomena shook her head pityingly. "No, I'm not going to hit you, but I will ask for my coin pouch back," she said, holding a hand out to the boy. The boy's eyes widened with fright, and his whole body tensed, ready to make a break for it.

"Please don't run," Philomena said. "There is a sergeant watching us from across the street,"

The boy flicked his eyes to the side and spotted the sergeant eyeing them. Reluctantly, the boy handed over the coin pouch he had stolen. Philomena dipped her head in thanks, and offered a hand to the boy. The boy stared at it suspiciously, but took it and allowed Philomena to haul him to his feet. The boy was light as a feather, and his hand was cold and thin. He stood just below Philomena's shoulder. His torn, dirty clothes clung from his skinny frame. His face was smeared with dirt.

"Might I ask you why you tried to steal my pouch?" asked Philomena.

The boy squared his thin shoulders. "My family's poor. We have nothing to eat," he said simply.

"Stealing isn't the answer to that though. Why can't you try to earn some money honestly?" asked Philomena.

"A poor boy like me isn't meant to have a job. That's what the other boys like me say," said the boy.

"You don't have to believe that if you don't want to," said Philomena.

The boy pursed his chapped lips doubtfully, perplexed by her words.

Philomena scrutinized him for a moment and considered her coin pouch. "I tell you what, I'll let you keep this pouch, no strings attached, if you do something for me in return,"

"Surely, ma'm," the boy said eagerly, his eyes brightening.

"Use the money to help your family. Help others if you can, and don't let this depression control you," said Philomena.

The boy considered this with disappointment. "I don't think I can do that," he said sadly, letting out a sigh.

"Can you try?" asked Philomena.

"If I try, it won't make a difference if I give up will it," the boy said hopelessly, shrugging his shoulders.

"If you try at a life better than what you are living, what is so wrong with that?" Philomena pointed out.

The boy's brow furrowed curiously. Her simple theory made sense, but it also baffled him. The world just wasn't as forgiving as she perceived it.

Philomena watched him steadily. "Will you try?"

"Y-yes," the boy said hesitantly.

"Then this is yours," said Philomena, extending the pouch to him. "Go on, take it,"

The boy accepted it tentatively, seeming fearful that the longer he held the pouch it might disappear.

"Don't let it get stolen," said Philomena.

He nodded, still dumbfounded. "Thank you ma'm!" he said gratefully. With that, the boy scurried off with the pouch, and quickly vanished amongst swarms of people. Philomena smiled after him.

"You know I can arrest you for what you just did," an arrogant voice said from behind.

Philomena turned on her heel and saw the sergeant she had spotted across the street before. He stood with his arms crossed over his breast plate with a cocky demeanor and a smug smirk plastered on his face.

Philomena's features twisted with a nasty sneer. "For what? Generosity?"

The sergeant laughed mockingly. "For encouraging the boy to rebel against his station in life that is perfectly clear: a worthless, low-life, street urchin,"

"Fine, arrest me," Philomena said carelessly throwing her hands up in the air. She abruptly turned away, throwing a disgusted glare over her shoulder at the sergeant as she went.

The sergeant smiled with pleasurable amusement, watching Philomena stride away with lust shining in his eyes. He unfolded his arms and followed after her.

Across the street, Lark McKnight pushed through the overwhelming market chaos having just finished delivering a horse Master Finn had sold to its new owner. Nothing on the market street had ever caught Lark's interest. Foreign merchants had passed through town with their exotic products, but none ever aroused Lark's curiosity.

Yet something today drew Lark's attention as he passed through the congested street.

Phyliss Stone stood out brilliantly from across the street as she stopped to admire an assortment of fruit. Although she was garbed in her plain, unusual apparel, she was the very definition of beauty in Lark's eyes. Every movement she made was full of delicate grace, yet was still strong and athletic.

Lark saw one of Commander Xavier's young sergeants following her, and seeming to speak to her most amorously. She seemed not to mind, but wasn't giving him any special attention. For some strange reason, Lark could feel a fiery resentment towards the sergeant for speaking to Phyliss the way Lark knew he was. Lark wondered why he felt this way. Why should he feel the way he did when he and Phyliss seemed to be constantly at each other's throats whenever they were near one another.

"Hey stable boy!" a voice far too familiar to Lark called out. Lark started out of his thoughts, and dreadfully turned around towards the sound of the voice, having unconsciously frozen in his tracks when he had first laid eyes on Phyliss. He saw Trez and his two friends, standing about a market stall selling woven baskets. Trez leaned against one of the tables holding several of the baskets with such negligence it was disturbing. A hearty and wicked smirk played at the boy's lips as he stared hungrily at Lark.

"Have you fallen for the fair maiden who just came into town? Or are you so ravishingly hungry that you don't have the time to think about wiping the drool off your chin?" Trez questioned cleverly, cocking his malevolent stare at Lark. His friends customarily broke into amused snickering.

"Why do you care?" Lark asked nastily. Trez and his friends cracked up with laughter.

"I think it's the first one you said, Trez," Horace snorted dumbly. "Yeah, he clearly loves her," Florez added, doubling over with another wave of laughter. Lark snarled at them.

"But he can't have her can he? It's bad enough that he's a stable boy, but it's even worse that he's a mutt, a half rogue. She wouldn't even consider him," said Trez with a mean grin.

"What do you want, Trez?" Lark asked grudgingly. Trez smirked.

"We just wanted to let you know that Commander Xavier has just entrusted to us our own swords this morning. We are now officially his sergeants, and *you* have to do as *we* say or else," Trez informed with great satisfaction and emphasis, his hand dropping to the pommel of his noted sword sheathed at his side. His friends too proudly showed off their new weaponry, their hands on their hips and their heads held high.

Lark did his best to stifle his snickering, but he couldn't help a grin spread across his face as he looked at the three of them.

"Sure Trez," Lark said, trying to keep a straight face. He started to walk away. "Just make sure you don't trip over your own ego,"

Trez stood dumbfounded for a second, and then turned beet red. Florez, Trez's red-headed friend, snorted with giggling, but a glare from Trez had him check his amusement. With a smoldering glower, Trez stormed after Lark, and giving no warning, pushed Lark into the alley between the basket and vegetable merchant.

Lark just barely broke his fall, but still tasted dirt. He spat and glared up at Trez.

"You are far too bold for your rank," Trez said, staring down at Lark.

Lark sneered at him. With a jolt of speed, he swung out his left leg, tripping Trez right out from under his feet. Trez yelped with surprise and landed with a solid thump on his backside. Lark jumped back to his feet and moved around Trez so he had an open shot for departing the alley quickly.

"You peasant swine," Trez growled, his eyes watering with the pain.

"Don't forget that you are of peasantry lineage as well," Lark said to him dryly.

"I will not remain a peasant," Trez argued, shifting himself stiffly. "You, you'll always remain low born filth," Trez said with disgust, putting a hand behind his back to where he felt bruised.

Everything happened fast. Lark bolted towards Trez, his fist balled. Trez looked up with little surprise. Trez's two friends came into view and started after Lark followed by a third figure who was smaller and faster than they were.

Trez pulled a knife he had stowed against the small of his back and smiled within as he watched Lark charge madly towards him. Trez stood and brought forth his knife to meet Lark, but someone wrenched his arm behind his back and twisted the knife from his grasp. Trez growled in pain and, grabbing his assailant with his free hand, flung his attacker to the ground before him. Lark skidded to a stop and stared with astonishment at Phyliss Stone who lay at his feet. She looked up at him with annoyance. "Don't just stand there!" Philomena barked at him. She stretched out her leg to trip over the rampaging Florez. He fell face first in the dirt with a yelp and a groan. Philomena sprung up onto her feet, her fiercely glittering eyes fixed on Trez who wore a shocked expression.

Lark rushed on Horace, who was attempting a maddened dash towards him with his sword. Horace swung out with his blade, and Lark ducked beneath the clumsy blow, and then straightened to slam his fist into Horace's nose. Horace howled angrily, and clutched his bloody nose. Lark heard another blade scrape against its scabbard and glanced over his shoulder to catch the sun's glint off of Trez's sword.

"Really? You want to do this?" Philomena asked with a pompous grin and a heedless outstretch of her arms.

Thinking quickly, Lark slammed his hardened forearm into Horace's wrist, causing the boy to drop his sword and shriek in pain some more. Lark snatched his sword.

"Phyliss!" Lark called, and he tossed the sword. Not so surprisingly, Philomena caught the sword with an expert snatch and flipped it over into her right hand.

"Make your move, Trez," Philomena encouraged with a confident smile, the point of her sword directed on him.

"You speak like a man," Trez said with repulsion. He lashed out his own blade against Philomena's.

Philomena blocked his hasty attack with one hand gripping her sword and her opposite forearm supporting the blade. Lifting her foot, Philomena shoved Trez in the chest, and then delivered an underhand cut followed by an overhead blow.

Sweat beaded out on Trez's face as he slowly retreated under Philomena's attacks.

Lark watched the proceedings in awe-inspired amazement. *Girls can't fight like this*, he thought. *Can they*?

Trez made a desperate lunge, which Philomena slashed aside, and twirled off of his blade. She came around and delivered a downward cut that smacked Trez's sword from his hand. His sword clattered to the ground between them. Philomena kicked it away and pressed the point of her blade against Trez's chest.

"Do you surrender?" Philomena asked with a triumphant grin, having not broken a sweat.

Trez's countenance was gnarled by self-loathing as he glared at Philomena. "I don't know what you are, but you have no idea who you're dealing with," he growled.

"Neither do you," Philomena smiled.

"We'll see about that," Trez said, backing away.

Lark stepped towards Trez, suddenly feeling a sense of loss for having not defeated Trez himself. "This isn't over, Trez," he called after him. Philomena blocked his way with an outstretched arm.

"You're right, it's not," Trez said, his eyes smoldering. "We'll see each other again soon, when your girlfriend isn't around to

protect you," he said, flashing a menacing look at Philomena.
Philomena gave a cocky smirk in return. Trez rushed out of the
alley. His two friends scrambled to their feet and followed after
him.

"Get back here!" Lark hollered after them, pushing passed
Philomena.

"Let them go," Philomena said, grabbing a hold of Lark's arm.
She was a lot stronger than Lark had anticipated. "Don't be such
an idiot. One must know when and when not to fight,"

"Oh, and I suppose you do know," Lark said, turning his temper
onto her.

"Yes I do," Philomena said confidently, releasing Lark's arm.

"You're a girl! You shouldn't even know how to hold a sword
let alone know the measures of when and when not to fight,"
Lark blurted out, gesturing earnestly.

Philomena regarded him with a light crinkle of her brow. "And
you shouldn't know how to toss a sword the way you did,"

"Why? Because I'm a stable boy?" Lark asked severely.

Philomena shrugged questionably and stuck the sword she still
held into the ground next to the one she had taken from Trez.
Lark narrowed his eyes and tilted his head as he considered her
thoroughly. Philomena stared back at him curiously, squirming
uncomfortably under his direct gaze.

"Why did you interfere anyway? I could have handled Trez on
my own," Lark said flatly.

"Perhaps Trez but not Trez *and* his ugly cohorts," Philomena
said. "I saved your life. You call that mere interference? Trez
could have gutted you if I hadn't stopped him,"

"Nobody saves someone just to save them," Lark said coldly.

Philomena sniffed disdainfully. "Just as you say nobody is kind
just to be kind?"

"Exactly," Lark said. "What is your motive?"

Philomena was taken aback. She struggled to provide a response.
Her fine lips parted but no words passed them.

Lark watched her carefully. He thought he caught a hint of guilt pass over the girl's fair features, but it was washed away in an instant to be replaced by defense.

"You honestly need to work on your character. Normally, someone shows a bit more gratitude towards the one who saves their life," Philomena said almost viciously.

"And you, I should note, need to show a bit more humility that is accustom to the fair ladies today," Lark said levelly.

Philomena snorted with laughter. "I'm not wasting my time on becoming a delicate lady as you put it. I have better things to do," Philomena said. She began to walk away, showing every bit of dignity she had in her stride.

"What things?" Lark tried.

Philomena smiled over her shoulder. "It's none of your business,"

Lark watched her stroll away with an easy air, and was reminded of how different she was compared to any girl he had ever met. She was confident in both speech and action. She was strong in her belief of who she was, and didn't seem to care what others thought of her. She had a humorous cockiness about her, much like her brother. Her unusual garment reflected her personality. Phyliss Stone was indeed far different, and yet Lark did not feel repulsed by her uniqueness.

Though despite Philomena's confidence, Lark sensed a heavy melancholy lingering within her which made no sense to him. Glancing up at the sky, Lark remembered the chores he still had left to do in Master Finn's stables and started walking out of the alley way, leaving the two swords and the dagger Philomena had taken away from Trez laying in the ally as silent witnesses of their fight together.

9

Philomena stepped inside the pub, the Tumbling Tankard, and was immediately hammered by the loud hollering and hooting of several boisterous, drunken men, enjoying a late evening. The pub contained many round tables that were filled with its hearty customers along with their tankards of rum and ale, and one or two plates of bread and cheese. The place glowed with the warm light of many candles from the walls and the tables, and the air was filled with the jovial music from the musicians playing near the bar.

Philomena sniffed, taking in the heavy aroma of burnt bread and the smoke from several pipes. She heaved a sigh and gathered herself as she looked around at the many, smiling intoxicated faces. A tankard flew through the air towards her and she ducked to avoid it. It slammed loudly against the door behind her. Straightening and glancing over her shoulder, Philomena rolled her eyes and shook her head before proceeding forward, making her way between the crowded tables.

The smells of sweat and alcohol filled her nose as she passed the drinking men. Crinkling her nose, Philomena wondered whether they even knew what the word 'clean' meant.

"Hey! Here comes the lovely lady!" called out a rough, admiring voice. Several eyes turned onto Philomena she walked towards the bar. Philomena kept her composure and did not meet anyone's eyes.

"Pretty thing! Where've you been?" another voice called. A couple of wolf whistles sounded from around. Philomena rolled her eyes and strengthened her stride.

"Oh come on now," a man close by said, clamping his callused hand on her arm and yanking her back. Philomena glared at him furiously, her teeth clenched together.

"Don't leave us so soon after you just come back," he said with a toothy grin, his words slurred. His breath reeked of alcohol. Philomena growled and drove her heel against the man's foot. The man howled and released her, clutching at his throbbing foot. Many angry protests rose from the onlookers. The drunken man flashed his eyes angrily at Philomena and rushed forward with a yell of fury. Philomena readied herself, not moving an inch.

Just as the rampaging man was upon her, a hard fist punched him in the face, and his crazed eyes glazed over. The man whimpered and he hit the floor with a crash and a groan. Philomena swung around and found her brother standing there.

Philip looked up from the drunken man. "Uncle has been worried sick. Are you alright?"

Philomena glared at him. "Why did you do that?" she demanded gesturing towards the man sprawled on the floor. "I could have handled him myself,"

Philip lifted his eyebrows. "Well, you are very welcome for being spared from an all out punching spree. It was no trouble at all," Philip said sarcastically. "Let's get to uncle before he explodes from anxiety," he added before Philomena could get in another word. He wrapped a protective arm around her shoulders and led her away, eyeing the men still watching.

"Where have you been?!" their uncle questioned demandingly when they arrived at his table which was nestled in the far corner of the pub away from everyone else.

"Doing exactly what my brother told me to do," Philomena said grudgingly as she sat down beside him. She directed a blaming stare at Philip who took a seat across from her.

"I told her to get acquainted with the young man I spoke to you earlier about," Philip said to their uncle. "The one I told you who might be able to lead us to Ezleon,"

Balin switched his gaze to Philip. "You mean the stable boy?"

Philip nodded. "I believe him to be trustworthy, so I sent Phyliss to see if she could find out more about him,"

Balin looked to Philomena. "And what did you discover?" he asked.

"Have you found a map yet, uncle?" Philomena asked almost desperately, ignoring his inquiry.

"No," Balin said flatly. "Answer my question; what did you find out about the stable boy?"

Philomena sat back in her chair disappointedly, folding her arms and setting her jaw defensively. Both Philip and Balin waited for her to reply.

"He fights," Philomena finally said. Their brows creased curiously. "He fights well for a stable boy,"

Philip grinned, leaning back in his chair satisfactorily. "So my idea worked did it? He came to your aide did he?"

"No," Philomena said with a shake of her head. "It was the other way around,"

Philip frowned, confused. "Huh?"

"*I* was the one who helped *him*," Philomena said. "He was being ganged up on by some snooty sergeants,"

"What?!" Balin blurted in an angry hiss, leaning towards Philomena from his seat. "You fought against some *sergeants*?"

Philip exhaled heavily and shook his head, running a hand through his hair.

Philomena felt a defensive surge rise in her. "Either of you would have done the same thing in my position," she said. "The one sergeant had hidden a knife in his belt. He could have killed Lark,"

"Don't tell me you like this boy now," Philip laughed.

Philomena reddened angrily.

"Here are your drinks, boys," said a tavern girl, planting two frothing tankards of ale on the table. She directed a favorable smile to Philip. "And will you be needing a third for your girlfriend?"

"No, I don't like ale," Philomena said flatly.

"And she's my sister, not my girlfriend," Philip said, taking up his tankard with grin and a wink at the pretty tavern girl.

She blushed and laughed. "Oh, I see," she said, smiling at Philip. Philomena stared with disbelief. She glared at the tavern girl. "Don't you have some more alcohol to serve?" she asked severely.

The tavern girl reddened with embarrassment, sensing Philomena's resentment. She pursed her lips and went away without another word. Philip looked to Philomena with a baffled expression. Philomena only gave a careless shrug. Balin cleared his throat and redirected their attention.

"What were you thinking going around and beating up on some sergeants," Balin lashed out in a hushed voice, staring upsettingly at Phyliss. "We don't need any trouble,"

Philomena flexed her jaw and glared down at the table, feeling mad and guilty at the same time. She could hear the worry in her uncle's voice, and the anger.

"Ugh, speaking of trouble," Philip muttered, his eyes locked onto the entrance of the Tumbling Tankard. Balin and Philomena followed his gaze.

"Sergeants," Balin whispered with dread.

Philomena felt her heart skip a beat as she laid eyes on the sergeants. There were three of them, wearing rough looking armor obviously crafted without any particular design or style with the insignia of the serpent and the rose of Salvador Corea poorly engraved into their breast plates. The sergeant in the center, standing a little ahead of his comrades, held himself commandingly, and slowly surveyed the pub with a mean gaze. Much of the noise in the pub had quieted, and nearly everyone was staring at the sergeants in a frightened daze.

Eventually, the middle sergeant spotted Philomena, and his cold eyes settled on her. Philomena shivered unconsciously. Balin and

Philip exchanged worried glances.

The sergeants began to walk over to them, their armor and weapons clinking with their strides. The general commotion and noise of the pub gradually started up again, and everyone went about their own business as they realized that the sergeants had no strife with them.

Philip met his uncle's eyes with a determined look as the sergeants got closer and closer. Balin shook his head, discouraging any resistance. Philip grinded his teeth.

Philomena let her gaze fall back to the table feeling lightheaded. The sergeants stopped before them as silent, stiff statues. The sergeant in the center flicked his eyes onto Philomena, and Philomena felt as though her breath was going to escape her lungs forever.

"Phyliss Stone, you're coming with us," the sergeant said.

*****

In Master Finn's traveling sable, Lark was feeling the same way as Philomena. He could see three sergeants wearing the same horribly forged armor coming from afar from where he stood in the stable pitching straw into a stall.

Panic threatened to overwhelm Lark's train of thought. He tried to concentrate on his work, but the sergeants were still coming. They strode into the stable with serious frowns and approached Master Finn who presently was speaking to a richly dressed traveler.

His heart pounding and his blood freezing, Lark ducked into the stall he had just pitched the straw into. He knew why the sergeants had come. He tried to seem engrossed in his work, chucking the fresh straw about the stall and bedding it down well.

Lark glanced up, peering through the gaps of the wooden poles that bared off the stall's windows. He could see the sergeant in front of the other two, an older man missing his left ear, attempting to gain Finn's attention. Master Finn though kept his pudgy eyes on the talking traveler, waving a hand over his shoulder in a shooing manner.

The sergeant eventually tapped the pig-headed horse master on the shoulder and Finn twisted around on him, ready to deliver a horribly smart comment. Finn's mouth slammed shut at the sight of the three sergeants, and Lark could see his meek apology.

"Hurry it along there, Lark," came a fellow stable boy's voice. Lark nearly jumped out of his skin. The other stable boy stared at him curiously from the stall door. His brown hair curled disorderly about his modest features, and his two front teeth were obviously larger than his others.

"You alright, Lark? You're awfully jumpy," the stable boy said to Lark.

"I'm fine," Lark stammered, struggling to conceal his concern. The fellow stable hand did not look convinced, but did not speak against the matter either.

"Well, Master Finn will be very unpleasant if these stalls are not bedded down in time for the new travelers," he said.

Lark nodded and began to pitch the straw around more ferociously.

The stable hand departed without another word, allowing Lark to check in on Finn and the sergeants. The richly dressed traveler had apparently left, and Lark now saw the sergeant with the missing ear speaking to Master Finn. He glimpsed a document being passed to Finn by the one eared sergeant. Finn skimmed over the words with an irritable expression. After a long moment, Finn shook his head angrily, returning the document. He pointed a directing finger Lark's way.

Lark felt like he might be sick from anxiety.

The one eared sergeant nodded his thanks and headed towards the stall Lark was in flanked by his fellow sergeants. Lark turned away, still pitching straw, and praying that he would not be noticed.

"Lark McKnight," came a voice from the stall's doorway.

Lark cringed. "Yes?" he said, his one-word response drawn out with dread as he turned around slowly to face the sergeants.

"We are to escort you to Commander Xavier's chamber," the one eared sergeant said.

"For what purpose?" Lark asked, even though he was well aware of the reason.

"That matter is to be discussed when you arrive at the Commander's chamber," the sergeant said somewhat impatiently. Lark hesitated, and unconsciously gripped his pitchfork tighter. The sergeant's eyes flicked to the pitchfork suspiciously.

"Know that if you try to resist," the sergeant spoke curtly, still watching Lark's pitchfork. "We are permitted to bring you by force, no matter how badly you are injured," The sergeant's unyielding gaze lifted to meet Lark's eyes.

Lark swallowed and shakily nodded his understanding. He tentatively set aside his pitchfork, and stepped forward towards the sergeants surrendering willingly and looking very scared about it.

The one eared sergeant gestured to his comrades and they led Lark out of the stall. Once out in the breezeway, the three sergeants stiffened into a triangular formation around Lark: two of them, including the one eared sergeant, on either side of Lark gripping his arms, and the last sergeant behind them doubly ensuring that Lark couldn't try to escape.

It was in this uncomfortable manner that Lark was led out of the stable.

As they passed through the usual commotion of the traveling stable, Lark's anxiety increased. Everyone who spotted him wedged between the muscular sergeants stared. Any traffic before them broke away quickly without request. Lark felt his stomach somersault several times. It was like he was contaminated.

No one wanted to look him in the eye. No one but Master Finn, and Lark recognized that pinched, overly concentrated frown of his that clearly said, '*You'll pay for this disturbance later.*'

Once out of the stable, the sergeants roughly steered Lark along the road leading towards the market street. The people they passed either stopped to stare curiously after them or gave pitying glances Lark's way before scurrying off.

Lark's spirits were sinking lower and lower with each nervous face he met.

They proceeded by an elderly man with long, straggly white hair and ragged clothes. He was holding what appeared to be a necklace of shiny blue beads. The old man did not flinch from the sergeants' presence like everyone else, but instead remained where he could meet Lark's frightened eyes with a steady, warm gaze.

"Peace be with you, and trust in Our Creator," he said to Lark in a kind voice. Lark stared at the man earnestly, silently crying out for reassurance.

"Mind your own business, old man," the one eared sergeant snarled, shoving the man aside. The elderly man stumbled and the beads he held fell to the ground with a gentle chiming jingle. Lark felt a pang of pity. He glanced down at the beads and caught a glimpse of a silver cross in the center. They were prayer beads.

Lark strained to look over his shoulder at the old man kneeling down to retrieve his prayer beads. When the old man straightened, he looked to Lark and nodded with an encouraging smile.

"Come on, boy," the one eared sergeant growled impatiently, yanking Lark forward. Lark's gaze was torn away from the old man. He hadn't even realized that he had slowed his pace.

The sergeants led Lark onward and sharply veered into a back alley going to the right. It took them down a shadowy little street lined with dark little shops all crammed together. They all had chipped stone steps leading to their doors. One shop had a sign hanging crookedly by a single rope over its doorway. The words 'Wonderful Dark Spells' were painted in gold against the black void of the sign.

A cloaked figure to their right was huddled against one of the many sets of chipped steps. Nothing could be discerned of the cloaked figure apart from a large crooked nose sticking out from the figure's gaping hood. Lark felt his skin crawl as he stared at the mysterious individual. He had always avoided this foreboding place, and for good reasons.

"Gosh, this place gives me the creeps," the sergeant behind Lark said in a whisper, clearly repelled by every dark secret the shadowy street had to offer.

"Remember how it used to be though," the one eared sergeant said, his sharp eyes shifting from side to side. "All those preachers and protestors filling up every corner and cranny they could find. You couldn't walk but five feet without being bombarded by some ludicrous speech,"

The sergeant on Lark's other side snorted with laughter. "The most ridiculous were those missionaries from the Old Religion," The one eared sergeant chuckled with hearty agreement. "What was it they'd always say? 'Come find peace' or something?"

"'Come find wealth in poverty and peace in spirit through Our Creator,'" the sergeant in the back provided mockingly. All three of them laughed.

Lark listened to all of this in silence. He had never been very religious, though his father often spoke of the Creator. For some reason or other, Lark felt a burning defensiveness for the religious men the sergeants were cutting down. Perhaps the missionaries had tried to raise the hopes of the people, but what was so wrong with that. The people had needed their spirits lifted a long time ago.

The road they were on gradually began to veer to the right, and a hum of many voices buzzed on the cool air. As they rounded the gentle turn, and came clear of the shadowy and malicious part of the street, Lark's heart sank heavily at the sudden sight of a long line of farmers with their humble carts of produce. Most of the carts looked as though they might fall apart any second, and several were only half filled with dusty sacks of flour or potatoes. The last harvest had been two weeks ago, and now nearly three-quarters of it was being delivered to Commander Xavier who would distribute it accordingly amongst the armies of Alamia.

The sergeants pushed Lark onward, passing by the unmoving line of farmers and their carts. As Lark stumbled on, he looked into the faces of the weary farmers and saw defeated souls: tired, hungry, and hopeless. Their clothes were torn and ragged, and they were covered with the soil they worked with. The animals pulling their carts mirrored their masters' hopelessness.

Although there was one farmer in particular who stood taller than his fellow men, like a large rock standing strongly above a rushing river. He bore a dreading expression like the other farmers, but yet there remained a glitter of determinedness in his eyes and stature. The man's features were strong and his skin was brown. Three hawk feathers stuck out from his long black hair, each of them painted half black. He led a shaggy, grey donkey that pulled a creaking cart.

Lark's eyes widened at the sight of the man, recognizing him instantly. The man was his father, Raven McKnight.

The sergeants pulled Lark along without a seconds glance at the poor farmers. As they marched by where Lark's father stood in the miserable line, the tall man's gaze rotated instinctively onto the sergeants and Lark. Raven McKnight's warm, dark eyes widened slightly at the shock of seeing his son being escorted like a criminal.

Lark trembled under his father's intense gaze, but managed a slight shake of his head, warning Raven not to interfere. Reluctantly, Raven remained where he was and attempted to draw his line of sight away from Lark.

At the end of the line of pitiful farmers there was a table with one sergeant seated behind it. A scroll was stretched out before him on the table, on which he tallied the amount of produce each farmer surrendered. Another sergeant worked to unload the carts, counting out loud as he stacked the produce. The farmer whose produce was currently being counted stood miserably to the side, wringing his hands nervously as he looked on without a word. He did not dare meet his superiors in the eye.

The sergeants led Lark around the table and pushed him up three stone steps that climbed to a thick oak door. The one eared sergeant opened the door and shoved Lark over its threshold just as the sergeant counting produce reached twenty sacks of potatoes.

Lark stumbled inside, feeling like he might topple over. A pair of strong hands caught him by the shoulders and broke his fall. Catching his breath, Lark peered up into a man's face. He was of middle age, with wavy dark hair. He did not look unkind, but tired and worn. His dark eyes flashed with abhorrence.

"Is that really necessary?" the man questioned the sergeants who had escorted Lark. The one eared sergeant folded his arms across his chest and shrugged his shoulders.

"You have no authority to lecture my men, Bazin," a thick voice said from across the room.

Lark flicked his eyes towards the voice and saw a heavily built man clad in a leather breast plate engraved with the same insignia as the sergeants' tunics. He stood superiorly behind a crude desk with his large hands planted on the rough wood. His eyes were sharp with calm alertness, shaded with suspicion. His wide jaw was taut. His chin was sprayed with dark stubble and his hair had been cropped short by an unprofessional hand. Lark recognized him as Commander Xavier, the man who controlled everything in Niche.

Lark stepped away from the man, Bazin, and surveyed the room he was in which he now knew to be the commander's chamber. The room was not especially large, and held a festering smell that suggested Commander Xavier wasn't fond of cleaning. The corners were filled with shadow, and the only source of light came from two torches blazing on either side of the Commander's desk, casting Xavier's rugged features with a shifting glow. Large dead rats hung on hooks from the ceiling close to the desk. The sight of the mangled forms made Lark shiver, and he wondered what kind of dark, torturing lair would display such unpleasant things in plain sight.

Taking his gaze away from the dead rats, Lark noticed Phyliss Stone being detained by two sergeants. She didn't look happy. Felix Stone was close by, his arms folded and his jaw set irritably. His eyes switched between his sister and the commander as if trying to figure out which one to be angrier at. Trez and his friends stood near Commander Xavier's desk. Trez smirked smugly at Lark, his eyes glittering with a malicious mischievousness.

"Do you know why you're here, boy?" Xavier asked Lark in a guttural voice. Lark's skin crawled as he felt the commander's sharp gaze pierce into him.

"It is clear to me now, sir," Lark said submissively.

"That's 'commander' sir where you're concerned," the one eared sergeant snarled, stepping towards Lark.

"For goodness sake, Renco, control yourself," Xavier snapped, glaring at his overly passionate sergeant. Renco froze, his face flushing. He took a step back, subdued, but still tried to hold himself with dignity.

Xavier shifted his dark eyes back onto Lark. "My apprentice informed me that you and this girl assaulted him in an alleyway today," Xavier paused for a moment to watch Lark who shifted uneasily. "Might you have a good reason for doing it?"

"Is that what Trez told you? That *we* attacked *him*?" Lark questioned. Xavier narrowed his eyes with annoyance, perturbed that Lark had not answered his question.

"Trez lied," Philomena put in haughtily. The commander switched his attention to her.

"Phyliss," Philip hissed warningly, looking quite angry.

"It's the truth I tell you!" Trez blurted out as he stepped forward. "Both of these two jumped me in the alleyway for no reason, just like I told you earlier commander sir!" he said, glaring blamefully at Lark and Philomena.

"That's enough coming out of you," Xavier said, staring coldly at his apprentice.

Trez swallowed his impulsiveness with difficulty, shuffling his feet and muttering under his breath. Xavier regarded Trez with deep irritability. Lark and Philomena exchanged curious glances and both understood the significance. Maybe they could get out of this with only a slap on the wrist.

The commander swung a calculating gaze about the room, as if he could smell the lies with his eyes. "Since this story of yours has two faces, let's discover which face is telling the truth . . . and which is telling the lies," His hard gaze lingered on Trez as he moved from his position from behind his desk. He walked over to a box-like crate that stood against the wall, his broad back turned to the company in the room.

Lark scrutinized the crate curiously. He hadn't noticed it before, and judging by Philip and Philomena's expressions they hadn't either. Maybe it was because the crate was veiled in shadow. The commander pulled a ring of jingling keys from his belt intended for the padlock securing the crate's door.

"Ugh, sir," one of the sergeants spoke nervously. Both Lark and Philip sensed the man's fear.

Commander Xavier ignored him as he selected the correct key on the ring, fitted into the padlock, and turned it. The key unlocked it with a sound click, but Xavier did not make a move to open the door the rest of the way. Lark happened to glance over at Trez and was shocked to see the bully's face paled over with fear as he stared wide-eyed at the crate.

"Now," the commander said, straightening and turning to face them once more. "I want you three to stay," He pointed to Lark, Philomena, and Trez. "The rest of you must leave,"

Everyone stared.

10

Philip broke the silence with a sarcastic chuckle. "If you think I'm going to leave my sister here with you, you must be smoking a bad weed," he said, his arms still crossed. A crooked smile played at his lips that somehow made him look more dangerous. Xavier raised his eyebrows. "If you are so concerned for your sister's well being, then you'll leave her with me. You do have reason to worry if you have little faith in her word,"

Philip grinded his teeth, uncrossed his arms, and clenched his hands into fists. "Why don't you take your smug remarks and shove-"

"Felix, Felix," Balin interrupted, hurriedly stepping in front of the angered boy with outstretched arms. "Cool yourself down," Balin advised through clenched teeth.

Xavier considered Philip with suspicious curiosity. "Escort these two gentlemen outside, men," he said.

Philip glared at the commander over Balin's shoulder. Lark feared that he might try to charge right through Balin.

"It's alright, Felix," Philomena reassured her protective brother confidently. Her perfect complexion remained smooth and unnerved. Philip wasn't convinced, but he allowed the sergeants to herd him roughly towards the door along with Balin.

"If something happens to her, commander," Philip said, his hardened gaze drilling into Xavier and his warning as cold as ice. "I'll hear it from you," Xavier finished.

The sergeants shoved Philip and Balin the rest of the way out of the chamber. A sergeant opened the door, casting a square of light into the dark room. The torches blazed and hissed fiercely against the fresh air. Lark could hear the sergeant outside still counting the produce from the poor farmers. He must have started on the next cart.

"You two leave as well," Xavier said, beckoning to the sergeants restraining Philomena. "She won't try anything now," he said, eyeing Philomena. The sergeants obeyed.

Philomena glared with offense. "Don't be so sure," she said grindingly.

Xavier ignored her. He didn't need to persuade Trez's two friends to leave. They followed the sergeants willingly and closed the door in their wake, cutting off the square of light. The torches settled once more.

A peculiar silence enveloped the dark room now that everyone else had departed. Xavier stared at Philomena, Lark, and Trez unnervingly. They didn't know what to expect. Trez kept his fear-filled eyes locked on the mysterious crate.

Lark turned his gaze calmly to the commander, and Philomena kept her usual confident stance. Trez was beginning to shrink away from the crate with almost invisible steps.

Xavier shook his head, perturbed by the ensuing quiet. He turned away, muttering and grumbling under his breath. Without any words, he unlatched the crate door. It opened with an eerie creak, sending shivers down the adolescents' spines.

A wave of cold air rippled from the crate and spread throughout the room. The torches' blazing flames dimmed against the sudden chilling breath of air. Lark and Philomena backed away instinctively. They unconsciously drew shoulder to shoulder to one another, their loath for one another forgotten for the time. Trez pressed himself flat against the wall, his breath coming in stabbing gasps.

Xavier assumed his position behind his desk. "I'm going to ask you three some questions and this time I want the truth," He acted as though the cold atmosphere was normal.

A rumble emitted from the crate, causing Trez to squeak with fright. Lark bared his teeth, his heart pounding in his chest. His eyes never left the opened crate. Philomena sucked in a breath, and dropped her hand where her sword usually was, but there was no hilt for her to grasp.

A clinking sound reached their ears, like chains moving with their prisoner. Then, two orbs of milky white appeared within the void of the dark crate. They locked onto them with all coldness and piercing malice. Another disturbingly quiet rumble and the white orbs advanced towards them.

Gradually, the dim light within the room revealed the hideous creature. Its skin was albino white, stretched tightly over the skull and sharp cheek bones. A nose and muzzle, much resembling that of a malnourished dog, jutted out before the deep pools of blinded eyes. Its mouth hung open, revealing the tips of large, yellowed canines. A massive paw like that of a giant cat stepped in to view.

The frightful creature stared at them as it slithered its elongated body from its prison. Its albino skin stretched over its body, scared and scraped in several places. Its ribs could be discerned, hip bones stuck out, and its chest was sunken in. Pointed ears flicked about like a horse as the creature listened for the tiniest of sounds.

"Meet the durjock," Xavier introduced placidly, extending an inviting gesture towards the creature.

The durjock responded to its name with its rumbling growl, crouching low to the ground as if about to pounce. Chains secured around its hind legs dug deep into its white skin and scraped noisily against the floor with the durjock's every movement. Its long, skinny tail twitched with nervous energy.

"What kind of cruel trick is this?" Philomena questioned. She stared horror-struck at the malnourished creature.

Xavier glared at her. "Judge all you want, princess,"

Philomena's gaze darted up to him. Xavier narrowed his eyes. "But the durjock is my special tool for handling sticky situations. My good friend here is blind as you can see. He can only hear and sense our movements. His frightful appearance does indeed help squeeze the truth out of people," Xavier walked around from behind his desk. "But they're even more willing to spill their sad little tales when I inform them that the durjock can sense lies," Xavier patted the durjock on top of the head, and the creature snapped at him viciously. Trez jumped with another squeal.

"How is that possible?" Philomena asked challengingly.

"Individuals tend to sweat more when they lie. They shake and twitch, and their heart races faster," Xavier said pleasurably.

"Yeah, well, we're already there," Lark said sarcastically, staring nervously at the durjock.

"The durjock knows the difference between fear and a lie," Xavier said, beginning to sound irritable. "He has sent twenty-three men to their deaths and another ten to the gallows,"

Lark frowned. "Isn't sending them to their deaths and sending them to the gallows the same thing?"

Xavier smirked coldly. "Let's just say it's hard to restrain the durjock once he smells a lie,"

Lark and Philomena exchanged worried glances. Trez gulped loudly beside them, whimpering pathetically as he pressed himself against the wall, his bulging eyes in danger of dropping out of their sockets.

Xavier perceived them with satisfaction. "Shall we begin?" he asked.

Outside, the sergeant counting produce was calling out fifty sacks of flour. Balin and Philip waited impatiently nearby, their nerves tightening with each passing second. Philip paced before the stone steps leading up to the commander's chamber, his hands on his hips.

"Shouldn't they be done by now?" he grumbled as he paced. An anxious frown wrinkled his brow.

"It's only been a few minutes," Balin said calmly, yet his

expression was just as agitated. His eyes were glued on the commander's door. Philip groaned anxiously.

Back inside, Xavier was beginning the interrogation with the durjock at his side.

"First question, I'll make it a simple one; is it true that all three of you had a fight in the alleyway?" he asked.

They hesitated, their weary gazes lingering on the durjock. Xavier stared at them with a sharp glare.

"Yes," Lark spoke, his throat dry.

"Yeah," Philomena put in with a nod, flexing her jaw.

To their relief, the durjock remained where it was, unmoving but alert. Xavier crinkled his nose with disgust when he looked to his apprentice who shivered beneath droplets of sweat.

"Trez, answer," the commander prompted firmly.

Trez started at his commander's voice, his scared gaze flicking to Xavier then back to the durjock. "Y-yes," he stuttered shakily. Xavier shook his head at the incredible amount of fear in the boy's voice.

"And you," Xavier said, narrowing his eyes on Philomena. "Did you knowingly take up a weapon against a sergeant apprentice?"

"Of course I did it knowingly," Philomena said flatly.

"Watch your tone," Xavier said quickly, his eyes flashing.

Philomena chewed at her lip irritably.

Xavier turned his attention to Lark. "Will you admit to taking up arms against my apprentices as mockingly as your friend?" he asked. Philomena huffed offensively.

Lark considered his words carefully. "I defended myself with my fists. I did not use any weapon against your apprentices,"

The commander looked down at the durjock, but saw no reaction from the lie-detecting creature. Xavier gazed back to Lark, looking disappointed. Lark stared back, confident in his words.

Xavier glared upsettingly over at Trez, but continued the interrogation. "Who started this fight?"

"The girl!" Trez blurted out. The durjock snarled and bared its yellowed teeth. Everyone looked to Trez. "It was the girl's fault!" Trez said, pointing a finger at Philomena.

"That's a lie!" Philomena yelled, glaring at Trez.

In the next instant the durjock sprang off the ground at Trez. Trez screamed and threw his arms up over his face. Philomena shoved him out of the way, knocking him to the ground. She looked up to see the frightening beast sailing through the air towards her, its large claws extended.

"Phyliss!" Lark yelled as he pushed her aside just as the durjock arced downward. A terrible rasping roar wracked their eardrums, and the durjock batted Lark with its giant paw and pinned him against the wall, knocking the air from his lungs. Trez cried and whined, burying his face against the floor where he lay.

"Lark!!" Philomena cried, suddenly frightened.

Forced to stare into the endless white orbs of the durjock's eyes, Lark felt his heart thud hard against his chest. The durjock's presence was overwhelming. It growled in his face, and Lark wrinkled his nose against the reeking odor of rotting meat. Despite the durjock's frail looking appearance, Lark could not budge under it's suffocating grip clasped around his throat. Philomena looked frantically to Xavier. "Do something!" she cried.

Xavier shifted reluctantly, undecided as he watched Lark's face slowly turn red.

Just when Lark thought he was about to be the durjock's next meal, Xavier called it off. The durjock released it's iron grip on Lark's throat and took a few receding steps backwards. Lark fell to his knees, coughing and spluttering as he gratefully sucked air back in to his lungs. He stared at the durjock. The creature stared back hungrily with its unseeing white orbs.

"Are you alright?" Philomena asked Lark worriedly, coming beside him.

"I'm fine," Lark panted, brushing aside her concern with an undertone of anger.

"The durjock doesn't appreciate sudden movements," Xavier said dryly.

Lark shot a poisonous glare at the pompous man. He became aware of something warm oozing down his cheek. Touching a finger there and peering at the liquid, Lark recognized blood. A gash made from the durjock's claws ran along his cheekbone beneath his right eye.

Philomena offered her hand to him and helped him to his feet. When she met his gaze, Lark was surprised to see gratefulness, even relief, on her face.

"Trez! Get off the floor!" Xavier demanded, his voice cracking like a whip.

Trez scrambled to his feet, still whimpering. He backed against the wall once more, his wide eyes staring at the durjock.

"Let's try this again," Xavier said, his voice edgy. "Who initiated the fight in the alleyway?"

There was a moment of uncomfortable silence. None of the three were eager to answer.

With an angry sigh, Lark finally provided a reply. "I did,"

Xavier straightened, his irritable expression smoothing over with satisfied victory. "How did you start it? By throwing a punch? By spitting at him?"

Lark shifted uneasily, feeling as though he were being backed into a corner. "I . . . I told him not to trip over his own ego," he said.

Xavier was taken aback. His eyebrows rose in surprise. He checked the durjock. The creature stood in silent passiveness, keenly focused once more. Xavier flicked his hard gaze back to Lark, and then to the whimpering Trez. "You threw the first blow, Trez?"

Trez nodded diligently, his face turned away, his eyes squeezed shut, and his lips pursed together unable to speak. Xavier shook his head in frustrated disbelief.

"And where do you come into all of this?" he asked, turning to

Philomena.

"I came in when Trez's two friends jumped into the fight," Philomena said.

"And the weapon? It was a sergeant's sword," Xavier said, his sharp eyes narrowing.

Lark and Philomena glanced at each other nervously.

"I disarmed Horace, and gave the sword to Phyliss because Trez had drawn his sword. Phyliss was weaponless when she came to help me," Lark said.

Xavier listened to him, though his expression was growing angrier by the second.

"Neither of us delivered any unnecessary blows. We merely fought Trez and his two friends till they ran off," Philomena added.

"So this whole thing was about you taking offense to Lark's words?" Xavier asked, his infuriated gaze piercing into Trez.

Trez looked pale as death. His mouth opened and shut a few times without any words passing his lips. He was completely flabbergasted.

Xavier leaned his face only inches away from his apprentice's. Trez slammed his mouth shut and pursed his lips together as he met Xavier's cold stare. His whole body trembled as sweat drooled down his face.

"Lying is a problem," Xavier said. "But lies coming from my very own apprentice . . . well, that just makes me angry," he said in a dangerously low voice.

Trez whimpered pathetically.

Lark shifted uneasily. Philomena watched with pity. Trez looked like he might pass out he was so frightened.

Xavier regarded him with disgust. "Get out of my sight. I'll deal with you later," he said with a jerk of his head, beckoning Trez to leave.

It took Trez a moment to unfreeze from his stiffened posture against the wall, and he glanced about uncertainly.

"Get out!!" Xavier bellowed. The durjock twitched agitatedly at the commander's side.

Trez didn't need any further encouragement. With great effort, he pushed himself off the wall and lurched passed Philomena and Lark.

The durjock emitted a rasping growl. Trez screamed and tripped, sprawling face first on the hard wooden floor with a solid thud. Xavier shook his head and turned away, unable to deal with such ludicrous happenings.

Trez looked about from his position on the floor, a line of blood streaming from his nose. His eyes widened when he perceived the durjock staring at him. Trez struggled to his feet, rushed to the door and stumbled outside, a square of light flowing into the room and then being cut off when he slammed the door shut.

Xavier ran a hand wearily through his poorly cut hair. He turned back to Philomena and Lark who remained where they were, uncertain of what would come next.

Xavier considered them with little interest but finally sighed and walked back behind his desk. "You two may go," he said. He took one of the dead rats dangling from its hook and whistled. The durjock jerked its head towards the sound. Xavier waggled the limp rat before the creature's nose.

The durjock snapped at it, getting only air. Xavier tossed the dead rat into the black void of the crate and the durjock eagerly pursued it, it's chains racing behind it. Xavier slammed the crate door shut and pulled out his ring of keys to secure the padlock. Over the sound of clinking keys, Lark and Philomena could hear the durjock devouring the rat. Lark winced at the horrible chomping and crushing sounds as the durjock enjoyed it's reward with satisfied grumbling. Philomena shivered from the disturbing noises.

Xavier straightened from his task, and seeing Lark and Philomena still standing there, said, "I misjudged your abilities, Lark McKnight. By what Trez and the boys told me, you fight well for a stable boy," Xavier hooked his ring of keys back to his belt and lowered himself into his chair behind his desk.

"Well, Trez and his friends don't fight very well," Lark said. Xavier narrowed his eyes, and Lark had a jolting fear that he had offended him. "What I mean is that they could use more practice." he added hurriedly.

Xavier laced his fingers together pensively. "Where did you learn how to fight?"

"My father," Lark said.

"You mean your Rogue father, who labors in the fields, taught you how to fight?" Xavier asked, leaning forward and cocking a disbelieving stare on him. Philomena glanced over at Lark with a new interest.

"You don't need to tell me who my father is," Lark said flatly. "And 'rogue' is not an agreeable term to us,"

Xavier leaned back into his chair in a none-too-happy silence. He now considered Lark with a new level of dislike, rolling his tongue haughtily over his teeth.

"Get out," he finally said. Lark ventured that Xavier spoke those two words more often than any others. "Neither of you think about casually slipping out of town for the next week," he added.

"Why?" asked Philomena.

"Captain Avador Corea will be arriving in Niche for an evaluation of the village," Xavier said, folding his arms atop his desk. A jolt of fear ran down Philomena's spine like an icy breath of air that made her shiver at this news.

"Lord Salvador Corea's son?" Lark said with a frown. "Why would he be coming to evaluate the village?"

"Lord Salvador Corea's coronation will be this coming spring. Captain Avador is his heir, his right hand. You do the math, stable boy, it's not that hard to figure out even for a half breed such as yourself," Xavier grumbled with a demeaning tone. Lark glowered at him, his dark eyes smoldering. The scratch beneath his eye was beginning to sting. Out of the corner of his gaze, he caught sight of Philomena's widened eyes and gaping mouth in shock of Xavier's prejudice statement.

What was the matter with her, Lark wondered. Such comments were normal and had to be tolerated.

Xavier lifted a questioning eyebrow at Philomena, obviously just as surprised as Lark over her reaction. Lark jogged her in the side with his elbow, and she hurriedly cleared her throat and shook off her shocked expression.

"We'll stay in town, commander," Philomena assured. Xavier nodded, but intrigue remained in his eyes as his stare lingered on her.

It was Philomena's turn to nudge Lark in the ribs. Lark understood the inclination and started for the door with Philomena close behind him.

"Don't get into anymore fights with my men, McKnight," Xavier said warningly after a gulp of ale from a crusty looking mug.

Lark stopped before the door to look over his shoulder at Xavier. "And if you do, I feel obliged to inform you that the durjock will eat well on that night,"

Lark didn't say anything. He turned away and departed out the door with Philomena following close behind.

11

"It's about time you two came out," Philip said with relief when he spotted Lark and Philomena descending the steps from the commander's chamber.

"We heard strange noises. We were about to bust down the door when Trez came falling down the steps." said Philip as he came over to them. His features crinkled worriedly as he noticed how uneasy they appeared.

Lark and Philomena both wore glum expressions, unable to meet each other's eyes. They just wanted to forget what had happened.

"Are you two alright?" Philip asked slowly, glancing uncertainly between them. He noticed the brutal gash on Lark's face and suddenly looked very upset.

His stare unnerved Lark. "See you later," he mumbled, trying to slip between them so he could hurry back to the stables. He hoped Finn wasn't too mad.

"Whoa, whoa wait a second," said Philip, lifting a discouraging hand to Lark's shoulder. With great reluctance, Lark stopped his countenance tight with impatience.

"You can't just leave. What happened in there? And why is your face all bloody?" Philip demanded, on the verge of distress.

Balin came forward, looking just as disturbed. "Did Xavier give you that gash?" he asked stiffly.

"That would be torture," said Philip, his voice beginning to fume.

Lark stared at them, his nerves twisting into tight balls of apprehension.

"Xavier used his creature called the durjock to interrogate us," said Philomena, folding her arms.

"The *what?*" said Philip and Balin.

Here we go, Lark thought with a sigh. He rubbed his forehead tiredly.

Philomena went on to explain what had happened in the commander's chambers. She told them how Xavier had used his lie detecting durjock to question them. Her description of the creature made them shudder. She also told them, to Lark's disappointment, how he had pushed her out of the way when they had triggered the durjock, and how it was the durjock that had given him the gash on his cheek.

"What a fowl, nasty little man Xavier is," Philip muttered haughtily once Philomena had finished. He eyed the door of the Xavier's chambers contemptuously. Despite his low voice, the sergeants still counting the farmer's produce directed vicious scowls his way.

"Felix," Balin said warningly.

"Oh, alright," Philip grumbled reluctantly. He glared at the dirt ground, folding his arms and fuming restlessly under his breath before lifting his gaze to Lark. "I believe we owe you our gratitude, Lark," he said.

Lark's insides were churning with the urge to leave now. "For what?"

"For what? For looking out for my sister," Philip said matter-of-factly. "If you hadn't taken the blunt end of that creature's attack, who knows what it could have done,"

"Indeed, you owe Lark a great deal, Phyliss," said Balin, looking pointedly to his niece.

Philomena did not reply. She was looking at Lark, her gaze regretful. She wanted to say something but a lump of reluctance welling in her throat kept her from doing so.

"And so do I; I'm indebted to you, Lark. Thank you," said Philip with a smile and a thankful nod Lark's way.

"I believe we all owe this boy our thanks," said Balin with a dry hint of a smile. Philip nodded in agreement. Philomena remained quietly brooding.

Lark was flabbergasted, and a little unnerved by Philomena's intent stare. "It was nothing, I just did . . . it was nothing," Lark said exasperated, and feeling very itchy to leave.

All of a sudden a strong, callused hand gripped Lark's shoulder from behind. Fear quickly ignited in Lark's chest. He swung his gaze around to find his father standing there.

Raven stared impassively down at his son for a moment, his dark eyes penetrating and making Lark gulp nervously. Raven flicked his attention to the gash across Lark's cheek and cupped his hand beneath Lark's chin. Lark could feel the roughness of his father's hand from working in the fields.

"Lucky we have something to treat this with," Raven said, tilting Lark's face to the side to study the gash. Lark hinted a relieved smile. "Mind telling me what this is all about?" Raven asked, lowering his hand from Lark's chin.

Lark bit his lip anxiously. "I got into a fight . . . with Trez," he added, looking down sheepishly.

Raven suddenly looked very upset. "I told you not to let Trez get to you," he scolded. He ran a hand restlessly over his long black hair. "For months you have not fought with that boy and now you fight him after he has been appointed a sergeant's apprentice?"

Lark cringed, shamefaced. He opened his mouth to reply, but was cut off.

"It wasn't his fault," Philomena said audaciously.

Lark looked around, surprised, and saw that Philomena, Philip and Balin still stood there, watching. Lark had almost forgotten they were there, having assumed they would have left.

"Trez is a bully," Philomena said.

Raven averted his attention onto her with an unmistakable authority encompassing him. Philomena stood her ground with an almost matching fearlessness.

"It may be true that Trez is a bully, but whose ever fault it was

that started the fight is for the commander to decide, which I am
sure he already has," Raven said, glancing over at Lark.
"He has," Philomena nodded. "The commander ruled in our
favor," she added.
Raven raised his eyebrows. "*Our* favor?"
"Yes, I was there when the fight broke out," Philomena said.
Raven looked back to Lark. "You were protecting her I
assume?" he asked.
"No, I . . ." Lark stuttered hesitantly. "She . . . actually helped me
in the fight," he finished reluctantly.
Raven chuckled, making Philomena frown with offense.
"You know how to fight?" Raven asked, his eyes crinkled with a
smile.
"Of course," Philomena said flatly. "I hear you taught Lark,"
Raven nodded. "He still has a lot to learn, and it is hard to teach
such things when we live in such oppressive times,"
Philomena shrugged. "Why do you live here anyway? You are
Rogues aren't you?" she asked, gesturing to the feathers in
Raven's hair.
Raven's countenance stiffened and his expression instantly fell
with what could have been detected as disappointment. Lark
rubbed the back of his neck with a troubled look.
Philomena's brow pinched confusedly, wondering what she had
said wrong.
Philip came alongside her. "Phyliss, you know 'rogue' is a
demeaning term to a native Alamian," he hissed through
clenched teeth. Understanding dawned upon Philomena and she
winced regretfully.
"Sorry about my sister," Philip said to Raven with a friendly
smile. Raven stared at him with interest. "She never knows when
to shut up," Philip added, still smiling. Philomena rolled her
eyes.
Lifting an eyebrow, Raven looked to Lark quizzically. Lark
could only shrug his shoulders. No matter how hard they tried

the Stone siblings would always draw unwanted attention. "Neither of you know when to shut up," Balin said stepping forward with an irritable expression. "Please ignore my niece and nephew's rudeness. Their words are in truth harmless. My name is Bazin Stone," Balin said kindly, extending a hand to Raven. Raven stared at him. Lark watched with taut nerves.

"It is somewhat hard to ignore them," Raven said. "Nevertheless, welcome to our poor little town. I'm Raven McKnight," Raven shook Balin's hand with a strong grip. Lark breathed in a sigh of relief.

"This is my son, Lark," Raven said, patting Lark on the shoulder.

"Yes, we've somewhat met," Balin said, shaking Lark's hand as well.

"You are not Phyliss and Felix's father?" Lark asked with a frown, taking note of Balin's earlier words.

"No, their father . . ." Balin hesitated, shaking his head. "Well, let's just say it is a long and complicated story," he finished with a forced smile.

Lark detected a deep pain in Balin's voice as he spoke. He glanced over to Philomena and Philip and noted their troubled expressions. The Stones' sudden change of mood made Lark burn with curiosity to know that long and complicated story.

"Hey!" hollered an irritated sergeant marching towards them. "Does this look like a place to just stand around and chat?" he said emphatically.

They all stared at him. "No it does not!" the sergeant said forcefully, glaring at them. "Get lost! Take up your conversation in the pub. There's better company in there than standing around with these Rogues anyway," the sergeant said, directing a disgusted sneer at Lark and Raven.

Anger swelled in Lark's chest as he watched the sergeant turn away. Philip started forward after the sergeant, a look of fury contorting his features. His uncle caught him by the arm.

"It would be a waste of time," Balin said to him, but he too glared after the rude sergeant.

"But uncle," Philip protested, scowling at the sergeant's back.

"Your uncle speaks wisely, young friend. You'd be just as wise to listen to him." Raven said to Philip.

Philip huffed haughtily, his eyes smoldering. Lark was surprised by his noble yet rash attempt to defend them.

"How can you take that, when you know it isn't right for him to treat you the way he just did," Philip demanded, looking at Raven.

"With patience," Raven replied simply.

"Don't you get tired of being patient," Philomena said with an emphatic gesture.

"Of course, but if he cannot see what we understand, than only the Creator can open his eyes now," Raven said, pointing to the evening sky that was beginning to burn with warm reds and oranges.

Philip seemed somewhat reluctant, but nodded his understanding. Philomena folded her arms and chewed at her lip thoughtfully.

"We should go," said Balin, noting the lateness of the hour. "It was nice meeting you both," he said kindly to Raven and Lark. He dipped his head in farewell, and did not hesitate in herding Philip and Philomena away from the front of Xavier's chambers. Lark watched them go, and for some odd reason felt regret nag at his chest.

"Let's go home," Raven said, putting an arm around Lark's shoulder and steering him around in the opposite direction. Raven's tired looking donkey and creaking cart stood patiently waiting for them.

"How harsh was the produce seizure this time?" Lark asked, looking up at his father.

Raven pursed his lips and gazed ahead. "We'll get by," he said determinedly. Lark looked persistent, but resisted the urge to ask exactly how much food the sergeants had allowed them to keep.

"Lark! Lark McKnight!" rose an exasperated voice over the general hum and the loud counting of the farmers' produce. Anticipation shot through Lark's mind. He knew that voice all too well. He turned around to see Master Finn, half running half waddling towards him, having trouble weaving in between the sergeants and the passers-by.

"I'll wait for you," Raven said to Lark, realizing the severity in the matter. Lark nodded thankfully and hurriedly went over to meet Master Finn.

Finn was breathing hard, his mouth gaped open like a fish out of water and his red face beaded with perspiration. He seemed very grateful that Lark covered the last few meters between them so he could slow his pace.

"Lark McKnight," Master Finn panted, trying to recover the breath that had long escaped his lungs.

"I'm coming back to work, Master Finn. There was no need to-" Lark began to say, but Finn cut him off.

"No," Finn managed, shaking his head and slicing the air with a negative gesture.

Lark stared confused.

"No," Finn repeated, trying desperately to compose himself. He bent over, hands on his stubby knees, trying to breathe normally.

"No?" Lark said, quite baffled. "What do you mean?"

Finn straightened and tried to reply but his air still hadn't returned to him. Then a horrifying realization dawned on Lark. The thought scared him, more than the sight of Master Finn, more than his memories of the durjock.

"You don't mean that you don't want me to come back to work do you?" Lark asked, horrified. Master Finn nodded eagerly, clapping Lark on the shoulder to thank him for saying it. Lark was dumbfounded for a moment.

"Look, I know I had to leave for a bit but I'll make it up to you," Lark said, angry and scared at the same time.

"Not that," Finn panted, shaking his head. He made a gesture towards the commander's chambers trying to make his reason more clear. Lark looked over his shoulder at the chamber behind him.

"Oh, come on," Lark said with frustration, pulling his gaze back around to Master Finn. "That's why you're letting me off? Because Commander Xavier needed to see me?" said Lark.

"Yes, exactly," Master Finn breathed.

"It was all just a big misunderstanding!" Lark blurted out frantically. "Trez lied. I wasn't blamed for anything,"

"My clients don't want anything to attract bad attention to the stables, and that includes stable hands on the wrong side of the law," Finn said heavily, blinking his eyes repeatedly like he might be fighting off nausea.

"I wasn't sentenced for anything!" Lark yelled in a panic, causing Finn to flinch.

"It doesn't matter, you're still . . . you're still . . . ." Finn frowned as he tried to complete the sentence.

"What?" Lark urged, his eyes flashing dangerously.

Finn shook his head, his heavy brow creasing. "Tainted with defiance," he finally said.

Lark stared. "I didn't do anything wrong!" he yelled desperately.

"Whatever," Finn said, holding up a hand to discourage Lark from saying anything else. "The point is that my clients don't want to see you working in my stables." Finn began to walk away. "I hate to do this to you Lark, but without anyone renting stalls my whole operation falls apart. Plus, people are beginning to dislike a . . ." Finn trailed off, gesturing uncertainly to Lark.

"A what?" Lark urged, feeling his face burning with anger.

"Well, a half breed," Finn finally said, scratching his head uncomfortably unable to meet Lark's eyes.

"That never bothered you before," Lark argued desperately, though a sinking feeling weighed in his stomach.

"Yes, but it's an issue now. My clients just don't approve of it anymore. That's all I'll say on the matter. I really hate to do this to you, Lark," said Finn, his voice anything but sincere. He turned away.

"But Master Finn," Lark said, taking a few steps in Finn's direction. Finn waved over his shoulder and hastened his step, not looking back.

Watching the stuffy horse master disappear up the street, Lark felt the whole world crumbling down with him underneath it. Everything around him blurred with motion as he turned back to his father with fright and hopelessness written on his face. Raven saw him and began to walk over, looking concerned.

His father . . . he'd have to tell him what just happened, Lark thought. The idea scared him. What could he say? That he lost his job; that he was sorry; that the money he always brought home to pay for their food would no longer be jingling in his pouch. Lark's stomach somersaulted.

"Is everything ok, son?" Raven asked interrupting Lark's jumbling thoughts.

Lark glanced about him, half way in a daze and half way into a nightmare. "I . . . I lost my job,"

12

It was getting late in Niche, and the sun finally sunk below the horizon. Everyone was returning to their homes or lodgings to eagerly start up a fire to ward off the chill of the autumn night. Candlelight glowed through the windows of homes and inns, squares of yellow warmth against the cold veil of night.

One by one the residents of the homes snuffed out their lights as the hour grew late. Smoke wafted plentifully from the rooftops, as well as the thick smell of the porridge that was a common dinner amongst the poor farmers.

Upstairs in the Tumbling Tankard, in one of its many rooms Balin, Philip, and Philomena sat about their own fire in deep conversation. Mugs of steaming coffee were in their hands as Philomena gave a more detailed account of her time with Commander Xavier.

She recited her story, telling them about how scared Trez was as if he knew beforehand about the horror of the durjock. She told them again of how Lark had pushed her out of the way of the monster's path.

Philip noted a change in her when she spoke of Lark. Her voice softened with regret and admiration, and she stared off into the distance, her expression glazed with reminiscence. Though Philip doubted he should mention his observation to his cantankerous sister. She would probably throttle him and deny the whole thing.

After Philomena gave Lark his well earned respect, she came to the part of what Xavier told them just before they had left his chambers.

"Avador is coming *here*?" Philip blurted with apprehension. He sat forward in his armchair, his serious gaze fixed on Philomena. Philomena nodded glumly in confirmation. She sat in a backwards facing chair, arms draped over its simply carved back. She watched Philip rub his chin with anxious pensiveness. Their uncle Balin showed no surprise to the distressing news, but his rugged jaw line flexed with disturbance. He sat stiffly in the armchair opposite Philip, leaning deep in the cushioned seat as if trying to trick himself in to feeling relaxed.

The fire crackled before them in its small fireplace, casting shadows that elongated eerily in their small, musty room.

Not standing the ensuing silence, Philip lifted a troubled gaze. "Did our friend Xavier happen to conveniently mention when the son of death and despair is arriving?"

Philomena winced. "Not exactly, he just emphasized not to leave Niche for the next few weeks. It must be soon, or otherwise he wouldn't have bothered mentioning it,"

"This could all just be a bluff to scare us," Philip muttered, staring into the fire and tapping his fingers together with nervous energy.

"There's no doubt that he is suspicious of your identities," Balin said. He turned a serious look to Philomena. "He directed this order to Lark, too, didn't he?"

Philomena nodded, sipping her coffee.

Philip leaned back with a frown. "I thought the whole country thinks we're dead. How would Xavier even suspect us to be who he thinks we are?"

"Because he is with Salvador; remember that the commanders of the towns and cities were recruited by Salvador after the siege so he could have control over every city in all three realms. They may not know the whole truth, but they could know some and I'm sure Salvador has them on the lookout for you," Balin reminded.

Drumming his fingers on the arm of his chair, Philip realized Balin was speaking logically, and was most likely right.

"He could jump us any minute. So, why hasn't he?" Philip murmured, running a hand restlessly through his hair.

"He's using Niche as our prison; we stay within its borders he won't bother us, we try to leave he'll throw us into his actual dungeon. Xavier is cunning," Philomena said.

"He knows that if we are who he thinks we are, we may still try to leave at the news of Avador's coming despite his order to stay," Philip said thoughtfully, his brow wrinkling.

Philomena lifted her shoulders in a light shrug, seeing their final decision on the matter as an obvious choice. "We have to wait for Avador to make our escape,"

"Easier said than done," Philip said with a tired sigh. "For one, we have no idea what kind of reinforcements Avador is bringing; second, his arrival could be weeks from now. We can't just sit around waiting for him to get here,"

"If we leave we'll be blowing our cover," Philomena argued.

Philip flexed his jaw, silently fuming as he glared at his sister. Philomena lifted her eyebrows, surprised by the haughty aggravation that shone in her brother's eyes.

"Uncle," Philip said after a moment, rotating his gaze to Balin. "What is your opinion on the matter?"

Balin scratched his chin pensively, the expectant gazes of his niece and nephew weighing heavily on him and unsettling his confidence. Exhaling through his nose, Balin lifted his eyes from the floor, shoving his uneasiness aside.

"You cannot underestimate Commander Xavier, or Avador for that matter. Philomena is right; Xavier is cunning. He has set words in your heads hoping for a reaction. Avador could be weeks away, he could not be coming at all, or he could already be here. The fact of the matter is that anything could happen. If it is true that Avador is out there somewhere, which I believe he is, than Salvador is definitely gathering his forces to strike the final blow and secure his victory," Balin looked pointedly at Philip.

"You mean . . . he's coming for me," Philip said, pointing an incredulous finger to himself.

Balin inclined his head.

"But I thought that I was suppose to duel Avador at Caelum," said Philip, panic threatening to overwhelm him. He didn't want to say he wasn't ready.

Balin looked upset. "You cannot be sure that is what Salvador intends especially since we took matters in to our own hands and escaped his control. He could have simply sent the order out for you to be killed. It would be convenient for him; the whole country believes you both to be dead already. But that all depends on what his plans are for Philomena. That has always been uncertain," said Balin, gesturing to Philomena.

Philomena stiffened and her gaze hardened.

Any fear that Philip might have felt instantly vanished. "I will kill or be killed before he comes within ten feet of her," he grinded out.

"Remember what I taught you," Balin said bluntly his brows furrowed. "Never rush in to a fight when you're angry. Your mind is-"

"Is moving too fast while your body is moving too slow. Yes, yes I know," Philip grumbled, rubbing his face tiredly. He sighed and stared in to the fire, cupping his hand under his chin. "I guess when Salvador heard that we escaped Tosh it made him pretty angry,"

"What should we do, uncle?" Philomena asked after a quiet moment. Philip looked to Balin hopefully, chewing at his nails.

Balin sat forward in his chair and looked at the pair of them.

"Plan our escape, stay close to each other, keep out of trouble," He shot a pointed look at Philomena. "And collect Lark McKnight," he added.

"Collect?" Philip frowned. "You make it sound like he's some overdue fee," he said, picking at a loose thread on his chair's arm rest.

"Why do we need Lark?" Philomena blurted irritably.

"You said Xavier directed this order to Lark as well as you. Just because we were seen with him, because you were seen talking to him, and especially since he saved your life from the durjock, he is considered connected to us. If we leave Lark behind, Xavier will definitely go after the boy. That will be his first move. Who knows what Avador would do to him, if he is anything like his father," Balin said looking away with deep disdain as memories flashed through his mind.

"Lark knows nothing about us; he's in no danger," Philomena said, somewhat defensive.

Balin gave her a curious glance.

"In truth he may not know anything but Xavier and Avador don't know that. Once they know for sure who you are, they'll think Lark has information concerning you," Balin said.

"Stop using the word 'you' like Philomena and I are the only ones in danger. You're a part of this, too," Philip said to Balin with light annoyance.

Philomena clenched her jaw, resentment beginning to fire in her chest. "So what, we just bring Lark along whether he likes it or not? Tie him up and gag him at night so he won't runaway? That'll just slow us down," Philomena said heatedly.

"Do you really want this boy's blood on your hands?" Balin said severely.

Philomena sat staring, his words hitting her hard.

"These men are willing to kill anyone who gets in the way, and anyone who they suspect is on your side whether they cooperate or not. I know these types of men. I've *seen* what they do," said Balin, his eyes smoldering.

"What did I just say about the word 'you'?" Philip asked casually.

Balin ignored him.

"We'll bring Lark along to protect him, for his own good, whether he likes it or not and whether you like it or not. Do you understand?" Balin said firmly.

Philomena pursed her lips and nodded, subdued and a little shamefaced. Balin's countenance softened as he watched his niece. He knew Philomena meant no harm to anyone, but she tended to be hardened due to her past.

"Right so," Philip spoke up, breaking the silence. He leaned comfortably into his armchair, as if he had nothing to trouble his mind. "What about our escape plan?" he asked, indulging in his coffee.

Balin dropped his eyes guiltily to the floor. "I was unable to find a map to help us. If there *is* one out there, I don't think it is possible for us to get a hold of it." Balin looked back up to Philip. "You understand what this means I'm sure, if we are to escape quickly,"

Philip dipped his head in understanding, his bottom lip protruding. "We really do need Lark McKnight with us," he said musingly.

"Yes, which is why you should go to him tomorrow, Phyliss," Balin said, looking over to her. Philomena gaped at him in aggravation. Her brow creased with an angry frown.

"Why does it have to be me? Why can't Felix do it?" Philomena argued.

"Because you unlike me, little sister, have the means of building the bridge of trust between us," Philip said with a teasing smirk and laughing eyes. Philomena glared at him.

"He's right," Balin said in a warning tone. "You can go over to him and thank him for what he did; that's not as suspicious as Felix going to him. Thanking him for saving you from that creature is a reasonable excuse for seeing him I believe,"

"I suppose," Philomena agreed grudgingly, her jaw taut.

Philip looked away to hide an amused grin.

"Than what's the problem?" asked Balin.

"I have no idea where he lives," Philomena pointed out, still aggravated.

"It's a small town, someone down in the pub might know," Balin said.

Philomena looked gravely disappointed as she realized she had nothing else to use as an excuse for not agreeing to the task appointed her. Fuming irritably, Philomena glared off in to space, silently surrendering.

"I think that's settled," Philip murmured, suppressing the urge to tease Philomena, but he couldn't stop the grin curling the corners of his mouth. Philomena shot a haughty sneer at him, sensing his amusement.

Balin grunted. "Good; and in the meantime I don't want either of you going anywhere by yourselves, and under no circumstances are you to go near Commander Xavier, or start fights with his sergeants. When I mean stay close, I *mean* it. Do you hear me, Felix?"

Philip spread his hands innocently. "I'm not deaf if that's what you're asking,"

Philomena snorted with laughter.

"I'm serious, this isn't a joke. This won't be like our training sessions in Tosh. If either of you die under my watch I won't be able to stand it."

Regret made Philip's expression falter. His gaze fell to the floor. Philomena's features were pained too.

Balin fixed his steely gaze on his nephew. "No heroics, Felix, promise me,"

"No heroics," Philip agreed hoarsely, meeting his uncle's eyes. His answer satisfied Balin well enough, though Balin still regarded him with light wariness. The fire crackled happily before them. A log fell and slowly disintegrated in to ash.

"We should get some sleep," said Balin, rising from his chair. They agreed readily.

As they stood, Philomena's eyes darted to the door, and she sucked in a breath at the sight of a shadow leaking beneath the door. She tugged at Balin's sleeve and gestured to the shadow that now shifted.

The three of them exchanged nervous looks. Philip cleared his throat. The shadow shifted again, as if the spy on the other side of the door was perplexed as to why it was suddenly silent. Balin motioned for them to move normally.

They stiffly went about getting ready for sleep. Philomena blew out the only candle on the window sill and placed her empty mug on the table. The lingering shadow made her tense.

Over near their beds, Philip and Balin were tugging off their boots in silence. It was very unlike Philip to be so quiet, but Philomena could tell by the tightness in his face that his thoughts were preoccupied with everything they had discussed. She wondered how much the spy had overheard, and if he worked for Xavier or perhaps a deeper, darker circle of villains.

Sitting at the edge of the bed she and Philip shared (there were only two beds in the room), Philomena pulled off her boots and let them plop disorderly on the floor. Philip slid on to the lumpy, straw mattress with a restless sigh, the scratchy blanket pulled up to his chest. His eyes remained open, and he laid his knife next to his pillow.

Balin was already in bed, laying on his side his back turned to them.

Glancing over at the door, Philomena found that the shadow had finally left. She climbed in to bed next to Philip, the tension within her lessening, but not vanishing. A tightness remained in the small of her back, like she felt as though there was still someone watching them. It was doubtful she would be able to sleep tonight.

Next to her, Philip seemed to feel the same way. He stared silently up at the ceiling, wide awake. Beneath the blanket they shared, Philomena slipped her hand in to his. Philip squeezed it reassuringly, but Philomena knew there was much to anticipate and much to fear.

With his free hand, Philip fingered the cross necklace he always wore. A pang of sympathy stabbed Philomena to see the evident sadness weighing heavily upon him, and the small pool of fury settling in his eyes. She wanted to reach out to him, get him to talk or simply say they would get through this, but the words snared in her throat.

Bitter guilt tasted metallic in her mouth as she turned her gaze to the ceiling. Her brother had always been there for her. Now she felt as though she were letting him down. She knew if he wanted to talk he would. That was something she cherished between them. Whenever they needed the other, they were there for each other. Still, Philomena felt she could do more.

"We'll be fine," came Philip's whispered voice so low Philomena could hardly hear it.

She tilted her face to the side to see him. He was still gazing upward, but his eyes sparkled with determination as though he were staring up at a diamond night sky of stars that reflected promise.

"As long as we're together, we can make it," said Philip. He gripped her hand and turned a soft smile to her.

Philomena pursed her lips, and nodded. Philip's contagious hope vibrated off him and slowly made her own faith rekindle.

Philip is right, Philomena thought. As long as they were together, they could survive anything. Exhaling with relief, Philomena lifted her gaze upward. Her and Philip stared at the ceiling together, imagining the twinkling sky they knew shone outside, until their eyelids grew heavy and sleep finally found them.

13

The following morning in Niche, Lark sat outside his home, his breath misting on the cool air. He had risen before the sun, having slept fitfully. He had tossed and turned most of the night in their damp, drafty house, troubled by yesterday's tragedy. The sun was just now peaking over the tops of the trees of Staleon Wood which had already shed most of their autumn colored leaves. A few radiant rays filtered through the thick woods and danced across Niche's sprawling fields. Bright orbs of gold light faded in and out between the faraway trees, and something on the tree branches themselves sparkled in the morning light like winking stars.

The townspeople were stirring in their homes, but none were venturing out to work yet. It was quiet, peaceful; the early morning's calm before the ensuing day's chaos. Only the sounds of the many songbirds could be heard for the crickets had long but vanished because of the cold. Lark welcomed the songbirds' comforting music. He sat on the damp dirt ground leaning against the wall beside the rickety door of his home, staring out to the golden fields.

The nasty scratch on his cheek left by the durjock still stung, and the blood had dried making it feel stiff and irritable; yet Lark ignored it. There hadn't been any thought of tending to the minor cut last night. Having returned home with the dreadful news that he had lost his job, his mother had been in an uproar and his father had spent most of the time trying to calm her down. Lark had sat at their poor kitchen table, miserably watching his fighting parents until they had finally exhausted themselves and slunk off to bed leaving him alone in the dark.

Lark watched a pair of sparrows flitter playfully about over the open fields, and longed to be one of them. He let out a despairing sigh, the smell of rotting wood filling his nose. He wondered whether the source of the smell came from the pile of stacked firewood beside him or the warped wooden boards that made up his home. It was probably both, he reasoned ruefully. He could feel splinters of the rough wood poking at his back through his tunic. He and his father had tried several times to save some money to afford to make repairs to their unstable home, but they never were able too. Now, they could hardly afford food to feed themselves.

The anguishing reminder weighed heavily upon Lark's conscious, hurling him into near hopelessness. He let his head hang, running a hand dejectedly through his hair. It was all his fault; because he lost his job, his family would suffer for it. Lark sniffed, wondering if there was any escape from such trifling things. The weight of the world suffocating him, Lark leaned his head against the wall, taking in a breath and trying to think clearly to come to some sort of solution to make up for his mistake.

There was a stirring sound behind him coming from within the house, and the shuffling of feet. The clanking of pots suggested that someone was at the hearth inside, putting something on the spit over the fire. It's probably mother, Lark thought. He remained where he was. He didn't feel like seeing anyone just yet.

Another pair of footsteps sounded from within. "It's getting colder," came Lark's father's deep voice.

"The worst time of the year for us," Lark's mother replied tiredly. "The worst time to be short on food," she said.

Lark felt guilt stab at him.

"We'll get by, like always," Raven said.

"How much food do we have from the harvest?" Lark's mother asked.

A few silent seconds ticked by before Raven answered. "Three sacks of flour and two sacks of potatoes,"

"We'll starve to death," Lark's mother said softly.

"You're forgetting the money I got from market, and Lark brought home fifteen silver pieces this week," Raven said.

"And you're forgetting that Lark lost that job. Those fifteen silver pieces will be the last he brings home. Thanks to him, we probably won't have enough food to last the winter," Lark's mother said severely.

"It's not Lark's fault, Leona," Raven said calmly. "You can't blame him for the way people are because of this depression,"

"Our son is considered a criminal; it's a reflection upon us. How are people going to treat us now?" Leona said. "Do you think he thought of his little sister when he was being dragged off to the commander's chambers? Kyla is so weak she can hardly get up to walk," she went on tearfully.

A lump welled in Lark's throat as he listened.

"Kyla will be fine," Raven said comfortingly.

"How do you know that?" Leona said chokingly.

"She has a strong spirit. She has faith," Raven said. "This is not Lark's fault, and you shouldn't think it is,"

Lark stood from the dirt ground. He had heard enough. His whole spirit ached with remorse and frustration. He started walking towards the Staleon Wood, yearning to distance himself from Niche and his family. He heard the familiar sound of that old rickety door groaning open and scraping against the dirt ground behind him.

"Lark," Raven said. Lark stopped, his shoulders sagging. Raven came up behind him, his features sympathetic. "Do not think ill of your mother for her words. This depression has burdened her in a different way,"

"I don't care," Lark said through clenched teeth, his hands curling into fists at his sides.

"Lark, this is not your fault," Raven said firmly, stepping closer to him.

"Because of me, we won't have enough food to last us through the winter. It will be because of me if something happens to Kyla," Lark said, his voice trembling with anger and self-loathing.

"It is not wrong to feel responsible, but it is harmful to punish yourself the way you are. Your mother is overreacting out of fear. Kyla will pull through her illness," Raven said with an easy confidence that annoyed Lark. Raven placed a consoling hand on Lark's shoulder. Lark batted it away, and turned abruptly to his father, his face twisted with hurt.

"Your reassurance isn't going to save us, father," Lark said hoarsely.

"You should have faith, my son, and not burden yourself," said Raven, peering at Lark with an underlining concern. "Your sister has faith,"

"Kyla is a child," Lark said, feeling angry and confused over the way he was speaking to his father.

"Sometimes believing and seeing things as a child is good," Raven said with an understanding nod. "A child perceives the world differently, with an innocence and trust that soon leaves us, but those childish ways may still live in us if we believe they can remain. Kyla is one that will always remain a child at heart. You, my son, left your childhood behind a long time ago, but you are a strong soul, you're a fighter, just like our ancestors before us," Raven said, gazing out towards the Staleon Woods.

"I don't need your Native Alamian wisdom," Lark said bitterly, feeling like the more he spoke of the matter the more his conscious was tangling with pain and resent. "I'm going to set things right . . . somehow," He started to turn away.

"I know, that's why I brought you this," said Raven bringing forth a coat made of fine buckskin. Lark stared at it for a moment, for he had never seen such a fine coat up close. It was well stitched with a gaping hood with two lines of fringe starting from the neckline to the shoulders.

"This use to be mine when I was a boy, but seeing that I can no longer fit into it, I think it's time for you to have it," said Raven with a smile. He handed the coat to Lark, who accepted it numbly. The coat was heavy, and Lark saw that it was because its many inside pockets were filled with small vials and jars of medicinal herbs.

"How did you know what I was going to do?" Lark asked quietly.

Raven grinned. "I use to be a boy your age. If I were you, I'd be doing the exact same thing,"

Lark pursed his lips knowingly. He started to pull out the herbal remedies from the coat but Raven stopped him.

"You need them more than I do. I can't take them all," Lark protested.

"Why? Are they too heavy for you?" Raven asked with a hint of a grin. "You'll never know when you need herbs out there," Raven added.

Lark hesitated, feeling wedged. His father's reasoning made sense. "Thank you, father, and-"

"I know you're sorry. Your apology is accepted," said Raven. Lark smiled weakly. He gripped his father's arm in gratitude and farewell.

"Come back whenever you can, and whenever you need help we'll be here," said Raven.

"I will," said Lark. He slipped on his father's coat and fitted the five bear teeth in their keepers to keep the coat closed. It fit him perfectly.

"Hunt well, my son," said Raven, slipping a bow and quiver from his shoulder and handing them to Lark. Raven gripped Lark's shoulders and looked him directly in the eyes.

"Remember that no matter how well you think you have planned something, the Creator has plans of His own. Things do not always go the way we expect them too,"

Lark gripped the bow, these words unsettling him but he nodded anyway and slung the quiver across his shoulder. His father waved one last farewell and Lark turned away and started for the Staleon Woods.

*****

Early morning in the market square was relatively busy, but not as boisterous. There were no bullying travelers out, and no thieves creating chaos. Xavier's patrolling sergeants yawned sleepily as they strolled along, paying little attention to the dull happenings around them.

The early risers went about their routine in an almost quiet politeness. Those buying goods were just as subdued. There was still a hum of voices on the air, but it was a stimulating sound instead of the usual jarring, nerve wracking buzz of noise.

Philip walked casually along the line of market stalls. He carried an oval shaped basket under his arm and he hummed a carefree tune under his breath. Occasional he stopped at a promising produce merchant of his choice to purchase a small quantity of the attractive food displayed.

Philomena trudged behind him moodily, her arms folded and her eyes downcast. She grumbled and fumed under her breath and kicked at a stray stone, sending it skipping to the side.

"I really wish you'd stop sulking back there," Philip said with a light grudging tone. He glimpsed his irritable sister over his shoulder.

"How do you know that I'm sulking?" Philomena questioned challengingly, firing a tight frown at Philip.

Philip ignored her inquiry. "I don't see why you're so grumpy anyway," he said.

"You want to know why I'm grumpy?" Philomena shot angrily.

"No, not really," Philip said, stopping at a merchant selling an interesting bright colored fruit.

"I'm grumpy because I was put up to the stupid task of gaining

Lark's friendship," Philomena grinded out.

"Here we go," Philip said with a sigh as he handed the merchant a few silver coins in exchange for some of the fruit. He added them to his basket which was beginning to take on the appearance of a colorful bouquet.

"Don't you think that you at least owe the poor lad a grateful thank you for helping you out in the commander's chambers," Philip pointed out, moving along down the line of market stalls. Philomena was silent behind him, her face contorted with frustration. Philip gave her a knowing look. He turned his gaze away to hide a grin.

"Why is this so painful for you anyway?" Philip asked curiously, trying not to sound amused.

"I don't know," Philomena grumbled her bitterness a burning anguish in her chest.

"Well, since you're being so open with your feelings," Philip said sarcastically, purchasing a couple loaves of bread and sticking them in the basket.

"You might as well go and tend to this stupid task that I can tell you are looking forward to," he said teasingly, distributing the heavy basket to her.

Philomena's brow pinched. "What are you talking about? You're coming with me,"

"Sorry, but I think I'll pass," Philip said casually, moving aside so some chatting ladies could go by. Philomena directed a startled frown at him.

"Uncle told us to go together. He doesn't want us to go out on our own," Philomena reminded seriously.

"Such an order never stopped *you*," Philip said flatly, lifting his eyebrows at her.

Huffing with frustration, Philomena shifted the overfilled basket on her hip and cocked a prying gaze on Philip.

Philip snorted and waved a hand dismissively. "Uncle worries too much. I need to find out more,"

"You mean, about Avador?" Philomena ventured guardedly, her eyes darting suspiciously about the few passersby.

Philip nodded. Philomena suddenly felt very perturbed . . . and concerned. She flexed her jaw and glanced around nervously.

"It's not something you should be doing alone," Philomena said with heated worry.

But Philip was squaring his shoulders and spreading his hands innocently. "I'm just going to poke around, see if I can hear anything. I'll be back in the square by the time you're done with Lark. Uncle doesn't need to know that we were ever apart,"

"No, he doesn't," Philomena said bluntly.

Philip gave a dry smile. "Do you have the directions?"

"Yes, I know where the stable boy lives," Philomena muttered. "What do you want me to do with all this food?"

"Give it to Lark," said Philip without hesitation.

Philomena stared at him. "I thought this was for us,"

"It was, but as we were walking and I realized how moody you are I unconsciously decided to put it together for Lark and his family. It's a great gift, sort of a thank you if you don't say it, and if you happen to talk meanly maybe it will help him ignore you," Philip said with a grin.

Philomena shook her head giving him a smoldering glare.

"Come on, it's not that bad," Philip laughed, patting her on the shoulder.

"Yes it is," Philomena glowered. "It's bad enough that I have to befriend someone I don't want to befriend but now I have to worry about you,"

"It will be fine," Philip reassured her. "Just another day in the village. We won't get in to trouble, I promise,"

"We always get in to trouble," Philomena said matter-of-factly.

"I have to do this, Philly," Philip said his voice suddenly quiet. He glanced nervously as a sergeant passed by giving them a suspicious sideways glance. The sergeants had probably been ordered to keep a close watch on them.

Philip stepped closer to Philomena. "I need to know when we have to make our move. I promised to take care of us, remember?"

Chewing her lip, Philomena reluctantly gave in with a gruff pent of air. She knew that straight faced determined look of Philip's. "Fine," she whispered. Philip grinned happily and kissed her cheek making her scowl.

"Make sure you don't let that get stolen," he said, gesturing towards the basket.

"That would be a lot easier if you let me have my sword back," Philomena grumbled.

"And make sure you're back in the square in an hour. We don't want Uncle Bazin finding out we disobeyed his orders. He'll do that silent anger thing of his," Philip added.

"Make sure you don't do anything too reckless," Philomena said through clenched teeth so no one else nearby could discern her words.

Philip smirked. "I'll try not to, little sister. No worries," he said. He waved and started walking in the direction they had come from going further in to the market, most likely to throw off the sergeants watching them.

Philomena watched him go till he was swallowed up by the flowing crowd, deep down feeling that they had made the wrong decision. There wasn't much she could do about it now though. They were set on their separate paths. *Please be safe*, she thought, glancing up at the sky in silent prayer.

With difficulty, Philomena directed her attention onto her own task. It took her forty minutes to reach Lark McKnight's home. The directions her uncle had gotten from the bartender were a little shady, and twisted her around a couple times before she finally discerned them.

She now laid her eyes on a small cottage standing alone fifty yards away from the clustered houses and shops of Niche. A skinny dirt path rimmed with yellowing grass broke off from the main road she was on and snaked over to the ram-shackle cottage. Philomena hefted the heavy basket of food and took a moment to survey the poor home. Most of the homes she had seen in Niche were run down and patched up, but this one was falling apart. It was like a wounded soldier, pushed aside to carry his own agony and pain.

Philomena started down the dirt path, looking on at the miserable home with sympathy for those inside. As she got closer, she noticed that the boards of the home were warped, and there were occasional large gaps between them. The roof was in dire need of patching.

The path took Philomena around the front of the home where a rickety door humbly offered entrance inside. An unstable overhang shaded the cottage's face. The overhang's right hand support post had a large rock beneath it to make up for the length it lacked. Philomena raised her eyebrows in amazement at the structure. When she finally lifted her gaze to the cottage's door she was somewhat startled to find a little girl crouched on a piece of firewood beside the door watching her. The girl was no more than seven years old. She wore a white night gown that was dirty and torn. Her face was pale, and dark circles were beneath her tired eyes.

"Hello," Philomena said kindly after recovering from her initial shock. "I'm looking for Lark McKnight. Is this where he lives?" The girl nodded.

"Are you his little sister?" Philomena asked, noticing the resemblance.

The girl nodded again.

"Do you know where your brother is?" Philomena asked.

"I'm right here," came Lark's voice.

Philomena snapped her gaze up and saw Lark standing at the end of the overhang, holding two dead hares and a bow. A quiver of arrows was slung over his shoulder and he still wore his father's boyhood coat. A look of astonished bafflement mixed with fright was plastered on his features.

Philomena considered him with curious interest.

"First hand to hand combat, now a bow," she said with light amusement, gesturing to the bow Lark gripped.

"It's just a hunting bow," Lark said steely. He moved closer to his little sister. "What do you expect from a Rogue, anyways," His sister glanced up at him with a confused frown. Philomena shifted uncomfortably, unsure of what to say in reply.

"What are you doing here?" Lark asked after a moment, his voice edgy.

"I, ugh . . . I came to bring you this," Philomena said, trying to sound cheerful as she brought forth the large basket of food. "Sort of a thank you for helping me," she added.

"How did you find me?" Lark asked seriously, ignoring the generous basket of food; although his sister stared at it hungrily. Philomena hesitated, not at all surprised by Lark's behavior.

"The bartender at the Tumbling Tankard," she said. Lark looked away with a knowing expression.

Philomena watched him curiously. "I heard you lost your job," she said.

Lark snapped his gaze back to her, bitter resentment flashing across his features. "So you brought your basket of food to show your sympathy?" he challenged.

"Frankly, no," Philomena said, not at all perturbed by Lark's tone. "The food is a gift, a thank you for everything. Really, it was Felix's idea,"

Lark stared at her for a moment, calculating every tiny emotion in her response. "Tell your brother thank you," he finally said, turning away to hang the pair of hares he held on a hook dangling from the overhang's ceiling.

"You're not going to accept this are you," Philomena said in a low voice, letting her gaze drop to the basket. Somehow, she found herself disappointed.

"No, I can't accept it," Lark said flatly, leaning his bow against the stacked firewood. He turned back to the hares he had killed. "My mother won't believe me if I try to explain it. She'd think that I'd stolen the food," he said, ducking his head to hide his own disappointment and shame. He pulled out a knife to start skinning and cleaning the hares.

"What am I going to do with all this food then?" Philomena asked exasperated, shrugging her shoulders.

"There are plenty of people in the area who are hungry. I'm sure they'd be more than happy to take it off your hands," Lark said, a slight edge of defense in his voice.

Philomena flexed her jaw, aggravation gnawing at her patience. "Perhaps explaining a gift of food would be far easier than trying to explain to her how you acquired those hares when hunting isn't allowed without proper registration through the commander," Philomena said heatedly.

Lark narrowed a vicious glare at her, gripping the hunting knife he was about to use till his knuckles whitened. His little sister watched them nervously.

Before they could enter a full out brawl, Philomena turned on her heel and strode away, down the skinny dirt path and out of sight. Lark grinded his teeth and dug his fingernails into his palms.

Philomena stormed down the path boiling with frustration, and yet guilt as well. She slowed as her guilt grew heavier, and looked back over her shoulder, then down at the basket she still cradled.

Heaving a sigh, Philomena looked about her and found a barrel standing at the corner of Lark's house. She moved over to it, rotating her gaze to be sure no one was watching. She knelt down beside the barrel and tucked the basket between it and the wall of the house. No one would be able to casually see it from Niche's streets and Philomena was certain that one of the McKnight's would find it. The barrel was used to store a day's supply of water, so when one of them would come to fill a pot or pale, they'd most likely stumble upon the basket.

Straightening, Philomena began to walk away again, feeling pleased with her decision.

14

A nervous sergeant proceeded cautiously down a blind alley alongside the storage house two buildings down from the commander's chambers. It was disturbingly quiet, and early evening was gradually settling in. The sergeant swore he had heard a suspicious sound come from this alley; scuffling feet or maybe a door creaking shut. The eerie sense that he was being stalked by whoever had made the noise had the sergeant's hairs standing on end.

Perspiration gathered on his face under his helmet. His sword shook in his trembling hand as he ventured further down the alley. He squinted his eyes, trying to see passed the jumbled piles of crates and barrels. Shadows lurked amongst the accumulated rubble. The silence vibrated against the air and the damp smell of mold and rotting wood filled his nose.

Feeling anxious to leave and return to the comfort of the main road, the sergeant turned back towards the alley's opening, deciding that whatever he had heard before was a puckish street urchin or merely a trick of his imagination.

"I'll take that," spoke a voice from the shadows. The sergeant spun towards the voice, his eyes wide and his mouth gaped open. He jumped when a hand shot out from the gloom and grabbed his sword. A balled fist flew out and punched him in the nose toppling him to the ground. Philip stepped out from the shadows, gripping the sergeant's sword with a cocky grin on his face.

"You need to go back to your first year of training, friend. A good warrior knows to never go down a shadowy blind alley alone," Philip said to the unconscious sergeant.

Glancing about him to be sure no one had witnessed his actions,

Philip knelt down beside the sergeant and began stripping him of his armor. As he unstrapped the miss-matched armor, he adorned it on himself, along with the black tunic stitched with Salvador Corea's insignia. Once he was finished, the sergeant wore only his trousers and a white tunic.

"I'll return these as soon as I'm done," Philip promised, fastening the leather strap of the helmet beneath his chin. The helmet's visor was small, but it would conceal his face enough for no one to recognize him.

Philip dragged the unconscious sergeant between some old crates so no one could see him from the road. For safe measures, he secured the man's hands and feet together with some twine. Just as Philip was tying the last knot, the sergeant groaned and his brow wrinkled. Before he could even open his eyes, Philip brought back his fist and slammed it hard against his jaw. The sergeant lay limp once more.

Philip grimaced, feeling somewhat bad. "Sorry, I'll be back shortly," he said, straightening and walking up the alley.

He reached the alley's opening and sheathed the sergeant's sword at his side. He glanced up and down the road. Only a few locals were passing by, and a traveler on horseback. Doubt started to swarm in Philip's mind, twisting his stomach into uncomfortable knots. If he messed this up, and Commander Xavier discovered him, the man would most likely throw his family in the dungeons. It would be over for them.

Philip swallowed his throat dry all of a sudden. He knew that Balin would be furious with him once he found out, even more so if he were caught, but he also knew that walking around disguised as a sergeant might lead to hearing vital information about Avador; information that in the end could save them. Feeling reassured that his plan was worthwhile, and hoping no one would be able to tell he wasn't really a sergeant; Philip let out a deep breath and started to stride up the road towards the commander's chambers that was just in view. He passed a circle of local villagers chatting. The villagers caught sight of him and instinctively ceased talking and lowered their gazes.

Philip pretended not to see, but beneath his visor he was pursing his lips pityingly.

The door to the chambers ahead clicked open and a real sergeant stepped out. He closed the door behind him and descended the few stone steps to the road.

Philip composed himself, inhaling to calm his nerves. He put on the eager, naïve obedience of a young sergeant and met up with the real sergeant. The older man noticed Philip and drilled a contemptuously irritated frown into him.

"You have a poor sense of time, Trycket," the sergeant said in a guttural voice. "Xavier has needed you in his chambers for the past fifteen minutes," he added, indicating the chamber's door with a jerk of his thumb.

Philip lifted his eyebrows, shocked that his plan was working and that his secret assumption the sergeants here were only sharp enough to recognize each other by their mismatched armor was correct.

"Yes sir, right on it," Philip replied enthusiastically. He passed the sergeant and hurried up the steps to the station. The older sergeant frowned inquisitively after him as if he had just noticed something peculiar.

"Just a moment there, boy," the sergeant called after Philip seriously. Philip grimaced, and turned around to face the sergeant's confused frown.

"What happened to that stubble of yours? It was getting close to being a beard," the sergeant asked, folding his arms and gesturing to Philip's chin.

"You noticed that did you?" said Philip forcing a laugh. "Yeah, well, I decided to delay my facial hair growth a little longer,"

"It was there this morning," said the sergeant, tilting his head slightly with a confounded suspicion that made Philip feel like a bear trap was slowly clamping shut on him.

151

"I went back home to shave," said Philip rubbing his chin. The sergeant's eyes narrowed and he flexed his jaw. Philip watched him for a moment, fighting to retain a calm demeanor.

"You see, I would have let it grow out, but a few girls said I'm better looking clean shaven. So, what are you going to do?" said Philip, spreading his arms in a vague gesture.

To his relief, the sergeant chuckled. "I guess that's a good reason. Maybe that's why the ladies never liked me," He indicated his own beard that was dark with flecks of grey.

Philip pursed his lips and shrugged, unsure of how to reply without offending him.

"Well, you better get in the chambers before Xavier explodes from impatience," the sergeant said, motioning Philip towards the chamber door.

"Yes, sir," Philip nodded, and eagerly left the sergeant standing there frowning after him.

Philip climbed the three stone steps to the chamber building. The old oak door creaked open and emitted Philip to the dark room inside. The two torches behind the commander's desk blazed defiantly against the gust of cool air from the open door. The firelight highlighted the silhouettes of two people; one man at the desk and another in the center of the room. Although he was able to keep a calm demeanor on the outside, Philip could feel his heart thudding with nervous excitement as he closed the door behind him. It felt like he was locking himself in a dungeon's cell with his enemies.

Once his eyes adjusted to the darkness, Philip found the first silhouette was Commander Xavier. The commander stared at him critically from where he leaned against his desk with his arms folded across his chest. The other silhouette was a young man Philip didn't recognize. Philip assessed him curiously. The young man stood with the confidence of a trained warrior, his hand resting on the pommel of his sheathed sword. His sleek black hair swept over his brow and dropped to his shoulders, and his steady gaze rested on Philip.

"You needed me, commander," Philip said stiffly, coming obediently towards Xavier and hiding his interest in the young man.

"Show some respect. This is your future crown prince," Xavier said thickly, gesturing to the young man.

The words slammed Philip like a battering ram. His eyes darted from the young man to Xavier and back, terrified shock threatening to overwhelm him. He swallowed his sudden emotions with difficulty and turned respectfully to the young man.

"It is an honor to meet you, Captain Avador," Philip said with a stiff bow. Avador watched him, but said nothing.

"You will also have the honor of assisting Captain Avador in his task here," Xavier said.

"Anything, my liege," Philip said, straightening. His increasing adrenaline felt like fire pumping through his veins. It was hard to keep his breath at a normal rate and his voice level.

Xavier gestured for Avador to take over.

"I need a meeting arranged in a convenient place, the market perhaps. The town's entire occupants, the travelers included, must be there," Avador said. Hearing his young voice, Philip realized that in truth he was just a boy.

"Everyone must be there?" Philip asked, managing to keep in character.

"Everyone," Avador said with a nod. "And I wish for all business to cease during this meeting to assure that everyone attends. I need you and your fellow sergeants to announce the meeting, spread the word, and make sure everyone comes. My men will help secure the square, and will be posted around the perimeter of the village to make sure no one avoids this meeting,"

"What is the purpose of this meeting?" Philip asked. He felt the itching desire the turn on his heel and fly out the door, but he had to stick it out. He had to find out what Avador was planning.

"If you do not know the purpose of my task here, then you'll never know, and neither should the occupants of the village. My purpose is to remain inconspicuous," Avador said guardedly, a harsh steel of defense shading his eyes.

"Understood, my liege," Philip said with a submissive bow. "I shall begin making the arrangements, if I might have permission to leave now?"

"One more thing, I expect the meeting to begin within the hour, no sooner and no later," Avador added. Philip nodded his understanding.

"I will see you in the square in an hour's time then. You may go, sergeant," Avador said, dipping his head in gratitude.

Philip bowed once more to Avador, and then turned away fighting the urge to rush wildly out of there. Once out of the chamber, he bounded down the steps nearly falling on his face. He stopped at the bottom of the steps his mind whirling, his heart racing, and his adrenaline forcing his breath out in gasps. Swinging his gaze around, Philip was torn in what to do. Agitation clouded his thoughts as he tried to swallow the fact that his enemy was in the chamber building behind him.

Taking a deep breath in an effort to calm himself, Philip caught sight of a couple of young sergeants conversing nearby. Philip's mind cleared instantly, and a clever grin spread across his face. He approached the two sergeants and addressed them formerly, informing them of the 'meeting' that Avador had requested.

"A feast?" the one sergeant questioned after Philip had filled them in.

"In thirty minutes?" the other sergeant added incredulously.

"Mmm hmm," Philip nodded with a smile. "It's sort of a celebration of Captain Avador's visit here, and since he'll be leaving earlier then he expected, he would like to make a presentation to the people before he leaves,"

The two sergeants looked at each other doubtfully.

"But, how are we to put together a celebration in thirty minutes time without anything planned?" the one sergeant asked skeptically.

"Well you certainly won't be able to with that kind of attitude! Now let's get to it, chop, chop," Philip encouraged, clapping his hands and causing the sergeants to jump. "You go rally up some chefs and food merchants, and you go start spreading the word. Everyone should be here. The feast will be in the market square," Philip said.

The sergeants nodded propelled into action, and trotted off towards the market street, chatting over their scheme to pull off the celebration feast.

"And tell the chefs that the bill is to be paid by Avador himself!" Philip called after them with a mischievous grin. He turned and made his way back to the blind alley in which he had stowed the unconscious sergeant. When he came to the alley's entrance, he shifted his gaze about to be sure no one was watching before slipping in the narrow path.

The evening sunlight was instantly cut off by the buildings leering over on either side, and once in the alley's cover Philip released a troubled groan. Avador was already here! He had to hurry and get back to Philomena and Balin. Philomena should be back from Lark's home by now.

Quickening his pace, Philip hurried to get moving, fumbling with the straps of the breastplate he was wearing. He made it halfway down the alley only to feel the tip of a sword poke against his back.

"Hold up there, boy, nice and easy," a deep voice said from behind. Philip froze, grimacing. A few silent seconds ticked by, and Philip's pulse raced.

"I believe I know who *you* are," the man mused. He reached for Philip's sword, pulled it out, and tossed it aside. His own sword he kept pressed against Philip's back.

Philip's hairs were standing on end, his already agitated

adrenaline churning even more.

"Trust me, sir, I don't think you know who I truly am," he said in a low voice.

Philip suddenly dropped to his knees and kicked his mysterious opponent out from under his feet. The man's sword flew in to the air as he toppled backwards. Philip caught the sword and stood over the man, pointing the blade's tip to his chest. The man was middle aged and dressed as a sergeant. His green eyes glittered with a fiery resentment beneath his helmet's visor.

"Now, what should I do with you," Philip said with mocking consideration, his own eyes glittering with an undeniable hardness.

"Wait! Please," a small, muffled voice said from somewhere on the ground. Philip tensed at the sight of something squirming beneath the man's tunic. A small pinecone-like creature with scales emerged from the tunic and sat up on the man's chest, staring up at Philip with beady black eyes.

Philip stared at the creature with intrigue, and his brow pinched with confusion.

"Forgive my friend's rudeness," the creature said, glaring pointedly at the man. "But we are not here to harm you. We are your allies,"

"You . . . you're a comae?" Philip stuttered with disbelief.

"Obviously, but yes. The name is Ramaro, and it is an honor to meet you, Prince Philip," the comae, Romaro said with a graceful bow. Philip stared with astonishment.

"You do know who I am," Philip said taken aback. He unconsciously lowered the sword he gripped.

"We do for certain now," the man grumbled with annoyance. He sat up, and Ramaro climbed onto his shoulder before he stood. Philip tensed, raising his sword to the man.

"Don't worry, prince, you won't be needing that," the man said, gesturing to Philip's sword. He dusted himself off. "My name is K'smet, and like Ramaro said we are on your side,"

"K'smet . . ." Philip mumbled, his brows coming together as he tried to remember. The man's name was familiar. Then it hit him. "K'smet as in *Sir* K'smet?" he asked.

The knight regarded him with something like approval. "I was sent here by your mother," he said.

"My mother?" Philip said a little breathless, the very thought of his mother making his mind go numb with disbelief.

K'smet dipped his head in confirmation. "She wanted me to find you before Avador Corea did, although I am cutting it a bit close," he said ruefully.

"K'smet," Ramaro hissed impatiently, tugging at the knight's tunic collar. "There's no time for idle chit chat," he said urgently.

"Yes, you're right," K'smet agreed. Philip looked to them with an expression of overwhelmed amazement. He felt as though someone had just slugged him over the head. It all was so much to take in.

"We have to get moving prince, before Avador finds out about that clever feast you're holding for him," K'smet said, moving to take Philip by the arm. But Philip backed away and raised his sword.

K'smet froze and lifted his hands yieldingly with a tight grimace. "How can I trust you?" Philip demanded, his eyes blazing and his palms sweaty.

K'smet cursed himself. He didn't blame Philip for reacting the way he was. "Easy, now prince," he said huskily, eyeing Philip's sword. "You can trust me; I'm here to help you. You remember me from the castle don't you? I was to be one of your weapons instructors. I'm one of your parents' best friends,"

"The question is whether you are still a friend," Philip said dangerously, making Ramaro gnaw nervously at his nails.

"I can tell I'll be wasting my time if I give you a pretty speech of why you should trust me," K'smet said grudgingly. "I've already seen your uncle and sister-"

"What?!" Philip growled, pressing forward. He could feel his temper rising. K'smet lifted his eyebrows, feeling a little nervous.

"K'smet, don't make him angry," Ramaro muttered in K'smet's ear.

"Your uncle and sister are both waiting for us in the stables, with our horses saddled by now I reckon. We're prepared to leave Niche now, only we can't leave without you," K'smet said with forced patience. Philip stared at him.

"Here," K'smet said, fishing something small and shiny from his trouser's pocket. "Maybe this will help. You're uncle said you wouldn't be easy to convince,"

K'smet handed the shiny object to Philip who accepted it without taking his eyes from K'smet. Philip rolled the object around in his hand, and looked down at it with a curious frown. What he held was a large silver ring, with the crest of Caelum in the center: a circle with a cross in the center and feathers on either side.

"The ring of Alamia's crown prince," Philip said pensively.

"Your ring, my prince," K'smet said, peering expectantly at Philip. A silent moment passed. "Are you satisfied now?" K'smet asked somewhat curtly.

Ramaro rolled his beady eyes. "You are so impatient,"

Philip considered the ring for another moment. He knew there was only one ring like this and that his uncle had been keeping it for him. Balin wouldn't just pass it over to anyone.

"Yeah," he finally said, looking up to K'smet. "I'm satisfied," Philip offered K'smet back his sword, tucking his ring into his pocket.

"Good," K'smet said, sounding rather relieved. He happily accepted his sword. "Now let's get to the stables," K'smet said, sheathing his sword and moving to leave the alley.

"No," Philip said flatly.

"What?" K'smet exclaimed, his eyebrows shooting skyward.

"We can't leave, not that way at least," said Philip hesitantly with a gesture to the alley's opening. "We should use the roof tops so that way we're not at risk of being spotted, and my prank feast can set in. While we're climbing on the rooftops, everyone else will be headed to the town square, even Avador,"

"That's a great plan if Avador remains locked up in Xavier's chambers long enough before finding out it's all a joke," K'smet said sarcastically, cocking his head and placing his hands on his hips.

"We'll have just enough time before Avador figures it out. If we just waltz out on the streets it will take us twice as long to reach the stables, and by then they'll be hot on our tails," Philip argued determinedly.

"Believe me, they'll be hot on our tails either way," K'smet said grudgingly.

"Five minutes, then," said Philip, with a frank gesture. "Give my plan five minutes to sink in before we leave,"

"Fine," K'smet grunted. "At least we can rid ourselves of this dreadful armor," he grumbled, turning away from Philip's triumphant grin. He started unbuckling the armor he was wearing which he had borrowed from Xavier's storehouse.

"I like this prince," Ramaro whispered happily into K'smet's ear. K'smet shot him a sharp look. "What?" the comae asked innocently, and K'smet grumbled under his breath.

Five minutes later and Philip and K'smet had abandoned their sergeant uniforms. The sergeant Philip had knocked out earlier still lay sprawled amongst the old crates and barrels, and was now snoring softly. The hour was growing late and the sunlight dimming.

"It's only a matter of time before Avador comes out of those chambers," K'smet warned. Without the sergeant's armor, K'smet's dusty blond hair fell about his rugged face, and Philip recognized him well enough to place him in his memories from Castle Caelum.

"Luckily, we'll be on the rooftops by then," Philip said assuredly. He was stacking barrels and crates to create a staircase to the rooftops, choosing the ones in the best of shape with the least rot.

"*Before then* is far more preferable to me," K'smet muttered, his arms folded over his chest. He glanced at the cross necklace that dangled about Philip's neck, his weather worn features twitching in recognition. He shook himself out of his thoughts. He glanced at the rubble Philip was stacking together, then to the rooftops which it towered to.

"What did your uncle teach you in Tosh?" K'smet scoffed lightly. He unfolded his arms and handed Philip the next crate. Philip chuckled half-heartedly.

"My uncle taught us how to survive," Philip said tersely.

"And creating makeshift staircases out of crates and barrels was in that category?" K'smet prompted. Philip looked at him sharply. K'smet lifted his brows innocently. Philip snatched the crate from him and positioned it as the last step in his staircase. Ramaro, still perched on K'smet's shoulder, grimaced at the exchange.

"I don't care if you ridicule me, *Sir* K'smet, but you don't need to demean my uncle. He's taught us as best as he could under the restrictions of house arrest, and he's sacrificed far more than you would ever think of," Philip cut harshly. The knight didn't even twinge. Instead he regarded Philip with a new respect.

"You'll need courage to break Salvador and all the lies he's webbed," K'smet said warmly, stepping forward and gripping Philip's shoulder. Philip met his stern gaze. "I meant nothing personal," he added.

"Right, sorry," Philip said, pursing his lips regretfully. K'smet waved aside his apology.

"And what K'smet really means to say is that he is the rudest, most inconsiderate knight that ever served under your parents," Ramaro piped in. A dark glare from K'smet quieted the comae, and Philip couldn't help but smirk amusedly.

Voices reached them from the main road. Snapping their gazes to the alley's mouth, they spotted a river of villagers going by. "They're headed for the town square," Philip said quietly.

Not needing to say anything further, Philip and K'smet hurriedly began to climb the tower of crates and barrels. They did so as quietly and quickly as possible. Ramaro leapt from K'smet's shoulder and climbed over the rough wood with ease, scurrying past Philip.

As they climbed, they could hear the voices on the road behind them grow louder. The smell of roasting meat wafted to them, making their stomachs growl.

Philip reached the eaves of the rooftop after Ramaro, and heaved himself up, feeling the rough shingles against his hands and knees. His gaze darted about seeing the neighboring rooftops and smoke spouting from the chimneys. The sun was a mere streak of bright orange and red on the horizon, the temperature sinking with it. Philip turned back around to help K'smet, his breath clouding the air.

K'smet stretched out his hand to grasp the roof's eaves, stepping up onto the last crate. With a *snap* the crate's boards broke beneath his weight and the entire structure began to crumble inward. Cursing aloud, K'smet scrambled to grab the roof's edge, but the collapsing crates and barrels were dragging him along. Philip shot out his hand and clasped K'smet's arm before he could slip out of reach. Philip hauled K'smet up to the roof, the staircase of crates and barrels tumbling end over end making an even more disorderly heap with some loudly smashing to pieces against the hard ground below.

K'smet exhaled in relief. "Thanks," he whispered gratefully.

"Don't mention it," Philip said with a smile.

"I think we better move," Ramaro urged, his wide eyes staring down into the alley. K'smet and Philip followed the comae's gaze downward, and saw the shadows of a couple men in the dancing firelight of the road. The two men were coming towards the alley at a fast trot.

"Let's go," K'smet whispered, pulling Philip along by the arm. Ramaro scurried behind them.

They moved swiftly, the roof beneath their boots rising slightly to meet the other side at a triangular point. When they reached the roof's center, they slid over to the other side on their stomachs where the roof angled downward again. Ramaro slipped between them and clambered fretfully aboard K'smet's shoulder. K'smet shot an annoyed glare at him.

They lay there silently, waiting for the two men to investigate the alley. They could faintly hear the footsteps of the men as they entered the alley, and then everything went quiet.

"Do you see anything?" they heard one of the men say, breaking the silence.

"Just the usual rubble," his companion said irritably. "Probably some stray crawling over the crates,"

There was a smashing sound, like the irritable man had just kicked at one of the rotten crates. K'smet and Philip lay patiently as a few seconds ticked by. Eventually they discerned the slight sound of footsteps once more.

"I hope there's enough roast at the feast," they heard the first man say hopefully, his voice fading away out of the alley along with their footsteps.

Both K'smet and Philip felt the tension in their muscles subside. Ramaro slumped on K'smet's shoulder with relief, looking rather weary.

"That was easy," Philip said happily.

"Don't expect them all to be that stupid," K'smet muttered, casting a knowing look to Philip. K'smet rose cautiously, staring over into the alley. Seeing that it was empty, he gestured to Philip that it was clear.

They began to move westward along the rooftop, stepping stealthily and their eyes darting around to be sure no one spotted them. When they came to the next building, a three foot gap separated the rooftops creating an easy jump from one to the other. A few stars were beginning to wink against the evening's velvet sky. It was getting colder by the minute.

"You sure you know where you're going?" K'smet whispered to Philip. Ramaro had huddled back inside his coat.

"This road leads into the market street," Philip whispered back, pointing down to the road running along their right hand side. "The shack at the end of this line of buildings is the blacksmith's. The stables are at the end of this road," Philip assured, jumping to the next building.

Glancing down at the road from the rooftops, it felt as though they were walking along a cliff and the road below was a fissure running through a canyon. The road was quiet, and lit by only a few torches creating great orbs of bright yellow light spaced unevenly along the dark street. Even the Tumbling Tankard offered no noise. Everything on the road below seemed to be sleeping. A few roads over though they could see an ebbing haze of yellow light pulsing from over the rooftops from several torches and fires right where the town square would be. They could hear the jovial hum of laughter and music, and the sweet scent of roasting meat mixed with other savory smells that made their stomachs rumble.

"Sounds like your feast is in play," K'smet said quietly, looking over the rooftops at the warm yellow glow coming from a street over. "How much time do you think?" he asked anxiously, already getting tired of jumping from roof to roof.

"Ten minutes," Philip said, slightly distracted. He stepped over on to the blacksmith's roof which creaked dangerously beneath his feet. He could feel the old wood and shingles shift beneath his boots. K'smet came right behind him, grumbling fussily when he felt the uncertain stability of the roof beneath him.

"There's the stables," Philip said, pointing to the three large stables standing just beyond a kilometer of open space.

"Great, let's get off this thing before it collapses under us," K'smet muttered eagerly. Philip smirked.

They lowered themselves to their knees and slid themselves over the edge of the shack's roof and dropped to the ground landing with a gentle thud. They cautiously rotated their gazes, feeling tense and anxious from the stillness of the road.

A muffled sound almost like someone grumbling under their breath caught Philip's attention. With a frown he peered into the shack and spotted Eric the blacksmith slumped on an old stool asleep, his head lolled against his large arms that were folded atop his workbench. A line of drool trailed from the corner of Eric's mouth to his chin. The grumbling sound was Eric snoring. Philip fought an amused snicker. "Looks like someone is going to miss the fun," he whispered over to K'smet with a gesture towards Eric.

"It appears he has had his own fun," K'smet whispered back, noting the bottle of rum half full next to the snoring blacksmith. "Let's go," K'smet said, starting towards the stables. Philip followed. They covered the dark open ground between the shack and the stables at a fast jog, their senses peeled for any movement that hinted a threat.

The traveling stable's double doors were open as they always were, and it was quiet as everything else was right now. The many horses slumbered in their stalls, and K'smet and Philip were grateful to find that it was warm inside. A few torches near the end of the stable were lit, providing sufficient light to make out the familiar surroundings. Philomena and Balin stood in the breezeway with four saddled horses waiting patiently nearby. Philip felt a weight of worry vanish from his shoulders at the sight of his uncle and sister. Any suspicion of K'smet's loyalty disappeared from his mind.

Philomena caught sight of K'smet and Philip and looked vastly relieved. "Thank goodness you guys made it, we thought something might have happened," she said stepping eagerly forward to meet them. Balin came forward as well, directing a scolding glare on Philip.

"Nothing happened, sister. At least nothing interesting," Philip said, draping an arm around Philomena's shoulder and steering her back around to the horses. He gave his uncle a nervous grin. Balin shook his head but said nothing, and followed them over to their horses.

"Are we ready to leave?" Philomena asked looking to K'smet.

"Yes, Princess Philomena," K'smet said to her, lifting the reins over his horse's head.

Philomena moved quickly over to the side of her grey steed sensing the urgency in the air, and hurriedly checked her horse's girth before swinging up into the saddle. Philip swung up onto his black stallion next to her and gathered his reins.

"I'm so glad I finally have my sword back," Philomena said to her brother with a hint of accusation. She touched the reassuring hilt of her sword sheathed at her side. Philip smirked at her in acknowledgement.

"You have a route in mind," Balin asked, hurriedly tightening his horse's girth.

"Whichever way leads us north will suffice, Lord Balin," K'smet said, quickly checking his saddle packs and his weapons his horse carried.

"Let's move then," Balin said placing a foot in his saddle's stirrup.

"Hold it," a young composed voice spoke. Everyone stiffened and snapped their eyes forward.

Captain Avador Corea stood in the stable's gaping entrance, a sword gripped in each hand. Six men were on either side of him, some with longbows knocked with arrows and some with knives or short swords. All six wore fringed buckskin garments and feathers in their long black hair. They all radiated the calm readiness of strong warriors.

Philip exchanged a worried glance with Philomena, feeling an anxious tightness pull at his chest.

"No one's going anywhere," Avador said calmly.

15

Captain Avador and his six native soldiers gave them no time to react in anyway. Before Philip and Philomena knew it, two of Avador's men were yanking them from their saddles and confiscating their weapons and horses. Balin and K'smet were stripped of their weapons as well, their hands quickly bound behind them and then pushed aside.

"Aren't you a little late for your feast, *Captain* Avador?" Philip spat venomously, fighting against the man who gripped his arms.

"Your prank wasn't enough to fool me, although I will admit that your idea of using the rooftops was clever," Avador said levelly, turning his steady gaze upon Philip. He strode over to him. "You may have dressed as a common sergeant a little while ago but it is clear you are not one,"

Philip held Avador's gaze, setting his jaw. He had to give the boy credit for being sharp enough to recognize him from Xavier's chambers.

Avador looked him slowly up and down, his dark eyes narrowing in consideration.

"I believe I can prove you are no mere sergeant," he said coolly. Avador grasped Philip's right arm and jerked back his sleeve. He turned Philip's forearm to reveal the exposed scar that burned as brightly as a beacon against Philip's skin.

The corners of Avador's mouth twitched satisfactorily. "The scar of the double beamed cross," he said quietly. He lifted his gaze to Philip who glared back.

"Prince Philip," Avador confirmed. The men restraining Philip and Philomena exchanged victorious grins.

"What do we do with their equipment, captain?" one of the men asked, holding up the swords he had taken from Balin and K'smet.

"Anything of use to us, weapons, food, we'll keep. Leave the horses to the horse master, we have enough to feed," Avador said sensibly.

His men obliged with loyal obedience, and began to go through the saddle packs starting with Philomena's horse. The grey stallion sidestepped and bobbed his head upsettingly as one man gripped his reins and another rummaged through Philomena's packs and pulled out anything that fit Avador's list of value. K'smet's face paled as he watched what the natives were doing, and flicked his eyes nervously over to his own saddle packs. One of the soldiers dumped the weapons he had collected beside Avador. Avador bent down to pick out a favorable looking sword from the pile.

"You men are natives," Philomena said, glancing around at Avador's men curiously, her voice tinged with disappointment. One of the natives passing by, a stocky built individual wearing three raven feathers in his long black hair, caught what she said and stopped abruptly.

Philomena shifted meekly under his penetrating stare, pressing her lips in a thin line as if to be sure no other comment passed them.

"Does that bother you, princess?" the native prodded cruelly, cocking his head indignantly. His dark eyes glittered treacherously in the torchlight, making Philomena swallow nervously.

Avador darted his attention to his vengeful sergeant. "Bright Sky, don't do anything rash," he cautioned, unsheathing the sword he had picked out.

Bright Sky wrinkled his nose disdainfully before walking away, throwing one last venomous glare at Philip and Philomena. Observing Avador interact with his men, Philip and Philomena could sense the near brotherly bond. There was loyalty and respect between them, as well as friendship.

K'smet and Balin surveyed the happenings from their own viewpoint, having had their hands secured and then forgotten, apparently not considered a very important priority in Avador's mind. Ramaro stuck out his pointed nose from K'smet's coat with caution.

"Clear?" Ramaro asked in a hushed whisper.

"Clear, hurry it up," K'smet whispered back.

"Don't get bossy with me," Ramaro said, climbing out of K'smet's tunic and scaling up and over his shoulder. He scrambled down K'smet's back till he reached his hands and began to gnaw at the bonds that secured them. Balin edged closer to K'smet so they were shoulder to shoulder.

They watched Avador and his men closely. It appeared though that the company was more concerned about guarding Philip and Philomena and stealing from their saddle packs than paying much attention to their other hostages, and Avador remained engrossed in the confiscated sword he held.

Avador tested the sword's weight and balance appreciatively. He turned it here and there, and rolled it over in his hands for a good deal of time without saying a word. Philip and Philomena watched him. Philomena especially glared at him with a jealous bitterness.

Inspecting the craftsmanship of the blade and the simple silver swirls engraved into the hilt and pommel, Avador flicked his gaze to Philip. "Yours, I take it," Avador ventured, but Philip shook his head.

"It's mine," Philomena said rigidly.

Avador turned to her, his eyebrows lifting in surprise. "A girl, with a man's blade," he said slowly, soaking in this curious notion. He strode over to them.

"The sharpest thing you should ever hold is a quill," Avador said, stopping before Philomena, and allowing her sword's blade to hover an inch from her chest.

Philip lunged at Avador, but the two natives behind him held him back with an iron grip.

K'smet watched tensely. He wriggled his hands, anxious to be free and flinched when Ramaro's sharp teeth caught his wrist. Balin glanced over at him with a frown.

"Stop moving," Ramaro hissed. K'smet growled impatiently.

"And perhaps the sharpest thing you should ever hold is a fan," Philomena replied to Avador crossly.

The sergeants restraining them 'oohed' and laughed at her boldness. Philip snorted with laughter himself, ducking his head to hide his amusement. Avador glared at Philomena, flexing his jaw. His knuckles turned white as his grip tightened on the sword.

Balin glanced over at K'smet expectantly. K'smet nodded, tossing aside his severed bonds and moving behind Balin to untie his. Ramaro crawled atop of K'smet's shoulder, his beady eyes darting about nervously.

"I did my part, gents," the comae said, slipping into the comfort of K'smet's tunic. "The rest is up to you," his muffled voice finished.

K'smet finished untying Balin and threw away the ropes.

"Thanks," Balin said, flexing his wrists gratefully.

"You go get them, I'll get the horses," said K'smet. Balin nodded, and they set to work. K'smet hastened towards the unsuspecting natives stealing their belongings, while Balin dashed to the pile of their confiscated weapons. Their sudden movements caught inevitable attention.

"Hey!!!" hollered one of Avador's men, who charged at Balin. Avador glanced up frowning, as did the natives guarding his prized prisoners. It was all the distraction Philip and Philomena needed.

Philip jabbed his elbow back and heard a groan. He spun on his heel and slammed his palm under his other retainer's nose. Philomena drove the heel of her boot hard against the foot of the native to her left, and turned to punch him in the chest knocking him backwards.

Just as Philip knocked down his second restrainer, the back of his neck prickled and he heard a shout of alarm. He ducked low and felt the blade of a sword swoosh over the top of his head, stirring his hair. Senses peaked and adrenaline pumping, Philip straightened and twirled around to see Avador. The young captain did not look happy, and his iced over features were that of a confident warrior who knew how to kill.

"I hope you've trained for this as hard as I have," said Avador, circling Philip stealthily.

"Yeah, me too," Philip agreed, glancing around for a weapon. Balin snaked his arm around a charging native's sword, flipping the man off his feet.

"Philip!!" he called, tossing the native's sword to Philip just in time for him to block an overhead swing from Avador. Their blades met with an ear shattering clash.

Over near their four saddled horses, K'smet easily took down the two natives who had been stealing their belongings. Bundles of food that they had already collected went scattering about the ground. The four horses snorted and pranced nervously, and K'smet moved to settle them.

Avador drew one of his own swords, and swung it in union with Philomena's for an arching overhead cut. Philip managed to block the two blades, leaning forward with all his strength and supporting the end of his own sword with his wrist. He strained to keep Avador's swords at bay, grinding his teeth with the effort. Finally, he managed to break their draw and push Avador back, pulling their swords down and locking their blades between them.

"Would you like to train for another year?" Avador asked. Philip growled, and pulled his sword free. Their swords screeched against each other and sent sparks flying.

Philomena took down the last native with a final arching kick to his jaw. The man jerked to the side, did a half twirl, and then fell senseless to the ground.

"Philomena!" Balin yelled as he hurried up to her.

"Are you alright?" Philomena asked turning to him.

Balin nodded, and hinted an approving grin down at the unconscious native. "Great kick, my niece, just as I taught you. Now get to K'smet and the horses. I'll get Philip," Balin said, handing her Philip and K'smet's swords. He turned away, drawing his own sword and rushing over to Philip and Avador. Philomena hesitated a moment, but an encouraging yell from K'smet galvanized her into motion.

Balin skidded to a stop before the two sparring boys, and called to Philip but he did not hear. He was engrossed in his match with Avador.

Avador slashed out with his right sword and Philip cut it aside. A flash came from Philip's left, and he flew out his hand to grasp Avador's wrist, stalling his clever side attack with his second sword. Their strength was at a draw once more, broken by shoving each other backwards and their weapons untangling. Philip attacked first this time with an overhead cut. Avador blocked it with his left sword and flung Philip's blade aside, bringing his right sword forward hilt first. He caught Philip behind the knee with the cross guard, and yanked Philip off his feet.

Avador swung his left blade around, his dark eyes sparking with contempt as they drilled into Philip laying at his mercy.

Balin rushed over and grabbed Avador's wrist with a bone crushing grip. Avador yelped in pain and dropped his sword. With burning anger he swung his remaining sword towards Balin.

Fear ignited in Philip. He kicked out his foot and tripped Avador out from under his feet. The young captain tumbled to the ground and Philomena's confiscated sword fell from his grasp. Giving him no time to recover, Philip leapt on top of Avador and smashed his fist against his nose. He came back with another hooking fist to the jaw then delivered a punch to his gut, forcing his air out in a gasp. After that, Avador lay on the ground in a daze, clutching at his sore stomach.

Philip straightened and stepped aside breathing heavily, his eyes lingering wearily on Avador.

"Philip!" yelled Balin, hurrying over to him and grabbing him by the shoulders. Seeing that he didn't have a scratch on him, Balin slumped with relief. Philip grinned at him.

"You did good," said Balin huskily. "But we've got to go,"

"No argument here," said Philip. He gathered Philomena's sword and left Avador groaning where he lay.

They made for their horses, jumping over the unconscious native soldiers. Philomena and K'smet rode forward to meet them, leading Philip and Balin's horses along with them. Philip and Balin hurried alongside their steeds.

"We don't have time for heroics," K'smet lectured as they swung in to their saddles. He shot a pointed glare at Philip.

Philip exchanged a frown with Balin and squared his shoulders inquiringly.

K'smet shook his head and grumbled irritably. Without another word, he clapped his heels against his horse's side and took the lead, galloping fiercely out of the stables with the others close behind.

Avador lifted his head groggily. His eyes widened when he saw the four horses stampeding towards him. Frantically, he rolled out of the way just in time, and felt the ground tremble underneath him as the horses pounded by. Avador punched the ground and cursed angrily. He scrambled to his feet and half ran half stumbled out of the stables. The four riders were racing down the street towards the market.

K'smet led the others down the unevenly lit street and then veered left onto the market street. The market stalls and shops went by in a confused blur, yet they could still tell that the entire market had been left completely vacant. Every commoner was at the feast Avador let happen.

They continued down the silent dark road at a strong pace, keeping together. The cold air whistled in their ears and stung their faces. It was officially night and a half moon shone radiantly above the village with winking stars to accompany her. Philip ventured a look over his shoulder, and saw the empty street behind them. He looked to the road ahead, breathing inward with the small relief that no one appeared to be chasing them.

Something made a dull strumming sound. Philip frowned and looked around to the side and caught sight of an arrow flying towards them.

"Duck!!!" Philip yelled, dropping low over his horse's neck. Next to him, Balin did the same and the arrow sailed harmlessly above their heads.

Philomena glanced back at them, and snapped her gaze to the rooftops where she could see more arrows taking flight as they rode by.

"K'smet!" she hollered to the knight riding beside her.

"I know!" K'smet called back over the pounding of hooves. He encouraged his horse to a faster pace. The loyal steed obliged stretching out his stride to a greater length, his breath fogging the air. The others followed eagerly, keeping low to avoid the arrows that split the air above their heads.

"STOP! STOP SHOOTING!" hollered a commanding voice from somewhere behind them. It sounded like Avador's voice. Despite his command, a few arrows still rained down on them. Philip yelped when one of them stabbed into his arm sending a stinging hot pain shooting up to his shoulder.

"Philip!!!" Balin shouted in alarm. Philomena looked over her shoulder, fright clutching her. Philip cringed and clenched his teeth against the pain. His wounded arm refused to move and was completely useless. His black stallion easily fought his waning hold and surged past Balin and his chestnut.

Struggling to get his horse under control, Philip could feel his strength dwindling quickly. Philomena came alongside him, reached over and grabbed the reins of his rampaging steed. Philip gratefully let her take control. She pulled the stallion alongside her own bringing him to a steadier gallop. Balin came on Philip's other side. Philip slumped against his horse's neck enduring the throbbing pain coursing through his arm.

K'smet cursed viciously, feeling their situation growing more dire. He led them onward, till the road broadened, lined on both sides with craftsmen's workshops. K'smet eased his horse to a trot and then stopped, rotating a perceiving gaze about the quiet road. No one had followed them.

The others halted behind him.

"What are you doing?" Philip questioned with exasperation, his pulse drumming in his ears. He was breathing heavily and his pale face was beginning to bead with perspiration.

K'smet said nothing. He wheeled his horse around and came alongside Philip. Without warning he grabbed Philip's wounded arm and expertly pushed the arrow the rest of the way through till the tip broke through the skin on the other side. Philip grimaced and chewed at his bottom lip. K'smet snapped the arrow tip off and quickly yanked the staff from Philip's arm. Philip growled and doubled over against his horse's neck refusing to yelp. He clutched at the bloody hole that the arrow had left. Philomena put a hand comfortingly to his shoulder, her brow wrinkled with worry. Balin tore part of his white sleeve off, and K'smet pulled his horse back to give him some room. Balin leaned over from his saddle to wrap the piece of cloth snugly about Philip's arm.

K'smet sniffed the tip of the arrow he still held. He licked the arrow head and swooshed his saliva about his mouth, his brow knitted with concentration. Philomena considered him with slight disgust.

Philip grimaced as his uncle secured the cloth around his arm with a tight knot. "You'll be alright," Balin said reassuringly to him. Philip nodded, clenching his teeth.

K'smet threw away the arrow and spat on the ground. "No poison, so I reckon you'll live," he said, considering Philip with light sympathy.

"There *shouldn't* be any poison; Salvador wants us alive," Philomena said. K'smet looked to her. "Doesn't he?" she asked, suddenly doubtful by K'smet's reluctant expression.

"We can never be sure, princess," K'smet said stiffly. "Not with a mind like Salvador's,"

The distant sound of pounding horse hooves from the road behind them caught their attention. Gazing down the dark road, they discerned nothing, but they knew Avador was coming.

"We have to go," Philip said urgently, wincing as he gathered his reins. His black horse chomped anxiously at his bit.

"Yes, you do," K'smet said, slipping down from his saddle.

"What are you doing now, K'smet?" Philip demanded.

K'smet ignored him. "Take my horse," he said, tying his horse's reins to Philip's saddle pommel. Philip stared at him with confusion.

"Inside the saddle bags is the key to all the information I've collected on Salvador. It should be all you need to defeat him and bring an end to this," said K'smet, taking his bow and quiver from his saddle and slinging them over his shoulder. He met the prince's eyes with a strong determination without fear or regret. The drumming of hooves was growing louder and approaching fast. Philip could feel his spine prickle with the pulsing urge to move, but confliction held him fast.

K'smet pursed his lips. "I am glad to have met you, both of you," he said with loyal warmth. With one final glance at them, K'smet turned away, pulling an arrow from his quiver as he went.

Philip watched him go with a heavy regret weighing on him. He longed to call out to the brave knight, but his words remained snagged in his throat.

"I'm staying as well," Balin said, stepping before Philip and Philomena, sword in hand.

Philomena's eyes widened with panic. "No! We can't just leave you here!" she cried frantically. She tugged at Philip's shirt, like she might climb over him just to get to their uncle in an attempt to stop him.

"We can give you enough time to get out of the village," Balin said firmly.

"No!" Philomena protested chokingly, moving as though she was going to dismount her horse. Philip stopped her. She tried to yank away from him. "Let go!" she yelled, trying to smack him away. A bitter lump swelled in her throat.

"There's no time to argue!" K'smet yelled huskily, raising his bow and pulling back the arrow till the feathered shaft tickled his cheek.

Riders suddenly rounded the bin and emerged from the lurking shadows of the road with Avador at the head of the party mounted on a fierce black stallion. Fear shot up Philip and Philomena's spines.

"For the love of God, get out of here!" Balin hollered at them. "GO! LEAVE!" he yelled, waving his arms frantically. Philip and Philomena still hesitated, their horses shifting nervously beneath them.

"BALIN!" K'smet yelled urgently, letting his arrow fly. The arrow sliced the air, and thudded against the side of an old cart cutting the rope that held its bulging load of barrels. The barrels came rolling out, tumbling over each other and bouncing across the road before Avador and his men.

Xavier's riders slid their horses to an abrupt stop, with one of the men sailing over his horse's head from the momentum. Avador forced his horse forward, jumping one of the barrels and galloping strongly onward. His native company followed easily, either dodging the barrels or sailing over them.

K'smet knocked a second arrow to his bow and pulled it back. "Get going!" Balin yelled, seeing Avador still coming. He brandished his sword and smacked its blunt side hard against the rear of Philomena's stallion. The stallion tensed and shot forward up the road, taking Philomena by surprise and leaving her breathless. She fought uselessly against her horse trying to turn him back around but the stallion's mind was made up to go forward. She tried to glimpse her uncle over her shoulder, with so many emotions stabbing through her it left her blinking back tears and chocking for air.

Philip clapped his heels against his own stallion and the horse lunged forward, racing after Philomena with K'smet's horse galloping beside him.

"DON'T LET THEM ESCAPE!" Avador bellowed.

Arrows arced through the air from Avador's men. K'smet released his second arrow hitting one of archers and making him crumple to the ground. Another rider yanked his horse back and dropped to the ground, frantically scrambling to his fallen comrade. K'smet saw him roll the still form over, saw his arrow sticking out from the man's chest, and heard the mournful cry rip through the night.

Avador came charging, and swung out his blade aiming for K'smet's head. K'smet ducked and grabbed the end of Avador's sword, yanking him right out of his saddle. Avador tumbled against the ground, his horse cantering off.

A rider raced by Balin after Philip and Philomena. Balin sidestepped and slashed out with his sword, cutting the saddle girth clean through. The saddle and his rider slipped from the horse's back and smashed to the ground.

Philip flung his gaze over his shoulder, and met his uncle's eyes. So much was exchanged in that brief moment. Philip's mind was a whirlwind of emotions that left everything around him in a dazed blur of motion, leaving only his uncle visible. It all was happening so fast and yet so slow, Philip wondered if it was real or just a horrible nightmare.

His horse bounded up the road that curved behind the buildings, and suddenly Philip's view of Balin was cut off. The loud sound of his charging horse and the whistling of the rushing air exploded against his ears. Philip swallowed with difficulty, blinking hard, but looked on ahead urging his horse to greater speeds.

Gradually, he caught up with Philomena so he was just behind her. They rode hard down the dark winding road lined with haunting shack-like cottages with heart pounding adrenaline surging them on.

Fear was a nasty culprit, and played tricks which their imaginations exaggerated. Shadows snatched at them with vicious black claws. The rare lit torch roared at them with teeth of fire and flying red embers hissed laughingly, swirling in their wake. The air hissed menacingly in their ears and jarred their nerves. Everything seemed to be against them.

The lines of ramshackle homes suddenly ceased, gaping open to the welcoming clear fields that stretched between Niche and Staleon Woods. Two sergeants on horses with pikes and flickering torches stood in the path before them. Seeing their swift approach, the sergeants crossed their pikes and held their ground firmly, blocking their way out of Niche.

Philip and Philomena pulled back on their reins to avoid a head on collision and their horses slid to a stop. They exchanged uncertain glances, breathing heavily with their fingers hovering over their weapons. Their horses blew hard, arching their necks, and chomping at their bits.

"There is no passage out of Niche at this time," said the sergeant to the left, his voice hollow against his helmet and his escaping breath fogging the air.

"We're in a bit of a hurry," Philip said, trying to catch his breath. The sergeants stared at him. It was difficult to tell what they were thinking judging by their expressions because most of their faces were covered by their helmets.

"It is best that we escort you back into the village," the sergeant to the right said.

"I don't think so," Philip said defiantly.

"For goodness sake, Philip, there are only two of them!" Philomena said determinedly, pulling out her sword and urging her horse forward. The sergeants tensed in their saddles.

"Wait, Philly!" Philip called to her desperately, drawing his sword as well.

A net suddenly sprang forth from the shadowy opening of the abandoned cottage behind them and smacked into Philomena. The round stones tied at the corners of the net swung around, wrapping the mesh about Philomena and dropping her to the ground.

The springing sound came again and a second net enveloped Philip. He landed on the cold ground with a hard thud, grimacing as hot pain flared in his wounded arm.

"Secure their swords!" commanded one of the mounted sergeants.

Philomena looked around through the mesh of the heavy net and spotted two bulky men half garbed in grubby, soiled clothing lumber quickly out from the gloom of the open doorways of the last two houses. Philomena frantically tried to pull her sword free from the netting it had been tangled in, but the blade was wrapped snuggly in the mesh and refused to budge from its prison.

The bulky man with an eye patch made of what looked like matted wool started for her, grunting as he hobbled towards her, his one good eye gleaming horribly beneath his heavy brow. She pulled a knife and brandished it through the netting, but the bulky man gripped it and bent the blade. Philomena gasped and tried to crawl backwards.

The other large man rushed at Philip brandishing a spiked mace, roaring loudly like an untamed beast. Philip yelled back and jabbed his sword through his netting, catching the man in the shoulder. The large man howled in pain, dropping his mace, and scrambling away down the street, clutching at his bleeding shoulder.

Philip slashed out his sword again and the net imprisoning him fell away. The two mounted sergeants came forward towards him, lowering their pikes against him.

The other bulky man stretched out his hairy arm to grab Philomena in his strong grip. Philomena tensed. She had nowhere to go and no weapon to use against him.

"Philly!" Philip yelled, desperately trying to fend off the two mounted sergeants who were encircling him tightly with their horses. He hacked off one of their pike tips and made a lunge at the sergeant before him. The sergeant kicked him in the chest, shoving him backwards against the other sergeant's horse.

"Face it boy, you've lost," the sergeant who had kicked him said, his breath clouding the air.

"I'll show you who's lost," Philip growled, wrinkling his nose angrily. He reached up for the sergeant's arm behind him and jerked the man out of his saddle. The man flipped through the air and landed on his back between Philip and his comrade. Philip knocked him unconscious with a boot to the cheek.

Philomena swallowed hard and her eyes widened as the burly man's filthy fingers hovered over her, hesitating as if he feared to touch her. A blur of grey suddenly slammed into him, and he stumbled violently to the side.

Philomena glanced about with surprise and saw her stallion standing there, ears pinned and eyes wild. Philomena couldn't help but grin with relief.

The burly man yowled with anger as he steadied himself and turned vengefully towards the horse. He pulled a wooden club from a loop on his thick leather belt and hefted it readily in his large hands. The stallion flattened his ears and flicked his tail determinedly.

Philomena felt the air prickle with tension and did her best to crawl further backwards. As she did, her burdensome net slipped over her head. Philomena glanced down at it with a frown, but didn't waste any time. She pulled herself the rest of the way out of the net and started to untangle her sword, looking around at Philip who was punching out the last sergeant.

The burly man raised his club. The stallion lunged forward and struck out with his front legs. His hoof caught the man on the shoulder crumbling him to the ground howling in pain.

The wounded man struggled to his feet, clutching his shoulder. He dropped his crude club letting it roll away, sniffling with watery eyes. Defeated, he lumbered down the road whimpering and sulked in to the shadows out of sight.

Philomena finally freed her sword and rushed over to meet her protective steed. She wrapped her arms around his neck in a grateful embrace, and silently promised to always take care of him. The stallion bobbed his head happily, his eyes glittering.

Philip delivered one last punch against the sergeant's cheek letting him crumple to the ground. Straightening, he circled his gaze searching for any other enemies. Satisfied that no one else needed knocking out, he hastened over to Philomena and her stallion.

"Are you alright?" Philip asked anxiously.

Philomena nodded. "Are you?"

"Fine," Philip said. "Let's get out of here," He made for his horse who stood by with K'smet's horse at his side.

Philomena kissed her horse's velvet soft nose before swinging up into her saddle. Philip sprang quickly onto his own horse and together they left the clustered buildings of Niche. They streaked across the vast fields towards Staleon Wood with the stars and moon lighting their way.

16

They charged into Staleon Woods, the dim brightness of the
night sky cut off from them as the gathered darkness of the trees
enveloped them. They could see nothing in the sudden gloom of
the woods. For their first few minutes in Staleon, all that their
senses could discern were the strong strides of their horses
beneath them, the pounding of their own hearts, and the warm
breath escaping them.

As their vision adjusted, they saw the cluttered trees flying by on
either side of the narrow road. They glimpsed the trees' mostly
naked branches reaching out over the path above them, set aglow
by the flowing starlight and moonlight. Fallen autumn leaves
swirled in their galloping horses' wake. Strange golden orbs of
light flew in and out of sight, illuminating the canopy. As they
advanced deeper into the woods, the ground beneath them began
to dip and rise wildly.

Everything was still obscured and uncertain as they rode through
the woods. Not only was everything in Staleon flashing by in a
blur of motion, Philomena's thoughts and emotions were a
scrambled mess.

Ahead of her she could see Philip bent over his horse's neck
urging him on eagerly with K'smet's horse at his side. The black
mane of her own stallion whipped in her face and tickled her
cheek. She could feel her horse's willingness to follow Philip,
and yet feel her own heart protest against it.

Tears leapt from her eyes and froze on her face stinging from the
cold of the night. She swallowed hard, and only succeeded in
swelling the bitter tasting lump that had formed in her throat. She
had to do something.

"Philip! Wait!" she called to her brother, slowing her stallion to a halt. She saw Philip glance over his shoulder with what looked like an irritated frown. He pulled back on his reins and his and K'smet's horses skidded to a stop.

"What's the problem?" he asked his frown still intact.

Philomena slid down from her saddle. "*Look*! What have we just done?!" she cried, stepping forward and fighting back angry tears. Philip stared at her in surprised astonishment.

"We just left Balin and K'smet behind for Avador. Our own uncle," said Philomena, the ache of guilt growing.

"They're willing to lay down their lives for us, Philly," Philip said, stiffly dismounting his horse and approaching her. He had his hand pressed to his wounded arm. His face was pale from exhaustion and beaded with sweat despite the cold temperature. Seeing him look the way he did, Philomena felt worried sick, yet she still couldn't help the feeling of confliction for leaving Balin and K'smet.

"I know, and that's why we have to go back," Philomena said with frustration. "Who say's we're worth dying for?"

"Philomena, we are the ones who can put an end to all of this deceit," said Philip, his voice heavy and tired. "We can end this depression,"

Philomena shook her head, not in the mood to be swayed. "Do you not care that we left Balin and K'smet? Does it even bother you that they might actually be *killed* because of us?"

"Of course it bothers me," Philip said defensively, his brow lowering.

"And yet we're still going to leave them?" Philomena demanded. Philip shifted uneasily, rotating his gaze as if he feared to be over heard. "We can't turn back now, if only for the sacrifice they made," he said wearily.

"I cannot turn my back on the people I love as easily as you," Philomena said, her voice tinged with disgust.

"I'm not turning my back on them," Philip said, suddenly flaring with anger.

"You're not?"

"No, I'm not,"

"What on earth are you two doing?" someone demanded.

Philip and Philomena tensed and snapped towards the voice.

Lark McKnight stood on the edge of the road across from them as if he had just morphed out of the trees. His hunting bow and quiver were slung across his back, and the gash beneath his eye from the durjock still looked ugly. He stared at the two of them with amazed bafflement. Philip and Philomena stared back, just as surprised.

"What are you two doing here?" Lark finally asked after a moment of silence.

Philip and Philomena glanced nervously at one another, their feud forgotten for the time.

"We . . . we're just out . . . for a ride," Philip stuttered forcing a smile and trying to sound casual.

Lark tilted his head wearing a suspicious frown. "With three horses?" he asked, gesturing to their waiting steeds.

Philip winced and pursed his lips. Philomena wouldn't meet Lark's or Philip's eyes, and looked anywhere else but at them.

"Are you two in some sort of trouble?" Lark asked, adjusting his bowstring that was strapped over his chest.

"No," Philip and Philomena said quickly. Lark lifted his eyebrows, not convinced by the siblings' response and suspecting that they were indeed in the worst sort of trouble. Frankly, Lark didn't want to know the details. Then he caught the sight of the blood soaked cloth wrapped around Philip's upper arm.

"What happened to your arm?" Lark asked, dipping his head towards the red stained bandage.

Philip's eyebrows rose as he glanced down at his wounded arm. Philomena shifted and swallowed nervously.

"Ugh, well, I . . ." Philip tried, clearing his throat noisily. Lark's brow wrinkled. "I sort of caught it on a thorny branch a ways back. Rather nasty, isn't it?" he said, directing a nervous smile at Lark.

"Sure," Lark said slowly, his voice skeptical. Philomena pursed her lips and glanced about anxiously.

Lark considered the pair of them with growing curiosity. "So, why were you two arguing?" he asked.

"Oh, you heard that did you," Philip said, scratching his chin diligently.

"You were loud enough for a deaf man with cotton stuffed between his ears to hear you," Lark said matter of factly.

"So you heard everything?" Philip asked, somewhat disappointed.

"Pretty much," Lark nodded. Philip looked perturbed. "Don't worry, I won't try to decipher what you were arguing about," Lark assured.

"Yes, but you can't very well go around pretending you didn't hear anything," Philomena said firmly, glancing pointedly over at Philip and back to Lark as if she were trying to tell Philip something.

"Why would I care what you two are yelling at each other for?" Lark asked, peering irritably over at Philomena.

"Then stop asking so many questions," Philomena shot, her eyes blazing defensively.

Lark glared at her with deep annoyance. "Any sane person would wonder why two trouble making idiots are riding at top speed through the woods in the middle of the night," he said, turning brusquely away to walk down the road.

Philomena rolled her eyes and sneered at his back. Philip heaved a sigh, his expression a confliction of weariness and consideration. Lark strode down the road, shouldering his quiver and bow. He walked a few feet and then froze in his tracks his brow furrowed.

"Ugh, are you guys sure you're not in trouble? Because

Commander Xavier doesn't send out a posse for nothing," Lark said over his shoulder.

"What?! Where?" Philip exclaimed, hurriedly joining Lark. Lark pointed out the posse to him. All Philip could make out were the flickers of bright torch light merging in between the trees, and the shifting of the dark shapes of horses. They were about a half a mile away down the winding dirt path, and it appeared that they were moving slowly. Philip knew it was no coincidence. Lark was right; they were a posse that was obviously tracking them or it could be Avador himself with his band of natives. Philip swallowed anxiously, clenching his sweaty hands and glancing about frantically as if he were a hunted animal trying to figure out which way to go. Lark watched him closely, seeing the panic in his eyes growing like wildfire. Philomena looked just as perturbed.

"You two really are in trouble," Lark ventured, glancing between the siblings. Philip looked over at him, chuckling nervously. Lark sighed and shook his head, moving to leave and this time heading towards the clustered trees bordering the road.

"Wait," Philip said catching him by the arm. Lark turned an angry frown on him. "Look, um, we need some help here. Can you get us through these woods without being caught by the angry sergeants?" Philip asked almost desperately, his eyes flicking occasionally towards the posse that was gradually getting closer.

Lark almost laughed with amazement. "Are you serious? You have the audacity to ask me for help?"

Philip grimaced and shrugged his shoulders helplessly which hurt due to the arrow hole in his arm.

"As it so happens I'm in enough trouble already, and I don't help troubled delinquents escape their fate," Lark said, shaking off Philip's hold on him and turning away to nearly collide into Philomena.

"We are not delinquents," Philomena said defensively. "And we need your help whether you like it or not," she added flatly.

Lark's face pinched with puzzlement.

"Point is, Lark, we need you to come with us," Philip said from behind him.

Lark jerked away from them as if they had struck him, looking completely bewildered and rather frightened by their insistence.

"I'm not going anywhere with either of you," he said defensively, taking a few more steps back.

"I'm not asking," Philip said, shaking his head and stepping carefully towards Lark as if he were approaching a frightened animal. Lark glared at him.

Philomena chewed at her lip, looking impatient. Out of nowhere, Philip threw out a hardened fist hammering it against Lark's nose. Lark crumpled to his knees and slumped against Philip.

"I'm insisting," Philip finished. He bent down and hefted Lark up, draping the unconscious boy's arm over his shoulder. Glancing upward, Philip could see the flickering torchlight and the dim shadowy images of the posse getting closer and closer. Muttering irritably under his breath, Philip started to drag Lark towards the horses. Philomena hastened over to help taking Lark's other arm to hurry the process along.

"That was effective," she said.

"Couldn't think of anything else," Philip replied, laboring as they hauled Lark onto K'smet's horse and draped him across the seat of the saddle so his arms and legs dangled on either side. He looked as though he were a slain stag ready to be taken to the butcher.

"Philip, your arm," Philomena said worriedly. Blood had soaked through the cloth and had completely drenched it in red.

"It will manage," Philip said, though he felt sick and lightheaded. He walked around to his own horse.

Philomena did not look convinced but they were in a hurry. She stripped Lark's bow and quiver from his shoulder and hooked them to her own saddle. She swiftly mounted up, swinging her horse around to join Philip only to find that he wasn't even on his horse. Philip shoved his horse's reins in her hands.

"What are you doing?" Philomena questioned severely, her voice filled with fright.

"It's senseless to outrun them, Philly. Take the horses and go into these woods here. Travel for about twenty minutes and then get back onto the road. I'll cover up our tracks and meet up with you," Philip said.

"What if you don't?" Philomena asked fearfully. "What if . . ." Her voice failed her and her words trailed off. The familiar lump in her throat swelled horribly.

Philip pursed his lips. "You know what to do," he said, gripping Philomena's hand.

After a brief moment, Philip turned away. He patted his horse on the head and then walked towards a branch that hung lazily out over the road with many of its colored leaves still clinging to it. Philomena hesitated as she watched her brother walk away, reluctant to leave him alone. Eventually though, she obeyed his wishes and urged her horse forward, leading Philip's horse who in turn pulled K'smet's horse along. She rode off the trail and into the trees. The thick layer of fallen leaves crunched beneath the horses' hooves and the bare branches of bushes brushed against their sides.

Philomena swallowed hard, feeling scared and vulnerable. It didn't sit well with her to be separated from Philip. In just a few minutes, the warm shadows of the trees embraced her and the horses and she could no longer see Philip.

Philip heaved a sigh and broke off part of the low hanging branch with his good arm. He hurried up the road a ways and began brushing away their tracks with the branch, stepping backwards as he proceeded. He lifted his gaze and spotted the bright burning torches of the sergeants emerging between the trees and growing larger by the second. He began to hear the voices of the men drift towards him. He brushed out the tracks

189

more fiercely staying low to the ground, feeling utterly exposed. Finally, Philip reached the part of the road where Philomena had taken the horses into the woods. The first few mounted men became visible down the road with more following. Philip's heart pounded and panic rose within him. He quickly brushed away the tracks leading into the woods. He threw away the branch and darted into the woods himself, taking cover behind a particularly large tree that was surrounded by bare brittle bushes. Philip crouched behind the tree and pressed his back against its trunk. He could feel the rough bark press against his coat and smell the crisp scent of the fallen autumn leaves that thickly layered the damp ground.

The steady sound of many clopping hooves came. Philip held his breath, waiting and listening and praying that none of the sergeants could see through tree trunks. The thudding of hooves suddenly ceased. Philip estimated that they were about ten feet away right behind him.

Silence lapsed. Philip swallowed nervously, not daring to move. His warm breath clouded before his face. He could hear the crackling of the sergeants' torches and see the glow of the firelight bounce off the surrounding trees.

"They had to have brushed out their tracks," said a deep voice, belonging to a native.

"We don't need you to point out the obvious to us, rogue," someone said grudgingly.

Philip listened carefully to the men's voices.

"No rogue is going to speak out in my company," said the man with the grudging voice.

Philip frowned. He recognized that voice. It was Commander Xavier. *Why wasn't Avador with them*, Philip wondered.

"Since it is clear that they are trying to disguise their true trail and throw us off course we should split up," said the commander. "Hugo, take some men that way and if you find their trail come straight back to report. Don't try to be heroes and do it all on your own. This is Captain Avador's hunt not ours, understood?"

Understanding dawned on Philip as he listened to Xavier speak. "Right, the rest of you come with me, especially you, rogue. I want to keep my eye on you," said Xavier.

"What? You don't trust me?" the native asked sarcastically.

"Enough," Xavier said in a hard guttural tone. "Let's get some good news for Captain Avador before he chops our heads off. God knows he has his father's temper," he added with an intact of breath. Philip resented his statement, but was certain it was true.

The rustling of brush and the crunching of dried leaves under foot sounded. Philip dared a peek around the tree he was crouching behind. Through the tangle of thorny vines and bare bushes he glimpsed Xavier and his men on the road, splitting into two groups. Three or four of the men were riding their horses into the woods on the east side of the road, and Xavier was leading the rest of them into the woods on the west side where Philip had concealed himself.

Philip slipped further behind the tree as he watched Xavier and his men track into the woods only ten feet away. He glimpsed the brown face of the native, hard and angry, with red feathers sticking out from his long black hair. Philip felt a cold breath breathe down his nape as he stared at the native's calm expression. The native snapped his dark, piercing gaze towards the underbrush that concealed Philip, sending an icy shiver down Philip's spine; then the native vanished amongst the trees and branches.

Philip slumped against the tree, leaning his head against the rough bark and letting a breath of relief escape him as he listened to the posse advance further and further into the woods. He watched the captivating orbs of gold light float high above in the canopy amongst the branches as he waited for the posse to travel into the depths of the woods.

Philip wondered what the gold orbs of light were. He found them rather beautiful and mesmerizing. They were like glittering stars only with a different life about them.

When Philip could no longer make out the rustling of the underbrush from the posse's passing, he cautiously rose to his feet. Glancing about, he picked his way around the bare bushes and thorny vines as quietly as he was able and got back onto the clear road. Taking a moment to gather his bearings, Philip broke in to a steady jog going northward up the road in the direction Philomena would have headed. His whole body ached with weariness and tension, and felt jarred as he forced himself onward. Philip gritted his teeth, ignoring his bodily aches and the searing pain that throbbed in his nearly unmovable left arm. He tried to focus his mind on the passing surroundings and the sounds of the woods.

In truth, Staleon Wood was mostly quiet. No crickets chirped. No frogs sang. Somewhere, the lonely hooting of an owl called out. The dreamy golden orbs of light drifting in the canopy made the shadows shift and dappled the trees in colors of yellow and grey. Frost accumulated on the hard road. The minute icicles crunched beneath Philip's boots along with the dried leaves. It was cold, but jogging with his coat on, Philip felt pleasantly warm.

The road curved to the left, and Philip's insides jolted at the sight of horses standing in the middle of the road. He recognized Philomena aboard her grey stallion and felt relief wash over him. She started at the sound of his sudden approach, but calmed when she saw him.

Philip waved reassuringly to her, and thankfully came to a stop, bending over to catch his breath.

"Are you alright?" Philomena asked worriedly, slipping down from her saddle.

Philip nodded straightening his posture. Philomena came over to him and undid the bandage around his arm. Blood still seeped from the hole the arrow had left. Philomena tucked away the old bandage and brought forth a fresh one.

"You know, it's incredible how one little hole in the arm can hurt so much," Philip commented musingly, turning his arm to peer at the wound himself and wincing from his own touch. Philomena flicked her eyes to her brother, uncertain how to behave after their argument. She cleared her throat nervously.

"How many are chasing us?" she asked.

"Seven to eight, but they're not exactly chasing us," Philip said, still wincing.

"What do you mean?" Philomena frowned.

"They're tracking us. Commander Xavier is leading them," Philip said.

"Xavier?" Philomena questioned.

Philip nodded. "Struck me as queer too at first, but Avador needs to tie things up in Niche and can't be in two places at once. He sent Xavier along with one of his native sergeants to sniff out our trail," Philip said.

"And have they made us?" Philomena asked, knotting the bandage securely about his arm.

"Nah," Philip said with a cocky smirk. "I diverted them off the main road, and they split up. Even the brilliant native sergeant won't be able to pick up our trail in the thick of the woods at night. I've bought us at least a day's worth of time," he said, starting to walk over to their horses.

"Brilliant," Philomena said, following him. "We can get ahead easily if you're plan works,"

"What do you mean, 'if'?" Philip questioned with offense, reaching his black stallion who greeted him with a prick of the ears. Philip fondled the stallion's forelock.

"How is our good friend, Lark, doing?" Philip asked, walking around to K'smet's horse who still carried the limp stable boy across his back.

"Still unconscious," Philomena replied, ducking beneath her

stallion's neck. "You knocked him pretty hard. He's definitely going to have a headache when he wakes up,"

Philip squared his shoulders innocently. "It's hard to use restraint sometimes," he said, walking back to his horse.

Philomena leaned against her horse's shoulder and folded her arms, her expression serious. "What are we going to tell him when he wakes up? He didn't want to help us in the first place as it is," she said.

Philip hesitated. "We'll tell him the truth," he said.

"He won't believe us," Philomena said, shaking her head.

"That's for him to decide. Either way though, he can't go back to Niche," Philip said. "For now, let's concentrate on getting away from this area. We'll ride for a good hour and then we'll stop for a rest, after which we'll sort things out with Lark." Philip said, swinging into his saddle and casting a knowing glance over at Lark.

Philomena nodded and did likewise, feeling her stallion's anxiousness to move matching her own. The thought of rest though threatened to make her mind feel heavy and her stomach growled hungrily.

They urged their horses into a steady trot up the road, feeling as though that the trail laid out before them was leading them to a distant strange place where no friends awaited to greet them and only their enemies lurked around every corner. Everything felt as though it were changing.

17

Lark drifted in and out of the gloom of unconsciousness. The first time he stirred he felt disorientated from the sensation of hanging upside down on what he thought might be a bouncy wagon; at least that's what it felt like. When he blearily squinted open his eyes, he found himself peering at a square of leather and a strap that dangled passed him. The jolting movements of whatever was carrying him made his head throb terribly, so he closed his eyes against the pain and allowed himself to drift back into the comforts of his conscious.

The second time he woke he could feel hands pulling and lifting him and then gently lowering him to the ground atop of what felt like a rough blanket. Lark never opened his eyes. He didn't know whether it was instinct or the simple weight of exhaustion that told him to slip back into a deep slumber.

The third time, Lark's mind stirred with a new energy. He lolled his head to the side and slowly opened his eyes. He found himself staring at Felix Stone who lay sleeping beneath the covers of a rough cloak only a couple feet away. Lark studied him and noticed how pale his face was and how his brow would pinch together every now and then as though he was in pain. Lark was rather surprised to see the cheerful young man look so ill and tired.

Lark looked away from Felix, and let his gaze roam about his surroundings. Tall trees encircled the small, sheltered opening they were in, and bristling walls of underbrush cluttered in between their trunks. Stars twinkled high in the sky, and the moon shone above, its light filtering through the branches. By the height of the moon Lark judged it was the middle of the night. The air had a wintery bite to it.

Lark let his gaze fall from the sky and found Phyliss Stone sitting on a fallen log across from him. A crackling fire flickered between them, sending pleasurable waves of warmth over them. Lark could see the three horses dozing close by, their heads down and their eyelids drooping.

Lark watched the girl that annoyed him so much for a moment. She sat there quietly, her chin resting in her palm while she fiddled with a silver ring in the other. Her gaze was downcast and she appeared to be deep in the thought. From Lark's point of view, he detected a deep melancholy that cloaked her. It was a peculiar mood to see her in.

Pain suddenly engulfed Lark's head and his nose tingled sorely. Lark cringed and tried to lift a hand to his face only to find his wrists bound together with thick rope. Groaning, he let his bound hands fall limply atop his stomach. He stared up at the night sky again to see the stars winking merrily down at him.

Philomena looked calmly to Lark, her features fraught with exhaustion. She stared quietly at him with no inclination of moving. Philip remained where he lay, resting fitfully. The fire crackled happily when Philomena tossed a dry twig into its hungry flames.

"You are awake?" Philomena asked Lark in a low voice. She pushed the ring she had been fiddling with on the index finger of her left hand.

"If you want to call it that," Lark moaned, feeling dreadful.

"Sorry about the bonds," Philomena said not unkindly. She rested a hand on her knee as she fixed him with a steady gaze.

"Why am I tied up anyway?" Lark asked, turning an annoyed glare at her. Philomena opened her mouth to answer but Philip managed to reply first.

"Because we can't have you running off to Niche," he said in a hoarse voice. Lark switched his gaze to the weary young man. Philip looked back at him with tired eyes, still lying underneath the cover of his cloak, appearing too sickly to move.

"How do you feel?" Philomena asked, walking around the fire and gently kneeling down beside him.

"Ugh, like I've been run over by a nasty mule, his drunken driver, and his rattling cart," Philip groaned, rubbing his forehead.

"You should rest some more, Philip," Philomena insisted. Lark's brow wrinkled with confusion. "It is still hours till dawn. We can start at first light." Philomena added.

"Wait, *Philip*?" Lark questioned with bafflement. Philip and Philomena looked to him.

"Your name is Felix," Lark said, trying to gesture towards them with his bound hands. "And why do you look like hell?"

Philip heaved a heavy sigh, propping himself up on his elbows and cringing slightly. "This is going to be a long conversation," he said tiredly. Lark stared at him with unnerved bemusement. Philip shifted, getting stiffly to his feet. Philomena helped him.

"Philip, you need to rest," Philomena protested firmly. The area between her brows crinkled with worry.

"I'll be fine, Philly," Philip assured, a hand to his wounded arm. "I won't be able to sleep right if we don't enlighten the boy of what he's been dragged into," he added under his breath, casting a troubled glance at Lark. Meanwhile, Lark was straining to hear what they were saying.

Philomena grimaced upsettingly. "Fine," she agreed reluctantly. Philip patted her gratefully on the shoulder and moved stiffly over to the dancing fire. Philomena clenched her teeth upsettingly and approached Lark with a scowl contorting her features. Lark scowled back at her with matching irritation. She reached down and heaved him to his feet by his bonds. Lark's mind swam sickly when he found himself standing and his whole world reeled dizzily. He closed his eyes and shook his head to try to clear his fuzzy mind.

"You alright?" Philomena asked thickly, her tone letting Lark know she didn't really care either way. Lark glared at her, but allowed her to lead him over to where Philip sat on the log indulging in the fire's glowing warmth.

"Sit down," Philomena commanded, gesturing for Lark to take the place beside Philip. Lark obeyed, but his whole being radiated the desire to be defiant. Philomena sat beside him, making his whole body tense.

Stillness lapsed, broken only by their crackling fire against the cold and the seemingly vibrating tension between them. Philip stared into the dancing flames, rolling over the notion of how to explain their shady circumstances to Lark without maddening him even more. Lark sat still without moving or breathing for that matter, waiting for one of them to break the uncomfortable silence. Philomena sat uncomfortably on the edge of the log, her jaw set with uneasiness. Taking in a breath, Philip finally spoke.

"Do you know of King Paul Stilwell, Lark?" he asked, speaking slowly and still staring into the flames. His voice seemed to echo off the quiet atmosphere.

Lark stared at him for a moment before finding his voice. "He's our reigning king," he answered.

"What of Salvador Corea? Do you know of him?" asked Philip, weighing the name down heavily.

"He's supposed to be crowned the new king this spring," Lark said. Philip looked perturbed by this reminder. Lark gave him a curious look.

"Where are you going with this?" he asked. Philip ignored him.

"What did you hear of King Paul's true heirs?" Philip questioned, turning a hard look on him. His steel blue eyes were penetrating and made Lark hesitate in his response.

"Only that they had died from some illness, and that King Paul went mad with grief. That's when the depression began, and Lord Salvador became his heir." said Lark.

"That's a lie," Philip said huskily with a shake of his head. "The king's children never succumbed to any illness. They never died,"

Lark stared at him, completely at a loss for words.

"What Philip is trying to say, Lark, is that we lied before in Niche," said Philomena. Lark switched a perplexed look on her, trying to read in between the lines they were drawing.

"Our names are not really Felix and Phyliss Stone," said Philomena. She looked expectantly to Philip.

"We're in truth Philip and Philomena Stilwell, the children of King Paul," Philip finished.

Lark blinked, taking in their confession with a blank expression. His mouth hung open in shock. Philomena looked to Philip uncertainly, and he gestured for her to keep quiet. They gave Lark a moment to take it all in. When he didn't speak or move for several minutes, Philomena leaned forward to look to Philip again, casting a questionable frown at him. Philip shrugged his shoulders and gave a helpless gesture.

Philomena peered into Lark's face. "Do you need us to repeat that?"

Lark suddenly snorted with laughter which made Philomena's frown deepen. Philip pursed his lips and rested his chin in his palm.

"You actually expect me to believe this?" asked Lark, glancing between them with a disbelieving grin. "No, you can't just plant the 'we're the prince and princess' line on someone. What a loud of rubbish!"

Philip's mouth tightened and he ran a hand through his hair. "What we just told you is the truth,"

"No it's not," said Lark shaking his head.

"Yes it is," said Philomena sternly. "We don't lie, Lark. Not twice anyway, and we wouldn't tell you unless it was absolutely necessary. We truly are the king's children,"

"If the prince and princess are alive than they can stay where they are. They abandoned us! To Alamia the prince and princess are dead!" Lark said severely, his gaze growing angry.

"Lark, you don't have to believe us, and the people have every right to be angry, but we really do need your help," Philip said, his voice surprisingly low and vulnerable.

"I don't want to help you," Lark growled clenching his teeth. "And why should I care about what you have to say? You knocked me out, tied me up and literally kidnapped me!"

Philip grimaced. "Point taken," he admitted.

A stubborn silence wedged between them. Philip's shoulders slumped and he exhaled a defeated sigh. His eyes lingered to the fire once more, having nothing to crumble the walls of Lark's distrust. Lark sat fuming and grinding his teeth surly. He couldn't explain his anger; he almost felt betrayed by these strange siblings. *This doesn't make sense*, Lark thought; *they were never your friends so how can you feel betrayed.*

Philomena chewed at her lip undecidedly. She looked to Philip's nearly overwhelmed expression to Lark's dogged and irritable features.

"Let me speak with him, Philip," she said calmly. Lark snapped his gaze to her, looking perturbed by such a proposal.

"If you like," said Philip with a careless wave of his hand. His head felt like a two ton boulder.

"You can have the fire to yourself," said Philomena, gripping Lark's arm so he was forced to stand with her. She walked around the fire and led Lark past the three horses towards the fortress of trees. Every grain in Lark's body screamed in protest as he was forced to follow her into the woods.

"Be nice to him, Philly," they heard Philip call after them.

Lark groaned dreadfully. Philomena hid a smirk and pushed aside a branch of a bristling bare bush. Lark followed her reluctantly. Prickly thorny vines and naked black berry bushes that were growing about the trees snagged their clothing. The shriveled leaves covering the forest floor crunched noisily beneath their boots. Philomena picked her way through the underbrush and in between the tree trunks, leading Lark into the woods till she knew they were out of earshot of Philip.

Lark's nerves were just about near bursting as he scowled at Philomena's back. "You know, I knew you two were weird but now you're just downright scary," he said.

Philomena suddenly stopped and turned to him, her jaw taunt in a determined line. She pulled a knife from her belt that gleamed in the filtered moonlight. Lark's eyes widened slightly.

"Not as scary or peculiar as our enemies, trust me," said Philomena lifting her knife and slicing through Lark's bonds.

Lark stared down at his liberated hands and then looked back to Philomena. She held his gaze, sheathed her knife and placed her hands on her hips. She could still make out the flickering yellow light of their camp fire through the trees over Lark's shoulder.

"I don't see how I can trust either of you," said Lark, his eyes narrowing.

Philomena let out an irritated breath and rolled her eyes to the tree tops. "You have to trust someone, and if anyone it should be us,"

"Why? For all I know these *enemies* you speak of are in truth the good ones. You could just be some twisted, deceitful secret agents working to destroy this country's last hope for peace,"

"We're trying to rid this country of Salvador Corea and his minions," Philomena said firmly.

"Salvador Corea *is* our last hope for peace," Lark said, his brows furrowing.

"He is not! He's a liar and a fake. It's not our father who's behind this depression its Salvador," Philomena said heatedly.

Lark stared at her. "All this nonsense you two have come up with is completely unbelievable, and I don't care to be a part of it,"

Philomena growled and stomped her foot with frustration. Lark lifted his eyebrows at her. Philomena took a moment to collect herself taking a few deep breaths before speaking. Lark waited patiently, watching her expectantly.

"I understand this is all hard to believe," Philomena began slowly. "But regardless of what is and isn't believable, the point is if my brother and I don't get to Caelum before Avador Corea does than this depression will suffocate everything. We need you to help us because we need to stop Salvador, and we can't navigate through these woods without your help,"

Lark's brow wrinkled. "What gives you the right to change anything of what you say besides the fact that you *believe* you're the lost prince and princess?" he questioned, speaking the last part with thick sarcasm.

His words pained Philomena. "We have to stop Salvador, because we're the only ones who know the truth and are willing to end his tyranny," she replied in a controlled voice. The determination reflected in her gaze was nearly contagious. Lark was nearly convinced but he shook himself stubbornly.

"Even if what you say is true, none of it makes sense," he said, gesturing in exasperation.

"Just because you don't understand something doesn't make it any less real," Philomena said defensively, folding her arms and sizing Lark up critically. "What we've told you is true,"

"That still doesn't convince me," said Lark, squaring his shoulders matter-of-factly.

Philomena vented an exasperated sigh, and fixed her hardened gaze on him, her mouth tightened in a determined line. "Look, I'm not telling you all of this because I'm hoping you'll believe us, but because I have too. I don't care if you believe our story. What we are may not be true to you, and in the end that doesn't really matter. But this depression," Philomena paused a moment, her voice cracking. "This depression *is* real for all of us. We can stop it if we can get to Caelum,"

Lark listened, Philomena's sincere filled words freezing him where he stood.

"The Creator gave us a great burden to carry, and it is heavier more for my brother than for myself. We may never understand why the Creator gave this to us, but we do know that it is ours to bear. I don't think that God gives us great burdens to watch us fail. I think He gives them to us because He believes we are capable of great things,"

Lark studied Philomena with a new perspective, surprised to have heard such inspirational words pass so easily from her lips, but he wasn't swayed. "A beautiful speech isn't going to convince me that what you're saying is the right choice," he said quietly.

"I can't force you to believe it's the right choice no more than you can convince yourself right now," said Philomena, squaring her shoulders. "I know this is difficult but . . . sometimes the right thing to do is not always our choice. Sometimes it is given to us so we must chose,"

Lark stared at her. Philomena ducked her head to break eye contact, feeling her face warm with bashful blush. She cleared her throat before lifting her gaze to his once more.

"So, just think of what I said. You don't have to believe that we're the king's children, or that Salvador is behind the depression. All I'm asking of you is your help. Help us navigate to Ezleon. Play the bigger role that is your calling. Help us end this depression," said Philomena.

"My calling? Is that flattery?" said Lark with a dry chuckle.

"From what I heard it is you and your brother's calling not mine. My own calling is to return to Niche where I must try to save my family from starvation,"

"You can't do that, Lark," said Philomena feeling a twinge of guilt.

"It's my fault that my family has no food for the winter, because I lost my job," said Lark with a hint of anger.

"You won't do them any good going back. By now Avador has the entire village locked down and under surveillance." said Philomena.

"Why would they bother with me when they're after you," Lark said with a slight shrug of his shoulders.

Philomena cringed. "Commander Xavier will have told Avador of our connection to you. He would happily invite you into Niche, but only to take you in to custody."

"You mean, he believes I have information that he could use to find you?" Lark asked fearfully.

"He'd torture you to get it, if he had too," Philomena said.

"But I don't know anything," Lark said desperately, his voice fraught.

"But Avador doesn't know that in truth you have nothing to do with us. He'll go by Commander Xavier's word, I'm sure," said Philomena.

Lark considered this, glancing around and flexing his jaw. "So really you just want me to stick around so Avador doesn't get a hold of me? Because you're afraid that I'll give you away?" he asked.

"That's true. We can't risk any leaks in our mission," Philomena said bluntly, her abrasiveness returning. "Plus, it would be a lot easier on our conscious' if we know you aren't harmed due to us,"

"Why do you care?" Lark challenged harshly.

"Frankly, I don't care for you much. You irritate me. But I know it would please my uncle and brother if you stayed with us," Philomena replied.

A jolt of panic suddenly stabbed Lark's mind. "What of my family?"

"I do not believe he'll harm them. He would possibly use them to get to you though, if you return to Niche," Philomena said confidently.

The corner of Lark's mouth twitched doubtfully. After a moment of thought though, he sighed inwardly. "I suppose I don't have much of a choice,"

Philomena's expression lifted slightly. "So you'll help us?"

Lark took a moment to reply, making Philomena nervous. "I'll help you, but only until we reach Ezleon. I don't want to spend any more time with you than what I have to," said Lark. "But keep in mind that you two drug me into this. Don't expect me to always be willing," he added.

Philomena pursed her lips, but she nodded her consent. "It's a deal,"

18

Morning dawned crisp and clear the next day. The welcoming sun rays filtered through Staleon's canopy and attempted to melt the frost that had blanketed the ground. A pair of cardinals flitted about the bare bushes and branches, joyfully sharing their morning songs.

Philomena stirred from her slumber. Her eyes flickered open and squinted in the brightly rising sun. She turned her gaze around their camp from where she lay. Philip was close beside her. He still slept with his back turned to her and the cloak he was using for a blanket a twisted mess covering only half of him.

Philomena's mouth twitched with a smile to see the disorderly cloak. She looked to her opposite side where Lark had fallen asleep.

But no one was there.

Philomena suddenly jolted upright, throwing aside her cloak and frantically searching the area for any sign of Lark. There was nothing; not even the cloak he had borrowed. Panic caused Philomena to think the worst. She shot to her feet and bolted towards Philip. She dropped down beside him and shook him violently.

"Philip! Philip! You have to get up *now*!" she hollered in his ear.

Philip's face crinkled and pinched with annoyance.

"Why?" he grumbled, his hoarse voice filled with lingering sleep.

"Because our loyal guide has disappeared," Philomena said.

Philip moaned and pulled his cloak over his head. Philomena stood, gritting her teeth, and yanked the cloak off of him.

"Oh come on, Philly," Philip groaned, sprawling on his back and glaring at her.

"Stable boy has conveniently vanished and you act as though you don't give a wart on a mud hog that he's gone. If he goes back to Niche, not only will he be dead, but we will be too and this entire country to top it off. We have to go after him," Philomena said impatiently.

"Wow, yeah, I hadn't thought of that," Philip said, sitting upright and rubbing the sleep from his eyes.

"Then what is wrong with you? Let's *go*," Philomena said emphatically.

"First, before we go rampaging off into the trees, you have to be sure stable boy is actually gone. Secondly, his name is Lark. I don't think he'd appreciate you calling him stable boy," Philip said.

"I don't care! And he *is* gone!" Philomena yelled, turning on her heel and storming towards their horses.

"Philomena, you have got to chill," Philip said sternly, but tiredly, with no indication of joining her.

"Good morning," someone said from somewhere to the side. Philomena spun towards the voice, drawing her sword in the process. She froze when she saw Lark standing just before the tree line with his bow and quiver slung across his back. He stared at her with little surprise and didn't even acknowledge the sword she had poking in his stomach.

"You see?" Philip said with a delighted grin. "I told you he hadn't taken off,"

Philomena grinded her teeth angrily. "Where have you been, stable boy?" she questioned severely. Philip rolled his eyes, and shook his head.

Lark's brow lowered with offense. "Off doing what any normal person does early in the morning," he said. He pushed aside her blade and brushed past her. Philip snickered.

"How long have you been awake?" Philip asked stifling a yawn and rising stiffly to his feet.

"Maybe a couple of hours," Lark replied with a shrug.

"A couple of hours? Didn't you sleep at all?' Philip asked with raised eyebrows.

"Not really,"

"I know I had no trouble sleeping," Philip mumbled, retrieving his and Philomena's cloaks from the ground. He neatly folded them so they could be stowed in their saddle bags.

Philomena turned towards them, her jaw set in a cantankerous line. "What are you doing with that bow and quiver?" she asked, glaring at Lark.

"It's my bow," Lark said simply.

"Yes I know, but I didn't give it back to you," Philomena said haughtily, taking a few steps towards him.

"I didn't think I needed permission since I'm on your side," Lark said levelly, somewhat taken aback.

Philomena opened her mouth to speak.

"Let it go, Philly," said Philip, walking by with their folded cloaks. "It's not like he's gonna shoot us in the backs or anything," he added, going over to their horses.

"Then what have you been doing these past two hours while we were sleeping," Philomena challenged, stepping closer to Lark.

Philip sighed heavily as he packed their cloaks.

"Why are you so angry all of a sudden? You seemed pretty thrilled when I agreed to help you last night," said Lark, his brow furrowed.

"I asked you what have you been doing?" Philomena repeated heatedly.

Lark gestured helplessly. "What do you think I've been doing?"

"Answer the question!" Philomena said angrily.

"Helping," Lark said, defense rising in him. "I brushed away most of our tracks and covered any other sign that might give us away, I filled all of your water skins, I packed up everything that I could and I took care of the horses,"

"He's not lying, Philly," Philip spoke up. "The horses are tacked and by the looks of them they have been well groomed under these saddles. And let's see here, yep, just as Lark said. The water skins are full. Nice work, Lark," Philip said with a grin, taking a swig of water.

Philomena's complexion reddened with embarrassment. She glanced at Lark's face and quickly looked away again. Lark watched her with light curiosity and much annoyance. She sheathed her sword and shifted uncomfortably.

"We should get going then," she finally said, walking away from Lark and moving over to the readied horses.

Lark breathed inward and followed, feeling rather unsolicited. Philip came towards him, leading the bay stallion that had belonged to K'smet. "Here, Lark, you'll be riding Spear,"

"Ugh, no thanks, I'll walk," Lark said, denying the reins Philip was offering him.

Philip snorted with laughter. "I don't think so. What will you do when Avador catches up to us? Climb up a tree?" He placed the stallion's reins into Lark's hands.

The corners of Lark's mouth twitched with discomfort. "It's just that . . . I don't really know how to ride," he said.

"You seemed to ride just fine last night," Philip said. Lark frowned making Philip smirk. "Look Lark, don't worry so much. Old Spear here will go easy on you, and if he decides otherwise, Philly and I are here to help," Philip winked, and patted Lark on the shoulder.

Lark tightened his lips grudgingly and considered the horse before him. That stallion stared back with a friendly glimmer reflecting in his warm brown eyes. A brilliant white diamond was centered perfectly on the stallion's forehead. Lark gave in reluctantly and carefully draped the reins over the horse's head.

"Spear?" Philomena asked as Philip came around the other side of his horse.

"The horse can't go around nameless now can he," Philip grinned.

Philomena huffed and shook her head. She climbed aboard her stallion, and Coursio pranced eagerly when he felt the weight of his rider in his saddle. Philip followed suite, as did Lark who sprung easily enough in to the saddle. He glanced nervously about him, feeling insecure and out of control of his own safety. He gripped the reins tightly unsure of whether he could shift in the seat of his saddle or not. Spear sidestepped beneath him uneasily.

"Relax, Lark. Don't think so hard," Philip advised. Lark swallowed, staring down at the firm unmoving ground below and longing to be standing on it instead.

"Easy Spear," Philip spoke soothingly, reaching over to stroke the stallion's neck. "He can sense your fear," Philip said, meeting Lark's frightened eyes. "If you're calm, then he is calm as well,"

"Aren't you a rou-, I mean native?" Philomena asked, catching herself from using the offensive term.

Lark switched an annoyed glare at her. "So?"

"So didn't you're father teach you to ride?"

"No," Lark replied flatly. Philomena drew back, looking somewhat surprised.

"Alright," Philip said cutting in. He cleared his throat noisily. "Just don't pull on the reins so much, and give your commands lightly. And remember, when you're afraid he's afraid, ok?"

Lark nodded his understanding, taking in a deep breath to try to calm his churning nerves. When he felt comfortable enough, Philomena led the way forward going in the general northward direction. They left their small protected opening and headed into the trees, going single file with Lark in the middle. As they pushed through the thick of the brush, they startled some birds that shot out of the bushes and flew up into the trees squawking loudly.

Spear tossed his head and reared on his haunches, spooked by the noisy flock of birds. Lark settled him down quickly enough, but his own heart was racing and his mouth was dry.

Philip came alongside him. "Nice work, Lark. You'll be a rider in no time flat," he said with a grin. Lark stared at him, his throat too dry to respond.

"Since you agreed to help us, how about doing that and leading us out of here," Philomena suggested dryly, casting an irritable glare over her shoulder.

"Give him some time, Philly," Philip said lightly. Lark though objected and pushed Spear forward alongside Philomena. He took a moment to study their surroundings.

"Why do you want to go to Ezleon anyway? Isn't it a bit . . . crowded for a supposed prince and princess on the run?" asked Lark.

"We'd avoid it if we could, but we need supplies to get through Twin Peak Pass. We were sort of liberated of most of our food by Avador's men," Philip said, with resent.

"Fair enough," Lark said. He surveyed their surroundings and glanced up at the sun shining through the canopy, calculating directionality. After a moment of thought, he pointed a finger slightly to their left. "It's this way," he said, gathering his reins.

Philomena snorted. "Isn't 'this way' a bit of a loose heading?"

"No," said Lark, nudging Spear forward to take the lead.

"But isn't north that way?" Philomena spluttered, pointing straight ahead.

"It is," said Lark.

"Well, isn't Ezleon in a northern direction?" questioned Philomena.

"Yes, but the quickest way through these woods without being caught by any of your so called enemies is to go northeast so we're away from the main road," Lark said over his shoulder.

Philomena exhaled irritable, drilling an annoyed glare into Lark's back. Philip rode by her with an amused smirk plastered on his face.

"Come on, Philly. You don't want you to fall behind," Philip said laughingly. Philomena glared after him. She brusquely turned her horse to follow, her nose crinkled with irritation. They traveled for almost half a mile in silence, with the trees stretching their exposed branches above them. Here and there an evergreen tree grew, it's lonely green needles standing out vibrantly against its grey brothers. The sun had not vanquished the chill in the air. The birds chirped happily and flitted from bush to bush and branch to branch. Squirrels chattered noisily and shook the braches, fussing amongst themselves.

Philip considered Lark ahead, and after a moment of hesitation, urged his horse alongside him. "Can I ask you something?" Philip asked. Lark glanced over at him uncertainly. "What made you stay?"

"What do you mean?" Lark asked with a frown.

"Last night you seemed pretty determined to leave. What made you change your mind?"

Lark contemplated his answer. "Your sister can be rather short tempered most of the time, yet she has a strange knack for being inspirational," he said reflectively.

Philip cocked an intrigued expression on him. "What did she say? Did she threaten you?"

Lark grimaced, feeling frustrated. "Let's just say she made me aware of larger things. But she is very annoying," he said grudgingly, not caring if Philip took offense.

"Oh, I know she's annoying," Philip agreed with a knowing grin. "Either way I know it wasn't an easy decision to help us,"

Lark shrugged uncomfortably.

"Well, what I mean is that you seem to care for your family a lot," Philip said, glancing over at Lark and noting his uneasiness and the fortification building in his eyes.

"You regret your decision already," Philip guessed.

Lark exhaled through his nose. "Yeah," he said, staring to the path ahead.

Philip pursed his lips, feeling sorry for this boy he was already fond of, and hoping someday he could return the favor.

19

It was dark and damp in Commander Xavier's crowded station, with only the two burning torches for comfort. The fire danced and flickered uneasily, as if it were alive enough to sense the boiling tension in the room.

Xavier leaned against his desk in a scornful manner with his arms folded across his chest. Captain Avador stood beside him, appearing cool and calm, as if he had no worries in the world to trouble him. Two of Xavier's sergeants stood silently to the side.

"I hope you know what you're doing," Xavier said sneeringly to Avador without looking at him.

Avador breathed in through his nose. "You need not to worry, commander. This is my mission, not yours. I'm going to do it my way."

"I think you're wasting your time here piddling your thumbs with questioning the captives. My men and I already tracked down the general path your prey took," Xavier said with disgust.

"You and your men couldn't track a fly over a dung pile. My men on the other hand are true trackers. I've worked with them before," said Avador.

Xavier sniffed disdainfully. "You're too fond of those rogue warriors you call your men."

Just then the door banged open and K'smet and Balin were shoved into the station. Four of Avador's men were escorting them, two for each of them. A fifth native came forward to Avador.

"The prisoners as you requested, captain," the fifth man said.

Avador dipped his head in acknowledgement. He directed a troubled look to one of his men in particular.

"Bright Sky, perhaps you should assist the others," he suggested levelly. Bright Sky's features contorted upsettingly.

"I'm more comfortable here, captain," said Bright Sky, switching a malevolent stare at K'smet and gripping the knight's arm till he winced. The corner of Avador's mouth twitched with reluctance.

"Is there something I should know?" Xavier questioned dryly, boring a hard stare into him. Avador gave a dismissive gesture. The natives steered K'smet and Balin roughly before their captain and Xavier. K'smet walked with a terrible limp. He and Balin glowered sourly at Avador. They looked like they had just gone through an entire war. Their faces were scarred and blackened with bruises though K'smet appeared to be in the worst of shape. One of his eyes was swollen shut, and blood trickled from the corner of his mouth. Balin's nose was crooked, most likely broken, and blood trailed from a cut above his eyebrow.

The natives kept their hold on them, and Xavier's two sergeants had their swords at the ready. Avador considered his captives for a moment. "It's been a long time, Lord Balin," he said.

"Yes, it has," Balin agreed. "You were but a small boy the last time I laid eyes on you; an innocent child. But I see that your father has turned you into a heartless wretch just as he longed for. A suitable heir to his despicable legacy,"

Avador's brow pinched slightly. "What do you know of such things?"

"What has become of your mother? Did she assist in your rearing, or was she even aware of what she married into? I'm sure if she didn't then it was an awful shock for her. She probably can't stand what your father has turned you into,"

"My father has raised me into a man," Avador said defensively.

"And a fine job he's done too," K'smet spoke, leaning to one side and cocking his head slightly to perceive Avador with his one good eye.

"You don't have to speak to be noticed, Sir K'smet, trust me. I warned my father of your true loyalty some time ago," Avador said, switching his dark eyes to K'smet.

"I don't believe he listened," K'smet said with a smart snicker, his white teeth flashing to reveal blood staining them on the one side.

"He'll believe me now. What I'm more concerned of at present is information on the prince and princess," said Avador, glancing at them both.

"Sorry, that information is confidential," said K'smet, leaning on Balin for support. His brain felt fuzzy and a sudden dizziness was making everything swim sickly. Balin looked to him worriedly, feeling horribly unhelpful.

Avador pondered the mangled knight uncertainly for a moment. "Get them some chairs, before they fall over," he ordered.

"You heard him, boys," Xavier said to his two sergeants, signaling them into action. "Give them some chairs, and don't forget the cushions,"

Avador glared at the smart-mouthed commander. The two sergeants smirked wickedly and stepped towards the captives. They pushed aside the natives and gripped Balin and K'smet roughly by the shoulders. They forcibly shoved them downward, till they were kneeling on the rough wooden planks of the floor. K'smet growled as white hot pain shot up his bad leg. The sergeant struck him hard against his cheek with a malicious grin, sending him toppling against Balin who steadied him.

There was a steel-like slither as Avador drew his sword. "Leave him be," he said in a dangerously low voice. The sergeant stared at the sword tip now pointed at him with surprise. His fellow sergeant looked to their commander expectantly. Balin stared at Avador with curiosity.

"You fool," Xavier hissed, smacking Avador's blade downward. "Why don't you try to remember what side you're on," He looked to his sergeants. "Leave them alone, boys. God knows we must be gentle with our enemies,"

The sergeants obeyed, but not without casting contemptuous scowls at Avador and the native sergeants as they passed by. Avador sheathed his sword. "Lord Balin," he addressed. Balin's eyes darkened as he met Avador's gaze.

"Think about the possibilities. Everything is at stake. You may think you have worked hard to train your nephew and niece for this, but how prepared could they be when you were under the restrictions of house arrest. They are two adolescences seeing the real world for the first time, against experienced and hardened soldiers. You'll be doing them a favor by telling me all that you know," Avador said appealingly.

The young captain's reasonable words stalled Balin's response for a moment as his mind sorted through it all. K'smet gazed at him nervously, worried that he had been swayed by Avador. Eventually, Balin directed a scowl at Avador. "I have nothing to say to you," he chewed out.

Avador's eyes burned, and his jaw tightened.

"Just as I said, this is getting you nowhere," Xavier commented arrogantly. He stepped forward, rubbing his stubble-covered chin. "I believe you should resort to torturing them into talking. How do you think we should start off? Ripping finger nails off, or burning body hair maybe,"

"That won't be necessary." Avador said, sounding disgusted. Anger was festering in his chest.

"You have a better idea?" Xavier questioned irritably.

"Yes as a matter of fact. I believe it is time to pay a visit to that stable boy's home you mentioned," Avador said.

"The McKnight boy?" Xavier said pensively, rolling over the idea. "That's certainly not the worst move you've decided upon. Gerard and Jarpikus will go with you,"

"I don't think so, commander," Avador objected flatly. "I believe you and you're men have helped enough. Send a hawk to Ezleon, let Commander Moth know what has happened. Tell him

I travel towards his city,"

Xavier glared at Avador with amazed disbelief, resentment flickering across his face. The two sergeants, Gerard and Jarpikus looked at each other. Avador gave them one last warning glance before turning away and walking towards the door. His own men shifted uncomfortably.

"What about the prisoners, captain?" one of them asked.

Avador stopped and looked over his shoulder. "Prepare them for travel, Night Hawk. They're coming with us,"

Avador turned away once more and departed from the station.

*****

The creaking rotten door of the McKnight's home collapsed without argue beneath the force of Avador's boot.

Leona McKnight jumped from the small hearth she was kneeling before, startled by the sudden noise. A thick porridge bubbled in a black pot hanging on the spit over the fire. A wooden spoon with half of its handle broken off was gripped in Leona's hand.

"What is the meaning of this?" she cried, frightened by the sight of Avador and his men filing into the room behind him with their weapons at hand.

"This is an investigation of your loyalty," said Avador, coming towards her. He casted his gaze about the room searching his surroundings.

"Our loyalty?" Leona questioned outraged.

There was a shuffling sound off to the left, causing Avador and his men to raise their weapons.

"Mama?" came a small voice, and Kyla appeared from the joining room. Leona picked up the spike from the hearth against Avador's sword and pulled Kyla close to her.

"You can lower your weapons, she's my daughter. She's just a child," Leona said with an underlining warning. Kyla peered at Avador from behind her mother's dirty skirts.

Avador stood fixedly, his muscles tensed for action as he stared at the innocent child who stared back without fear. After a moment, Avador signaled for his men to ease their weapons as he lowered his own.

"What's wrong with her?" Avador asked, noting Kyla's pale face and weary countenance.

Leona glared at him as if he had said something terribly offensive, the spike gripped tightly in her hand. "She's ill. She has been for a long time,"

Avador looked at Kyla for a drawn out moment, with pity almost reflecting in his features.

"What do you want?" Leona questioned, perturbed by Avador's behavior.

Avador lifted his gaze from Kyla. "Your son," he said.

Fear struck Leona like a battering ram smashing through a barred gate. The spike trembled in her hand. Kyla made a sound between a gasp and a whimper, and she looked frightfully up at her mother's terrified face.

"Our son is no longer here," a voice spoke from the open doorway. Avador and his men spun towards the voice, their weapons tensed again. Raven McKnight stood in the doorway with a calm demeanor. Avador narrowed his eyes suspiciously, about to speak but one of his men spoke first.

"I don't believe it," the native said in a hushed voice as he lowered his knocked bow. His eyes grew wide with disbelief. Raven glanced about him just now realizing that the other men in his home were natives. He attempted to fight it but apprehension gradually contorted his features.

"Its Raven Wing," another young native said with a gleeful grin. The other six natives nodded and murmured agreement. The younger natives looked excitedly joyous, while the older natives appeared despondent and displeased.

"What do you mean?" Avador queried, rather confused.

"Raven Wing is son of Water Wing, *chief* Water Wing," the native Night Hawk explained who stood closest to Avador.

Raven swallowed nervously, but remained standing firmly.

"He's a dirty rotten traitor," another native spat with disgust, glowering at Raven. "A deserter and a coward is what he is. He's no son to our chief."

"He should be dealt with properly, and given the penalty all deserters receive," another native said.

"Yeah, a good scaring across the back," a third growled in agreement.

Raven barred his teeth and clenched his hands into fists, ready to fight. The three natives pressed forward towards him, and just as a cat stalks its prey they pounced with lightning speed. A chaotic brawl ensued. Crushing blows were exchanged as the natives tried to wrestle Raven under their captivity.

"NO!!" cried Leona as she rushed forward. Avador caught her by the arm. "Let me GO!" she yelled, beating a fist against his breastplate.

"Stop this insanity, Night Hawk, before someone gets hurt," Avador demanded, holding Leona back and keeping Kyla behind him.

There was a bone shattering sound as Raven flung a punch at one of the natives who reeled backwards. The three young natives charged into the chaos to help him.

Night Hawk strode forward sheathing his blade as he went.

"Stop this! Enough!" he commanded, gripping one of his fellow warriors by the arm. The native turned and glanced a blow against Night Hawk's cheek.

"Bright Sky!" Night Hawk hollered, anger set in his eyes as he felt the sting of Bright Sky's blow. Night Hawk swung back with a hardened fist, and Bright Sky's nose crushed beneath his punch. The other warriors suddenly ceased their senseless struggle, all of them panting for breath.

"I said knock it off!" Night Hawk yelled angrily, glaring at his fellow men. Raven shrugged off the natives' hold on him and scowled crossly.

Bright Sky wiped the blood that now streamed from his nose. "You know as well as us, Night Hawk, that Raven Wing is a deserter and a traitor to our people."

"He is not worthy to wear the hawk feathers of the chief's son," said another, casting a contemptuous glare at Raven.

"Swift Deer and Bright Sky are right, Night Hawk. Raven Wing should be punished properly for abandoning us accordingly to our tribe's law," a third native spoke, stepping forward.

"Especially since he left us in a time of need, he was just about to be made chief. He deserves to be punished, or are you as naïve as our young brothers who defend him?"

"I understand your bitterness towards Raven Wing, Fall Leaf, but I also remember that we swore an oath to take up service under Captain Avador's command. His mission is our priority," said Night Hawk, looking loyally to Avador.

The three older natives went quiet when their superior reminded them of their responsibilities. Fall Leaf lowered his gaze shamefully and took a step back from Night Hawk. "Our apologies, captain. We meant no disrespect," he said meekly, looking to Avador.

Avador dipped his head in acknowledgement. He turned his attention upon Raven and released Leona's arm. "If it is true that your son is no longer here, then where is he now?" he interrogated, advancing towards Raven.

"Certainly not in this home, and most likely not anywhere in Niche," Raven said.

Avador assessed Raven's answer with a suspicious air. Leona knelt beside Kyla and wrapped her arms comfortingly around her.

"I feel inclined to inform you that your son has been associating with . . . a certain pair of fugitives for the past week." said Avador.

"Fugitives?" Raven questioned, his eyes narrowing.

"Yes, I am hunting them down to bring them back to Caelum

where they will be dealt with accordingly. You should know now that if your son is caught with them, he will be punished with equal harshness."

Raven took this in with darkening features.

"Are you certain there is nothing you wish to tell me?" Avador asked.

Raven's eyes hardened. "I have nothing to say. You're on your own, captain," he said huskily.

Disappointment settled over Avador. He breathed inward submissively.

"We will leave you then," he said. He signaled for his men to depart, and the native warriors began to file out of the ramshackle home. As the older warriors passed, they casted malevolent glares at Raven; Avador was the last to leave.

"If you hurt our son, captain, there will be no where for you to hide," Leona warned, her voice trembling.

"And I'll make sure that promise is kept," Raven said coolly.

"I believe you," Avador said. He pulled a small pouch from his belt and gave it to Raven who stared at it curiously.

"Why don't you take your daughter to a physician," said Avador. He then departed just when Raven discovered that he had given them a pouch of gold.

20

The sun was dipping behind the trees of Staleon in a beautiful sunset. The oncoming night was dragging the temperatures down to freezing. Frost would definitely lay its fine crystal carpet over the land more thickly tonight. Autumn had departed. Winter had officially arrived.

Lark led Philip and Philomena onward still. They rode alongside a bubbling creek that sparkled brilliantly in the evening sun.

Philip lagged behind Philomena and Lark with drooping eyelids and paling skin. "This looks like a good place to camp," he said, looking wearily down at the stream. He gently pulled back on Nimbius' reins.

"I thought we agreed to travel till nightfall. We can't stop now. It's not dark," said Lark, turning his horse (who he had become comfortably acquainted with), to face Philip.

"We *should* keep going, Philip," Philomena said over her shoulder.

"I don't think I can," Philip said with difficulty, beginning to breathe heavily. He bent over his saddle pommel, his eyes glazed with a tiring pain. Philomena frowned at his words and turned towards him. When she saw him, pain-filled eyes and weak appearance, her countenance instantly contorted with fearful worry.

"Philip?! Are you alright?" asked Philomena, her voice nearly faltering.

"We have to stop," said Philip weakly, sliding down from his horse. He held onto his saddle, not having the strength to hold himself up. His horse, Nimbius, bent his head to him and nudged him, nickering with concern.

"Philip!" said Philomena worriedly, jumping off her horse and rushing to his side. Lark stood by uncertainly, sensing the urgency in the air but not sure whether to help.

"What's wrong?" demanded Philomena, trying to help Philip stay on his feet.

"My arm," said Philip, slamming his eyes shut against the pain. "It really hurts," he said through clenched teeth. Lark's brow furrowed and he climbed down from his horse. Philomena lifted her hand from Philip's arm to find blood blotched on her palm from his wound. She lifted her gaze to Lark, and he could see her raw fear.

"We'll stop for the night," said Philomena firmly, her voice cracking slightly.

Lark offered no protests but instead went over to the siblings, still doubtful yet having a sneaking suspicion. "What really pierced your arm?" he asked Philip.

"An arrow," said Philip.

Lark pulled away the bloody bandage. His stomach clenched into uncomfortable knots when he revealed the puncture wound that was now horribly swollen and beginning to fester. Lark glanced worriedly at Philip, knowing there was no time to waste. He looked over at Philomena.

"Can you get him settled while I start a fire?" asked Lark. Philomena nodded and they both set to work in a prompt fashion. Philomena laid out Philip's bed roll, and Philip collapsed on top of it shivering violently. Lark made a circle of large rocks he found alongside the creek and then began to hurriedly gather sticks, bark, and pinecones which he piled inside the ring of stone. He brought out his flint and steel kit and slashed them together, sending bright sparks flying. The sparks landed amidst the kindling and hissed and crackled as they brought forth tiny tongues of flame that quickly grew larger.

Every cloak and blanket they possessed Philomena took and covered Philip with in hopes of ceasing his trembling. All the

while she spoke comforting words to him even though her voice
was fraught with panic.

Lark plopped a large flat rock in the fire, not caring if the hot
flames licked his fingers.

"Can I borrow a knife?" he asked.

Philomena pulled the knife from her belt and gave it to him
without question. Lark wiped its blade against his coat sleeve
ensuring that it was clean and then laid it upon the flat rock in
the fire. With that done he rushed over to their horses and
snatched the water skin from Philip's saddle pommel and then
frantically began to rummage through the saddle bags.

"What are you looking for?" asked Philomena, her voice still
panicky.

"A pot or pan, anything to boil some water in," said Lark.

"In my saddle bag on the left, there's a pot," said Philomena.
Lark hurried to her horse and found the pot where she had said.
He returned to the fire, all the while pouring water into the pot as
he went. Some spilt over the rim and streamed down his hand.
The droplets fell onto the fire and sizzled angrily. Lark
practically dropped the pot of water onto the fire for it to boil.

"Here, let him drink some water, and then wash the wound clean.
There can be no dirt or grime in it," said Lark handing
Philomena the water skin. "Do you have anything we can use for
bandages?"

"There are some shirts in my other saddle bag," said Philomena.
Lark went and retrieved one of the shirts, a clean white one that
was obviously Philip's, and began tearing it into thin strips.
Bubbles were already beginning to form in the water Lark had
set on the fire. Philomena's knife was beginning to ebb with a
burning red glow as it grew hotter and hotter.

Lark stuffed a few of the strips of fine cloth into the pot, wincing
as the hot water splashed his skin. He then brought out a pouch
gathered at the top by a drawstring, opened it, and emptied its
contents of dried leafy herbs into the pot as well.

With a stick Lark stirred the bandages and dried herbs, then allowed them to boil together.

Philomena cradled Philip's head in her lap and uncorked the water skin. Philip drank eagerly. His eyelids were too heavy for him to open, and any movement he did make was lethargic. Philomena used a corner of one of the cloaks to mop the sweat from his face. With trembling hands she cut away his sleeve to uncover his wound.

Philomena's stomach coiled into sickened knots as she stared at the puncture made by the arrow. The blood was so dark it looked black, making the wound appear far deeper than what it truly was. The flesh around it was a bruised purple splotched with a sickly yellow, and the entire upper arm was swollen. Philomena touched Philip's arm with her fingertips and sucked in a breath. His skin was burning hot.

Gathering herself, and mustering her strength, Philomena moistened the sleeve she had cut off from Philip's shirt, and began cleaning the wound with the wet cloth.

"Philly," spoke Philip, his voice groggy. It took all his strength to open his eyes to look at her.

"I'm right here, Philip," said Philomena softly.

Philip let out a deep breath, doing his best to keep his concentration. "I'm so sorry," he said.

"For what?" Philomena asked with a small frown.

"Everything, making us stop like this, bringing you into danger, forcing you to use a sword," said Philip, closing his eyes.

Philomena's brow knitted with sympathy. "You're talking nonsense, Philip," she said, touching his cheek.

"Am I?" Philip said with a tired grin.

Lark came over to them and knelt beside Philomena. "Pour some of this onto the puncture," he said, handing Philomena a small bottle of clear liquid.

"What is it?" asked Philomena.

"Do you ask out of curiosity or distrust?" Lark asked meanly.

Philomena stared at him with surprise. She uncorked the bottle without another word. Lark grimaced as guilt suddenly jabbed him.

"It's a tincture of St. John's Wort, an herb that helps stop bleeding and prevents infection," said Lark, finding it difficult to meet Philomena's gaze.

She poured some of the tincture onto Philip's wound, making him wince and clench his teeth.

"Are you here, Lark?" asked Philip through meshed teeth.

"Yeah, I'm right here," said Lark, accepting the bottle back from Philomena.

Philip grinned. "I thought you'd be gone by now," he said.

"You and me both," said Lark.

"I thank you though for everything. I knew we could trust you," said Philip, his voice hoarse and his tongue feeling heavier by the second.

"Don't thank me yet," said Lark. He went back to the fire and, with great care, picked up Philomena's knife by the hilt. The blade was glowing red and burning hot. Lark could feel the heat of the blade ebbing to the hilt and down to the pommel. He returned to Philip's side with the steaming knife.

"What are you doing?" asked Philomena, staring frightfully at the knife.

"Give him something to bite on, and do your best to keep him still. I'm going to cauterize the wound," said Lark. Philomena moved out of his way, and went around to Philip's other side. Lark knelt on Philip's forearm with his knee. Philip grimaced and grinded on the stick Philomena gave him to bite.

"Sorry," Lark winced. He looked up to Philomena. She lay across Philip's chest and nodded that she was ready.

Lark heaved a steadying breath and pressed the red hot blade against Philip's wound.

Philip's muffled scream of agony pierced the night air, startling the sleeping birds and in turn their horses. Shivers ran down

Philomena's spine as she used all her weight and strength to keep Philip as still as possible.

Steam coiled and rolled off the knife and Philip's arm. Lark grimaced as he put pressure on the blade to sear the wound shut. After an agonizingly painful moment, Lark lifted the blade from the wound leaving a red burnt scar that steamed with heat. Philip spat out the stick and panted heavily, hardly remaining conscious. His face drooled with sweat.

Lark sat back off of Philip's arm and breathed an inward sigh of relief. He met Philomena's gaze and saw the fear kindling there, not knowing whether to subside or burst into flames.

"Did it work?" Philomena asked tentatively.

Lark nodded, feeling rather tired. "After it cools down, we need to wrap it in those bandages I have prepared," he said.

They stared at Philip for a moment, taking in the peaceful stillness that had suddenly settled over their camp. Philip now lay unmoving, having finally given in to unconsciousness. Philomena lifted a hand to his face, feeling very relieved.

"He'll be fine," assured Lark. "But he needs rest and food,"

"Avador and his men took all of our food," said Philomena almost despairingly.

"Then we'll have to find some," said Lark, standing.

Philomena looked around them with a growing frown. "Its winter time; how are we going to find anything edible out here?"

"There's plenty to eat in these woods if you know where to look," said Lark. Philomena gave him a doubtful look. Lark didn't bother supporting his argument. "Why don't you stay here with your brother while I go find some food," he said, giving back the knife he had borrowed.

Suspicion instantly crept over Philomena's countenance as she accepted the knife. "Ugh, how about instead you stay here and I go find some food," she said, gesturing with her knife.

Lark frowned, glancing down at the moving blade and then back up at Philomena. "But you don't know where to look for food,"

"You don't know that," Philomena said huffily.

The frown deepened across Lark's brow, and then suddenly lifted as understanding dawned on him. "I do not believe you have to be concerned about me trying to run off from your pleasant company anymore," said Lark.

"Why is that?" asked Philomena.

"Because I am far too tired to try, and really there's nothing you could do about it if I did feel like trying anyway," said Lark in a matter-of-fact tone.

A shrug and a smart snicker were Philomena's reply.

Lark narrowed his eyes. "You'd tie me up again wouldn't you?" Philomena said nothing, but chewed at her lip and stared at him with distrust.

Lark huffed impatiently. "Look, are we really going to argue this point all night?"

"I suppose not," said Philomena slowly, looking him up and down. In truth, it was their own hunger that helped speed things along.

"Good," said Lark, picking up his bow and quiver and strapping them across his back. "Keep the fire going, and I would let him rest for a while before bothering him," he added.

Too tired to snap a smart remark in return, Philomena nodded instead. Lark turned away towards the shadowy trees, stepping with hardly a sound.

Philomena returned to Philip's side, and when Lark had gone from sight, she let the tears she had been holding back flow freely.

"Why are you crying?" asked Philip huskily.

Philomena hurriedly wiped away her tears. "Because, I thought I had lost you, before . . ." she trailed off.

"Before what?" Philip prompted, peering at her and feeling utterly weak.

"Before I had the chance to say sorry; I was such a jerk to you after we escaped Niche," Philomena sniffed, still wiping away tears.

"Nonsense," Philip smiled. "You love uncle very much and we're both indebted to K'smet. I cannot hold that against you," he said. Philomena smiled back and gripped his hand warmly.

"But you can't just be crying over that," Philip went on, looking at her blearily. "Why are you so upset?"

Philomena glanced around uncertainly. "You should be resting," she said softly, still holding his hand.

"Come on, Philly, I know you too well," Philip prod gently with a weak smile.

Inhaling with slight annoyance, Philomena frowned at the ground. Her brow pinched with emotion, and when she lifted her eyes back to him, they reflected regret and pain.

"It's just . . . getting so much closer to Caelum after so long, I sometimes wonder if mom and dad remember us." Philomena said slowly. Her gaze strayed to their surroundings.

"Do we ever forget them?" Philip asked simply.

"No," Philomena replied.

"Then they remember us, Philly," Philip smiled.

Philomena nodded, pursing her lips. She didn't want to say that she could barely remember what their parents looked like, or how they were. Philip needed to rest so he could recover. He didn't need to be worrying about her. His eyes were already closing with heavy sleep.

"Where's Lark?" Philip asked, straining to look around. Philomena quieted him and put a hand to his shoulder to keep him still.

"He went to find some food," she said.

Philip relaxed again. "You shouldn't be so hard on him, Philly. He's not so bad. I don't think I would have made it without him," he said. Defensiveness rose in Philomena, but she chewed at her lip to fight the urge to protest.

"I'm tired," Philip said wearily, letting out a deep sigh. He was suddenly conscious of the heavy weight of his ring he kept safely hidden in his pocket, the ring of the Alamian prince.

"Sleep, I'm watching you," Philomena whispered. She gripped his hand reassuringly. It was only seconds later that Philip's conscious plunged into a deep slumber, escaping the burning pain of his arm and the burden of his identity.

21

By the time Lark returned to their camp thirty minutes later with a small pouch in his hands filled with the edible things he had found, Philomena had already tended to the horses and collected more wood for the fire. It's warm glow gave a great deal of comfort. Lark stepped into the fire's orb of light without a sound startling Philomena from where she sat beside Philip.

"It's only me," said Lark, kneeling across from her on the opposite side of the fire. "How's your brother?"

"Better," Philomena breathed settling back down. "I think he'll pull out of this just fine thanks to you," she said. She was trying to sound grateful, yet Lark still sensed the reluctance in her words.

"He'll need lots of sleep tonight, and that arm should be kept clean and covered." Lark said with an undertone of annoyance. There was nothing left to say, for Philomena did not know how to express her gratitude to him, and Lark wasn't sure what to think of her yet.

Philomena took up the pot of boiling water which still had the bandages and herbs bubbling together.

"Here, this should help as well," said Lark, pulling out a small bottle that was labeled 'aloe vera'. Philomena accepted it with a grateful nod and pursed lips. She went over to Philip and busied herself with dressing his arm. The area of flesh which Lark had cauterized was burnt and tender. A scar in the shape of the knife Lark had used could faintly be discerned.

As Philomena rubbed in the aloe she was relieved to feel that the feverish heat had already begun to leave Philip's skin.

Over at the fire, Lark untied the pouch and brought out its

various contents to be cooked for their supper. Using a flat rock, he chopped the few roots he had unearthed and the leafy herbs that had managed to survive the frost. He crushed the flakey white pine bark, and cut up the other questionable things he had gathered. All of these ingredients, Lark plopped into the cooking pot that Philomena had returned which already had fresh water bubbling inside. Lark stirred everything together with the knife he had used for chopping. The stirring enticed the water to boil and sent steam gushing into the air.

When Philomena had finished bandaging Philip's arm the intriguing mixture of smells wafted over to her and made her stomach growl. The sweet, savory aroma stirred Philip from sleep.

"Is that food I smell?" he asked, sniffing the air with brightening eyes. Lingering sleep was quickly vanishing from him.

Both Lark and Philomena looked to him. A joyful smile spread on Philomena's face to see him look so lively so soon.

"How do you feel? Any better?" asked Philomena.

"Lots better," said Philip, propping himself up stiffly. He still cringed and put a hand to his sore arm and shoulder, but the sluggishness of the fever had left him. "Ah, there's the man who burnt my skin," he said, beaming over at Lark.

"Are you hungry?" asked Lark, stirring the contents of the pot that billowed savory steam.

"Enough to eat a herd of cows," said Philip, attempting to get to his feet.

Philomena pushed him back down on. "I'll bring you some food," she assured.

Shortly after, Philomena had laid out three small wooden bowls and spoons, and by then the stew was ready to be served. Lark ladled out the food equally, filling the bowls almost to the brim. Philip eagerly accepted the bowl Philomena brought to him and hungrily tucked into the stew, slurping it noisily and hardly taking the time to breathe.

Lark and Philomena watched him. An amused smile played at Philomena's lips. Lark remained straight faced, but he was satisfied to see Philip's enthusiastic appetite. He met Philomena's gaze and suddenly their content expressions vanished and they quickly looked away from one another. Philomena stirred her stew, and Lark cleared his throat uncertainly.

"I thought princes were supposed to have manners," said Lark without looking up.

"He does have manners, he just forgets that he has them," said Philomena. Philip didn't even acknowledge their comments.

"This is really good," said Philip happily between slurping mouthfuls. He smiled up at Lark, his empty stomach finally beginning to feel full. "How'd you conjure up such a great meal without anything to cook?" he asked.

Lark shrugged modestly. "My father taught me what the woods provide when I was a boy," he said.

"Really? What's exactly in this then?" asked Philip, pointing at his bowl with his spoon.

"Just some roots, a couple of herbs, pine bark, earthworms, few grubs and snails," said Lark picking up his own bowl. There was a choking coughing sound as Philomena spat out the disturbing things she had almost swallowed. Lark gave her a knowing look, not at all offended. There was a hint of pleasure in his features in fact.

"Huh," said Philip, intrigued. "I never imagined those things would taste so good," He continued eating, not at all bothered by what the stew contained.

They sat in content silence for the next few moments, indulging in the hot meal. Philomena was only able to stomach eating half of her stew before handing the rest to Philip who happily finished it for her. Lark did not mind and so took no offense towards her. Their horses munched on the foliage that grew in between the trees they were tied to, seeming just as content as their masters. Beyond the orb of their camp fire, the nocturnal world of Staleon flourished in the cold air. They could hear an owl hooting somewhere in the distant trees. Guttural growls and various yowls sprung from the brush faraway and sometimes a little to nearby for their comfort.

Still, they were too tired, and too full from the stew, to allow the sounds of the night to trifle them for very long. And not all of Staleon's nocturnal inhabitants suggested death and fear, a few were enchanting and rather beautiful, especially to Philip and Philomena who had never seen such things. Such as the creek, which glittered with the moonlight also sparkled with bright green and blue lights that danced up and down the bubbling water. Every time there was a significant ripple in the water, music played that sounded like watery flutes corresponding to one another the way crickets do in a meadow.

"What *is* that?" asked Philomena, staring at the creek in nervous wonderment.

"Minnows," said Lark. Philip and Philomena stared at him curiously. "You've never heard of the singing minnows of Staleon?" he asked.

"No," they both said. Lark frowned at them, absolutely bewildered. Yet the matter was dropped and nothing else was said on the subject.

After supper, Philip felt warm and satisfied, and easily drifted off to sleep.

"We shouldn't disturb him," said Lark, adding more wood and kindling to the fire.

"Yeah," Philomena agreed, smiling at Philip as she cleaned the pot and the bowls they had used with water and sand from the nearby creek.

Lark looked to Philomena. Even though he could barely tolerate her, he could tell she was exhausted. "Why don't you get some sleep. I'll keep watch," he said.

"No, I'll take the first watch," said Philomena firmly without meeting Lark's gaze.

"You still don't trust me, even after all I did," said Lark.

"Perhaps, though it doesn't matter whether we trust each other or not, as long as we get what we want from the other," said Philomena, packing away the pot and bowls. Lark stared at her. "Anyway, I don't know why you helped us in the first place." she added.

"Did you see anyone else who could have helped you at the time?" asked Lark, his voice cross.

"No, but even you said that no one is ever kind simply to be kind," said Philomena levelly.

"Yeah, and I still stand by that," said Lark, glaring at her.

"Good, because we don't care to gain your trust and vice versa," said Philomena, buckling her saddle bag and setting it aside. "We're simply three people who happen to be traveling together, with you as our guide,"

A log fell in the fire and spit red sparks. The fire crackled hungrily as it devoured the wood piled onto it. Lark poked at the embers. He flexed his jaw and looked haughtily at Philomena. She sensed his gaze boring into her, but only stared into the fire.

"You know, being kind simply to be kind is for the people. I don't direct such a saying to you or even me," Lark said slowly, in hopes to clear some of the tension.

"Why do you even bother telling me this?" asked Philomena irritably.

"Because it's the truth," said Lark firmly. "And whether trust is between us or not, things hardly ever work out the way you plan them too; and whether you and your brother are royalty or not, I believe you to be good people,"

"*Good* people?" questioned Philomena with a smirk.

"With a few faults that are accustomed to princes and princesses," Lark added sarcastically.

"You still don't believe us do you?" asked Philomena, looking to him.

"Would you believe you?"

"No,"

A piece of the awkward, competitive wall between them melted away, but it was indeed a small piece. They both could sense this, yet with the wall crumbling away there was something new beyond it that was a different awkwardness. It felt warm and intoxicating, and neither of them could identify it, so they pushed it far away in the very corners of their minds and the rest of their repulsion remained intact.

"Go to bed. I'll wake you in a while," said Lark, breaking eye contact and gesturing for her to obey.

Philomena rose to her feet, suddenly realizing she was exhausted. Before she could turn away she looked back to Lark, hesitating a moment. "I hope you know how much I appreciate what you did for Philip. I know you didn't have to help us, and I'm glad you did." she said.

She turned away before Lark could say anything in return. Her words pleasantly surprised him, and he was sure it wouldn't be the last time.

For Philomena, something like relief had settled within her as she brought out her bed roll and laid it close to Philip. In only a few minutes she was peacefully asleep, leaving Lark alone by the fire with his thoughts.

At first, Lark felt soothed, feeling the warmth of the dancing fire's glow upon his face. Then suddenly, the black thorn of resentment bore a gaping hole in his contentment. As the black thorn dug further inward, his jaw tightened and his eyes grew angry, as his disturbing thoughts frolicked furiously inside him. Something had changed. That's why he felt angry. He had spent only a day and two nights with Philip and Philomena and already he could feel a change. It was only small, but he was beginning to have doubts of what he thought of them. Perhaps there was *some* truth in their story.

This consideration only served to confuse Lark further. He

snapped a twig in half and angrily tossed it into the fire. What now? If there was truth to their words, what sort of future was in store? Should he really help them?

They had kidnapped him and pretty much forced him to act as their guide. Why should he help them? They weren't his friends; especially Philomena.

Lark sat there fuming, feeling his temper rise inside him like bubbling lava. A single answer was vivid in his mind. He turned his gaze to Philip and Philomena. They remained still, sleeping underneath the rough covers of their cloaks.

Lark switched his gaze to Spear, the horse they had given him. Spear was resting beside the other two horses, his head low and his eyes closed. Shifting to his feet, Lark walked silently around the fire away from Philip and Philomena. He grabbed a bridal that was stashed with the other tack as he went and moved over to Spear. He didn't know if he could ride bareback. He didn't really care. He just wanted to go back home and leave behind the possible truth that made everything he knew to be lies. He wanted things the way they had been; less complicated with a brighter future.

Spear lifted his head at Lark's approach. The horse's kind eyes shone in the firelight. Lark pursed his lips and stroked Spear's nose.

"You can't expect me to want to help them," Lark whispered. The horse stared at him steadily. Lark lifted the bridal to put it on, but then something distracting him.

A gentle tingling like many little bells sounded from above. It was a soothing sound that fell into rhythm with the bubbling creek and the singing minnows. Listening to the gentle music, Lark's anger began to diminish as if it had never been. He looked up and saw several golden orbs of sparkling light glowing amongst the trees, illuminating the canopy.

They flitted and frolicked and danced with one another, radiating fleeting joy and happiness. Some came very close, but they dared not come too close. Lark knew fairies were shy, fragile beings and they disliked fire.

He stood there mesmerized, watching them and listening to them. It was as if they wished to help him understand his own feelings. They wanted to take away his confusion. After a minute, Lark's confusion and doubt ebbed away and the fairies' beautiful music filled him.

"Lark?" came Philomena's voice. Lark glanced around and saw her half sitting up from her bed roll looking at him with a knitted brow.

"Is something wrong?" she asked.

"No," Lark replied, hiding the bridal he still held behind his back. "Everything's fine. Go back to sleep,"

For a moment, Philomena stared at him uncertainly, but then nodded and laid back down. Lark watched her and waited for her breathing to be deep and restful. When it was, he patted Spear and went back to the camp fire. He dropped the bridal back with the other tack and looked up at the glowing fairies.

"Alright, I got the message, but I hope I get to go home eventually," he whispered to them. They glowed brighter in response and their wings tingled happily. Lark wasn't sure if fairies could understand the common tongue, but these ones seemed to understand just fine. He sat back down beside the fire and soaked in their reassuring company.

22

Captain Avador came to the decision that it was time for he, his
men, and their prisoners to leave the town of Niche. After
sending a message to Lord Salvador by the fastest falcon, they
happily left Niche behind with lifting spirits. They now traveled
across the stretching fields and into the dark Staleon Woods
under the light of the moon and stars.

Their prisoners, K'smet and Balin, even seemed to be in better
moods as Niche vanished from sight behind the brush and trees.
At least, in the best moods they could be in considering that they
were tied securely to the saddles of the company's pack horses
and lead by the natives Bright Sky and Fall Leaf.

"I still think we should make them walk," said Bright Sky
grudgingly as he casted a glare over his shoulder at K'smet.
K'smet glared back haughtily with his one good eye. His other
eye was still terribly blackened and swollen shut.

"That would only slow us down," said Avador from the front of
the company as he ducked beneath a low hanging branch. Bright
Sky grumbled upsettingly, but the matter was dropped for the
time being.

Night Hawk, Avador's second in command, glanced worriedly
from his comrade to his captain.

"Do you not think it unwise for Bright Sky to lead that
prisoner?" he whispered to Avador so Bright Sky couldn't hear.
"The man killed his cousin," he reminded.

Avador breathed in a steadying breath. "Bright Sky is a warrior,
as are all of we, and so was Red Moon. We know the
consequences of such a life, we know the risks. Not all of us will
return home in the end,"

"Hardly any of us will see home again if your father becomes king," Night Hawk put in. Avador didn't argue.

"We put Red Moon to rest. Bright Sky will be resentful towards the knight, but it is to be expected. We will keep an eye on him. For now, let him be," said Avador, turning a calm look to his second in command.

The corner of Night Hawk's mouth twitched reluctantly, but he nodded. He sneaked a glimpse of Bright Sky behind them and saw the vengeful anger in him. Bright Sky was cantankerous by nature; now he was dangerous.

When the company reached the area that Commander Xavier had described, they halted gazing around down at the ground in confusion. The dirt road was covered in horse tracks going every which way, overlapping and disappearing into the woods.

"There are no clear tracks to lead us," said Night Hawk, gazing around.

"What a shame," spoke K'smet mockingly. Everyone looked to him with angry scowls and contemptuous glares. Bright Sky spat abuse at him, and Avador silenced him.

"What do you make of it, Silver Stream?" asked Avador, directing their attention to the more important matter. He gestured for Silver Stream's opinion.

Silver Stream swung down from his pinto horse and knelt upon the dirt road amidst the many tracks. Despite being the second most youthful member of the company, second only to Avador, Silver Stream was respected for having the sharpest eyes to pick out and discern the tiniest marks and tracks on the ground. Everyone waited patiently while he analyzed the tracks before him that criss-crossed confusingly.

"These happened just the other night," said Silver Stream after several long moments of silence.

"That would be accurate to Xavier's account. This must be where they lost their trail," said Avador, sounding not at all impressed by the commander's work.

"Can you find their trail, Silver Stream?" asked Night Hawk. Silver Stream shook his head doubtfully. "It appears that they brushed away their tracks, and then Xavier and his men rode over it all,"

"I told you he couldn't track a dung beetle," muttered Avador to Night Hawk.

"But if I were them," said Silver Stream more to himself. He rose and moved silently towards the trees, glancing down at the ground every now and then. He entered into the woods and brush and their shadows swallowed him up. The rest of the company remained where they stood, exchanging curious glances. When several long moments passed, Avador began to feel edgy. When he came to the decision to go after Silver Stream, the young tracker appeared from the woods.

"Blood," said Silver Stream striding towards them and lifting a hand to show the smears of red that stained his index finger.

A jolt of fear penetrated Balin.

"It was just behind this tree here, and judging by the amount it is not a fatal wound," said Silver Stream indicating the tree.

"It's the prince," said Avador, remembering the arrow that had hit Philip.

Silver Stream nodded. "I reckon he was the one who brushed away the tracks and diverted Xavier and his men off course."

"You found the trail?" asked Avador earnestly.

"Yes, but it is hard to make out. We could easily loose our way and then we'll have to back track," said Silver Stream.

"We cannot waste anymore time," said Avador, chewing at his lip as he weighed out their predicament.

"Well, there is one way to be certain of our path," said Swift Deer. They turned to look at him. Swift Deer dug in his buckskin coat and brought out a small furry ball. Everyone frowned.

"You brought Teaco?" questioned Night Hawk.

Swift Deer shrugged and looked to Avador who appeared just as displeased. Teaco shifted and lifted his little head. He looked like a cross between a weasel and a hound with floppy ears, droopy yellow eyes, and a big wet nose neighbored by long wiggling whiskers. His coat looked dense and fluffy, and brilliantly colored in shifting shades of blue and green. Teaco yawned and blinked sleepily, his eyes nearly glowing in the dark.

"Swift Deer, you know how much my father detests the creatures of this country. If he were here now he'd be arranging for your hanging on the highest tree he could find," said Avador chidingly.

"Yes, I know but your father is not here and frankly he can be rather in-" Fall Leaf elbowed Swift Deer painfully in the ribs. Swift Deer cleared his throat noisily and furrowed his brow in concentration. Avador eyed him impassively.

"Lord Salvador is just not the kindest person in the world, captain," Swift Deer finally finished rather meekly.

"I'm well aware of his personality. Though for yours and that creature's well being, I beg you not to be caught with him in my father's presence." said Avador.

"Yes, captain," Swift Deer said crestfallen. Balin was rather intrigued by the chemistry between the company's members.

"So how does this little guy work?" asked Avador, looking to Teaco who stretched in Swift Deer's arms. The atmosphere instantly lightened.

"Glad you asked. Will you do the honors, young friend," said Swift Deer, who handed Teaco to Silver Stream.

Silver Stream placed Teaco on the dirt ground, where he unraveled revealing his long tail tipped with a tuft of fur. His back bristled as he stretched and yawned. Silver Stream let him sniff the blood on his fingers and gave him the command to find the trail. Teaco sniffed the cold air distractedly, than dropped to roll around in the dirt. He yawned and stretched again, shivering and paying little mind to his surroundings. Everyone watched him as he took his time to gather his bearings.

Swift Deer chewed at his thumbnail and shifted in his saddle anxiously, noting his comrades' uneasiness and dwindling patience as the minutes ticked by.

They watched Teaco sit up to scratch his ear with his hind paw. They pretty much lost hope when Teaco plopped on the ground and closed his droopy eyes.

"Okay, that doesn't mean what it looks like it means," Swift Deer assured with an uncertain chuckle.

"I believe it means exactly what it looks like," said Avador, somewhat disappointed.

"Yeah, yeah that's true," Swift Deer said, chewing at his thumbnail again. He let out an angry, dejected breath. "I'm sorry, captain, I thought he could do it," he said, his shoulders slumping.

"Its fine, Swift Deer; we'll just have to do our best by our own skills." said Avador. Hope rose within K'smet and Balin.

Teaco's eyes suddenly shot open and his nose and whiskers wiggled excitedly. He pushed himself off the ground and lifted his muzzle as he scented the air. His sudden activity drew everyone's attention and they watched in silence as Teaco sorted out the many scents. He circled three times, sniffing the ground. He licked the dirt with a long tongue, swished his saliva around with bulging cheeks and then spat it out. A few of the company members grimaced at such a disgusting act, or chuckled at the sight. Avador lifted his eyebrows and exchanged an inquisitive glance with Night Hawk who squared his shoulders unknowingly.

With bright glowing eyes and his nose to the ground like a hound, Teaco set off down the road, still sifting through the many different smells.

"He's found their trail!" said Swift Deer excitedly.

"Are you sure?" asked Avador, somewhat doubtfully.

"Positive," said Swift Deer with an eager nod.

With a sigh, Avador gave a reluctant gesture. They all followed after Teaco in pairs with Avador and Swift Deer in front. Bright

Sky and Fall Leaf led the prisoners in the center of the group. With Teaco having picked up Philip and Philomena's trail, hope had been suddenly dashed from Balin and K'smet. They had no plan or means of escape from Avador, and so they had not the slightest clue what to do. Yet even though there seemed to be no hope, Balin wasn't giving up. Balin was patient in the light of his restless companion. He knew that if they were to bide their time, a window of opportunity just might arise.

So the company followed after Teaco and vanished into the shadows of the trees.

23

Philomena could no longer sleep. She was far too restless. It was still dark and very early in the morning. Philip still slept soundly close by. Philomena turned to lie on her back so she could see the night sky. The millions of stars winked above beyond the reaches of the tree tops. She stared up at them for a time before deciding to quietly slip out from under her blanket. She stepped softly around Philip so as not to wake him.

Lark sat before the fire, his back turned to her and Philip. Philomena hesitated a moment, but eventually went over to him. The soft crunching of leaves under her boots alerted Lark and he quickly looked around at her. He relaxed when he saw it was her.

"Sorry, I thought you might have forgotten to wake me," said Philomena, taking a seat near him though making sure there was enough space between them.

"You only slept for two hours," said Lark.

"Yeah, well I can't sleep anymore," said Philomena. She drew her knees to her chin, indulging in the waves of warmth rippling from the fire Lark had kept going. Its heat was a luxury, and gradually ceased the shivers of the night's cold.

The two of them sat in silence for a time, which grew to be somewhat awkward and uncomfortable. Philomena chewed at her lip and glanced over at Lark. She felt on edge, and was beginning to speculate whether leaving her comfortable bedroll was such a good idea. Lark on the other hand was use to not talking, and sometimes preferred it that way.

"Do you miss your family?" asked Philomena, not able to bear the silence any longer.

Lark looked over at her, his expression nearing offensive. "I suppose," he said. He tossed a pinecone into the fire. Another agonizing moment of silence rolled by only broken when Philomena conjured up another question.

"So, why were you in Staleon the other night instead of in Niche?" asked Philomena.

It took a few seconds of consideration on Lark's part before he answered. "I was hunting,"

"That's not allowed though," Philomena said pointedly.

"No, it's not," he said without care.

More silence, and it took Philomena twice as long to think of another question. She noticed his buckskin coat for the first time. She took in the fringe on the shoulders, and the bear teeth that kept it snugly in place, and the neat stitching work.

"You truly are a native, aren't you?" she asked, still staring at his coat.

"Do you think I lied to you about it before?" Lark asked offensively, breaking some twigs in half for the fire.

"No," said Philomena. "I know your father is a native. What about your mother?" she asked, her curiosity building. These words drummed soundly, and froze Lark in his movements. He lifted his gaze slowly to the fire, his jaw set in a hard line.

"No, she's an Alamian," he said, bad memories seeming to flash in his eyes.

"Oh, I can see it now. You and your sister have paler skin, and your features are not as sharp," said Philomena, noting the blend of race.

"Yeah, I know. I've heard it all," said Lark, his voice stony and his expression growing harsh and cold.

Philomena frowned at his sudden change of mood. "What's your problem? I didn't mean it as a bad thing. Your father seems like a nice man, and I'm sure your mother is just as good of a person,"

Lark grimaced, and ran a hand through his choppy black hair.

"Why are you being so defensive?" Philomena went on, feeling frustrated. "If I were you, I would be rather pleased with such parents. Not everyone gets to be both Alamian *and* Native Alamian,"

"Such an ancestry is not to be bragged over. It is to be kept a secret, if that is at all possible," Lark said grudgingly.

Philomena huffed disapprovingly. "Why? It's not like people will bombard you with degrading comments all the time, or stone you in the streets,"

No reply came from Lark this time. He simply sat there, staring in to the fire like a hardened stone obviously reliving haunting memories. This unsettled Philomena, and despite her tough demeanor she couldn't help but feel sympathy for him.

Not wishing to damper the night anymore then what she had, Philomena cleared her throat and allowed silence to envelope them again. This time she welcomed it. She directed her attention to their surroundings. Their horses were dozing side by side. The singing minnows still sang like watery flutes. Casting her gaze upward to the stars, Philomena caught sight of the gold orbs dancing overhead. One in particular hovered only a few feet away from them. Philomena flinched and bumped Lark's shoulder.

"What?" Lark questioned, frowning over at her still irritated.

"What . . . what are those?" she stammered, staring at the gold sparkling orbs. Lark gazed skyward at the orbs as well.

"They're fairies," said Lark, perplexed.

"Fairies? You mean little winged people?" questioned Philomena looking to him.

"That's not exactly appropriate, but I suppose that's one way to put it," said Lark. "You've really never seen a fairy before?" he asked with a creased brow.

"House arrest doesn't exactly give you much time to go sightseeing," said Philomena, gazing in wonderment at the fairies.

"House arrest?" asked Lark, rather baffled.

"Yeah, my brother and I have spent the past eight years in house arrest in Tosh. Salvador wanted us kept out of the way, and with us in enemy hands our father was more compliant to obey him. Really, it was our uncle who arranged it. If he hadn't, Salvador would have killed Philip that very night of the siege. Uncle gave up everything to be put in to house arrest with us so we might have someone to teach us what we needed to know," Philomena explained.

"You mean your uncle Bazin," said Lark.

"It's Balin actually," Philomena corrected.

"Ahh, right, Balin Stilwell, lord of Woodrid," said Lark sarcastically. Philomena glanced over at him, noting the disbelief in his tone and manner. She said nothing of it though, for she couldn't really blame him for not believing their story.

"What happened to your uncle anyway?" asked Lark, remembering that Balin was no longer with them. Philomena's gaze dropped to the ground.

"When we were trying to escape Niche, Philip got hurt and Avador was closing in on us at the square. Uncle and K'smet stayed behind to give us time to get away," said Philomena.

"So you don't know if they're okay or not?" Lark asked.

"No," said Philomena with a shake of her head. Her voice was quiet and her gaze faraway as she reflected back to that night in Niche's square. It had happened only two nights ago, but it felt like eternity had passed.

Philomena shook herself out of her saddened thoughts and straightened. "It will work out somehow. All things happen for a reason," she said. Lark gave her a hard sideways glance of uncertainty.

"You have a lot of faith for someone who claims such a tragic past and for someone who has a tendency to doubt," he mused mildly.

Twisting her mouth uncomfortably, Philomena glared at the ground between her boots. "Sometimes the reality of our situation gets to me," she admitted reluctantly. "What about you? Don't you have faith?" she asked.

Looking away, Lark let out an uncomfortable sigh. "There never seemed to be time to acquire faith. There was always . . . something happening," His voice was pained. Philomena could sense all of the hard times playing by in Lark's mind.

"Do you believe in the Creator?" she asked in a low voice. Lark fixed her with a hard stare and she thought he was going to snap back a smart remark.

"Yes, I do," he said, gazing in to the fire. His expression was still glazed with the reminiscence of the past.

"Then your faith will come; you probably already have it and you don't even know it. You've never given up after all," Philomena said reassuringly. Lark felt a hint of warmth in his chest, but he turned a frown on Philomena.

"Your moments of inspirational speech baffle me," he said frankly. Philomena sat back and squared her shoulders, not offended.

"I suppose I just don't trust anyone. You least of all," she said, tilting a teasing grin at him that reminded him so much of her brother.

"Of course because I have done nothing at all to earn your trust," Lark said sarcastically. He threw some more wood on the fire. "As you said before, it doesn't matter if we trust each other anyway,"

"True," Philomena agreed.

"Cause we hardly know one another and we don't want to be friends," Lark added.

"Right," said Philomena, pursing her lips. "We'll be rid of one another before we know it," she added with a grin.

Lark looked to her. She put on a good front, but Lark could see the near dejection underneath her clever mask. Her eyes reflected the firelight, and her dark braid of hair wrapped in leather glowed over her shoulder.

Sighing, Philomena lifted her gaze back to the treetops.

"They really are beautiful," she said after a long moment, smiling up at the many dancing fairies. "Can they talk at all?" she asked.

Lark pondered this for a moment. In truth, this was the closest he'd ever been to a fairy. "They communicate in their own way," Lark finally said.

"You've heard them before then?" asked Philomena.

"Once," said Lark, remembering earlier that night. Philomena looked to him inquisitively, sensing something more behind his single word reply, but again she decided not to say anything.

They sat there for a while watching the fairies and listening to the minnows. After a time though, Philomena caught sight of Lark stifling a yawn and remembered what time it was.

"It's your turn to get some sleep. I'll keep watch till first light," said Philomena.

"It's three hours till dawn," said Lark.

"I can handle it," Philomena assured. "You can use my bedroll," she added. Lark nodded his gratitude, too tired to argue. He stood to leave, eager to pass out even if it was just for a few hours.

Philomena stood as well and moved quietly over to their horses. She went to her grey stallion, Coursio, and patted him gently on his dappled back. The stallion lifted his head and turned his bright eyes to her. Philomena smiled and stroked his soft nose. "Sleep well, friend. We have a hard ride tomorrow," she said to him softly. Coursio nickered and went back to dozing when she left his side. Philomena went about gathering some more kindling and wood for the fire. She glanced up and looked to Philip and Lark. Neither of them were so much as stirring underneath their blankets. Philomena smiled and went back to gathering fuel for the fire.

Yes, Philomena thought as she picked up prickly pinecones; it would be a long hard ride tomorrow. They would have to make up for the time they had lost. Philomena knew Avador and his men would be tracking them by now. Philip would have to be strong.

24

Light of the fresh dawn filtered through the trees hours later.
Birds sang happily. The frost that had been created during the
night lingered, for the sun's light was not yet warm. Fire still
crackled steadily in the ring of stone, eating away at the wood
Philomena had fed it. Their horses wandered in the small
opening, eating any vegetation they fancied.

Over at the bubbling creek, Philomena sat staring in to the
rippling water with her chin resting in her palm and her elbow
planted on her knee. Dejected uncertainty clung to her, though
whenever one of the singing minnows stirred the water with its
brilliant light and song her expression lifted with fascination.
She must have been sitting there for half an hour, maybe an hour,
she didn't know. Everything seemed to be happening so fast. It
was only three weeks ago that she, Philip, and Balin had escaped
their imprisonment in Tosh. Already their plans had been led
astray. Balin was in Avador's custody, and Philip had been hurt.
It was all so suffocating, Philomena felt like running back to
Tosh and shutting herself back in the comfortable quarters that
had been their prison. At least they had had good food and a
warm place to sleep. Feeling such a pathetic longing, Philomena
mentally kicked herself. She had always prided herself in being
tough and strong. Now she doubted how strong she truly was.

"Hey," said a warm voice.

Philomena jumped and looked around to see Philip standing
behind her. Philip laughed and lifted his hands in an innocent
gesture. Philomena released a breath of relief and shot an
annoyed glare at him.

"I've appeared to have broken a chain of serious thought," said

Philip, easing down next to her and grimacing slightly.

"How are you feeling?" Philomena asked worriedly.

"Better," said Philip with a nod. "Still sore, but I reckon it will be like that for a while," he said, putting a hand to his cauterized arm.

"I guess we have Lark to thank," said Philomena, fiddling with some moss growing on the rocks along the stream. A minnow murmured a watery tune, stirring the stream with green light.

"Yep, it's a good thing he knew what to do," Philip agreed, casting a grin over at Lark who was still sleeping. "Though, I hope I never have to experience being cauterized again. It's not very fun,"

Philomena smiled in reply, but it was a distracted effort. She sighed and stared in to the stream once more. Philip's grin faded. He corked his mouth and pinched his brow as he considered Philomena.

"Alright, out with it. What's wrong?" said Philip.

Philomena frowned and shook her head. "Nothing's wrong," she said.

"Oh, that's incredibly convincing. Now all you have to do is convince yourself of that story," Philip retorted sarcastically, tilting a prying stare on her. Philomena groaned and slumped her shoulders. She knew better then to try to hide things from Philip.

"It's just so much has happened since we escaped Tosh," she said, staring at the moss covered rocks.

"I can't say I miss Tosh," Philip said, shaking his head and wrinkling his nose. "Another year in those lovely quarters of ours and I would have died of boredom,"

Smirking, Philomena nodded in agreement. "I don't miss being under house arrest, I just . . ." she trailed off uncertainly.

"You didn't think it would be this way," Philip finished gently. Philomena looked to him with gratefulness and nodded.

"It usually never works out the way we think it will," Philip added. His words were both reassuring and unsettling.

Philomena chewed at her lip and switched her gaze back to the stream. Another minnow sang and this time the water rippled with blue.

"Did you think the world would be like this?" Philomena asked quietly, dipping a finger in to the stream and feeling its smooth, cold sensation.

"This world is far more beautiful than what I thought it would be," said Philip, gazing around at the forest surrounding them, hearing the birds and seeing the sunshine dance with the trees.

"The world that Salvador has made though is far uglier than what we imagined, I'm sure," he added glumly.

The corner of Philomena's mouth twitched with regret, but she knew Philip was probably right and it was a depressing thought. She let out a sigh, and withdrew her hand from the stream.

Something rustled behind them and they twisted around to see Lark kneeling by the fire. The flames disbursed with a cloud of steam under a pale of water Lark threw on it. He met their gaze, his expression serious and impassive as ever.

"It's time to go," he said, gathering the stones that had made a ring around their fire.

"Good morning to you too," Philip grinned. Lark ignored his cheery greeting.

"We have a lot of ground to cover, and a lot of time to make up for," said Lark, carrying the stones over to the stream and letting them drop. Philip and Philomena watched the stones fall in the water with a splash and a clonk. They lifted questioning gazes to Lark.

"If anyone is trailing you, it's best that we disguise our presence as much as possible," Lark explained. He turned around and went to collect the rest of the stones.

Getting to their feet, Philip and Philomena joined in. They packed their clocks and bedrolls. They filled their water skins from the stream. They scattered the ashes of their fire till it mixed with the soil. Lark and Philip brushed away their tracks while Philomena saddled the horses.

"You know, there's no way you can cover all of our tracks," Philomena told them thickly, buckling Spear's girth.

"The more we can cover, the more confusing it will be for any tracker to find our exact trail," Lark retorted smartly, swinging his leafy branch back and forth as he moved backwards. Philip was doing the same. They brushed away the tracks until they reached Philomena and their horses at the edge of the tree line. Making sure they hadn't forgotten anything, they then climbed onto their horses. Lark did this rather gingerly, quite stiff from their hard ride yesterday with having no experience of being in the saddle.

"You okay?" Philip smirked over at Lark, having noticed his grimacing. "You're sore aren't you?"

Lark scowled at him. "I think you should know what being sore feels like right about now," he said, gesturing to Philip's bandaged arm.

"Nah, it's not that bad," Philip shrugged his lower lip protruding. "Nothing I can't handle,"

"Don't act like a hero, Philip," Philomena scolded, her brow lowered. "You have to heal completely before pushing yourself. If we have to stop for a rest, we're going to stop,"

"I'm fine, I won't need a break," Philip insisted, squaring his shoulders. Philomena shot a prying stare at him.

"Easy with the intense staring, I'm fine," Philip said more forcefully. This didn't convince Philomena.

"If you don't take it easy I'm going to pound you in to the ground before you can do it to yourself," she warned, her eyes flashing dangerously. Philip sighed, and nodded in acknowledgement. He knew it was her way of showing her concern. He looked back to Lark who appeared bored.

"You don't have to be embarrassed, you know. Everyone gets a little stiff now and then," Philip told him with a reassuring grin. Lark fixed him with a defensive glare.

"Are we going to get moving or are we going to talk all day?" he demanded crossly. He didn't wait for Philip to reply. Nudging Spear forward, he headed in to the woods.

Philip met Philomena's gaze. "This is going to be fun," he said sarcastically.

They trotted their horses after Lark, resuming their journey through the thick of Staleon's brush.

Every step they made, they could feel it bringing them that much closer to Ezleon and in turn the northern realm of Lacemore.

Lark led them well. He never needed to stop to be sure that the landmarks he knew were pointing them in the right direction. Lark was familiar with Staleon, for he had memorized its ways when he was a boy. He knew the best route without thinking and Philip and Philomena raised no questions against his guidance.

Philip was admiring the splendid elements of the woods that were new and exciting for both him and Philomena. Looking up at the trees, something particularly interesting caught Philip's eye. Something that appeared to be moss clinging to the tree branches only it sparkled with every ray of sunshine.

"Hey, Lark. What's that green sparkly stuff in the trees?" asked Philip when his curiosity met its peak.

"Its glitter moss," said Lark, not even looking to be sure.

"Is it edible?" asked Philip, the thought of food making his mouth water. He gazed longingly at the abundant moss. They hadn't had any breakfast, nor would they have lunch. They would have to wait till this evening to eat.

"No," said Lark, actually laughing at such a ridiculous idea.

"Oh," said Philip, disappointed.

Lark looked over his shoulder at him, smirking laughingly. "You really have been in house arrest," he mused.

"Yeah, for eight years," said Philip.

"Now do you believe me?" asked Philomena, coming alongside Philip.

"I never said I didn't believe you," said Lark.

"You don't believe anything else we've told you," said Philomena flatly.

"If someone doesn't know what glitter moss is then I can believe that they've been jammed in a dreary, dark cell for most of their lives," said Lark, leaning forward to help his horse up a steep incline. Philip followed with Philomena close behind.

Atop the incline was a narrow ridge which offered a skinny path that was bordered by a seemingly endless, impenetrable thorny vine forest. The ridge dropped off on the other side of the path where the incline became steeper and steeper as they went. The path only allowed them to travel single file and took them along the ridgeline and thorny vine forest, winding further into Staleon.

"So, what is glitter moss good for if you can't eat it?" Philip finally asked.

Lark grinned to himself and shook his head. "Toymakers use it in their craft," he said.

"Toymakers?" Philip frowned thoughtfully.

"Do they make dolls with glittery dresses or something?" Philomena asked, snorting with laughter at such a thought.

Thinking for a moment, Lark shook his head. "I've never seen a doll with a glitter dress. They sell a lot of glitter balls and horse figurines. I'm sure they'd love your idea though,"

"I'm surprised Salvador's depression hasn't plunged crafters like them in to extinction," Philip said derisively.

The mention of Salvador's name blanketed the atmosphere with a scathing sense. Even Lark looked angry, but Philip figured it wasn't for the same reason he and Philomena felt. Everything Lark had thought was true, he suddenly had been told was a lie. They went on in silence for a time. The impenetrable thorny vine forest suddenly dwindled, and the ridgeline descended into the ground and vanished. Their path widened and went down into the company of neatly spaced trees. An immense amount of ivy carpeted the ground and climbed up several of the trees covering the bottoms of their trunks and trailing into their branches. The trees grew wide and tall here and gave them ample room to ride abreast if they wished. Sun light filtered in through the canopy and danced about the ivy and trees. A chirping flock of sparrows flew over head, rejoicing in their wondrous home.

Lark halted Spear just at the top of the path before it descended, and waited for Philip and Philomena to come alongside him as he assessed the forest that was now spread out before them.

"Whoa, that's a lot of ivy," said Philomena, taking in the sight of the rich green ivy vines with widening eyes.

"And some big trees," added Philip, staring skyward.

"The Ivy Forest of Staleon; it's rather quiet in the winter," said Lark, with a light smile. Their reactions pleased him.

"So a forest within a forest," Philip considered out loud.

They stood in awe for a few moments, soaking in the incredible view from their vantage point on the incline.

"How faraway is Ezleon?" asked Philip, looking expectantly to Lark.

"A three days ride," said Lark. "When we clear the Ivy Forest, we'll only have a day left,"

"Isn't there a quicker way?" asked Philomena.

"There is, an untraveled route," said Lark.

"Lead us there and it will be traveled," Philomena said determinedly.

"No," said Lark flatly. An amused smirk twitched at the corner of Philip's mouth as he listened, yet he kept his laughing eyes appraising the Ivy Forest.

Philomena huffed and gawked at Lark. "No? Don't you understand that we have to get out of here as fast as possible?"

"I do, but not at the cost of traveling the untraveled path through Poacher's Land. There's a reason why no one goes that way," said Lark, switching his hard hazel eyes onto Philomena which silenced her. She looked away from him to hide her aggravated scowl.

"Poacher's Land?" said Philip. "That doesn't sound very

pleasant," he mused.

"It's not supposed to be pleasant," said Lark. Philip chewed at his lip pensively. Anxiousness nagged at Lark as he watched Philip and Philomena exchanged questioning glances.

"Look, I know you have the right to question whether I'm helping you or not, but I give you my word that I am. I assure you, this is the safest and second quickest way to Ezleon," said Lark, gesturing towards the trail before them.

Philip looked to Lark and breathed inward. "I believe you, Lark," he said.

Philomena's mouth twitched with reluctance, but she could not go against her brother's wishes. "If we have too, we'll travel by night as well," she said submissively.

Lark nodded, confused that he felt better by their assurance of confidence in his guidance.

"We need to pick up the pace," said Philip, gathering his reins. "I don't want to see Avador and his band of native soldiers anytime soon,"

"Philip, you're not healed yet. There's no point in rushing things if it's only going to make you weaker," Philomena objected worriedly.

"Did you just imply that I'm weak?" asked Philip, lifting his eyebrows at her.

Philomena shook her head. "No! You know I don't think that, but if traveling hard is too much than we need to pace ourselves for your sake,"

"What if Avador catches up to us?" Philip retorted.

"What if he does? If you're rested at least you'll be able to fight," Philomena pointed out.

"You even said yourself just now that we have to get out of here as fast as possible. What happened to that notion?" Philip questioned with a demanding gesture.

Huffing irritably, Philomena rounded on Philip. "Not at the cost of your life. We're going to go as slow as we have to, and we're going to stop as often as you need,"

Philip looked away, flexing his jaw and grumbling impatiently. Philomena switched her gaze to Lark with a need-for-help expression.

"She's right," said Lark, looking to Philip. "You can't push yourself,"

Chewing at his lip irritably, Philip decided quickly. "Fine, but we're not going to go slow," He looked to Philomena and she nodded satisfactorily.

"Lead the way, Lark," said Philip, gesturing for Lark to go on ahead.

Spear started forward at Lark's command, and they trotted down the path with Philip and Philomena following.

They rode down the slight incline, leaving the foreboding walls of thorny vines behind them. They encouraged their horses to go faster, breaking into a canter, upon which they entered the richly colored, leafy domain of the Ivy Forest.

25

Avador's company had traveled through the entire night following Teaco. The faithful little creature sniffed out the prince and princess' trail, leading them over rises and through thick brush. Teaco never seemed to tire, and trotted along persistently with his nose never leaving the ground. Now the sun's first light greeted them and warmed the damp shadows of Staleon.

"We'll rest here for a short time," said Avador, stopping his black stallion as they entered a small, bright opening amidst a grove of closely growing trees with thick tangled roots. The company filed in behind him.

"Why must we stop?" questioned Running Buck.

"He's right. I can keep going strong all day and into the night even," boasted Hawk Eye with an eager grin.

"You may be able to keep going, but remember it is your tired horse who carries you," said Avador, climbing down from his saddle and patting his horse on the neck. Running Buck and Hawk Eye both reddened bashfully and slid down from their horses, their youthful eagerness subdued.

"Don't bother taking off the tack. Just loosen their girths so they can rest," Avador said, loosening his horse's girth as he spoke.

"What about the prisoners?" asked Fall Leaf, gazing at Balin and K'smet who remained tied to the saddles of the company's pack horses. They both looked weary and irritable and their sore, stiff bodies cried out for sleep.

"Let them come down for a time, but keep them tied," said Avador, looking pointedly at his captives. Fall Leaf nodded and began to undo the ropes that bound Balin and K'smet to the pack horses.

"Why don't you assist Fall Leaf, Night Hawk," said Avador seeing that his second in command had already finished tending to his horse. "Take the prisoners some water as well," he said, handing Night Hawk a plump water skin.

"Give them water? Why should we give them water? They are our prisoners, not our friends," Bright Sky said grudgingly, shooting a nasty glare at K'smet and Balin.

"If I am to get anything of use out of either of them, they need to be at least half alive, and that requires them to have something to drink," Avador said firmly, meeting Bright Sky's challenging attitude with a stony, unwavering stare.

The atmosphere sparked with a dangerous air as Avador and Bright Sky glared at one another for a time. Night Hawk and Fall Leaf exchanged nervous glances, both of them frozen in their tasks.

"Take them water, and be sure to tend to the pack horses," said Avador, breaking his strong stare with Bright Sky and gesturing for Night Hawk to obey.

"Yes, Captain," said Night Hawk, happily obliging in the order. Bright Sky sniffed disdainfully, his vengeful stare lingering on K'smet. "Why don't you show some respect for the warrior who that man killed,"

Avador narrowed his eyes upsettingly. "Red Moon has my respect. He has the respect of this whole company,"

Bright Sky shot a nasty glare at him and turned away, grumbling under his breath.

"Bright Sky, you have to keep your personal emotions under control. I understand you're hurting over your cousin's death. We all admired him and miss him, but we have a mission to complete," Avador said, coming behind Bright Sky and hoping to smooth things over.

"That's easy for you to say," Bright Sky snapped, turning to face Avador. "We have a mission to complete, we have a job that's needs to be done. You can bury yourself in an impassive stone cold shell that has no feeling and go home to a castle where you're going to be a prince with all the security in the world; while we don't get to go home, and we suffer the loss of our loved ones alone,"

His voice of bitter anger and regret held Avador speechless, his painful words stinging him. The rest of the company watched and listened, completely stunned. K'smet and Balin listened too. Bright Sky exhaled in disgust, his dark eyes sparking. "But what do you care. You don't care about anyone," he said, turning away again to loosen his horse's girth.

Resentfulness threatened to burst within Avador's chest. With effort, he spoke in a level tone, "If you cannot control yourself, I'll be forced to banish you from the company."

No reply came from Bright Sky. Glancing around, Avador realized the others were still watching. "Get some rest all of you," he told them. His throat had gone dry.

Slowly, the company unfroze and went about tending to their horses.

Avador looked back to Bright Sky and watched his defiant warrior for a time, listening to him grumbling to himself. The temptation to confront Bright Sky was strong. Avador felt for him, but Bright Sky's temper made it hard to show him sympathy. Shaking off the aggravating matter, Avador turned his attention back to the rest of the company.

"Thirty minutes, men. No more than that," said Avador. He went to his horse and dug in his saddle bags for their meager breakfast. The young captain kept an unemotional expression, knowing that his men were glancing at him worriedly. Inside though, conflicted feelings raged a battle in Avador's mind. Avador swallowed hard, fighting the tightness that was building in his chest. He couldn't show weakness. He focused his energy on tending to his horse and bringing out the company's meal. Once their horses were watered and settled, the company looked to seek a bit of luxurious comfort for themselves starting with the food their captain brought out for them. Hunks of bread and dried pork were passed around and water skins were retrieved from saddle pommels. They took their breakfast and lounged on the large curving roots of the trees around them, or sat cross legged on the leaf covered ground that was damp with the morning's chill. They sat in silent content as they ate and drank their fill. Their energy slowly returned to them, and any stiffness that hindered them gradually melted away. Their horses stood quietly, their heads hanging low and their eyelids drooping. Some of their riders were doing the same, catching some sleep before they had to move again.

K'smet and Balin sat stiffly on a moss covered log between Bright Sky and Fall Leaf. The generous offer of water Avador insisted that they have had done them wonders and had partly rejuvenated them. K'smet felt well enough to ponder on his contempt for their retainers and glowered nastily over at Avador who sat beside Night Hawk. He savored the thought of pounding Avador into the ground. Bright Sky, still moody, noticed him glaring at Avador and was haughtily perturbed by this.

Balin on the other hand showed no interest in openly displaying his hatred for the company. Instead he took the opportunity to study them, taking mental notes of how many weapons they carried, who favored what weapons, and what part each of them individually played in the group. It was all very useful information, Balin thought, and might help in his future plans.

The young native, Hawk Eye, finished eating his breakfast first. Finding that he had nothing to do but sit there and not tired enough to doze like some of his companions, he looked to his friend, Silver Stream, who sat next to him. Silver Stream hadn't touched his food and appeared very pensive. His deep thoughts had obviously flown him off somewhere faraway for he stared down at his food as if it weren't even there. Apparently it was a happy place, Hawk Eye considered, for his friend wore a blissful smile.

"What are you grinning about?" asked Hawk Eye when he could no longer resist. He peered curiously at Silver Stream eager for an explanation.

Silver Stream started out of his thoughts and looked around at Hawk Eye. "Oh . . . I was just thinking," said Silver Stream, still smiling.

"About what?" Hawk Eye probed. To his surprise, Silver Stream ducked his head with a bashful smile and blushed brightly.

"White Doe," said Silver Stream.

A teasing grin spread across Hawk Eye's countenance. "You mean the girl you've been courting?"

"I plan to marry her when I return to our islands," said Silver Stream still blushing, his happy thoughts sweeping him away again.

Running Buck, who sat on the other side of Hawk Eye, spluttered with laughter when he heard Silver Stream's announcement. Both Silver Stream and Hawk Eye looked to him incredulously, as did a few other members of the company.

"What?" Silver Stream prompted.

"You're not serious I hope," said Running Buck grinning as if it were all a joke.

"Of course I'm serious," said Silver Stream defensively.

"Silver Stream, you're a warrior," began Running Buck in a lecturing manner. "You have years of service left to Lord Salvador. Have you not forgotten the contract that binds you to your servitude?"

"No, I haven't," said Silver Stream sourly.

"I don't see how any of us could forget. Twenty years as Lord Salvador's warrior slaves, and if we try to run from that servitude we face the penalty of death by his choosing. Three quarters of us will be killed, either in battle or by some other cause. You know this. Why do you think Hawk Eye and I never courted,"

Guilt filtered across Avador's features as he overheard the

adolescents' conversation, and a familiar weight pressed painfully hard between his shoulders. He knew all too well about the contract his father had made to bind the natives. If Red Moon had survived, he would have been able to return home in three years.

Silver Stream squared his shoulders and shook his head unknowingly and frankly without care at Running Buck's words. "Why raise hopes for a life of family when we most likely will be dead in the next year? Accept the fact that you are one of Lord Salvador's men and will probably never be a husband or father," continued Running Buck.

"I know all of this, but there is still a chance I'll return home," said Silver Stream with a rather naïve innocence reflecting in his now faint smile.

"Did you not hear me?" Running Buck questioned critically. "If you have a chance then it is a slight chance which is hardly a chance at all if you ask me. You didn't speak to White Doe of your intentions did you?" asked Running Buck suddenly frightened.

"Why ever should I have not? I intend for her to be my bride, and she promised she'd wait for me," said Silver Stream.

"Because!" Running Buck cried flabbergasted. Hawk Eye flinched from his sudden outburst.

"You've lifted her hopes of being with you when you may not return to her thus ruining her chances to be with another, and if you don't return she'll absolutely refuse to marry someone else because she feels obligated to be faithful to you and so she will be left to live out the rest of her days in total misery without a family of her own," Running Buck preached.

At this powerful speech, Silver Stream's happy hopes for the future were dampened thoroughly. He slumped his shoulders and stared depressingly at his untouched food.

"Oh leave the boy alone, Running Buck," said Fall Leaf. The entire company had overheard the teenagers' conversation. "He's always been a dreamer. It's probably a better way of thinking than us 'warriors'," he said. A few of the members chuckled. Silver Stream's spirits were not lifted despite his superior attempting to lighten the atmosphere for him.

"Where is Teaco?" Swift Deer suddenly asked, casting a worried and confused frown about the small opening. Everyone went quiet and glanced around them for the little creature, but Teaco was nowhere in sight.

"He's certainly not around here," said Fall Leaf stating the obvious.

"Perhaps he's gone off to chase a hog," suggested Hawk Eye.

"More likely a rabbit." grinned Running Buck. Everyone laughed heartily except for Swift Deer and Silver Stream, and of course Avador.

"He's probably continued to follow the prince's trail," Swift Deer corrected, boring a warning glare into his fellow comrades.

"Go look for him, Swift Deer. We'll wait here," said Avador with an encouraging gesture. Swift Deer nodded thankfully.

"I'll go with you," said Silver Stream standing. He was rather tired of his boyhood companions. Avador nodded in agreement. Swift Deer didn't waste any time and started off immediately over the tangled roots to leave their small opening. Silver Stream returned his uneaten breakfast to his captain and hurried to catch up with his anxious comrade.

They picked their way over the tree roots and out of sight of the company. They walked for several minutes in the general northward direction which was the direction the prince's trail had taken them thus far. The further they went though, the more the certainty that they were going the right way dwindled in their minds. Luckily, for their sake, Silver Stream found a tuft of Teaco's hair caught on a low branch thus assuring them that they were on the right path.

A few minutes later, the two warriors came to a rise overlooking another small clearing neighbored by a bubbling creek, very well sheltered by closely growing trees and brush. Looking down into the sheltered opening that was alit by morning sunlight, they found themselves gazing upon a peculiar and rather disturbing sight. There was Teaco beside the creek racing rapidly around in circles chasing his tail.

"What on earth is the matter with him?" asked Silver Stream bewildered. Swift Deer shook his head wordlessly, just as baffled and bemused as Silver Sream. He hastened down to his crazed pet.

"Teaco! Come to your senses!" cried Swift Deer. The little creature acknowledged him with a gurgling, growling sound but only raced in circles faster than before.

Silver Stream came down from the rise and watched as Swift Deer desperately tried to stop Teaco from his crazed dance. He hollered his name over and over again, and threw a pinecone for him to chase, but Teaco continued to spin dizzily. Swift Deer stood over Teaco and attempted to pick him up but the feisty little beast snapped at his hands with needle sharp teeth. Swift Deer jerked away from him, and Teaco went back to racing around in circles.

Silver Stream sighed and shifted his gaze to the side when the sight of familiar markings in the ground drew his attention. The markings were faint, but he knew they were there and he knew they were the distinct imprints of a camp.

"Swift Deer! Look!" cried Silver Stream, rushing over to the markings and kneeling before them.

"What?" questioned Swift Deer irritably. He had finally managed to get a hold of Teaco, who now wriggled in his arms. Teaco was emitting a loud gurgling, whining sound, begging to be released.

"These markings, there was a campsite here," said Silver Stream studying the ground. "And it's not very old. Last night most likely," he said, holding a hand over the faint markings as if they were telling him their story.

"Last night?" asked Swift Deer, kneeling beside his young friend.

Silver Stream nodded, and then looked to Teaco in Swift Deer's arms. "That's why he was going crazy. It's the prince's camp," he said, excitement building in his voice.

"How far ahead of us do you think they are?" asked Swift Deer, the excitement growing in him as well.

"Half a day, I'd say. But they were going relatively slow before. By the looks of it, they camped here all last night. They have probably picked up their pace, and it also appears that Captain Avador's assumption was right," said Silver Stream, studying the ground with narrowing eyes.

"What is it?" Swift Deer prompted impatiently.

"It appears that Raven Wing's son *is* traveling with the prince," said Silver Stream.

"He's no threat to us," said Swift Deer, the disgust evident in his voice at the mention of Raven Wing.

Silver Stream frowned disturbingly over at him. "He is the son of chiefs, Swift Deer. Are we going to be lowered to threatening our own?"

"Not now, Silver Stream," snapped Swift Deer, standing with Teaco still in his arms. "We have to get this news back to Avador,"

Though Silver Stream wished to clear the clouded disagreement between them concerning Raven Wing and his son, he knew they were pressed for time and so pushed himself off the ground with an irritable huff. The two native warriors raced up the incline together to the point of the rise and traced their trail back the way they had come with Teaco squalling in protest.

26

By the time evening had come and night was beginning to
breathe its cold breath across the land, Philip, Philomena, and
Lark were deep amidst the Ivy Forest of Staleon. They had
galloped and jogged most of the way, but now they could feel
their horses beginning to tire beneath them.

"I think we've made good progress," said Philomena, pleased, as
they slowed their horses to a walk.

Lark, who rode beside her, said nothing but looked to Philip who
was on his opposite side. Philip's countenance was drained of
color. His breath came in heavy gasps, and he half slumped with
exhaustion over his saddle pommel. Guilt and worry instantly
stabbed at Philomena when she caught sight of her brother.

"Philip, you should have said something if you started to feel
bad," said Philomena, her voice both worried and harshly
chiding. Philip straightened abruptly when he realized that they
had noticed him and tried to slow his breathing to normal.

"I'm fine," he insisted, his voice husky.

"We agreed that we'd stop as much as you needed," Philomena
retorted, her brow furrowed upsettingly. Grimacing, Philip
shifted stiffly in his saddle.

"You need to rest," Lark put in.

"Is that concern I hear, Lark," said Philip, grinning weakly over
at him.

"Seriously, you need to rest for at least an hour," said Lark,
meeting Philip's grin without humor.

"No," said Philip. "We don't have time for that. I've slowed us
down enough," he added.

"That arm of yours still needs to heal. Cauterizing isn't a miracle cure," said Lark.

"It doesn't feel too bad," Philip lied. In truth, his wounded arm was feeling worse and worse as the evening progressed.

"I think you need to rest, Philip," Philomena said sternly.

"And you need to eat," Lark added. Philip moaned and rubbed his face tiredly.

It took Lark and Philomena a few more tries before they persuaded Philip and convinced him that he wasn't invincible and that he needed to rest.

"Just for an hour," said Philip, feeling weak and drained.

"No more than that," Lark assured as he and Philomena helped Philip down from his horse.

They guided him over to an area that was free of the extensive ivy and instead covered in soft moss and lichens.

Nimbius, Philip's black stallion, followed closely nickering worriedly for his friend. Philip gratefully sank to the ground and immediately fell unconscious atop the soft carpet of moss.

Philomena and Lark knelt on either side of him. They watched his sides rise and fall with his breathing, his breath becoming deeper and steadier as he fell further into sleep.

Philomena clenched her jaw and curled her fist, feeling responsibility suffocating her. "I should have been watching him more closely," she said in a low voice.

Lark lifted his gaze to her. Her brow was knitted with guilt.

"He's always been hardheaded," she said, a hint of a fond smile touching her features. She felt so helpless sitting there staring at Philip and unable to do anything to ease his pain.

Lark could see the vulnerability straining against her features, and felt conflicted for feeling the slightest bit of brotherly worry towards Philip.

"He's going to be fine," Lark said suddenly, in a soft reassuring voice. Philomena met his quiet, confident gaze. "It's not your fault. This is only part of his healing. He's going to feel like this. We just have to make sure that he gets enough rest and food,"

"Even if we have to battle his stubbornness?" Philomena asked. Lark nodded with pursed lips. "Even if we have to yank him from his saddle, pin him down and tie him up, we'll make sure he gets enough rest,"

A grin lit Philomena's features at the humorous notion and she nodded thankfully. "In that case, you can do the pinning, I'll do the tying," she said, and swore she caught a ghost of a smile on Lark's face, but only for an instant and then it was gone. She looked back down at her brother. He was always so strong. It was strange for her to see him weak and tired.

"I'll go get a fresh bandage for his arm," said Lark, getting to his feet and walking back over to their horses. He patted Nimbius as he went by to Spear and Coursio. The black stallion was standing very still, his warm eyes locked on Philip. Seeing this love that the horse had for Philip, Lark felt his trust for the supposed prince grow a tad. Animals never lie Lark knew, and was reminded why he loved them so much.

Reaching the grey stallion, Coursio, Lark went along his side. He spent a minute digging in the saddlebags searching for what he needed. He returned to Philomena with the bandage and also a blanket which they covered Philip with. They then set to work re-bandaging Philip's arm together. The arm was still somewhat swollen, and the cauterized wound itself buried with a burn mark shaped like a knife's blade was ugly and sensitive. On the bright side, it was healing well and the terrible scar would certainly diminish over time.

Lark brought out a tiny jar sealed with a cork. The jar contained a light green poultice which Lark smeared over the burnt skin till a considerable layer covered area. The poultice smelled strongly of mint, making Philomena crinkle her nose.

"This should help with the pain and speed the healing," Lark explained.

"Exactly how many magical remedies do you carry around?" asked Philomena.

"They're not magical remedies, they're medicinal herbs, and this is my father's coat not mine," said Lark, wiping his fingers clean against his trousers.

Once Lark had finished with the poultice Philomena wrapped Philip's arm with the fresh bandage. Lark gathered the old bandage and moved towards the horses to pack it away when something on the ground caught his eye. With a frown, he knelt on the ground to study the markings in the moss and ivy covered earth.

"It appears there are mud hogs in the area," said Lark, casting his gaze around as if hoping to find an especially plump mud hog materialize before them.

"So," said Philomena without care as she tied Philip's bandage in place.

"So your brother needs to eat. A nice slab of pork will do him some good and us as well," said Lark. He moved to retrieve his bow and quiver when something else demanded his attention. He paused and pushed aside a couple of large ivy leaves to reveal markings that leapt out at him with terrifying significance. Horse tracks were stamped into the ground; horse tracks belonging to horses with shoes. Were their horses shod? Lark couldn't remember.

Moving hurriedly to Spear, Lark lifted one of the horse's front legs and peered at the bottom of the stallion's hoof. The hoof was bare. Galvanized to be thorough, Lark checked Nimbius and Coursio for shoes. All three horses were barefooted.

An icy claw clutched at Lark, and he fixed his gaze on the tracks of the shod horses like they were poison. The tracks were fresh, no more than an hour old. Lark casted his gaze around now, fearful that he'd see horseman clad in armor bearing wicked crossbows and swords. Philomena said something which Lark failed to hear.

"Hey Lark? Didn't you hear me?" asked Philomena sounding annoyed as she tried to gain Lark's attention.

"Get your brother up," said Lark, still searching their surroundings. He could've sworn he saw a shadow move and disappear behind some trees.

Philomena frowned. "What?"

"We have to get out of here," said Lark. He stuffed the old bandage his still held in the nearest saddlebag and rushed over to Philip and Philomena.

"Why?" Philomena demanded bewildered.

"There are horse tracks around us," said Lark.

"Ugh, the last time I checked, we *have* horses," said Philomena sarcastically gesturing to their steeds.

"I know that. These tracks did not come from our horses. These horses were shod," said Lark, burning with impatience.

"Our horses don't have shoes," said Philip fighting grogginess as he forced himself to sit up. He had overheard them, and understood the significance in Lark's argument. Both Lark and Philomena bent down to help him. The world spun sickly beneath Philip as they lifted him to his feet.

"Philip," said Philomena worriedly, peering at Philip's pale face. "I'm fine," Philip assured, though his weak, tired voice did not settle his sister's fears. He shook himself, fighting off a wave of nausea. "If the tracks are of shod horses, then we must assume its Avador. Lark is right, Philomena. We have to get out of here," said Philip in a hushed voice so their assumed enemies nearby could not hear him.

"Why must we assume its Avador? There could be any number of travelers coming through here," Philomena hissed, her expression rigid with anger.

"No mere traveler could afford a horse to ride let alone shoes for it," Lark argued, his voice matching theirs.

The corners of Philomena's mouth twitched reluctantly. She knew Lark was right, but what irritated her was that Philip had sided with him so quickly. "Fine, then what do we do?" she asked grudgingly.

"We get out of here," said Philip, his gaze flicking from side to side, sensing unfriendly eyes watching them. He started stiffly for the horses. Another wave of nausea hit him and he swayed dangerously. Philomena hurried to steady him, and he gripped her arm gratefully.

"Maybe we should take hold up somewhere," Philomena suggested, peering at Philip with concern.

Philip shook his head, his face paling even more with the effort of moving. "If we go and hide somewhere, they'll just surround us and wait for us to surrender. We'll be cornered. We have to go now," he said, breathing heavily. Sweat was beginning to bead his face.

"You're in no condition for this," Philomena argued, gripping his hand in hers and willing him to listen.

"If you take cover somewhere, we can lead them away from you," came Lark's low voice on Philip's other side. They both looked to him, somewhat surprised. Lark met their gaze with a calm, steady confidence that made them believe he could take out a whole army without help if he had to.

"He's right, Philip," Philomena caught on eagerly. "We can do better than just lead them away, we can take them down," she said determinedly. This gave Lark a jolt of fear and his gaze dropped to the ground, but he said nothing and neither Philomena nor Philip noticed.

The fire lighting Philomena's eyes was intoxicating. Philip was drained, exhausted and sore and he doubted he could fight anyone right now. He sighed inwardly, coming to the conclusion that Lark and Philomena were right.

But before he could agreed, their concealed enemies ran out of patience. The twang of bowstring vibrated against the air. Snapping their gazes around, they caught sight of three blurred arrows flying towards them. Lark felt his breath freeze in his chest.

"On your horses!" yelled Philip, completely forgetting the

thought of sitting the excitement out. He rushed to Nimbius and leapt in the saddle, finding new strength with the sudden surge of adrenaline.

Two arrows thudded harmlessly into nearby trees, and the third flew towards Lark. Lark braced himself for searing pain for he had no time to move and the arrow was aimed for his chest. A streak of silver flashed before him and the arrow disappeared. Lark looked around stunned and saw Philomena on her grey stallion with her sword in hand. That cocky irritable look that was becoming familiar to him was plastered all over her face. "Next time don't hesitate to duck. I may not be there to save you," she said. Lark frowned and then caught sight of the arrow that would have killed him if it hadn't been for her. It lay on the ground cleaved in two.

More arrows hissed their way, some thudding into the trees and others whizzing dangerously close over their heads.
"Hurry, Lark!" Philip demanded, pulling his sword from its sheath. Lark clambered on top of Spear, feeling clumsy and anxious.

Swinging Nimbius around, Philip clapped his heels against the stallion's sides and shot away. Lark and Philomena encouraged their horses to follow and they galloped fiercely through the ivy. From where the arrows had come, three mounted warriors came charging from their cover to pursue them.

Sensing their enemies behind them, the three flew passed the ivy covered trees. Philip led the way his sword grasped with his good arm. Philomena and Lark followed closely behind galloping abreast with weapons at hand. For the first time, Lark's bow felt clumsy in his hands. Flinging his gaze over his shoulder, Lark's brow pinched with confusion.

"They're falling back," Lark yelled to Philomena over the pounding of hooves. They glimpsed the figures of their pursuers fading behind them.

Just then arrows whistled towards them from ahead. Philip felt his chest tighten as he pulled Nimbius to a stop. The black stallion slid, rearing on his haunches. Lark and Philomena just managed to pull up their own steeds before they could collide with Philip and Nimbius.

Three natives atop galloping horses burst forth from the waterfalls of ivy before them sporting long bows and short swords and shouting battle cries. Seeing clearly that their attackers were natives, they knew for sure now that it was Avador's company.

Two arrows instantly sprang from their bows making Philip flatten himself against Nimbius' neck. The arrows whistled over his head and stirred his hair. Philomena growled angrily and pushed Coursio forward to charge at the native warriors.

"Get back!" Philip hollered at her, steering Nimbius between her and the natives and shoving Coursio to the side. The native, Running Buck, rushed forward at Philip with a threatening blade. Lark fitted an arrow to his bow, aimed and fired in seconds. The arrow found Running Buck's sword and bounced off the blade, distracting him just enough for Philip to move out of the way. Running Buck cursed and turned an angry glare at Lark.

"Lark! This way!" Philip called to him, and Lark clapped his heels against Spear's sides and shot after Philip and Philomena. They raced away to the east with the three angry natives pursuing them. Seeing the space beginning to grow between them and their pursuers, Philip felt confident that they could outrun them. Looking ahead, his hopes were dashed as quickly as they had formed. Three other natives charged at them from the shadows. Philip cringed and veered Nimbius away from them with the other three natives still on their heels. Their horses slid, tearing and ripping the ivy and nearly colliding into one another and bringing them uncomfortably close to their enemies. Lark jerked back to avoid a dagger thrown by one of the natives which flew by him stirring the fringe on his coat. Fright tugged at Lark when he saw the dagger zoom at Philomena. The warrior princess however wasn't fazed, and cut away the dagger with her sword just as she had done with the arrow before.

They then shot away to the north with all six natives rampaging after them. The air rushed by them, whistling and murmuring loudly in their ears. The breathtaking Ivy Forest was nothing but black and green blurs around them, and their enemies chasing after them were burning significantly bright like torches in the dark.

Keeping away from the natives behind them and dodging the occasional arrow or dagger for what seemed like eternity, the three of them wondered how long this futile chase would last and even pondered whether or not they'd survive it.

Suddenly, a net made of rope as thick as a man's wrists sprung abruptly from the cover of the dense ivy and rose swiftly to create a wall between two trees before them. For a third time, Philip slowed Nimbius to a sliding stop as did Lark and Philomena. Their horses reared, pranced, and chomped anxiously their breath fogging the air. The six natives tailing them closed in and circled around them giving them no open gap to escape. They were trapped.

Philomena clenched her teeth and raised her sword. Lark knocked an arrow to his bow, the uncertainty he felt before gone. Philip gripped his sword and pulled out another, feeling a burning pain tug in his wounded arm as he did so. The three of them stayed close to one another, guarding each other's blind sides as the natives tightened the space around them. Just when they thought there would be an all out battle, the natives caught sight of their captain and instantly froze, relaxing their weapons but keeping them at hand.

Captain Avador Corea walked his black stallion forward from behind the trees that held the netted wall behind them. Philip met Avador's dark eyes, knowing he should feel trapped and even fearful, but all he felt now was anger.

"Prince Philip," said Avador coolly. "We meet again,"

27

Being trapped is a bad feeling; but being trapped with your arch enemy standing in front of you is even worse. Philip didn't know how they were going to get out of this one. His skin prickled with anticipation and adrenaline, though somehow the feel of his swords in his hands kept him from acting on his emotions. Seeing his companions just as calm also reassured him. Lark had his bow aimed at the native Fall Leaf who was closest to him. The native's fixed gaze on Lark was starting to make him feel uncomfortable, for Lark saw recognition and anger there. Philomena gripped her sword determinedly, her gaze shifting from one native warrior to the other.

"I see you are fairing quite well even after your experience in Niche," Avador mused casually, his gaze locked on Philip.

"And why shouldn't we?" Philip said offensively, his jaw flexed. Avador considered him for a moment before replying.

"Your arm must be hurting you a great deal," he said, his eyes dropping to Philip's bandaged left arm. "It's amazing you can even lift a sword with it. How is that possible?" he asked curiously.

"Stop pretending you have concern for us. There's not a large enough mask of lies to cover your inheritance," Philip said, deep disdain filling his voice.

Keeping his temper at bay and retaining a calm expression, Avador lifted his chin to perceive Philip in a new sense. "Truth always unfolds eventually, just as blood leaves behind a bright red trail,"

Philip glared at him, his eyes narrowing. Avador's twisting, condemning words made Philomena angry and she looked to him with a burning glower.

"What are you trying to say?" she demanded through clenched teeth, swinging her sword point around at Avador. He looked to her with a light frown. "Speak plain you pompous devil brat!"

"Philomena," Philip growled in warning, never taking his eyes off Avador.

"Bold speech for a girl," Avador commented, considering Philomena. "I think my words were plain enough to decipher, princess. Your brother may have the truth on his side, he may have some help along the way, but he metaphorically bleeds leaving a clear trail for me to follow, and with me and my company close behind you that will eventually lead to your destruction,"

A murmur of agreement rippled through the native warriors. Philomena gritted her teeth and shifted as if she was going to charge at Avador, but Philip put a hand on her arm to stop her. She reluctantly obeyed, scowling menacingly at their enemy.

"I thought your father wanted a grand audience when we finally fight, Avador," Philip said, remembering something his uncle had said back in Niche.

"Don't worry yourself. We'll get to fight one another, but not at this moment. Our orders are to collect the both of you, and bring you back to Caelum alive and unharmed. Though, I doubt my father will be too disappointed if we bring back your dead body instead," Avador said coolly.

"Alright, that's it!" Philomena snapped furiously, urging Coursio forward. Both Philip and Lark hurried to stop her, Philip grabbing her reins and Lark blocking her way. The natives raised their weapons threateningly, ready to strike, but Philomena didn't care. Her infuriated gaze was locked on Avador. The young captain considered her with new amusement, but then his gaze shifted to Lark.

"Your stable boy can do as he chooses, of course," said Avador, casually resting his hand on his sword pommel. There was a tightening feeling within Lark at the mention of himself. "Though I believe my men wouldn't mind a chat with him," Avador added.

Another murmur of agreement came from the native warriors. Lark felt his heart begin to race. What had he done to deserve special attention from these angry looking natives? He had never met any of them before.

"Why?" Philip asked before Lark could.

Avador lifted his eyebrows and pressed his lips in a tight, considering line. He turned an expectant look to his second in command, Night Hawk. Philip narrowed a frown on him.

Night Hawk exhaled reluctantly. "The boy probably doesn't even know," he said, shaking his head with an almost pitying gaze on Lark.

"He's old enough to know his own tainted birth by now," Bright Sky scoffed moodily next to Night Hawk. His comrades chided him.

Lark felt greatly disturbed. The way Bright Sky had said 'tainted birth' was like he should never have been born. "What is it that you know about me?" he demanded gravely.

Everyone seemed to look at him at once. It was Night Hawk who finally answered.

"Your father is Raven Wing, son of *Chief* Water Wing," Night Hawk explained. "Raven abandoned our people just when he was to become chief,"

"What?" Lark stuttered in shock. Philip and Philomena exchanged surprised expressions.

"Raven left us in a time of need. Our people fell apart because of him! You're the son of a coward!" Bright Sky spat nastily.

"You're lying!" Lark yelled raising his bow and firing before Philip or Philomena could stop him. His arrow flew at Bright Sky. The native warrior jerked in his saddle, but the arrow still ripped his coat sleeve and grazed his arm. Blood seeped from the shallow cut. Bright Sky roared with rage, but Night Hawk pushed his horse in front of his to block his way.

"Bright Sky!" Avador snapped warningly, shooting an angry glare at him.

With difficulty they settled Bright Sky down.

Lark watched with a smoldering stare, his bow gripped in his hand and his breath coming fast with adrenaline. Philomena placed a hand on his bow arm and whispered something that appeared to calm him.

"I doubt you ambushed us just to chat, Avador, so why don't we get down to business," said Philip, getting edgy. He could sense the air prickling with tension.

"Yes, lets," Avador agreed gruffly. "As I said before, my father's orders are to capture you both alive and you are to be kept fresh for future events if that's possible,"

"You always do you what your father tells you too," Philip challenged.

Avador's countenance hardened like a stone as he stared resentfully at Philip, flexing his jaw with his building anger. For a moment, it seemed as though the two young men were on the verge of pulling out their swords to start their promised duel early.

"Where are Balin and K'smet?" Philomena blurted out at Avador, breaking the concentrated tension between the two boys. It took Avador a moment to pry his attention away from Philip.

"They are alive if that is what you wish to know," he said. That was all he would say on the matter and it left a longing desire gnawing at Philomena.

Avador turned his attention back to Philip. "This is how it is going to be," he began. "You are going to drop your weapons and surrender yourselves and we'll escort you to Caelum peacefully,"

"That's not going to happen," said Philip.

"Why would we make the stupid mistake of surrendering when you could kill us the minute we drop our weapons?" questioned

Philomena.

"Look around you," said Avador gesturing lightly to their surroundings. The six natives had closed in tightly around them, and the thick netting loomed menacingly over them.

Philip circled his gaze around at their enemies and realized how bleak their situation was. They were surrounded and outnumbered against experienced warriors.

"Do you really think you have a choice?" Avador asked coolly. The black ravine of near hopelessness yawned threateningly inside Philip which frightened him more than their delicate situation.

"You have already lost the war, prince. The only thing you need to give up now is your will to keep trying at a futile mission. Let's not drag on the inevitable," said Avador convincingly. The dark shadow of defeat began to leak out from the ravine of hopelessness and started to cloud Philip's mind with whispers of surrender, making him feel tired from his heavy burden.

Philomena saw the uncertainty on her brother's face and snarled at Avador. Could her brother really be considering surrendering?

"Don't believe his words," said Lark, his bow drawn once more with the arrow aimed at the natives.

Just when Philip thought he was going to drop off the edge of the ravine into endless hopelessness determination suddenly burst forth and scattered the doubtful shadows. Strength filtered and flowed through him, and Philip knew what he had to do. He lifted his determined gaze to Avador.

"Like hell will I ever give up," he said.

Disappointment instantly settled over Avador. Relief washed over Philomena at Philip's words and she smirked with satisfaction.

Frustrated irritation boiled on Avador's countenance. He set his jaw in a haughty manner as he glowered at Philip. The tension everyone felt became taut. The natives drew their bows and shifted their weapons. Lark, Philip, and Philomena stayed back to back to one another, feeling the atmosphere spark with the oncoming fight.

"We can always do it the hard way, prince. I have no gripe with that," said Avador. He drew his sword from its scabbard. The short blade came out with a menacing hiss.

Fowl words were about to spew from Philomena's mouth when the heavy, thick netting that they were trapped against suddenly dropped with a whooshing sound and fell in a disorderly heap on the ground.

Shock left Avador and his company frozen.

When Philip met Avador's eyes he could see the bewildered rage. All Philip felt was relief. The fallen net offered a window of escape. They took this escape with hooting yells and the pounding of hooves. Their horses leapt over the fallen net and raced onto their route of freedom.

Avador cursed. "AFTER THEM!!!" he shouted brandishing his sword and leading the chase after the prince.

The natives pushed their horses over the fallen net following their enraged captain. Their prey had a head start and grew smaller as they distanced themselves even more. Avador urged his horse greatly pushing the black stallion to go as fast as he was able.

Ahead, Philip, Philomena, and Lark were kept close together, weaving between the wide trunks of trees and ducking beneath low hanging branches that trailed ivy vines. They jumped over a fallen log and continued to crash through the forest.

A slight descending of the land came upon them to their left with high ridges bordering either side which had cascading waterfalls of ivy dropping in to the small pass. Many would have ridden by without having even noticed this half concealed pass, but Lark knew it was there and knew where it led.

"This way!" Lark encouraged taking the lead and steering Spear down the pass. Philip and Philomena did not argue. They followed Lark down the descending trail.

A few moments later, Avador and his company pulled their steeds to a sliding stop before the descending pass. The company glanced around, panting hard from the pursuit.

"They went this way," said Avador, directing attention to the freshly torn ivy left from their prey. He steered his lathered steed towards the mostly concealed pass.

"No!" Night Hawk exclaimed, pushing his horse in front of Avador to block his way. This action infuriated Avador greatly. "We cannot go that way,"

"The prince went that way," Avador said with angry desperation, his features dark and violent.

"That is the way to Poacher's Land. It is far too dangerous," Night Hawk protested sternly.

"It doesn't seem to be too dangerous for *them*," said Avador, jerking his head towards the pass. He tried to get around Night Hawk.

"No!" said Night Hawk, swinging his horse to keep Avador where he was. Avador glowered at him breathing heavily with impatience.

"You must understand, captain, we have to be alive to capture them. Going through Poacher's Land is far too much of a risk. If they survive going through there, then we can intercept them at Ezleon," Night Hawk told him.

It took a long moment for the logic of these words to sink in for Avador. He stared at the pass he knew the prince had gone down still feeling the burning overwhelming desire to gallop after him. With great effort Avador averted his gaze to his second in command. "Very well," he said reluctantly. He looked around at the rest of the company. "We head for Ezleon with all speed possible," he confirmed, turning his stallion back around.

"What of Swift Deer and Silver Stream?" asked Hawk Eye, casting a concerned gaze over his shoulder.

"They'll catch up," Avador replied flatly. No one offered any protests.

The company regrouped and began galloping through the Ivy Forest to take the safer route to the city of Ezleon.

28

They could not slow their pace; at least not for some time they couldn't. Philip knew this. Avador would be pursuing them even more persistently now that he and Philomena had escaped his clutches not only once but twice now. Lark had no complaints about keeping a rapid speed, though he knew he would soon have to explain why he had urged them to go this way.

All night long they rode stampeding through the woods startling small hunters and sleeping birds. Exhaustion crept within them, only kept at bay by the adrenaline of being chased. The fairies flitted and flashed alongside them as if trying to offer their help and guidance.

After some time when they thought that the darkness of night itself would engulf them what appeared to be a crooked post suddenly came into view ahead.

Philip's brow crinkled as the post became more visible.

As they galloped onward the post grew larger, and they found that it was not a post at all but a tree; a gnarled, mangled bare tree that was hunched over to one side like an old man with corkscrew branches twisting about.

The sight of the tree brought the three of them to a stop. Whether the tree was so frightening or hauntingly intriguing to bring them to a halt, only they knew. The swarm of fairies that had been accompanying them thus far suddenly zipped away out of sight, sensing the menacing presence of the lifeless land that lay ahead. The tree stood withered before them, only tall enough to reach their horses' shoulders.

The ugly thing bore several planks of broken and splintered wood nailed to its trunk scratched with nasty threats and chilling warnings written in more than one language. One of the planks read, 'THE SOIL OF THE ASHEN LANDS WILL DEVOUR YOU ALIVE'. Another said, 'THE GLOWING EYES OF THE DRAGONS WILL BE THE LAST THING YOU SEE.'

The three looked to each other uneasily. Out of all the warnings though the one that read, 'AHEAD BE POACHER'S LAND' screamed out at Philip the most. The warning was nailed on top, as if it deserved a pedestal above all the others.

Philip snapped his gaze to Lark with a demanding quizzical stare. "You took us to Poacher's Land?!"

There was an evident grimace in Lark's features as he noticed the Poacher's Land warning.

"I thought you said Poacher's Land is far too dangerous of a risk to cross," said Philomena in a scolding manner. Lark was quite in a pinch now. The siblings were both glaring at him expectantly for an explanation.

"I won't deny that I said that, but now things have changed. Avador is chasing you," said Lark. The siblings only looked more perturbed and impatient.

"We haven't forgotten, and I'm sure Avador has enough sense to take a much less life risking route," argued Philip.

"Exactly," said Lark, gesturing knowingly to Philip as if he had explained their reasons for being on the edge of Poacher's Land in full.

Philip looked confused and sat quiet for a moment, thinking it through.

"Exactly what? Are you agreeing that Avador is making us look like complete idiots as we run around Staleon as if we've been beheaded like chickens," Philomena flared, motioning sharply. Lark rolled his eyes and shook his head, too tired to untangle the misunderstanding that had ensued.

"Oh, I see," said Philip as understanding dawned on him.

"Avador will not risk going through Poacher's Land but we will," he said, grinning at Lark.

"That's what I said," said Lark with a tired nod.

"Ingenious, Lark," Philip beamed.

Lark squared his shoulders modestly. "I have my moments,"

Philomena still remained baffled and not agreeable. "Ingenious? You've got to be kidding me!"

The boys looked to her.

"We are willing to travel through a place that is hardly ever traveled just to avoid Avador who is smart enough to steer clear of it. Where is the logic? If Avador will not go through Poacher's Land then it must be a death trap. I would personally prefer to deal with Avador himself and his band of knife throwing natives," Philomena said rapidly.

"Before you were quite eager to be one of the few to travel through Poacher's Land. What makes it so different now?" Philip said innocently.

Philomena shot an irritable glare at him. Philip lifted his eyebrows and shrugged.

Lark sighed heavily, pleased that Philip had pointed out Philomena's absurd contradiction. "My father taught me well enough how to track and disarm all sorts of traps. I'm sure I can manage getting us through Poacher's Land unharmed," he said.

Philip nodded in confident agreement, still wearing a lopsided smirk. "He's right, Philly. If we can get to Ezleon safely without anymore run-ins with Avador, than Poacher's Land sounds like the best route," he said.

Stubbornness squirmed across Philomena's fine features as she chewed her lip obstinately. "I suppose that does make *some* sense," she said reluctantly yielding to their notion.

"Yes, it does," Philip said grinning.

"But what about this talk of the Ashen Lands and glowing eyed dragons?" Philomena questioned severely, gesturing at the other warning signs that spoke of another terrible land.

"The Ashen Lands are the bare lands before Poacher's Land. Only dragons live in that area," Lark explained.

"And how in the hell do you expect us to fight off fire breathing, man eating dragons?" Philomena demanded, glaring at Lark. "There's nothing that says they are literally man eating," said Lark wryly. He tapped Spear's sides gently and the loyal bay steed walked forward passed the gnarled, hunched over tree that held all of the warning signs. Philip filed in behind him.

"Oh, sure," said Philomena with disbelief. Absolute loathing filled her as she reluctantly urged Coursio to follow after Philip and Lark.

The three of them traveled together, distancing themselves from the crooked tree and advancing further onward. They noticed that as they continued on their journey the land around them gradually became barer and less filled with life. The trees that loomed over them were suddenly drained of their rich color to be replaced with a bleak grey, and they were noticeably diminishing in height. Only a few birds broke the eerie quiet with their lonely songs, and a single squirrel chattered noisily and shook the dry branches overhead.

This prolonged silence allowed Philip to ponder about what was ahead. The image of a terrible fire-breathing dragon popped into Philip's mind creating a worm of uncertainty to squirm within him. He looked ahead with suspicious uneasiness, setting his jaw and chewing at his lip.

Riding beside him, Lark noticed his perturbed expression and instantly deciphered his thoughts. "Having second thoughts?" asked Lark. Philip flicked his gaze to him. "We can always turn back,"

Philip shook his head. "No," he said, sounding skeptical.

"You're thinking of the dragons," said Lark, switching his gaze back to their path ahead.

Philip squared his shoulders innocently. "Well, yeah," he said. "Who wouldn't contemplate the idea of coming face to face with a grumpy dragon?" Philomena put in sarcastically, still fuming over the fact that they were taking a deadly dangerous route.

No comment came from Lark on this.

"Is there by any slightest chance that you've seen these dragons?" Philip asked Lark with the smallest hope.

"I've heard rumors," said Lark. He could tell he had Philip and Philomena's full attention now and so continued. "Most folk say they are actual minions of the devil charged to recruit those who are evil at heart and bring punishment to those who still hold hope for peace. Others say they are merely ghosts troubled by Alamia's depression and so are beginning to haunt the woodlands. Few others believe that none of this is true and there really are no dragons only hallucinations exaggerated by those who claim to have seen them,"

None of these stories made Philip or Philomena feel better; in fact they made them shudder even more.

"And what do you believe?" asked Philip.

Lark took a moment to think, breathing inward. "I do not take any of the rumors seriously, so I am not sure whether there are dragons or no dragons at all," he said.

"Well, if there are dragons and they are evil I do hope they are real and made of flesh," said Philomena.

"Why is that?" Lark asked.

"You can't harm a ghost with a sword now can you?" said Philip with a crooked grin. "If they are living breathing monsters we can at least be assured that our swords will have some effect against them,"

Lark said nothing. He could tell that Philip and Philomena were comfortable with situations that could be settled with a blade; situations that he had hardly any experience with.

"Oh, that reminds me," spoke Philip. "You don't have a sword do you?" he asked Lark.

"Stable boys tend not to carry weapons," said Lark matter-of-factly.

"You have a bow," said Philip, gesturing to the bow slung across Lark's back.

"It's just a hunting bow," said Lark, glancing over his shoulder at his bow.

"But still a bow, and you're quite a good shot with it if I might say so myself," Philip complimented, directing a praising grin at Lark that appeared almost brotherly. His kind words left Lark unsure of how to respond.

"Anyway, back to your sword-less state, I have a gift for you," said Philip, undoing a few buckles and bringing forth a sheathed sword. "It's not much to look at, but it is a reliable little blade. It will defend you well," Philip added.

On the contrary to Philip's words, it was in truth an impressive short sword, with an elegantly honed mahogany hilt and pommel with a silver cross guard shaped with twisting knots and vines which together made a pleasing design. The scabbard was old and battered, but still in usable condition.

"What about you? Don't you need the sword?" asked Lark, glancing down at the weapon and back to Philip.

"Oh please! He has about five of them," laughed Philomena.

"Not true, I have three now," Philip corrected, offering the sword to his friend.

Lark was astounded by the generous gift, and was unsure of what to say as he accepted the sword. Numbly, he drew the sword from its sheath. The silver blade came out with a metallic slither, beautifully reflecting the moonlight.

Gripping his new weapon, Lark felt the graceful sword's strength and endurance. The image of the sword slicing through an opponent in battle suddenly entered Lark's mind and he realized that the sword did not only look beautiful and feel strong, but was also capable of great pain. It was deadly, this elegant blade he held. Lark felt suddenly repulsed by the sword.

"No worries," came Philip's voice causing Lark to resurface from his thoughts. "I'll teach you how to use it effectively. Philomena will help you too," he added.

Philomena scowled and shot a nasty glare at Philip.

Lark felt his heart thud hard against his chest. "Do I really need a sword?" he asked, looking to Philip.

At first, Philip felt insulted, but when he saw the look on Lark's face he understood why he was asking such a question. He had felt the same way the first time he had held a real sword, and he knew there were no pleasant thoughts going through Lark's mind presently.

"Well, I suppose you don't have to have it, but when you come face to face with something that is pure evil and wants to kill you, you want a good sword at your side," said Philip kindly.

The corners of Lark's mouth twitched with reluctance, but he found logic in Philip's words. Without another word, Lark accepted the sword he held and buckled it about his waist. The sword felt heavy at his hip, but Lark was sure he would get use to it. He'd have to.

Philip regarded Lark with something that resembled sympathy. Lark met the prince's eyes and an understanding passed between them. Not all who carried swords chose to carry them.

Sometimes it just befell upon them and Lark was one of those individuals as was Philomena and Philip.

Lark felt his former life of a stable boy the son of a farmer in a small village fading away. His new life just coming to being was still blurred with uncertainty leaving inside him a sense of anxiety . . . and fear.

Nearly everything that was familiar to him was gone.

29

When morning came they could not tell for the sun hid behind
thick curtains of grey clouds that threatened early winter
weather. They huddled atop their horses with the hoods of their
cloaks pulled over their heads. The Ivy Forest was behind them,
and sadly their new scenery reflected the dreary weather. The
trees appeared to be dead and it seemed as though that their
trunks had been blackened by fire. Do to this, the trees were
pretty much just ash, and so were slowly disintegrating. And
instead of a bed of fall leaves on the ground, there was a thick
grey carpet of ash.

"This is an awfully cheerful place," Philip said thickly, gazing
around at their bleak surroundings.

He sniffed and crinkled his nose. The smell of burnt wood
polluted the air.

"We are in the Ashen Lands now," said Lark, riding just behind
him.

"Obviously," Philip said dryly, watching as the tree they were
passing suddenly crumbled drastically, its ashes blowing away
with the light breeze.

"Is Poacher's Land as bad as this dreadful place?" asked
Philomena, pulling her cloak closer to her as if it might help
distance herself from the repelling burnt trees and ashen ground.

"I hope it's not," said Lark, shuddering within from the sights
around him, and yet a tugging sadness and urge to fill in this gap
of loss kept his eyes locked on the burnt land.

As they traveled onward, they found that no birds flew over head
or sang in the trees (if there were any trees to sing in that is). No
living creature of any kind appeared to be near, and the three

young travelers could not blame them for avoiding such a depressing place.

They were mostly quiet as they rode by the black trees, for even the smallest sound made had an ominous effect. Philip though could not handle silence for too long of a time; he squirmed in his saddle from the prolonged silence and so could not take it anymore.

"Where are those fiendish creatures you were speaking of?" he asked, though he kept his voice just above a whisper. Lark looked to him, and then casted his gaze around unsure of how to reply.

"Perhaps it *was* all just rumors," suggested Philomena. This idea lightened their moods and lifted their spirits a tad.

A crumbling shifting sound from behind them raised the hairs on the back of Philip's neck. He swung his gaze around, his hand hovering over his sword hilt, but all he saw was a line of mounded dirt as though a giant mole had just tunneled behind them. Philip frowned at the mounded earth, confused. Beneath him, Nimbius shifted uneasily and chomped at his bit.

"What is it?" asked Philomena. She and Lark stopped their horses to look back at Philip.

"Did you hear that?" asked Philip still staring at the risen dirt and putting a calming hand to his stallion's arched neck.

"Hear what?"

"That sound . . . like the ground shifting," said Philip, feeling his pulse pound harder.

Lark and Philomena directed perturbed frowns at him. Before either of them could say anything a giant snake-like creature with glowing green eyes burst forth from the earth before them, hissing and spewing dirt and ash. Their horses whinnied and reared in fright.

"A dragon!" yelled Lark, pulling his bow out from behind him and trying to keep Spear steady.

Philip felt the familiar rush of adrenaline. He pushed Nimbius forward between Philomena and Lark, facing the monstrous dragon. Philip and Philomena drew their swords.

The dragon slithered its scaly body further out of the ashen ground, dwarfing them. Its head was just as large as one of their horses, towering above them. Short legs and scaly fingers tipped with curved claws emerged. The dragon gaped its toothy mouth open, the yellow light of fire glowing in the back of its throat.

"This is just great," said Philomena, gawking at the dragon and gripping her sword nervously. Coursio danced anxiously underneath her and flattened his ears.

The dragon roared at them, rippling their clothes and causing their horses to reel back. The ashen trees closest to them crumbled under the sheer volume.

"Move! Now!!" Philip bellowed, pushing Nimbius into Spear and Lark to get them moving. Philomena gave Coursio his head to follow and felt the rush of air behind them as the dragon struck the place where they had just been standing. The dragon only got a mouthful of dirt, his missed strike stirring up a cloud of ash obscuring their surroundings and making it difficult to see. An irritable roar emitted from the dragon and he dove head first into the ashen ground as though he were a sea serpent in a vast ocean. The ground surrendered to the dragon and mounded as it burrowed after them.

Their horses galloped wildly, needing no urging to go fast. A terrible crumbling sound filled the air as the dragon tunneled fiercely behind them, its trail of mounded earth getting closer and closer.

They didn't get very far when a second dragon suddenly burst out of the ground before them blocking their way. They quickly pulled their horses to a stop. The dragon behind them erupted from the ground hissing angrily and slithering its body out and around them, trapping them where they had been forced to stop. Philip gulped his breath coming quick. "Oh, this is bad," he said wide eyed.

Philomena huffed in reply, and pushed Coursio forward flourishing her sword. Instantly, the dragons roared in protest, stomping the ground and tightening the circle they had formed around them. Philomena shuddered regretfully and lowered her sword.

The dragon before them that had blocked their way hissed suspiciously, flicking its tail. Its icy blue eyes shimmered menacingly in the gloom and seemed to pierce through them like knives. Twice as large, this dragon was far fiercer than the first.

"Now what?" Philomena grumbled hoping one of them had an idea.

Lark knocked an arrow to his bow, aimed and fired at the first dragon's head. The dragon snatched the arrow out of the air with its jaws, chomped and spat the broken arrow on the ground with an angry hiss. Lark lifted his eyebrows, a jolt tugging at his gut. He knocked another arrow to his bow simply for comfort.

Philip and Philomena raised their swords, ready to defend against either dragon that might attack. Their horses sidestepped and pranced anxiously.

The dragons glared down at them with their glowing eyes for what seemed like forever as if waiting for them to try another attack. Their mighty presence was irrepressibly overwhelming and made them shrink under their piercing gaze. When several nerve crushing seconds ticked by in silence, the dragons became impatient.

"Why have you entered this land?" asked the blue eyed dragon with a deep guttural voice.

They gawked in shock, rather taken aback and astounded to hear the dragon speak with a very human-like voice.

"You can speak?" asked Philip, intrigued.

"Of course we can," said the green eyed dragon from behind them, his own voice being younger but just as deep.

"Our kind could always use your words, as my brother and I are conversing with you now. But you did not answer my question.

Why are you here?" the blue eyed dragon asked again with narrowing eyes. His demanding tone made them shudder.

"We are just passing through to get to Ezleon," said Philip, his throat going dry as he met the gaze of the dragon towering before them.

The blue eyed dragon sniffed ruefully, yellow flames flickering from his nostrils. "If you wish to get to Ezleon, than turn back the way you came and take the safer path," he said.

"Don't you think that if that path were safer we would have taken it?" Philomena said pointedly.

"We will see to it that the path you are on is far more dangerous," the blue eyed dragon said flatly.

The three exchanged nervous glances, knowing without a doubt that the dragons would see that promise kept.

"Now turn back the way you came," the green eyed dragon demanded from behind them.

They stood uncertainly between the brother dragons, unsure of what to do. Philomena looked to Philip expectantly, already knowing full well his decision. Meeting his hardened expression, she could see that her assumption was right.

The dragons watched them with their penetrating glares, waiting for them to turn around and leave.

Their expectancy made Philip's insides roil with frustration melting away any fear. He lifted his sword, gripping its hilt till his knuckles turned white.

"I'm getting so tired of being pushed around," he growled through gritted teeth.

With a sudden flare of determination, Philip leapt from his saddle and charged at the dragon before them with a loud cry. The blue eyed dragon frowned at his insanity.

"Philip?!!" Philomena shouted after him. Philip paid no mind and raised his sword to swing it at the dragon's leg. The other dragon behind them arched his neck over Lark and Philomena and opened his jaws after Philip.

"Look out!" Philomena cried. Lark fired an arrow at the dragon's neck but the arrow only thudded harmlessly in the dragon's hide not daunting him at all. The dragon snatched at Philip.

"No!!" Philomena yelled.

The dragon lifted Philip up by the scruff of his jerkin. Philip shouted out as the ground fell away from him. His sword slipped from his grasp and fell on the ash filled ground. The dragon brought Philip eye level with his brother. The blue eyed dragon leaned his muzzle close to Philip, and Philip braced himself for the searing pain of being chomped on. Surprisingly the dragon merely sniffed him, his large nostrils flaring. The smell of soot was thick on the dragon's breath. His shimmering blue eyes that were somehow both beautiful and belittling were terrifyingly large; so large Philip could see his own frightened reflection in the dragon's pupil.

"Rather brave, this one, huh?" said the dragon who held Philip through meshed teeth.

"Or perhaps he's simply reckless," the blue eyed dragon said ruefully.

"He doesn't smell like a poacher though does he, Kirfen?" said the green eyed dragon.

"No, I suppose not, Kirken," said the dragon Kirfen, his gaze moving curiously over Philip. Philip frowned confusedly as he listened to them.

"Come to think of it, none of them smell like poachers," said the dragon Kirken.

"True," said Kirfen, staring at Philip with a deep curiosity which made Philip's skin tingle though somehow he wasn't afraid.

"What should we do with them, brother, since they aren't poachers?" asked Kirken.

"Poachers? What are you talking about?" Philip questioned, absolutely baffled.

Kirfen's brows lowered over his irritated gaze and he signaled to his younger brother with his eyes. Philip felt suddenly worried that he had offended them.

Kirken did not hesitate to obey his brother's command, and eased his bite on Philip's jerkin. Philip yelped as he plummeted to the ground and fell hard beside his sword. Pain shot up his still healing arm and shoulder like a hot iron rod. He rolled over groaning and groping for his weapon and silently cursing the dragons. Lark and Philomena rushed over to him, helping him to his feet and asking if he were alright.

Kirfen lowered his magnificent head to be eye level with them. "Speak the truth, why have you come here?" he asked.

The three exchanged glances before deciding to reply truthfully. "We came this way because we are being chased by a posse which is meant to either kill us or take us to Caelum. The leader of the posse is Avador Corea, the son of Salvador Corea who-," Philip went on to explain, but Kirfen cut him short.

"My brother and I know full well who the Coreas' are, and what they are doing," said Kirfen with deep disgust evident in his voice. Lark sucked in a breath at the dragon's words.

"So you know the truth?" Philip asked, astounded.

Kirfen dipped his muzzle in confirmation. "And since we do know the truth, it is surprising to hear Salvador directing so much attention on to you. If what you say is true, why are you so important to him that he has sent out his own son to collect you?"

Philip hesitated. "My sister and I are the lost heirs to the kingdom. We are the children of King Paul and Queen Catherine. We are the only ones who can stop the tyranny of Salvador Corea,"

"Philip, don't tell him everything," hissed Philomena, elbowing him in the ribs.

Kirfen sniffed disdainfully. "The lost heirs to the kingdom of man, you mean, not the world of the other creatures who live along side them,"

"My family has always loved and respected the creatures of this world," Philip said defensively.

"Listen well, prince of man," Kirfen spoke forcefully. "My brother and I are the last of our kind. The end of the dragons is the fault of man, but it is our burden as well for we trusted man and allowed them to pass through our forest. They abused our trust, and laid down their sharp traps for the creatures of the forest to tread on. They took many innocent lives only to sell their skins, teeth, and claws in their markets,"

"Poachers," Lark said under his breath, the poisonous word heavy on his tongue.

"Yes, young one, poachers. They lied to us and our kind as well as the entire forest has paid for our mistake," said Kirfen.

"You are the ones who have burnt the forest," said Lark, looking up at Kirfen. Kirfen nodded.

"But why?" Philomena asked outraged.

"Because," spoke up Kirken. They turned to face him. "We have burnt the forest to drive the creatures away from Poacher's Land. We did it to protect them, and ever since we did the poachers have suffered for hardly any beast has been snared in their vile traps anymore. Not here anyway,"

This explanation blanketed a sadness and regret over their souls. Knowing that fellow humans could be brought so low as to destroy innocent life was a shameful knowledge.

"Why do you stay in this place though?" asked Philomena. "If you have succeeded in protecting the rest of the forest, can't you move on for the sake of your own kind? I'm sure there must be other dragons somewhere out there,"

Kirfen and Kirken exchanged glances. "We are the guardians of the forest. We belong here, and we will remain here and continue to burn the land to protect what life remains until our time is done," said Kirfen.

"Besides, allowing the poachers to enter our part of the forest was an unforgivable mistake on our account. We do not deserve to flee for our own sake, but instead remain here in the Ashen

Lands we have created. Perhaps such a burden we have forced upon ourselves will help atone for our sins," said Kirken.

"It is on honorable act. I hope you will find peace afterwards," Lark said sincerely.

The dragons were surprised by Lark's understanding and sincerity. They bowed their heads to him in acknowledgement and gratitude.

"So what will you do with us? You said yourselves that we smell nothing like poachers. Is that sufficient enough for you to let us pass unharmed?" asked Philip, stepping forward.

"What does it matter what you look or smell like? You are still capable of killing," Kirken said.

"Kirken," Kirfen warned.

"He has a point, Kirfen," Philip said regretfully. Kirfen looked to him. "We are still capable of killing," said Philip.

Kirfen appraised Philip with an approving expression. "And since your appearance or scent is not satisfying enough proof that you are not poachers, what shall be solid proof of your good nature?" he wondered out loud.

Philip, Philomena, and Lark looked nervously to one another, waiting awkwardly as the brother dragons began a whispered debate between themselves.

Impatience quickly settled over Philomena and had her tapping her foot and chewing at her lip. Philip and Lark stood quietly, having far more patience for the situation than Philomena.

Finally, the brother dragons finished discussing the matter and came forth with their answer.

"My brother and I agree that you are not poachers, but as you said yourself, still capable of taking a life. We have found that the most peaceful way to avoid any brutality is for you to surrender your weapons to us," said Kirfen.

Philomena's jaw dropped. "You've got to be joking!" she blurted out. The brother dragons narrowed their glowing eyes on her. Their cold expressions panicked Philip, and he hurried to reassure them.

"What she means is that it is surprisingly generous of you to give us passage on such painless terms," Philip said in cheerful hurry, putting an arm around Philomena's shoulders and directing a friendly grin up at the dragons. They did not appear especially convinced that Philomena wasn't being rude, but Philip's words satisfied them well enough. Philomena sniffed disdainfully and brushed Philip's arm away.

"All we ask in return is that you do not abuse our generosity," said Kirken.

"We won't. We promise," said Lark, not giving Philomena's scornful behavior any attention at all.

"We learned long ago that promises are empty words, young one. They mean nothing to us anymore. Now surrender your weapons," said Kirfen in a hardened tone.

With a great deal of grumbling and muttered complaints from Philomena they surrendered all of their weapons over to the dragons. For Lark, this took only a few seconds, but for Philip and Philomena it took several minutes. They took their time unsheathing their many swords, knives, and daggers.

By the time they had finished, there was a good sized pile of blades set before the dragons. The dragons leveled confounded looks at them and their weapons for a moment.

Lark knew exactly what they were thinking; why does one need to be a walking arsenal?

Kirfen shook his head and swept their weapons away with his tail taking them out of their sight and far out of their reach.

Philomena cursed angrily, feeling utterly vulnerable. Philip felt this too, but like Lark he understood that their vulnerability was a necessary sacrifice.

"You may pass now," said Kirken.

"But we warn you, we no longer know what lies ahead in Poacher's Land. There is no telling what you may encounter in that heathen place." said Kirfen.

"We understand," said Philip. He hesitated a moment, his brow crinkling as he thought of how to put his thoughts into words. "I'm sorry for what happened here, and what you have to do to protect your home. I wish I could make things better for you," he said.

Kirken's shimmering blue eyes lightened with intrigue.

"You amaze me, prince of man," the dragon said. "Never have I met a human with a heart as brave and enduring as yours, and still you are kind and understanding. If ever I can help you I will, nature's prince, but if I am never to see you again I will remember you till the day I breathe my last breath," Kirken gracefully bowed his head low to Philip.

A warm fondness swelled within Philip, and he returned the dragon's gracious bow. *A prince of nature am I,* Philip thought. He felt undeserving of the title.

With this, the young travelers climbed aboard their waiting steeds and steered them around the dragons. They rode forward on their route to Poacher's Land with Philip leading them. The dragons followed them with their glowing eyes.

Philip glanced over his shoulder to look upon the magnificent creatures for what he thought might be his last time. Kirken met the prince's gaze, and they held eye contact until they disappeared from each other's sight.

30

Far away to the north in the towering structure of Castle Caelum, Salvador Corea was finally receiving word from his son by a hawk that had arrived ten minutes ago. Salvador snatched the small, tightly rolled scroll that the hawk had faithfully carried and strode away, deciding to read the scroll in the privacy of his own quarters.

Being in such a large and roomy castle as he was, it took Salvador several minutes to reach his quarters. He went down a long hall and turned left into a branching chamber where he found a stone staircase which he climbed to get to the hall above. Having lived in Caelum as long as he had, Salvador could easily navigate through her twisting halls, chambers, and staircases. He walked the length of the hall he had come to, passing by closed doors on either side that was warmly illuminated by torches. At the end of the hall, Salvador swiftly climbed the spiraling staircase which brought him to a narrow landing. At the end of this small landing, he opened the great oaken door to his quarters. He slammed the door behind him, startling his wife, Avriliana, from her chair beside the round window that looked out upon the hills of forest that were now veiled with the dark of night.

Salvador gave Avriliana no acknowledgement and brusquely marched over to the door that lead out to the balcony which he roughly yanked open and stalked through. A gust of cold wintry air blew into the room making Avriliana shiver and reach for her white fur cloak.

Though Salvador showed her no attention, Avriliana was a beauty with no equal. Her long wavy hair was a rich black that shimmered with the candle light. Her complexion was smooth and fine and her bright eyes were calm pools of sea green beneath thin eyebrows.

Out on the balcony, Salvador untied the scroll with haste, unrolled it, and read the words in hungry earnest.

Avriliana wrapped herself in her cloak and went to the open door way. She dare not go out on the balcony, and so waited in fearful impatience as she watched her husband read the message to himself.

A fiery boldness tempted Avriliana to go over to Salvador and rip the scroll from his hands, just so she might glimpse her son's neat and curved handwriting for herself. But fear of Salvador kept her from acting on this temptation, and for this she hated herself and loathed Salvador even more. Avriliana could hardly believe she was united in marriage with the hateful monster she now watched. She could not believe that the son she loved so dearly belonged to Salvador as well.

Suddenly, Salvador emitted one of his usual curses in a loud growl, and balled up Avador's message hatefully. Cursing again, Salvador flung the scrunched letter over the balcony. It sailed through the air and disappeared in the night sky on its descent. Seeing the scroll fall out of sight increased Salvador's rage. He would have thrown it back into his chambers if his wife wasn't standing in the doorway. But she was, and he'd rather get rid of the scroll entirely and miss out reading it over again so to be sure *she* wouldn't be able to read it at all.

Avriliana shifted uncomfortably, her nerves quivering and her stomach feeling queasy just as she always felt when she sensed Salvador's bitter temperament. Salvador turned a dreadful glare on her, as if everything were her fault. His cold stare made her shiver.

Salvador snorted with disgust and stormed back inside, stalking passed Avriliana. She timidly followed him at a cautious distance. She watched him stomp to his desk and begin rummaging through its drawers for parchment. She desired to ask of Avador but was too afraid to present such a question. After several long, dreadfully silent minutes though, she could not wait any longer.

"What of Avador?" she asked with great longing. "What of our son?"

"No need to worry for *your* cowardly son. He has already failed at his first opportunity to catch the prince," said Salvador scornfully without looking at her.

"Where is he?" Avriliana dared to ask. Salvador was getting annoyed already.

"He and his worthless company are most likely traveling through Staleon Wood by now. They have the prince on the run. They're headed for Ezleon. Avador isn't even capable of doing a boy's job of bringing in a runaway prince. It's pathetic," scoffed Salvador, finally finding some parchment.

Angry defense rose within Avriliana, yet she still spoke gently. "He never wanted this life. Avador is a kind boy. All he wants to do is find his true place in the world. He doesn't want to know the way of the sword anymore,"

"I don't care what he wants!!!" Salvador bellowed, snapping a boiling glower at Avriliana. "He is of the Corea family. His forefathers demand that he plays his part in seeking revenge against the Stilwell's."

"Our son did not ask to be born. You cannot force him to live the life you want him to live. He has to decide for himself," said Avriliana, mustering her courage.

"He is my son, whether he likes it or not or I like it or not. He has no choice but to go forward with these plans," Salvador said harshly, roughly dipping his quill into an inkwell. He started scratching his message onto the parchment.

"Or what, Salvador?" Avriliana said angrily, stepping towards him. "Will you kill him if he doesn't obey? Or perhaps throw him in the dungeons for the rest of his life?"

"I said he has no choice in the matter. If he is defiant I may be tempted to do either one of those punishments," said Salvador without looking up from his parchment.

Despair clouded Avriliana's mind. Hot tears threatened to leak from her eyes as she imagined her beloved son chained down to a fate that he wanted no part of. For this, she hated Salvador greatly.

"Just as you tricked me in to marrying you?" she said her voice low and hoarse. Salvador looked around at her, his black eyes narrowing. "You have to control the fate of our son too,"

"I never forced you to marry me. You agreed to the arrangement," Salvador said haughtily.

"You tricked me. You never loved me. You just wanted a son," Avriliana insisted, her voice cracking with emotion.

Something inside Salvador snapped. He snatched the inkwell from his desk and threw it across the room. It flew over Avriliana's shoulder and shattered the round glass window behind her. Ink and splinters of glass flew every which way. Avriliana did not so much as flinch. She stared at Salvador who glared back, his chest rising and falling with his roiled anger. Before they could speak again, the door to their chambers banged open emitting five armored guards with risen spears and swords. Salvador and Avriliana turned to look at them.

"What the hell do you think you're doing?" snapped Salvador. The guard in front shifted his gaze around nervously. "We heard a crash, and thought maybe the rebels had tried to attack," the man stuttered.

"You thought wrong. Get out of here," Salvador said cruelly, sharply motioning them to leave. The guards behind the first did not hesitate. They turned on their heels and scurried down the stone stairs, eager to get far away from Salvador. The first guard though seemed petrified by fear and stood there his mouth opening and closing wordlessly. Salvador glowered at him with disgust.

"Why don't you do something useful and send a maid up here to clean this mess," Salvador said to the guard. The guard nodded rapidly, and began backing away sweat starting to drool beneath his helmet.

"GET OUT!!" Salvador hollered.

The guard's eyes widened with fright. He fled without a word. He was in such a hurry to leave that he left the door to Salvador's chambers wide open. Salvador huffed irritably.

Avriliana shook her head, pitying the poor guard. She gathered her dress and cloak and started for the open door wanting to find an isolated place away from Salvador.

Salvador rolled his eyes to the ceiling. "Close the door," he said gruffly. Avriliana obeyed, and hurried down the spiraling staircase.

Salvador stayed in his chambers, muttering and grumbling to himself. He went back to his desk and brought out a new inkwell to finish his message.

Half way down the staircase, Avriliana stopped abruptly clinging to the stone wall for support. Despair twisted her features and tears started to spill down her face as she sank to the steps. Avador, her beloved son, was going to be forced to live as a ruthless villain like his father; or if he refused, he would be killed or imprisoned for his defiance. There was no future for him. There was nothing to look forward too.

Sorrow clutching her, Avriliana buried her face against her knees and cried. What sort of life was this? If all was to end in tyranny and sadness, why linger?

Sniffling and pulling her face back, Avriliana glanced around. No one was ascending or coming down the stairs. She pulled the small knife she kept stowed in a secret sheath she had made that was secured to her right calf. Salvador disliked her carrying weapons, but she had managed to keep this particular knife hidden.

The knife gleamed in the dancing torchlight. Avriliana could see her tear stained reflection on its blade. Inhaling a shaky breath, Avriliana raised the knife above her head. She had thought of doing this before, but now seemed like the perfect time.

She closed her eyes, prepared to feel the cold steel of the little knife penetrate her heart. But the knife refused to budge, as if something had frozen her arms to keep her from plunging in to her chest.

Never is there a perfect time for this, a warm voice spoke from the air. Avriliana didn't know if she had imagined the voice, but the wish of the speaker was clear. With a shuddering breath, Avriliana let the knife fall. It clattered to the stone.

Breathing heavily, Avriliana shook the hazy feeling that had almost taken her in full. Pushing herself to her feet, she knew what she had to do. She wasn't going to leave her son in the horrid clutches of Salvador's plans, even if it meant giving her life to ensure that hope for Avador. At least he could have a chance at a better life.

Determination suddenly swelled in Avriliana as she stowed away her knife and hurried down the stairs, her footsteps echoing off the walls. She was going to save her son no matter what it took.

31

It was not till midday when Philip, Philomena and Lark reached Poacher's Land. This now marked Lark's time with Philip and Philomena as three nights and two and a half days traveling together. Lark let out a sigh at this fact, for the short time spent felt more like eternity had passed. Several times Lark pondered on why he had even agreed to help them. Though thinking over this only served to frustrate him, so he would shake himself and tuck away his aggravation for the time being.

It had been an easy ride to the Poacher Land border, except for the fact that Philomena had muttered under her breath most of the way, complaining over the dragons forcing them to surrender their weapons. Philip and Lark had remained quiet about this and had let her complain to her heart's content.

After an hour or so, she had grown tired of it. She now rode silently atop her grey stallion, her expression set stiffly with irritation and annoyance.

When the Ashen Lands they were traveling over began to morph into Poacher's Land, what appeared to be a brown sack hanging from a low tree branch came into view. Several things poking out of the sack shone dully in the dim light of the afternoon and made the sack appear as though it were a pincushion stuck with many needles.

They squinted at it suspiciously.

"What is that?" Philomena asked apprehensively, feeling on edge and terribly vulnerable without her sword.

No reply came from Philip or Lark for they had no way of knowing what it was.

Cautiously, they approached the mysterious sack that dangled in the trees before them. When they got close, Philip volunteered to investigate.

Edging Nimbius slowly closer to the strange bundle, Philip found that it was in fact a leather satchel. Carefully, he turned the satchel to the side gritting his teeth all the while and fearing that some sort of vicious spiny creature might fly out at his face. Instead of a nasty little beast though, the familiar pommels of six swords were sticking out of the satchel along with a bow and quiver.

Philip breathed inward with relief. "It appears that the kind dragons decided to return our weapons," he said.

At this, Philomena eagerly joined him. They brought down the satchel, which was rather heavy, from the tree branch. Philomena beamed happily at the bundle, very much relieved. She turned a blaming look on Philip.

"I cannot believe you agreed to this in the first place," she said critically. "What if we had been attacked? We traveled defenseless for hours!"

"But we weren't attacked were we?" Philip pointed out, cocking a smirk at her. Philomena bit at her lip crossly.

"We still could have been, and we would have been killed," Philomena argued. "I'm never parting with my swords again," she said, gripping the reassuring hilt of one of her swords.

Philip sighed. "Your fondness for weapons scares me sometimes,"

Philomena shrugged carelessly. The three of them climbed down from their saddles. After making their horses comfortable, they sat in a circle to divide their weapons.

Philomena gladly took back her two curved swords, and immediately buckled them to their proper place at her side. Philip accepted his three swords, happily assessing his favorite which was a broad sword with a cross guard, hilt and pommel shaped as a single soaring dove. Lark received his bow and quiver as well as the sword Philip had bequeathed him. What was left in the sack were about eight various knives and daggers which Philip and Philomena began fussing over.

"No, Philomena! That pair is mine," said Philip annoyed, snatching the two daggers from his sister.

"You are so dimwitted sometimes! Mine are the ones without leather on the hilts. These ones *have* leather," said Philomena, waggling the other pair of daggers at Philip which indeed had leather wrapped hilts. "Now give me back my daggers," she demanded, tossing the daggers at Philip and seizing the ones she claimed to be hers.

Lark listened to them in silent amusement while he restrung his bow. The bow, as he had said before, was a mere hunting bow and not very powerful. It was strong enough for small game, but not suitable for battle. No wonder why it hadn't effected the dragons, Lark thought ruefully. He slung the small bow across his chest and stood to buckle his sword about his waist. Looking back to Philip and Philomena, Lark smiled inwardly for the siblings were still sorting out their weapons.

"Now, you had the one with the green jewel," said Philip, tapping the mentioned green jewel that was embedded in a curved knife's pommel.

"No, I had the one with the blue jewel," said Philomena, seizing the knife with the blue jewel without hesitation. Philip grumbled under his breath as he stuffed the green jeweled knife into a sheath that hid in the folds of his coat beneath his left arm.

"What about this one then?" he asked, holding up the last blade that measured one and a half feet long.

"That's mine," said Philomena, grabbing the knife. Philip pursed his lips and clenched his hand irritably.

"Why do I feel that you've taken most of my knives?" he asked, forcing himself to sound patient.

Philomena cocked a smug smirk to him. "Come on, Philip. Everyone knows I carry more blades than you," she said with a giggle.

Huffing in surrender, Philip corked his mouth upsettingly. "It's not funny, Philomena. And who do you mean by everyone? There's no one who knows us except Lark," he grumbled.

Philomena shrugged unknowingly, sheathing the last of her knives. "Yeah I guess you're right. No one knows us but they will for sure if they ever cross my blades. And no, it's not funny," she said.

Philip shook his head and rolled his eyes hopelessly. Even Lark had to snicker at them as he sat back down.

"Speaking of funny," Philomena began remembering something and directing a curious look to Lark. "What were those natives talking about back in Staleon?"

Frustration and anger darkened Lark's features as he looked away.

Philip raised his eyebrows. "Here we go," he mumbled uncomfortably, ducking his head.

"You know, what they said about your father being-" said Philomena, but Lark cut her off, his gaze snapping back to her.

"I know what you're talking about," he said sharply. His smoldering stare and angry voice surprised Philomena. Checking his temper, Lark looked away and breathed in a steadying breath. "I'm surprised you didn't ask earlier," he said in a calmer tone.

"Is it true what they said?" asked Philomena.

Lark picked up a small stone and tossed it away getting ash on his fingers. "I don't know," he admitted gruffly.

Philip glanced sidelong at him, sensing the bitter incredulousness in his behavior. Philip couldn't blame him.

"You don't know if your father is the son of a chief and abandoned his people in a time of need?" Philomena asked insensitively. Lark lifted a hardened stare at her, his jaw set in a dangerous line. Philip winced, knowing Philomena had crossed a line.

"No, I don't," Lark replied levelly. Philomena considered him skeptically, but his level response clearly closed the topic. There was nothing left to say.

Pursing her lips and clearing her throat awkwardly, Philomena changed the subject. "So, what now? We should probably keep going," she said.

"I believe we deserve a short break," said Philip. "What we really deserve is some food," he added grudgingly, rubbing his growling stomach. It ached with emptiness, though he knew well enough that it was doubtful that they'd find anything edible in Poacher's Land. The land was dead after all.

"We can take an hour or so, but when we push through Poacher's Land we can't stop," said Lark, still moody from the previous conversation.

"Sounds good to me," Philip agreed. He looked to Philomena. "Take a rest, Philly. We'll wake you when it's time to go," he assured, gesturing for her to go and sleep.

Secretly relieved, Philomena nodded, her entire being suddenly aching for sleep. Only a few minutes later and she was sound asleep. Philip went over and covered her with her cloak.

"Shouldn't you rest as well," Lark suggested, feeling terribly drained himself.

Philip grinned over at him. "And shouldn't you, Lark? You've hardly slept since you joined us. I've gotten more rest than either of you. I can manage just fine. You can get some sleep," he said standing. He began collecting the dry brittle branches that littered the forest floor for a fire.

Instead of giving in to Philip's generous offer, which indeed was tempting, Lark went over to join him, helping gather the wood they needed.

"You are rather stubborn, aren't you," Philip commented when he noticed Lark helping him.

Lark pursed his lips. "You're one to talk. Your wound still hasn't healed and yet you still push yourself,"

"Runs in the family, I suppose," said Philip, squaring his shoulders.

"I know," Lark said shrewdly, his arms nearly loaded with wood already.

Philip glanced at him with a light smile. Noticing the deep hurt set in Lark's expression, Philip's smile faded apologetically. "Listen, Philomena didn't mean anything before about your father. She just . . . doesn't know how to handle sensitive matters,"

Inhaling glumly, Lark shook his head. "Its fine," He picked up another three pieces of wood. "I really don't know, I don't know what's true," he said morosely. The pain was evident in his voice.

"I can only imagine how difficult it is," Philip said. Lark lifted a quizzical stare at him. "At least Philomena and I know the truth of our past. It might not be the greatest truth, but at least we know where we came from,"

"If that truth really is true," Lark said cynically, carrying the gathered wood to where Philomena and their belongings were. Philip pursed his lips in a tight line, his eyes following Lark with a critical stare.

"What I'm trying to say," Philip went on patiently, following Lark. "Is that I feel sorry for you," he said, kneeling down and dumping the armful of wood on the ground. He met Lark's distrusting stare with a sincere expression.

"I hope you find the truth," Philip added kindly, helping pile a portion of the wood for a fire.

Lark brought out the flint and steel kit, and struck the rocks together. The bright sparks sprayed over the brittle wood, and flames lunged forth vigorously. "Even if the truth isn't what I want to know," he said tersely, the fire reflecting in his eyes.

"Truth hurts sometimes," said Philip, spreading his hands apologetically.

At this, Lark gazed faraway in to the fire immersed in his own thoughts. He had kept himself from thinking of what the natives had revealed to him. The possibility of it being true, that his father was the son of a chief and had left his people, ignited a fear in Lark so great that he preferred to hide from it. He actually was grateful at the moment to be on the borders of Poacher's Land with Philip and Philomena far away from Niche.

Sensing Lark needed time to contemplate over things, Philip kept the silence. He offered Lark a cloak and grabbed one for himself, wrapping it around his shoulders and huddling close to the fire for warmth. Even though it was still day time it was cold and dreary. The whole sky was blanketed by clouds.

Neither of them had the appetite to sleep despite the fact that they were tired. Across from them, Philomena had not stirred and remained sleeping soundly underneath her cloak. Philip smiled warmly at her.

"You love her very much, don't you?" asked Lark, having noticed Philip smiling at Philomena.

Philip looked around at Lark. "Despite her forward manner and cantankerousness, yeah I do," he said fondly. "We've been through a great deal together."

Lark nodded understandingly, remembering his own little sister and wondering if she was doing any better.

"It's just . . ." Philip trailed off. He shifted and cringed, longing to speak what was nagging at his mind.

"What?" Lark prompted. It took Philip a moment to reply.

"I had promised our father that I would keep her safe," he began. "I didn't realize that teaching her the things I made sure she learned would cause her to live like this,"

Lark picked up the implication quickly. "*You* are the reason why she acts like a boy?" he asked critically, not entirely astounded but somewhat taken aback by the confession.

Shamefully, Philip nodded in confirmation. "I thought that when I had forced our uncle to train her in combat, I was keeping my promise to our father. It never occurred to me then that it would only drag her further into this mess," he said, snapping a twig in half and bitterly tossing the broken pieces into the hungry flames.

"What did she think of the idea when you wanted her to learn combat?" asked Lark, pulling his cloak closer around him. He cautioned to keep his voice low as did Philip.

"Frankly, she didn't seem to care either way," Philip admitted, reminiscing back to his time spent in the comfortable yet stifling chamber in Tosh in which they had been imprisoned. "But the more Balin trained her, the more . . . fascinated she became of the way of the sword. She could never gain the physical strength of a man despite her efforts, but her speed and cleverness tipped the scale for her," A proud glint sparkled in Philip's eyes and a smile spread across his face as he spoke fondly of his warrior sister.

"You know she was the one who made sure we escaped from Tosh," Philip continued, looking to Lark. "It wasn't me or Balin who freed us, it was Philomena. She dressed herself as a lady and actually *flirted* with the guards. She stole the weapons and clothes we needed, and took the lead out of the castle. She had made herself so breathtaking that the guards were too distracted to realize what was happening," Philip laughed, remembering that night. Lark had to smile too, but then Philip's expression darkened and his smile faded.

"Of course when we were almost through the gates, the captain saw us," Philip's voice became grim. "Fighting broke out, and that was the first real action we had ever seen. Luckily our uncle taught us well. It was almost scary to find out how capable we were, and that doubles for Philomena. She was as able in the fight as any man would be. She'll never have a normal life because I made sure she knew how to defend herself," Philip's voice cracked and his hands balled in to fists.

Lark could literally feel Philip's regret, his pain, and his bitterness towards himself. It was a poison Lark knew had been festering deep down for a long time. Realizing his sincere guilt and regret, Lark's critical feeling towards Philip for teaching his sister to fight quickly subsided. He felt obliged to offer the supposed prince reassurance, but was unsure of how.

Philip smirked to himself half-heartedly. "I suppose if I hadn't forced her to know how to fight, she wouldn't have had to do what she did and she wouldn't be going through what she's going through now,"

Lark's brow furrowed at this. "Indeed. She would be a fragile lady like any other young girl if you hadn't made sure she knew how to defend herself," he said. Philip's brow pinched with stinging guilt, contemplating on what could have been.

"But she isn't just any other young girl," Lark went on in the most comforting tone he could manage. "She is your sister and I may have met you both only last week, but I don't believe she'd have it any other way,"

Philip smiled warmly, relieved by Lark's words. "That's true," he said, turning his smile to Philomena. "Thanks," he added, directing a grateful look to Lark.

Lark squared his shoulders modestly and poked at the fire with a spare stick. Philip peered at him with sudden curiosity, his smile lingering on his features.

"Do you miss home at all?" Philip asked.

"Home?" Lark said with a frown, looking at him with an almost startled expression.

"Yeah, home; where you live back in Niche. Don't you miss it?" asked Philip.

Lark winced as he rolled the thought of missing home over in his mind. "What brought this about?"

Philip shrugged. "Just answer the question," he said.

Bewilderment scrambled Lark's train of thought. He took a moment to collect an answer. "I don't know," he finally said sincerely. "In a way I miss my family, but part of me is glad to be away from Niche,"

"Well, maybe it is because Niche is too small for you," Philip said pensively, resting his chin in his palm.

"Too small?" Lark repeated doubtfully.

"Small, as in it doesn't provide much opportunity for someone like you," Philip explained matter-of-factly.

Lark snorted with dry laughter. "Someone like me belongs in the stables or the fields alongside my father,"

"Come on Lark," said Philip, directing a perceptive grin at him. "You don't really see yourself mucking stalls for the rest of your life do you?"

"It's where I belong, so it's where I'll stay," said Lark in a stony tone that warned Philip to drop the matter.

Philip's face fell with disappointment and he switched his gaze to the fire to stare into the flickering flames. The fire hissed and crackled as one of the logs fell, breaking in half and slowly crumbling away into ash.

Somewhat regretful that he had spoken harshly, Lark felt obliged to restore the more conversational atmosphere. "What about you? Do you miss home?" he asked. Philip stiffened and his expression hardened as a thousand memories flashed through his mind; not all of them good.

"Hmm, I sort of forgotten what home is like," Philip mused slowly.

"You do remember home though," said Lark.

"I do, I just don't remember . . . what it feels like to be home," Philip replied in the same drawn out way. His somewhat saddened expression showed Lark how truly lost he felt on the subject.

"We've been training so hard for so long that it's all we know anymore. We know how to handle a sword or throw a dagger or pass by someone without being seen, but feeling at home is something foreign to us. I think that last night at Caelum . . . will be a scar we will always bare," said Philip, taking an intact of breath as more memories flooded his conscious.

"What happened?" Lark ventured, not sure if Philip would tell him or not.

Philip considered him with a curious frown. "You really want to know?"

"Yes I do," Lark said with a nod.

Philip was silent for a moment as he weighed things out. When he decided to enlighten Lark of the truth, he collected his thoughts and began the story.

"It all started in Woodrid, in Castle Terra where our uncle resided. Salvador had been Balin's advisor, under a false name. On the night that our aunt was giving birth, Salvador confronted Balin and his true identity was revealed. Under threats from Salvador, Balin took him to Caelum. The guards at Caelum allowed Balin entry of course, and in doing so emitted their enemies as well.

To make a long story short, Salvador threatened our father with our lives and so persuaded him to surrender. Salvador had planned to kill me then and there, but Balin had cut a deal with him; I would be trained in combat while under house arrest until brought back to Caelum to fight Avador to the death. Of course our uncle hadn't trusted Salvador from the beginning, which is way we planned our escape years ahead. So here we are now, at least two of us," said Philip, placing another log into the fire.

Lark nodded, his brow slightly furrowed as he took this all in. Whether Lark believed the story or not, Philip couldn't tell.

"And that scar of yours that's on your forearm," said Lark, gesturing to Philip's right arm where he knew the white scar of a double beamed cross was. "I assume that was Salvador's work as well,"

Philip looked down at his arm, the scar covered by his sleeve burning heavily into his skin. "Salvador's natives did it on our way to Tosh," he said.

"Most likely for Salvador to identify you," Lark said thoughtfully.

"I suspect so," Philip agreed. "Philomena has been hounding on me to alter it, but it would be pointless. I don't plan on running away from this, and it wouldn't matter anyway now that Avador has seen me,"

This was understandable for Lark, though he could easily imagine Philomena being thoroughly frustrated with Philip over the matter.

"Why'd you want to know more, Lark? I thought you didn't believe us before," said Philip, looking expectantly over at him. Chewing at his lip, Lark suddenly felt frustrated and conflicted. "I can't say that I believe your story, but I think I see that you are good people, and honest enough,"

"If that were so then you'd believe every word we have said without a doubt," Philip said with a smirk and a clever glint in his eyes. Lark grimaced with frustration. Sometimes Philip had a way of turning things around for you to regret having ever said anything on the matter, somewhat like his quick tempered sister. "You know what I mean," Lark said thickly. "I feel like I can believe you, but everything you've claimed to be true is difficult to believe. What I have thought to be true about this country you're telling me is all a lie. It's just a lot to take in,"

"Yeah," Philip said with a sigh. "I guess that's what happens when you knock someone out, kidnap him and pretty much force him to help you," he added with a crooked grin.

"That too," Lark agreed lightly. A companionable silence settled over them, warding off the dreary emptiness of Poacher's Land. For the first time in his life, Lark felt he had gained a friend and a true one at that.

"Go get some sleep, Lark," Philip finally said. "I'd feel terrible if you remain sleep deprived because of me,"

Lark was going to argue, saying no matter how much rest they could get they'd still feel sleep deprived, but he was far too tired. Eventually, after a bit more urging from Philip, he suddenly found himself beneath the rough but warm covers of his blankets.

It did not matter how ashy the ground was, how cold the night was, or even the fact that a rock was jabbing him in the side; sleep was impossible to evade.

Once Lark had drifted to sleep, Philip let out a long drawn out sigh and pulled his cloak closer. The night was deathly silent. Not a sound came from an owl, a fox, or even a cricket. Even the crackling of the fire seemed to be keeping as quiet as possible. Dipping a hand beneath his jerkin and tunic, Philip brought out the cord about his neck. He fingered the simple wooden cross, remembering his father and the promise he had made. Saying a silent prayer, Philip tucked the cross away feeling his promise weighing heavily upon his shoulders.

32

Avador and his company had traveled hard and covered a great distance from the time they had lost the prince and his companions till now. Only a day and a half worth of fierce traveling lay between them and Ezleon City. Avador's determination to intercept the prince kept his company at a blazingly rapid pace.

Since they had come a great way in a short period of time, Avador finally brought them to a halt, deciding they deserved a small respite. Gratefully, they all dismounted from their weary steeds, their own legs wobbly from being in the saddle so long. After tending to the needs of their faithful horses, they tended to themselves with cold water and dried pork.

Both men and horses were exhausted. Their leader however showed no signs of weariness. Instead he sat in silence staring straight ahead, his attention fixed on his unfinished mission. His youthful features were draught with anxiety and restlessness. Everyone knew he was upset, so they gave him space.

When the sudden sound of approaching hooves reached their ears they stirred from their lounging postures. The sound had them snatching their weapons and facing the south where they sensed the unknown visitors coming from.

Avador had not moved an inch from where he sat on an ivy covered log. He simply watched the excitement with little interest.

The pounding of hooves came right on top of them without revealing their mysterious visitors. The native warriors frowned at one another, perturbed by this bafflement. Just as they thought that they might be facing ghost riders entered their spooked minds, the drumming slowed and the mountainous waterfall of ivy vines before them split apart to make way for four riders. The company raised their weapons at the ready, but as the four riders came forward they recognized Swift Deer and Silver Stream escorting Balin and K'smet between them.

An enormous tension lifted at the sight of their comrades and they exchanged relieved grins and even hearty laughs.

"It's about time you joined us," said Night Hawk relaxing his sword at his side and grinning at the new arrivals.

"About time you say?" scoffed Swift Deer, bringing his horse to a stop and slid down from his saddle. "You should tell that to yourselves. You left us in the dust. It's about time *you* all came to a stop for once," he added, helping K'smet down from his horse. Silver Stream followed suite and helped Balin. The two prisoners were herded into the center of the group and urged to sit amongst the company members making it impossible for them to try anything without being noticed.

Swift Deer and Silver Stream greeted their fellow warriors and happily accepted some dried pork from them.

Their captain watched with something resembling loathing.

"Don't get to comfortable. We'll be leaving shortly," Avador said moodily.

Swift Deer and Silver Stream were taken aback by his tone. Everyone else though was not at all surprised and stiffened nervously.

His brow furrowed, Swift Deer looked to Avador critically. "What happened with the prince?"

Balin tensed at this and listened closely. Avador ran his tongue fumingly over his teeth and glowered at Swift Deer.

"The prince managed to escape. Our tactic now is to intercept him," said Avador, turning his gaze away and trying to fight back his growing temper.

"Intercept?" Silver Stream questioned curiously. Avador flexed his jaw for the very subject was infuriating to him.

"The prince took the path to Poacher's Land," Night Hawk spoke up. "We would have caught up with him if I had not advised our captain to avoid Poacher's Land all together,"

"And if I had rigged the net right we would have had their hands bound before they could have gotten within a hundred feet of the very route that offered them an escape," said Avador angrily, standing and facing away from his company. The warriors shifted, sensing the shame as well as the boiling rage that radiated off Avador.

"You're saying this mess is your fault?" Swift Deer said audaciously.

"I'm saying I don't know!!!" Avador thundered, wheeling around and making Swift Deer flinch. Somehow, the company detected fear in their captain. He stood there, his chest heaving from his pent up anxiety. He flicked his dark eyes onto Balin and K'smet.

"But what I do know," Avador began coolly, stepping towards his captives. "Is that if either of you had anything to do with your beloved prince's escape, you're never going to see him again," Balin stared calmly back at him while K'smet scowled haughtily his nose wrinkled.

"How could they have caused anything to have gone wrong?" Swift Deer protested pointedly. "They were with me and Silver Stream the entire time and they were never out of our sight,"

"It's true, sir," Silver Stream concurred.

"Are you defending them?" Avador demanded, turning a dangerous glower on them.

Swift Deer shook his head in disbelief. "We're simply trying to put you straight on the matter,"

"I don't need you to put me straight," Avador grinded out heatedly, bringing his face only inches away from Swift Deer's.

"Their prince is far too precious to them. They would have found a way," Avador said flatly, turning back to the prisoners. He knelt in front of them and locked his gaze onto Balin.

"All hope is lost if the prince is in enemies hands, right? You love your nephew don't you Lord Balin. You wouldn't want anything to happen to him, or your lovely niece for that matter. Without them, there is no point in you resisting my father's reign," said Avador in a quiet tone.

The native warriors exchanged perturbed looks. Their captain's odd behavior was making them shift and itch nervously. Being a more independent and confident individual, Swift Deer was not disturbed by Avador's mood; he was disgusted.

"You sound just like him," he said.

"Like who?" Avador demanded sharply, averting his attention back on to Swift Deer with a crinkled brow.

"Like your father," said Swift Deer with a sharp gesture. His words had a stunning effect. All of the natives had agreed that their captain was nothing like the evil Salvador.

"You talk a great deal, pretending to be nothing like him but in truth you are exactly like him. No matter who you hurt in the process you're going to finish what you set your mind to and nothing will stop you," Swift Deer went on.

Avador stared, his darkened features lifting to be replaced with shaken shock. He hadn't realized that his frustration had caused his temper to run away from him. This realization settled upon Avador like a rock in a pond and had him surface from his maddened behavior.

"Swift Deer, leave him be," Night Hawk stepped in, feeling inclined to defend his captain.

"No," Avador objected with a wave of his hand, sounding as though he were coming out of a fog. "He's right, Night Hawk," he said in surrender.

Night Hawk suddenly looked worried as did several others of the company. The confliction and the sense of vulnerability was evident in Avador's features especially to Balin. He recognized Avador's feelings and understood them for he had felt the pain of them himself. What confused Balin was why of all people would the son of Salvador Corea feel this way.

Guilt and exhaustion tugging at him, Avador circled his gaze about his uneasy warriors. He could see that they were just as tired as he was. "We'll camp here for the night. Get a good's night's rest. We'll start again at first light," he said.

The company members shrugged and murmured agreeably. They began un-tacking the horses and unpacking their bedrolls almost cheerfully.

Stepping away from the group to some closely growing trees, Avador secluded himself so he might collect his thoughts somewhere quiet. The familiar rage still murmured deep within his chest. He knew this nearly uncontrollable anger came from his father. It was something he despised.

Dried leaves crunched from behind and Avador spun to find Night Hawk standing there. Avador closed his eyes and let out a relieved sigh. Night Hawk's brow pinched with deepening worry.

"Were you fearful that I was Swift Deer maybe," Night Hawk suggested, coming alongside the young captain.

Avador hesitated. "Swift Deer does not bother me," he said.

Night Hawk wasn't convinced, but said nothing. He lifted his gaze to the emerging stars. The bare tree limbs seemed to be trying to reach up and pluck the twinkling jewels from the velvet sky so they might wear them themselves.

"What do you make of it, Night Hawk?" Avador finally broke the silence.

"Capturing the prince you mean?" Night Hawk asked, looking back to Avador.

"Everything," Avador said, longing for reassurance.

Night Hawk pondered this for a moment. "It depends on what side you're looking from. Capturing the prince will settle things between you and your father. The rebels will then need to be subdued and the new authorities secured, after which my fellow warriors and I will be released from servitude and be free to return home," said Night Hawk, a smile lurking on his lips at the thought of home. Avador soaked this all up eagerly.

"But you know what your father is doing is wrong, Avador. He has destroyed many good lives and balances which cannot be ignored. Though all of the blame has been placed on King Paul for this tyranny, it is your father who is responsible," Night Hawk added sternly.

"And us as well, don't forget. We have undertaken many of the raids and torn down many forests. We are responsible for bringing pain to these people just as much as my father," Avador reminded glumly.

"Ah, yes we did. But we were merely following orders. We are nothing but tools to Salvador," said Night Hawk.

"Capturing the prince will win back our freedom, and hopefully we can begin mending the wrong we were forced to do," Avador said, the confidence in his voice restored.

Curiosity tugged at Night Hawk as he peered at the young captain he was becoming fond of. "You are quite intelligent despite your young age, and we have seen you grow. I am certain, when the time comes you will know what to decide to restore peace," he said surely.

At first, Night Hawk's carefully chosen words troubled Avador, but he felt certain that his loyal second in command was right.

Meanwhile, Balin and K'smet sat tiredly where they had been assigned too on the ivy covered ground. Though they were centered amongst the native warriors, the company was quite occupied with their own activities of settling down for the night. They were conversing in a lightened mood with one another, enough for Balin and K'smet to exchange quiet words.

"At least we accomplished what we had been hoping for," K'smet whispered. "Philip and Philomena are safe,"

Balin nodded. "For the most part,"

"Yes, with *my* help don't forget," Ramaro reminded cockily, sticking his snout out from K'smet's tunic. His beady eyes glittered with something beyond self recognition.

"We know already," K'smet hissed with annoyance, his nose crinkled. Ramaro scowled.

"And we're very grateful for your service," Balin said sincerely. "I know you are grateful, Lord Balin, but this arrogant knight here is not. He cannot handle the fact that someone twenty times smaller than him accomplished something he could not have with as much ease as I," Ramaro said smugly, shooting a poisonous glare at K'smet.

"Oh, you are such a fowl little beast," K'smet muttered.

Swift Deer, who was laying his bedroll close by, caught wind of their hushed voices and looked over to them. Sensing the native's gaze on them, Balin rotated his attention to him. The two of them met each other's gaze. No hatred, no bitterness, not even anger was exchanged between them. It was pity that they knew they were enemies.

Breaking eye contact with Swift Deer, Balin looked back to K'smet. "We should get some rest," he said. K'smet glanced over at Swift Deer who still watched them, and nodded in agreement. Silently, they did their best to make themselves comfortable for the night with bound hands. Ramaro slithered back inside the folds of K'smet's tunic and out of sight. Swift Deer breathed inward and went back to his bed roll.

Laying on his back and gazing up at the bare trees against the twinkling night sky, Balin felt the warmth of gratefulness that Philip and Philomena had escaped once more. It was a comfort to know they were safe and on their way to Caelum. Even so, the tiniest prick of fear nestled in the center of that gratefulness. A fear that Balin knew would grow with each passing day, for though he was certain that his niece and nephew were safe tonight, what about tomorrow?

33

Just when Lark caught sight of the trip wire glinting in the dim sunlight Philip snapped it against his boot. A creaking, groaning sound like that of a giant yawning drew their attention to the trees. Lark dreaded what was coming but it came anyway with an impressive swoosh: a rod of vicious spikes swinging down from the trees straight at them.

"Holy smokes!" said Philip wide-eyed.

"Get down!" Lark yelled, pushing Philomena to the ground. The rod of spikes swung over them with a deadly whoosh stirring their clothes and hair and sending their horses flying backwards. The rod swung over them a few more times, hissing through the air, determined to snatch them up on one of its sharp spikes. As if it felt defeated, the rod finally settled to a stop above them only hanging a foot over their heads.

"Phew," Philip breathed, lifting his face from the dirt. "That was a close one," he said, crawling out from under the rod. He helped Philomena and Lark and then brushed himself off.

"You didn't have to push me you know," Philomena said to Lark with an annoyed frown. "I could have handled myself just fine without you,"

"Next time move faster, because I might not be there to save you," said Lark, making Philomena scowl. "Let's just call it even, alright," he added, remembering the arrow she had saved him from.

Reluctantly, Philomena nodded curtly, and then busied herself with straightening her sword belt.

"Check this thing out," came Philip's voice. He was kneeling in front of the rod of spikes that had almost impaled them, peering at it with intrigue. "It looks like a mouthful of teeth only without the mouth," he said, putting a fingertip to one of the longer spikes.

"It looks like it's been kept busy," Philomena said with disgust, pointing out the dried blood that coated many of the murderous spikes.

"That's a kind way of saying that it's killed too many," Philip said bluntly, looking up from the spikes at her.

Lark came over to join them, feeling grateful and relieved that they had survived; yet when he took in the sight of the terrible trap, something more than anger washed over him. "This is definitely a poacher's trap," he said in a hollow voice.

"Is there any other kind?" Philomena questioned sarcastically.

"Poachers design their traps carefully to make sure that the animal doesn't get too . . . mangled. That way, they can sell the skins at market." explained Lark.

"That's kind of sick," said Philip, wrinkling his nose with disgust.

Lark agreed with a nod. "This trap has long, thin spikes," he noted, gesturing repulsively to the trap.

"Suggesting it's a poacher's," Philip figured.

"Yes, it most certainly is," said Lark, staring at the wicked thing. Hatred for the poachers reddened his face and set dark stones in his eyes.

"Well, this nasty thing doesn't need to hang around for its master to come back and reset it. Let's say we cut it down," Philip suggested with a hearty smirk.

They agreed.

"Lark, why don't you do the honors," said Philip, turning expectantly to him.

Pulling his sword from its sheath, Lark took great pleasure in chopping the rod of spikes from the ropes it swung on. Lark happily thought it was the most appropriate way to use his sword for the first time.

Together, they carried the heavy rod away to a spot where the land dipped inward like a bowl. They tossed the rod in and covered it with branches, leaves, and dirt. They buried it until they were sure no one, especially poachers, could easily find it. This pleased Lark, but he would never forget the blood stains of all the creatures the trap had killed.

"At least that nasty piece of work is out of service," Philip said, leading their horses to them.

"Too bad there's probably a hundred more of them in these woods, if you want to call it a wood," Philomena said gruffly. She accepted Coursio's reins from Philip who gave her a disapproving stare. What resembled saddened helplessness had washed over Lark at her words, and his usually quiet calmness sunk to simply being silent.

"What?" Philomena asked looking between them and not realizing what she had done.

"Never mind," Philip said, shaking his head and turning away. Lark followed, somewhat crestfallen. Philomena squared her shoulders and spread her arms in an innocent confused gesture before falling in behind them.

Moving onward, they discovered the black bleak heart of Poacher's Land. They were soon touring a living nightmarish array of sprung traps which, unfortunately, still clasped tightly onto their prey. The mangled carcasses of unrecognizable creatures lay impaled or strangled. Bones of those passed littered the ground.

"This is awful," said Philip, holding his nose from the stench. Lark and Philomena were silent, but they couldn't agree more with Philip as they scanned their trap-filled surroundings. Their horses stirred uneasily from the foulness that pulsed off everything around them. The Ashen Lands may have been unpleasant, Lark thought, but Poacher's Land stooped to intolerable. It was a living hell; a grave yard.

"It looks like the poachers just laid out their traps here. They didn't even care about . . ." Philip hesitated, not sure how to put his thoughts into words that wouldn't make them hurl. "About scavenging,"

"If the poachers are going through a rough time, they may have just abandoned everything. The dragons said that they were not sure what was happening here anymore. Maybe their plan of cutting off the poachers is working," said Lark, his insides beginning to squirm uneasily.

They hoped this notion was correct and that the poachers had moved on, or even gone out of business.

Philomena's face had paled from the sights around them, and her whole body felt shaky. She took a few unsteady steps to keep up, only to break another trip wire she had failed to see. The sound snapped Lark and Philip's attention to her. She sucked in a breath as something crashed down from above, but she was too petrified to move. There was a meaty *smack!* And a gnarled carcass suddenly dangled an inch away from her face. Philomena jerked back with a scream, releasing Coursio's reins. Philip rushed towards her, and she slammed into him thoroughly frightened.

"Philly! It's okay," said Philip, wrapping his arms around her. She buried her face against his chest, the image of the mangled animal flashing over in her mind, silently torturing her.

"It's alright," Philip soothed, holding her tight.

Lark stepped swiftly forward and cut the poor creature down from the trap it had been entangled in. It landed with a dull thump at his feet. Gazing skyward, Lark saw ropes and cords hanging from the trees. Some of them ended with black claw-like hands.

Lark sheathed his sword, and looked back down to Philip. "We should get moving,"

"Good idea," Philip agreed.

They took up the reins of their horses and moved away from the traps. Philip kept a comforting arm around Philomena, assuring her that it would be okay and they were moving away from Poacher's Land. Lark led Coursio for her as well as his own horse ahead of her and Philip, keeping a watchful eye out for any traps in their path.

After being comforted by Philip for a time, Philomena was able to gather her wits and recover. She took Coursio back from Lark and walked alongside Philip, her usual abrasive personality deflated from her experience.

"I've never heard you scream like that before," Philip grinned. "You sounded like a girl,"

"Shut up," Philomena snapped, punching him in the arm and knocking him sideways. Philip rubbed his arm and laughed. Thankfully, she had hit his good arm. His other arm and shoulder were still healing from being shot by the native's arrow, though thanks to Lark cauterizing it, it was healing rapidly.

Out of nowhere the faint noise of what sounded like chiming bells reached Lark's ears. Lark froze in his tracks and tilted his head to listen better. Philip and Philomena stopped behind him, confused.

"What's the matter, Lark? Another trap?" Philip asked, glancing around him, expecting to see something large and sharp swinging down from the trees or springing from the ground.

"Let me guess, it's something that is going to attempt to kill us," Philomena said sarcastically and with slight boredom.

"No," Lark said distractedly, straining to hear the chimes. "Its . . . it's more like . . ." he trailed off. Philip and Philomena waited patiently, though anticipation was boring into their features.

"Like something is struggling in a trap nearby," Lark finally finished, catching wind of the chimes again.

"You mean something that's *alive*?" Philomena questioned, astounded. Lark nodded, trying to determine which way the chimes were coming from. He turned to the east, and the bells chimed strongly. "It's this way," he said, setting off in that direction.

Philip followed without question. Philomena stared after them with her jaw set in angry disbelief. "Are you serious?" she questioned, bewildered. "We have no idea what it is yet we're walking towards it? This is backwards!"

The boys ignored her and only continued to walk away.

"Do I hear bells?" Philip frowned.

"They are attached to the trap. It lets the poachers know when they've caught something," Lark explained.

"Oh, okay," Philip said enlightened.

Behind them, Philomena huffed angrily and stomped her foot. She hated being ignored. Muttering under her breath, she went after them, not having much of a choice.

Following the sound of the chiming bells, they trod through a surprisingly thick yellow grass that reached passed their shoulders. Thorny bristles in the grass bit at their skin and tugged at their garments. Once they cleared the tall yellow grass, they picked their way over some thick tree roots, and ducked beneath several curtains of a strange trailing brown moss that was nowhere near as pleasant as glitter moss. Various winged insects flew out from the mossy coverage and buzzed irritably around their heads. One particular insect that looked like a giant gnat bit Philip in the neck. Philip cursed and squashed the bug with a slap of his hand.

"Hasn't the cold killed these things yet?" he grumbled irritably, swatting more of the insects away from his face. Lark and Philomena were too busy battling the insects and trailing moss to offer a reply.

Gratefully, they pushed through the last of the strange brown moss, and came to a small clearing that was filled with a strange sight. Thin cords of string that were barely discernible criss-crossed in a confusing pattern before them and disappeared up into the trees or behind tree trunks. What lay beyond the criss-crossing cords was a sack hanging from the trees drawn together by its edges like a pouch with a drawstring. Something was wriggled inside, desperate to escape. The chiming bells that had led them there danced and rang against the wiggling sack. A disturbed gurgle emitted from the poor creature as it struggled to be free.

"Well, whatever it is, it's alive," said Philip.

"Yeah, whatever it is. We have no way of knowing what it is exactly," Philomena said pointedly, staring almost contemptuously at the wriggling sack.

"It will certainly die if we leave it," said Lark, watching the sack with pity. Philomena turned an outraged look on him.

"Are you crazy? Don't tell me that you're going to waste your time trying to save that thing," Philomena blurted out flabbergasted.

"I'm thinking about it," Lark said absently. He knelt down to study the cords that zigg-zagged before them. Philomena gawked at Lark's back. She turned an expectant look onto Philip, her expression clearly propelling him to force Lark to leave the trap and the creature caught in it alone. Philip's response though was a helpless shrug. Philomena snarled at him. They didn't have time for this nonsense, she thought.

"This is a typical cord maze," said Lark, peering closely at the cords.

"A what?" asked Philip.

"A cord maze. Poachers use them to discourage other poachers from stealing whatever animal is caught in their trap," Lark explained.

"Can you disarm it?" asked Philip. Philomena shot a glare at him.

Lark quirked his mouth thoughtfully. "The thing about cord mazes is that they are all different depending on the individual. The only way of knowing how to disarm it is if you're the poacher who rigged it,"

"Of course," Philomena said sarcastically, folding her arms and shifting her weight to the side.

"What makes these things dangerous anyway? They look pretty harmless from where I stand," said Philip, cocking a smug look on the seemingly harmless cords. He put a hand to his sword pommel like he might just pull out his blade and start swinging. Lark casted a disapproving look at him. "If you were to touch one of these cords let alone cut one of them anything could happen,"

"Anything?" Philomena asked skeptically. Lark nodded.

"So you could tug on one of these cords and the ground could fall out from underneath our feet," said Philip, sounding both irritable and almost fascinated at the same time.

"You could say that," Lark agreed with a casual shrug of his shoulders. He looked to the still wriggling sack that contained the unfortunate creature snagged in the trap. The creature emitted another pitiful cry that tugged at Lark's conscious. He could hear the fear in the animal's voice. In that instant, Lark made up his mind.

"Hold this," he said, handing the reins of his horse to Philip. He unslung his bow and quiver from his shoulder and hung them on his saddle pommel. Philomena shook her head and ran her tongue fumingly over her teeth.

"Here, Philly," Philip said in turn, giving Philomena the reins of his and Lark's horses. Philomena gaped at him in disbelief. "But Philip-" she protested. Philip cut her short.

"I can't just let him do this on his own, Philomena," he said in a tone that told her he was set in his decision.

"You shouldn't put yourself in unnecessary danger. You're the prince, not some forest warrior. You're far more important than some dumb creature caught in a trap," Philomena said under her breath so Lark couldn't hear her words.

"Your concern is most flattering, sister," Philip grinned. "I'll be fine," he assured her, gripping her shoulder.

Philomena growled irritably, her face reddening. "This is ridiculous," she muttered, turning a blaming glare on Lark.

Lark held her gaze for a moment and then looked away to hide his opposition. He didn't like the idea of Philip aiding him anymore than Philomena. He didn't want to be responsible for Philip being hurt or killed, especially if he really was the prince. Following Lark's example, Philip stripped off his belt of sheathed swords and hung them on his saddle pommel.

"Okay," he said, rubbing his hands together. "How do we do this?"

"Very carefully," Lark replied smartly. Philip raised an eyebrow at him. "Just don't touch the cords," Lark added.

With great care, Lark stepped over the first cord and slowly maneuvered inside the complicated maze. Philip followed tentatively, his warrior's blood pulsing within him and making it difficult to keep calm and steady. Philomena watched from where she stood with the three horses, nervously shifting her weight from one side to the other.

Gradually, Lark and Philip advanced further inside the cord maze. They ducked and twisted, leaned and slid to avoid coming in contact with the cords. Sometimes they came within centimeters of the cords which seemed to laugh menacingly as they just barely passed.

They reached the center, and somehow the cords seemed to grow closer together. The two of them slowed their pace, holding their breath every time they wove around a tight space that brought them uncomfortably close to the cords.

Philip ducked underneath a waist-high cord, bending so low his nose nearly touched the dirt ground. He slid forward and breathed inward with relief to have made it, but he did not perceive Lark right in front of him. Consequently, Philip bumped into him. Lark stumbled, and the cord closest to him snapped against his chest. A black dart whizzed towards him from out of the dead trees.

Sucking in a breath, Lark jerked back and the dart flashed by, thudding harmlessly into a nearby tree.

Yet Lark's reflex only caused him to break another cord. A ballad of thronging sounds accompanied the whistling of a volley of arrows.

"Down!!!" yelled Philip, yanking Lark to the ground. The arrows flew over their heads, peppering the dead trees. Philomena grimaced and bit at her nails.

"I don't like arrows," Philip muttered. He shifted slightly and a third cord snapped. They looked to each other, horrified. Something clicked beneath them and both boys cursed. They vaulted to their feet just as vicious spikes sprang out of the ground where they had just been with a solid *clang*!

They paid no mind to avoiding the rest of the cords and pelted towards the sack together, spikes springing from the ground in their wake and more arrows flying out from the trees. Philomena could have pulled her hair out as she watched from the safety of the opposite side.

The last set of spikes snagged the toe of Lark's boot and sent him sprawling face first into the dirt. He lay there for a moment, his whole body tingling with anticipation. He discerned no whoosh, no whistle, and no click. The poacher's traps had all been spent.

"That's one way to get through an obstacle like that," said Philip, not even breathing hard. He offered a hand to Lark and heaved him to his feet. Lark cringed from stiffness. Pain shot up his leg from a long cut on his shin, most likely from the spike that had tripped him.

"You alright?" asked Philip.

"I'm fine. You?"

"Just another day in paradise," Philip shrugged.

Lark looked at him. His nonchalant air after what they had just been through made it seem like they had just returned from a stroll in a garden. They turned to survey the disruption of traps they had caused and their eyebrows went up. Where the cord maze had been there was now a small field of spikes, many of them splattered with dry blood. The dead trees that lined the spike field bristled with numerous arrows and darts.

"Very nicely done," Philomena called to them sarcastically.

"You try dodging cords that are so close together there may as well be a brick wall there," Philip shot back.

Philomena rolled her eyes and gave a dismissive gesture. "Just hurry up and do what you need to do," she said.

Averting their attention back to the sack, Philip and Lark found that the creature trapped inside had stopped moving. They shared a disturbed look, wondering if their efforts had all just been a waste of time. Philip pulled a knife from his belt and stepped forward to cut the sack down.

"Let me do it," said Lark.

"All yours," Philip said with a submissive gesture. He handed Lark his knife and moved aside.

Lark gripped the knife and began cutting away at the sack, making a large slit near the top. The net suddenly thrashed, and Lark's hand slipped inside. He felt a pair of claws brush his hand, and saw a flash of brown patterned fur. Lark yelped and jerked back.

"What?" Philip asked in alarm. Lark winced and lifted his hand. Three bright red scratches were etched into his skin just below his thumb.

"Little bit feisty, huh," Philip said considerably, fixing a stare on the sack. His hand instinctively dropped to his sword.

"It's not his fault. He's just scared, and I know what he is. He's an ocelot," said Lark, putting his scratched hand to his mouth.

"I don't know what that is," Philip admitted with a frown.

"It's a small forest cat. This one is young, just a cub. He shouldn't be away from his mother yet," Lark explained, directing a pitying look to the sack where the ocelot cub remained inside.

Philip nodded with pursed lips. "So what do we do?"

Lark shook his head uncertainly, pondering on what was best to do for the cub.

"What's taking you two so long?" came Philomena's impatient voice from across the field of spikes.

Galvanized into making a quick decision, Lark squared his shoulders and spread his hands submissively. "I guess the best thing we can do for him is free him," he said.

"Right," Philip agreed. He received his knife back from Lark and quickly hacked through the rope that held the sack suspended in the air. Lark held onto the sack so it wouldn't drop with the cub, careful not to get scratched again.

Once Philip cut the sack free, Lark gently but quickly laid it on the ground. They backed away a few steps and the ocelot cub shot out from the folds of the sack. Not even wasting the time to look behind him, the cub scurried to the dead trees and out of sight.

Lark heaved a sigh, glad to see the cub free. Still, he felt a pestering ache that made him wish he could do more.

"That wasn't so hard," Philip said happily, sheathing his knife and placing his hands on his hips. He looked to Lark and noted his regretful expression. "We did what we could, Lark. Most people wouldn't even think about helping him the way we just did. At least he's free. He's a wild animal. He'll find his way,"

"Yeah," Lark agreed huskily. What Philip said made sense, he thought.

Philip studied him for a moment. "Come on. We should get going," he said. Lark nodded and pried his gaze from the way the ocelot had gone. He started back with Philip, carefully picking their way around the spikes they had triggered to surface.

"Are you two finally ready to go?" Philomena asked when they reached her. "We've wasted enough time doddling around the way it is," she added with annoyance.

"Don't be so annoyed, Philly," Philip smiled at her as he took back Nimbius' reins. "We did something good. And yes, we are ready to go,"

"It's about time," Philomena said moodily. She tossed Lark Spear's reins and shot a scowl at him before turning to climb onto Coursio. Lark frowned at her attitude, still thinking about the ocelot cub, but he deciphered the message she sent him in that stare: *if anything bad had happened to Philip it would have totally been your fault.*

Lark sniffed disdainfully and shook his head wondering if he'd be able to survive Philomena's abrasive behavior much longer. He and Philip swung up onto their horses and the three of them rode back the way they had come.

34

They walked the rest of the day and most of the night just to get through Poacher's Land. After all, there would have been no reasonable argument that could have convinced them to spend the night in that nightmarish place.

When Poacher's Land was finally behind them, the mangled dead trees were suddenly gone from their view. The bare trees and dry brush of winter once again surrounded them with comforting arms, and the bed of autumn leaves on the ground was like a warm blanket compared to the ashen ground they had just traveled over. The constant tension that Poacher's Land had created within them lifted and they gratefully sank to the ground, exhausted.

It was very early in the morning, still dark. The stars winked above and the shimmering moon was low. Philip, Philomena, and Lark lay sprawled on the ground beside each other, far too drained to move. Their horses moved over to the trees and hungrily began to devour what vegetation remained from the frost.

"How faraway is Ezleon now?" Philomena asked tiredly.

"About a day," Lark replied hoarsely. Philomena groaned for a day's worth of traveling seemed far too much right now.

"Excellent," said Philip, sitting up. By some miracle he didn't sound tired at all. "We can rest for a couple hours and start again in the morning,"

"It is morning," Lark said grudgingly, his eyes closed.

"Later morning," Philip corrected with a dismissive gesture. "We can reach Ezleon by tomorrow evening," he said cheerfully.

"Today," Philomena and Lark both corrected.

"Whatever," Philip said carelessly. "Sound like a plan?" he asked.

"It sounds great, Philip. Now can you please be quiet so we can sleep," Philomena moaned.

No arguments came from Philip, and he happily obliged her request. In the silence, Lark and Philomena easily drifted to sleep. The freedom to rest even if it was just for a couple hours was enough to content them. They didn't bother to unpack their bed rolls or cloaks, or even unbuckle their swords from their waists. They simply fell asleep where they lay.

Sleep did not befall Philip though. Instead, he reluctantly pushed himself to his feet and went about unsaddling their horses. He replaced their bridals with rope halters and watered them. After making sure each horse was well, Philip went back to where Lark and Philomena were sleeping and settled back down between them with a sigh. An owl hooted in the trees above. There was no real need to keep watch, Philip figured as he closed his eyes. They would have to wake soon enough anyway. In a matter of seconds, Philip was asleep.

While the three young travelers slept soundly, oblivious to their surroundings, the sun crept closer and closer to the horizon coloring the sky with cool pinks and yellows. The rays of sun poured onto them, and birds began to sing.

Lark was the first to stir. His weary mind gradually lifted out of his deep slumber. As he woke, he became aware of something warm nestled beside him. Feeling that whatever it was was soft and furry, cuddled in the nook of his arm, and definitely alive. Lark could feel the animal breathing deeply.

Frowning, Lark opened his eyes and peered down to find a small ball of light brown and white fur. Lark yelped and the creature jerked awake, its yellow eyes flying open. Philomena quickly sat up, pulling a knife out.

"What's wrong?!" she asked in alarm. Her voice was slurred from sleep. She in turn woke Philip who yawned and blearily blinked his eyes.

Lark was too shocked to speak. He stared at the animal who stared back with bright eyes. Looking at the creature for a moment, Lark's brow pinched in recognition. It was the ocelot cub he and Philip had rescued from the trap earlier. The ocelot cub sniffed curiously at Lark, its innocent stare locked on him as if questioning why he had been so frightened.

"Is there something after us again?" Philip yawned with little interest, running a hand tiredly over his tousled hair. Lark looked helplessly over at him. When Philip finally averted his attention onto Lark, his eyes widened in alarm at the sight of the animal. He scrambled for his sword.

"Don't," Lark managed, holding up a hand to stop him. Philip frowned, his reflex tingling as he fought against it. He peered closely at the creature.

"Well, all be, it's the ocelit," Philip grinned.

"Ocelot," Lark corrected.

"Too early for that," said Philip, still looking fondly at the cub. The ocelot stared back as it had done with Lark. When Philip stretched a hand out to the cub, he made a chirping sound and licked at Philip's fingers. The cub yawned, exposing his sharp needle-like teeth and settled back down.

Both Lark and Philip were thrilled. Philomena on the other hand was not so excited. She let out an irritable sigh and closed her eyes once more. She let herself fall back on the warm area of ground she had been sleeping on, her knife landing at her side clutched limply in her hand.

Over the next fifteen minutes, Philip and Lark took turns petting their new animal friend. The cub's fur was soft, and beautiful. His back and sides were a sandy brown patterned with black chain-like spots and lines. His belly, chest and throat were white. He was about the size of a house cat, but Lark assured that he would grow to the size of a small hound.

"Shouldn't we give him a name?" Philip suggested.

Lark shrugged. He had never named anything in his life. "You'll have to make it a girl's name," he said.

Philip's bottom lip protruded and his eyebrows lifted incredulously. "It's a girl?"

Lark nodded in confirmation. Gazing pensively up at the trees, Philip thought for a long moment. He tossed parts of names around, mumbling thoughtfully under his breath. He drummed his lips and circled his gaze about them looking for inspiration.

"Oh do take longer," came Philomena's dry remark. "It is a very important decision to name a furry fuzz ball that just won't go away,"

Lark scowled at her around Philip. She was still sprawled on the ground with her eyes closed. Philip paid no mind to her, and continued to contemplate a name. Lark wondered how he found the patience to tolerate his infuriating sister.

"Oh, I got it!" Philip said excitedly, snapping his fingers. He turned to the ocelot cub still dozing at Lark's side. "How about Arican,"

Philomena snorted amusedly. "That's not even a real name," she said, propping herself on her elbows to look at Philip and Lark. "It is now," Philip retorted mildly. Philomena rolled her eyes and laid back down.

The name had a ring to it, Lark had to admit, and once it was said it stuck. In that instant, Arican became part of their group. The little cub made herself at home with her chosen guardians, and treated them as if she had always been in their company. She let them stroke her, and swatted at a twig that Philip wiggled before her pink nose.

After spending a few minutes with the newly named ocelot, Philip's stomach grumbled with a hungry growl. Lark looked to him with little surprise. Philip bashfully put a hand to his empty stomach and shrugged his shoulders helplessly.

"We haven't eaten in two days. There's no doubt we are all hungry," said Lark figuratively. "I'm sure I can find something for us out here," he added, casting an evaluating gaze about them.

A light breeze blew. It rattled the brittle brush and whispered through the bare tree branches above. The cool scent of winter was carried on the breeze and nipped at their faces. The waving grass excited Arican and the cub lowered herself to the ground to pounce.

"Are you going to make that grub stew of yours again?" Philip asked cheerfully. His excitement for Lark's stew perturbed Philomena, who unlike her brother, did not enjoy the slimy taste of grubs and worms.

"That ocelot cub of yours looks fat enough," she suggested with implication, sitting upright.

"No!" Lark and Philip objected. Philomena raised her hands in a surrendering gesture.

"Sorry," she said sarcastically. Lark scowled at her. "But we have to eat something," she added matter-of-factly.

"Get a fire going," Lark said bluntly as he rose to his feet. He wrapped the cloak Philip let him borrow about his shoulders. "I'll be back," He started off towards the surrounding trees with Arican padding after him at his heels.

Lark was out of sight before Philomena could argue, materializing amongst the trees in his native fashion. Philomena didn't have much of a choice but to do as he had asked, or more like commanded. She grumbled with annoyed defiance, making Philip smirk with amusement.

"I'll collect some wood," he said standing and doing his best to hide his grin. Philomena grumbled some more before reluctantly getting to her feet and turning towards their horses to retrieve the flint and steel kit. But when she came to their saddles and saddlebags, her brow creased. Their saddlebags were sprawled messily on the ground like someone had gone through them and then threw them away. Their saddles were caked with mud and the stirrups were missing. She knelt down and peered inside one of the saddlebags and found it was empty. Frantically, she checked the other saddle bags and they too were empty.

"Philip, where's all of our stuff?" asked Philomena, her anxiety growing. She still fumbled through the saddle backs with hurried movements.

"On the ground over there," said Philip, his back to her as he began loading his arms with sticks and twigs.

"I *know* that," Philomena said emphatically, tossing aside the saddlebags. "Our *stuff* is gone,"

Philip frowned. "What?" He turned and went over to Philomena. His eyebrows lifted in astonishment at the sight of their muddy saddles and their obviously vacant saddlebags. Philomena stood and stared at him expectantly, looking quite disturbed.

Philip's mouth hung open, stunned, as he stared at their tampered equipment for the longest time. "I put everything there," he finally stuttered with a weak gesture.

"I'm pretty sure our saddlebags were filled the last time I checked, Philip," Philomena said pointedly, sounding upset.

"I know! Everything's gone!" Philip said flabbergasted, his voice rising.

"I can see that!" Philomena said steely.

"Do you think someone just came along and stole everything?" Philip questioned, casting his bewildered gaze around.

"How should I know? You were the one who unsaddled the horses last night. You should have kept watch," Philomena argued heatedly.

"I was tired!" Philip raged defensively, glowering at Philomena and letting the wood he had gathered fall to the ground with a clatter.

"We were all tired!" Philomena stormed.

"My point exactly," Philip said, with a matter-of-fact shrug of his shoulders.

They glared at one another, their faces flushed with frustration. There was no argument left to fuel the brawling exchange between them, so they stood silently glaring at each other and glancing about them from time to time. The situation that all of their possessions were gone was quite problematic and planted a weight of discomforting tension upon them.

Dry rustling sounded, and Lark stepped out from the thick of the woods. His pouch was in his hands and plump from his time searching for edible things the wood had to offer. Arican came trotting close behind him with a piece of pine bark in her mouth. Lark directed an inquisitive look to Philip and Philomena, who remained standing before the mangled saddles and saddlebags.

"I thought I asked you to start a fire," said Lark, glancing at the ground around him where he expected a fire to be.

"We were going about that," Philip said diffidently, scratching the back of his head.

"Only someone took all of our things from our saddlebags and messed up our saddles," Philomena said brashly, folding her arms and tilting an annoyed stare at their remaining belongings. Lark quirked his mouth uncertainly. His brow creased when his gaze rested on their three horses. "Don't you find it strange that if *someone* took your stuff that they left the horses behind," Lark reasoned, gesturing to their steeds. Arican slumped on the ground at Lark's feet, and chewed on her prized bark. Philip and Philomena rotated their gaze onto the dozing horses.

"What's your point?" Philomena asked demandingly, her brow lowered with irritation.

Understanding though dawned on Philip. "If it wasn't someone it was something," he said thoughtfully. Philomena suddenly appeared outraged.

Lark dipped his head in agreement, and moved over to join them. Arican scrambled clumsy to her feet and hurried after him, forgetting her piece of bark. Reaching the mud filled saddles and the sprawled saddle bags Lark knelt before them and studied the ground closely with a scrutinizing expression. Philip and Philomena watched him for a passing moment.

"Do you really think you'll be able to figure out who stole our stuff by staring at the ground?" Philomena questioned harshly, boring a critical frown into Lark's back.

Lark could feel the sting of her sharp stare which made him extremely uneasy. "Do you have a better idea?" he shot back without looking over his shoulder at her.

The corners of Philomena's mouth twitched with resent. She shot a haughty glare at Philip when she noticed the smirk plastered on his face. Philip cleared his throat and looked back to Lark, though his amused grin did not totally disappear.

After another minute or so, Lark deciphered the confusing marks imprinted on the ground. "Imphoids," he mused out loud, touching the tracks in the ground.

"What the hell are imphoids?" Philomena snapped impatiently. Philip gave her a chiding look.

"Small creatures of the woodlands," Lark said, ignoring Philomena's blunt remark. He straightened from his kneeling position. "They are quite intelligent, but they enjoy the occasional prank," he added, glancing around.

"Prank? As in stealing someone's things and covering their saddles with smelly mud," Philip figured.

"They've been known to steal," Lark said, nodding. "They find it rather amusing to watch people flip out over their belongings being stolen,"

"It might be funny to them, but I'm definitely not amused," Philomena said irritably, placing her hands on her hips. Her face flushed with anger again.

"Can't we find them?" Philip asked, turning to Lark.

Lark squared his shoulders helplessly. "If they want to be seen then they'll show themselves eventually,"

Giggling suddenly reached their ears. They exchanged curious looks and they swung searching gazes about them. Finding no one to their sides, in front or behind them, they exchanged dumbfounded frowns. Their perplexity only caused the giggling to heighten. Philomena was obviously frustrated, the giggling contorting her features with irritation. Lark's brow pinched ponderingly, and he lifted his eyes to the tree branches above them. Philip and Philomena followed his gaze, and they stared in wonderment, for on the large tree branch stretching out above them sat four small beings.

The four beings shook the branch with their giggling, and they peered down at them with laughing yellow eyes. Their skin was a light brown blushed with pink, and they appeared to be dressed in feathery, auburn colored outfits that even when up to their heads and framed their childish features. They swung their skinny legs and bare feet dangling over the branch.

"Are those?" Philip questioned wonderingly.

"Imphoids," Lark confirmed.

They stared up at the giggling creatures. The imphoids stared back with mischievous grins. They started to exchange whispers, cupping their hands about their mouths so the young travelers couldn't hear. The imphoid in the middle suddenly appeared angry and he shoved his fellow imphoid next to him who had been whispering in his ear.

The imphoid yelped, and wind-milled his skinny arms to regain his balance but to no prevail. A brown tunic fluttered down from his lap, and a shiny object flashed in the morning light as it dropped to the ground. Philip, Philomena and Lark glanced down at the fallen objects before looking back up to watch the one imphoid follow his treasures in their descent, flipping over in the air twice. The other two imphoids squealed with alarm and bombarded their friend with disapproving remarks.

Philip, Philomena, and Lark watched with stunned expressions as the imphoid fell. Though just when they thought he would slam on the ground and probably break a leg, the imphoid stretched out his arms and long feathers extended from his forearm passed his elbow. The feathers shot out and caught the light breeze, breaking his rapid descent and gliding him softly to the ground where he landed with an elegant grace.

Straightening, the imphoid directed a curious look up at Philip, Philomena, and Lark with a hint of mischievousness glinting in his yellow eyes. The creature stood only three feet in height, though his structure resembled that of a person's. Seeing him up close, they found that the feathery outfit was not garments at all, but in fact auburn colored feathers that densely covered his body and head. Furry, pointed ears like that of a cat's stuck out from the top of his head and flicked occasionally.

"Welcome, human travelers," the imphoid said in a young, playful voice with a wide welcoming gesture.

35

The imphoid who had greeted them gave them a gracious bow and a crooked grin. Philomena considered him fumingly, becoming more impatient and irritated by the minute. Philip though looked at the imphoid with intrigue, not at all perturbed. Lark stood impassively between them.

"I'm Papk, and that's my colony in the tree," said Papk the imphoid, pointing to his fellow imphoids perched on the tree limb above him.

An empty water skin fell from the tree and smacked Papk in the back of the head.

"This is *my* colony, Papk," said the imphoid who had shoved Papk earlier. His feathers flared and flushed a fluorescent red. Philip lifted a regarding gaze at the officious imphoid.

Papk ignored him and rubbed the back of his head where the water skin had hit him. "Though we have stolen most of your things, the bright side is that we may be willing to return them basically in the same condition we found them in," said Papk with a happy grin that irritated Philomena even more.

"Cut the maybe and give us our stuff back," Philomena said demandingly. Lark grimaced from her words and shook his head. Papk clicked his tongue chidingly. "A mindless beast is its own worst enemy. We have a process that allows you to regain your belongings, so everyone goes home happy!" the imphoid said cheerfully, spreading his arms to indicate everyone.

"We don't have to regain anything. *You* stole *our* things, so you should give them back," Philomena said firmly, stepping towards Papk. The little imphoid held his ground and peered fearlessly up at Philomena who loomed threateningly over him.

Philip moved to intervene, but Lark held him back by his arm. Philip frowned upsettingly over at him. Lark shook his head, discouraging any action and urging him to remain where he stood. Philip swallowed his impulsiveness with difficulty, and stayed beside Lark grinding his teeth with reluctance. They watched unmoving the happenings between Philomena and the imphoid.

"I take it you would use force to make us return your belongings," Papk figured calmly, looking up at Philomena who was three times bigger than he.

"Yes, I would, shorty. We're on a bit of a tight schedule," Philomena said flatly.

His bottom lip protruding, Papk examined his fingernails with distracted interest. "Hmm, and what would you do if we were too resist?" he asked musingly.

Philomena smirked. "I don't believe you're in any position to argue," she said smartly, reaching down for her sword, but there was no pommel for her to grasp. Frowning down at her waist, she found that both sheaths were empty and her swords missing. "What?" she said bewildered. She flung her gaze around.

"Looking for these?" a girl's voice asked. Philomena turned back to Papk and snarled angrily. A girl imphoid stood beside Papk with a sweet face and a smile on her lips. In her arms she held one of Philomena's swords while Papk held the other.

"Oh no," Philip muttered with dread, scratching the back of his head and staring down at the ground. A ghost of a grin flickered across Lark's face as he looked on.

Philomena's face reddened. "Give those back you little rats!" she yelled, lunging forward. But ropes with small rocks at their ends flew out, wrapped about her ankles, and yanked her off her feet. The imphoids laughed.

Sitting up, Philomena growled with infuriation, wanting very much to punch the little pranksters and send them flying. The other two imphoids stood at her side, holding the other ends of the twine snaked about her ankles, laughing just as hard as Papk and his friend.

Philip grimaced and looked to Lark, who reluctantly nodded. They stepped forward to intervene.

"Alright, that's enough. How about we all chill out and cut to the chase here," Philip said, his hands spread out in a peaceful gesture. The imphoids stopped laughing, and looked to one another. Philomena worked on unwinding the twine from her ankles, grumbling and cursing under her breath.

"Tell us what you want, so you can return the things you've stolen and we can leave," Lark said levelly, looking steadily at the imphoids.

"We do what we want, when we want," one of the imphoids holding the twine said cockily. Lark and Philip directed indignant glares at him.

"Don't be so rude, Soja," the girl imphoid next to him chided.

"I'm in charge, Sionni," Soja grinded firmly.

Philomena finally freed herself of the irritating twine. Looking smolderingly at the imphoids, Soja and Sionni, Philomena gripped the twine and jerked it hard. Soja and Sionni, holding the opposite ends, gasped in surprise as they were yanked off their feet. They sprawled on the ground face first before Philomena. Philip shook his head hopelessly and Lark let out a sigh. Philomena brushed her hands off and stood with a satisfied smirk.

Groaning, Sionni lifted her face that was now smudged with dirt. Soja scrambled to his feet and glowered at Philomena, his jaw set in an angry line. Papk suddenly burst with laughter. Soja's feathers flared on the back of his head and flashed their fluorescent red. He shot a warning stare at Papk who slammed his mouth shut and suddenly found interest in the trees.

Philomena gave that careless tilt of her head. She moved over to Philip and Lark and snatched her swords back from the first girl imphoid and Papk as she passed.

Soja stomped after her, his sharp teeth clenched and the feathers on his back puffing out.

Philomena turned on him and stopped him short at sword point. Soja hissed, his eyes smoldering like yellow coals.

"Watch yourself little guy," said Philomena. "The world is a whole lot bigger than you,"

"That goes for you too; you gluttons are so selfish," Soja spat. The other imphoids shuffled their bare feet uncomfortably.

"Are you calling me fat?" Philomena asked heatedly.

"Fat in your mind with desire and greed that chokes out any compassion you might have," said Soja. Vengeful hatred flashed in his eyes. "You take what you want, you do what you want, and you don't care,"

"Kind of like you," Philomena noted meanly.

Soja wrinkled his nose in disgust. "We are not gluttons! We may play pranks but we are not as hostile as your kind,"

"I think your attitude needs to be cut down a size," said Philomena, brandishing her sword threateningly. Soja growled and flattened his ears.

"Whoa, Philomena!" Philip said hurriedly. He rushed over to his sister and grabbed her sword arm. The other three imphoids scurried to Soja and gathered about him, the girl imphoids looking rather alarmed.

"Let's just everybody simmer down," Philip suggested firmly, looking pointedly at Philomena and Soja.

Lark stepped forward beside Philip. "Is what they stole that important, or can we just let them have it all?" he asked in a low voice, staring at the imphoids who were doing their best to calm their quick tempered leader.

Philip's features squirmed with reluctance. "I would agree that what your saying is brilliant and lets run for it, but whatever was in Spear's saddlebags is vital to our mission,"

"Don't tell him that, Philip!" Philomena hissed upsettingly.

Philip's brow furrowed irritably. "I think Lark has been with us long enough to know, Philly. And I don't think he really cares," he said.

"I don't care," Lark confirmed carelessly. He then frowned. "I thought those saddle bags were empty," said Lark.

"They're not, though we don't know exactly what they contained," Philip said with a wince.

"But whatever was in those saddle bags, we need it back," said Philomena sheathing her swords and turning a blaming look on the group of imphoids.

Lark pursed his lips with dread. "Let's get this over with then," They turned to the imphoids. The little creatures were huddled together, whispering to one another like they might be strategizing. Soja caught sight of them staring, and tapped the girl imphoids next him to get their attention. The imphoids straightened and faced the young travelers.

"Do you wish to regain your possessions by our regulations now?" Papk asked skeptically. Soja elbowed him in the ribs and glared at him with disapproval.

"I am aware of your regulations," Lark spoke. "My companions however are not," he added, gesturing to Philip and Philomena.

"You don't say," Soja said dryly, staring at Philomena. Philomena crinkled her nose in response.

"What regulations are we talking about?" asked Philip.

"We steal things, not because we want to keep the stuff, but because we find amusement in making people do humiliating things to get their belongings back," Soja explained so seriously that Philomena had to fight from laughing.

"It is all rather amusing," Papk added with a grin.

"Basically you're pranksters," Lark said levelly.

"Yup, and we have a great knack for telling what gluttons are most uncomfortable doing," said Sionni with a proud grin.

"Some gluttons are afraid of water, some don't like eating grubs, others are just afraid of dirt," said the other girl imphoid. Sionni nodded in agreement.

"You're serious?" asked Philomena with disbelief. The girl imphoids nodded in confirmation, their sweet faces beaming.

"Can you believe they actually call us gluttons?" Philip whispered to Lark.

"There are worse names," Lark whispered back.

"And we always like to chose something special for the gluttons who defy us," said Soja pointedly looking to Philomena.

"You haven't seen defiant yet, fur face," Philomena snapped harshly.

"Enough, Philomena," Philip chided. "You'll only make matters worse," he said through meshed teeth. Resentment roiled across Soja's face as he scowled at Philomena.

"So," Lark spoke up to divert the cantankerous imphoid's attention. "What prank do you have in mind,"

"Don't worry yourself none; Give us a moment to contemplate the idea," Papk assured with a mischievous grin.

The one girl imphoid nudged Soja with an eager energy. "It's my turn to choose, Soja," she said in a determined whiney tone. Soja stared at her with annoyance. She was practically hopping from one foot to the other as she waited for his response.

"Fine, you can choose this time, Soji, but don't come up with something ridiculous," said Soja, folding his arms across his chest.

Soji grinned happily, exposing her sharp white teeth. She stepped before the travelers and considered them. A long quiet moment drug on as Soji stared at them. She tilted her head to one side, then to the other, pensively rubbing her round chin with her forefinger.

"*This* is ridiculous," Philomena muttered, shifting impatiently. Soja exhaled irritably, and rolled his eyes, actually finding himself in agreement with Philomena.

Soji paid no mind. She walked closer to them, and stared at each one of them for a minute starting with Philip, then Philomena, and then Lark. Her stare was soft and innocent, but somehow nerve-wracking.

Finishing her silent analyzing of Lark, Soji looked back to
Philomena, and then back to Lark finding some sort of invisible
connection there that was most thrilling to her. A grin of
recognition lightened her face as she deciphered the connection
she was looking for.

"I know," Soji announced cheerfully. "I think you and you
should kiss!" she said, pointing to Lark and Philomena.

Their faces fell with astonishment, and their jaws dropped in
disbelief. Philip tried to contain it but he snorted with laughter.
The imphoids Sionni and Papk rolled over, cackling. Soja
frowned, not looking very agreeable.

Philomena was so shocked by the implication, she couldn't
absorb the idea. "Oh come on! There's no way *you* think this
will regain our stuff," she said defensively, gesturing to Soja and
hoping his serious attitude would save her. Soja stared at her
with light curiosity.

"You guys even said yourselves you like to make us do things
we are very uncomfortable with, and I have no problem with
Lark. I mean, he's . . . he's my friend. He's great actually," she
said diligently, forcing a smile Lark's way. Lark gave her a
confused frown.

"Superb friend," Philip put in, pursing his lips to refrain from
laughing, though he couldn't stop grinning.

The imphoids stared at them blankly.

"I think you having to kiss is the most uncomfortable thing we
can make you do. Brilliant choice, Soji," Soja complimented,
smiling approvingly at Soji.

"Thanks," Soji beamed, folding her arms behind her back and
blushing, the feathers on her head flushing pink as well. She
looked quite pleased with herself.

"So, you two kiss each other once on the lips, and we'll give you
your things back. That's our only and final offer," said Soja, all
business.

Philomena and Lark looked at one another. Philomena cringed with repulsion, and looked away. Lark folded his arms and crinkled his nose like he smelt something bad.

"I'll eat a grub," Philomena suggested to Soja, sounding a little desperate. "I *hate* grubs. I *hate* their slimy taste and the way they squirm. I'll eat a whole bowl if you want,"

"I know I could eat of bowl of grubs right now," said Philip to himself, remembering how hungry he was.

Soja shook his head and placed his hands on his hips. "No. Kiss or kiss your belongings good-bye," he said.

Papk chuckled.

Unfortunately for Lark and Philomena, the imphoids were no fools to fall for smooth talk. The imphoids were bound firmly in their 'brilliant choice'. There was no way around it, and Philomena knew they couldn't just leave their stuff with the little pranksters. She remembered what K'smet had said to them back in Niche, that he had given them as much information on Salvador as he could and that he had packed it in his horse's saddle bags.

Moaning, Philomena kicked at a rock. Lark shot a blaming glare at her, unfolded his arms and walked away. Arican chirped and followed after him.

"Someone go get him," Soja demanded, pointing after Lark.

Papk and Soji obliged, hurrying after Lark.

"There's no way you're making me kiss him!" Philomena said defiantly. Soja shrugged carelessly. Philomena looked desperately to Philip who held up his hands and shook his head negatively.

"Don't look to me for help," he said. Philomena slumped with disappointment.

It took the imphoids a few minutes to bring Lark back over to them. He didn't look too happy as the imphoids pulled him along, one tugging on his sheathed sword and the other simply gripping a fistful of his pants.

Soja smirked satisfactorily. With great effort the little imphoids drug Lark all the way over to Philomena. Lark dug in his heels so he wouldn't collide into her.

"Now kiss!" Papk commanded, still tugging on Lark's sword while Soji pulled at his pants.

Soja ordered Papk and Soji to stop. They obeyed but with deflated expressions.

"Now you can kiss," said Soja with a go-ahead gesture.

"You may as well get it over with," said Philip, standing with the imphoids. A grin flickered across his face. Philomena silently swore she would pay him back for enjoying this too much.

"You can do it!" Papk said teasingly.

Grinding her teeth, Philomena drug her gaze around to Lark. His expression was as stone faced as ever, yet a hint of uneasiness and irritation wavered in his features. Philomena shuttered within when she met his hazel eyes that stared steadily back at her with a mixture of calmness and hardness. They must have stared at each for a significant amount of time, for their eager audience began to become impatient.

"We're waiting," Sionni said tauntingly.

"It's just one kiss," Soji reasoned with little care.

"We don't have all day though," Soja grumbled. He sat down cross legged, and rested his chin in his palm with a look of boredom.

"Maybe it *is* too hard for them," suggested Papk. He sighed. Philomena's face reddened with anger as the impish beings discussed them as if they weren't even there. Intolerance was building on Lark's features as well. He set his jaw irritably and breathed inward with annoyance.

Papk suddenly spluttered with laughter. "Isn't it funny how the gluttons behave? Their faces flush red and their jaws shift when they get moody," he said, pinching his cheeks and moving his jaw around in a poor imitation.

"Or how they stomp around and slash those big knives," Sionni added, giggling.

"Maybe it's the way they think they are so smart and know what they're doing when they're actually quite lost," Soja said dully, staring off in to space. The other three imphoids cackled.

That's it, Philomena thought grudgingly. She didn't know if it was the infuriating comments the imphoids were blurting out, or the way Lark was looking at her that said I-know-you-hate-me-too-much-to-kiss-me that propelled her into action. She determinedly stepped toward Lark and kissed him.

The imphoids gasped excitedly. Philip's eyes widened with surprise.

At first, Lark stood there stiffly as he endured the humiliation. Though Philomena's soft lips against his melted his mind, and for a few seconds he was kissing her back.

When they broke apart, they stared at one another, both of them blushing beet red. The imphoids exploded with laughter and rolled on the ground clutching their sides. Philip laughed too, but painstakingly, his brain still deciphering what he had just seen.

Lark and Philomena surfaced from their daze. Philomena looked around as if she had forgotten where she was. She saw the imphoids laughing and realized Lark's arms were around her. Anger and humiliation slammed Philomena, and she shoved Lark away, which only made the imphoids laugh harder. Philomena growled furiously and stomped off.

Lark walked over to Philip sheepishly, still in shock. Philip folded his arms and considered him critically. "I saw that," he said seriously, sounding very brotherly.

Lark looked at him, puzzled. "What?"

"You kissed her," said Philip, narrowing his eyes observantly.

"I thought that was what I was supposed to do," Lark tried weakly.

Philip chuckled dryly. "Yes but you kissed her *back*," he said.

Lark squared his shoulders and pursed his lips uneasily. "Is there any difference?" he asked.

"Oh yes there is," said Philip with a crooked grin. "Most young men find my sister attractive. It's not unusual,"

His direct approach made Lark uncomfortable.

"But none of them get the pleasure of kissing her. I can't say I blame you for enjoying the moment," said Philip, cocking another perceiving look at Lark.

"A momentary set back I assure you," said Lark, regaining his calm steady voice.

"Ugh huh," said Philip, not convinced.

Looking back to the imphoids, the impish beings were still rolling around on the ground, clutching at their aching sides. Tears of laughter squeezed from the corners of their eyes and their round cheeks were rosy red. Philomena came marching back, her expression set seriously.

"You've had your fun, now give us our stuff back before I hang you in the trees and bury you in the ground myself!" she demanded.

The imphoids laughed harder.

36

Once the imphoids recovered from their fits of laughter which required some stern urging from Philomena, they scurried up the tree they had originally come from and brought down everything they had stolen. Water skins, cooking utensils, clothes, pouches of coins, navigating tools, flint and steel kit, a small sack of grain, and the stirrups from their saddles were all dumped in a heap on the ground at the travelers' feet.

"There," said Soja with a straight face. Papk stood beside him, mocking Soja's serious demeanor with a goofy grin plastered on his face while the girl imphoids discussed what kind of mud was the best to bathe in.

"That's everything we stole from you," said Soja, gesturing frankly.

Philip looked down at their stuff with pursed lips. "You wouldn't happen to have any food would you?" he asked, nearly on the verge of sounding desperate. Soja appeared surprised by his question.

"Unless you want to eat our insect riddled bread, we've got nothing," said Papk, cocking his head and shrugging his shoulders helplessly.

The idea of eating insect bread made Philomena shutter with disgust. Gravely disappointed, Philip slumped slightly with an almost pouting countenance. His stomach ached with a vengeance from being empty for two days, and his desperate hunger was making him cranky and melancholy.

"I can still cook the food I found if you like," Lark offered, noting Philip's downcast behavior, not to mention the occasional rumble emitted from his stomach.

Philip brightened at this generous gesture.

"Yeah, that sounds good. We have time, and we can still reach Ezleon tonight," said Philip cheerfully. Philomena flung a furious glare on them.

"No! We don't have time to act like a bunch of girls at a tea party!" she barked with deep opposition.

"Ugh, the last time I checked you are a girl," said Lark with a tight lipped smile. Philomena fumed, drilling a blaming stare into him. Lark bent down and retrieved the flint and steel kit and one of the cooking pots, Philomena's stare not bothering him. He straightened and walked away to start their fire with Arican frolicking at his side.

"You have to calm yourself, Philly. We're going to get to Ezleon," said Philip stepping towards his fiery tempered sister and placing his hands on her shoulders, trying to sound soothing. Philomena switched her steely look on him.

"But if I don't get something to eat right now, I'm going to pass out from hunger," he said with mocking humor.

"That's not the only way you could pass out in the next few minutes," grumbled Philomena, her underlining intention quite clear to Philip.

"You're going to the city?" asked Papk, diverting their attention. They nodded. Papk grimaced with repulsion. "Boy, I feel sorry for you," he said sincerely.

"Why feel sorry for them? They're gluttons, they'll fit right in that scummy little hole," Soja said stingily, staring nastily up at Philip and Philomena. The girl imphoids literally squealed in protest at his grim comment.

"I tell you what you spicy little shrimp," Philomena grinded out through meshed teeth. "You're starting to irritate me so you best scamper off before I give in to the temptation of sitting on you and plucking your feathers out one by one!"

The girl imphoids screeched fearfully and hurried up the tree with Papk close behind. Soja though took the opportunity to hiss and flare his red flashing feathers one more time at Philomena before following his friends.

The imphoids climbed to the first limb of the tree and then leapt off one by one. Their long feathers extended from their arms caught the slight breeze and glided them in between the trees and deep into the forest. Philomena bore a resentful stare after them. "Wow, what a sheer waste of time," she said, placing her hands on her hips.

"Yep, but what can we do about it? At least we had a good laugh," said Philip, grinning over at her. Philomena turned a cold killer stare on him in reply. The memory of being forced to kiss Lark was still far too fresh for jokes.

"I'll go start tacking the horses," said Philip, clearing his throat and eagerly departing.

Philomena watched him go, grinding her teeth fumingly. Lark looked up from his cooking pot and the two of them made eye contact. They scowled at one another and quickly looked away. Lark went back to cooking their breakfast and Philomena went to work on cleaning the mud off their saddlebags, reattaching the stirrups, and repacking their belongings.

The three of them worked in silence, concentrating on not wasting any more time. It was now late morning, and grey clouds drifted across the sky. The air was crisp with winter, making them grateful for their coats. Arican buried herself in Lark's cloak, rather frightened by the plummeting temperatures. Beside her, Lark stirred their breakfast of roots, bark, and worms. The stew wafted a savory smell despite the strange ingredients. Lark sniffed ruefully as he thought of the one person who would most likely complain about the meal.

Having finished tacking their horses, Philip went back over to help Philomena, only to find her in a flustered state. The saddles were freed of mud but she hadn't gotten very far with repacking their things. She was now frantically rummaging through everything her brow knitted in a concentrated manner as she searched for something that obviously wasn't there.

"Something wrong, Philly?" asked Philip, wondering if he would regret speaking. Philomena tossed aside one of their saddlebags and swung a grudging gaze on him.

"Whatever K'smet gave us . . . it's not here," she said, her voice on the verge of panic.

Philip stared with stricken shock, his mouth dropping open. "What?"

"It's gone!" said Philomena, sifting through their disorderly things. "Those little pests must have lied to us," she added sourly through clenched teeth.

"Have you checked the saddlebags?" Philip asked hopefully, looking to their three sets of saddlebags beside Philomena.

"They're empty," said Philomena, dashing Philip's tiniest remaining hope for finding the mysterious object.

"But K'smet said the thing he left us will help us defeat Salvador. We *need* whatever that thing is! We're two half-trained teenagers against an army of evil minions!" Philip blurted out frightfully.

"I know!" said Philomena, throwing her hands up in the air. "I mean this is just great! We are officially the laughing stalk of this annoying, creature infested forest!" she grinded out angrily.

"What's wrong now?" came Lark's reluctant voice. Philip and Philomena turned to him. A rueful look was etched into his features. Philip heaved in a sigh, his mouth set in a tight line.

"Something's missing from our belongings," he said with dread.

"What's missing?" asked Lark.

"We don't exactly know what it is," said Philip, scratching the back of his head.

Lark stared at him blankly. "And yet somehow you know its missing?" he questioned sarcastically.

Annoyance prickled inside Philomena. "You know what the problem is? You're little friends lied to us," she said, her voice blaming.

"*My* little friends?" Lark questioned, his eyes narrowing with outrage.

"What if the imphoids didn't lie though?" said Philip, trying to keep them on track of their true problem. His suggestion made Philomena's face twist with disagreement.

"They didn't lie. Imphoids don't do that," said Lark, sure of his ground.

"Why are you defending them?" snapped Philomena, firing an aggravated and disgusted look at Lark who sneered back. Philip closed his eyes and shook his head, knowing their remarks would lead them into an argument.

"Alright, just shut up the both of you," he said firmly. Lark and Philomena averted their irritable looks onto him. "Let's just stop and think logically for a second okay?" he suggested.

The two of them went quiet, both seeming a little sheepish but their expressions obviously read that they still were fuming inside with hostility for one another.

"You say the imphoids don't lie?" asked Philip, looking to Lark. Lark nodded in confirmation. "If they didn't lie, and what K'smet gave us is not here now, then Spear's saddlebags were empty to begin with," said Philip, his mind racing.

Philomena soaked in his assumption, following his train of thought.

"Do you think Avador emptied the saddlebags?" asked Philip.

"No, his men never got to K'smet's saddlebags. We made sure of it, or at least Balin and K'smet did," said Philomena with a pensive frown as she played their fight with Avador and his men in Niche over in her mind's eye, her resentment for the imphoids forgotten.

They were thrust into a pondering silence. Lark's curiosity was building, but he kept respectfully quiet as the siblings weeded for an explanation for their missing object.

Confusion pinched Philip's brow as he weighed the possibilities out. He remembered what K'smet had said back in Niche:

'Inside the saddlebags is the key to all of the information I've collected on Salvador. It should be all you need to defeat him and bring this to an end.'

Maybe K'smet had spoken code, and since the saddle bags were empty, he was pretty much telling them that they were on their own. Perhaps he had simply forgotten to pack the information or . . .

Philip and Philomena met each other's gazes, the next possibility disturbing them deeply.

"Maybe K'smet is really our enemy," said Philip, accusation filling his low voice. Philomena looked to him with something like dread, for what he spoke was what they feared.

"Maybe his job was to separate us from our uncle," he said heavily.

Philomena's features squirmed. What Philip said was a great possibility, but it simply wasn't tangible, not for K'smet. "No, it's not possible. There's no way K'smet could betray father. They've known each other for . . . well, forever," she said.

Philip let his eyes drop to the ground guiltily. He inhaled a deep breath. "Yeah, you're probably right," he said hoarsely.

Philomena pursed her lips and knitted her brow.

Lark couldn't restrain himself any longer. "Who's K'smet? And what was supposed to be in those saddlebags?"

"K'smet is a family friend, a knight," said Philip. "He said that he had given us some information that would help defeat Salvador. *Whatever* he gave us, it couldn't have been insignificant," he said distractedly, biting his thumbnail. His explanation wasn't surprising to Lark.

They lapsed into a thoughtful silence again. The perturbed looks on Philip and Philomena's faces told Lark how torn they were about their predicament. Philip shook himself out of his thoughts, realizing they were wasting time.

"Well, standing around isn't going to solve anything. Let's eat quickly so we can get to Ezleon," he said.

Before going to eat, they all pitched in to repack the saddlebags and once filled they slung them behind their saddles, securing them in their proper places.

Afterwards, they happily went over to the small fire Lark had built where the small pot of stew simmered welcomingly. Philip drooled as he watched Lark dish out a bowl of the hot meal for each of them. He eagerly accepted his bowl and settled down to eat it. Lark served himself last and sat down on the opposite side of the fire. The folds of his cloak next to him shifted and Arican stuck her head out, her yellow eyes bright and her pink nose sniffing the air. Lark stroked her between the ears.

They ate in content silence. Philip was already serving himself a second bowl, his stomach growling loudly enough for Lark and Philomena to hear it.

Philomena ate more diligently. Lark noted only the slightest hint of disgust in her features as she ate the stew.

After finishing, Lark poured out the rest of the stew into his bowl and set it on the ground for Arican. The cub chirped happily and started to lap up the brown broth. Philomena stared with disapproval, her mouth a gap as if she were about to say something against the ocelot cub sharing their meal. She glanced up to find Lark's hard gaze narrowed onto her.

His stare read easily: '*This is happening, and there's nothing you can do about it but I just dare you to say something.*'

Philomena shut her mouth, swallowing any smart comment on her mind. She looked away from Lark and finished her stew.

"I am so glad you know how to cook," said Philip with a satisfied smile, having finished his second bowl. Lark dipped his head in acknowledgement. He accepted the empty bowl from Philip and brought out a water skin and rag.

"I'll clean the dishes," said Philomena more demandingly than generously. She took the water skin and rag from Lark without meeting his gaze and poured a small portion of water into the empty bowls and cooking pot.

Lark gave her a curious frown and looked over at Philip for an explanation. Philip shook his head slightly, and forced a smile when Philomena looked their way.

"We'll go get the horses then," he said standing and gesturing for Lark to join him. Somewhat confused, Lark obeyed, scooping Arican in to his arms and following Philip to their horses. Philomena watched them go with light interest, and went back to scrubbing the dishes, her brow knit together as if she were trying to figure out a frustrating problem.

"What is wrong with her?" whispered Lark as they reached the horses. "I know she is quick tempered but now she is just being plain angry," he said, shooting an annoyed stare over at Philomena.

Philip chuckled and met his gaze. "She's just confused. Give her some space, and she'll go back to just being plain quick tempered as always,"

"Confused?" Lark frowned. Philip raised his eyebrows with a hint. "You mean about what the imphoids made us do?" guessed Lark, his voice hardening.

Philip smirked which told Lark he had guessed right. "Listen, Lark, you are an intelligent guy. You have the ability to do whatever you set your mind to whether you like it or not and not let it bother you. Philomena is not like that. She's more complex, and even though she acts tough she has a tendency to let things get to her. What the imphoids made you do was something she had never even considered doing before. Now, she just feels blown off course,"

Lark contemplated Philip's words for a moment, and then something like fear washed over his features. "You don't think . . . that . . ." he trailed off uncomfortably. Philip read between the lines.

"That feelings for you stirred in her? No, don't worry. She can't stand you," assured Philip. "I wouldn't take it personally though. She doesn't take a liking to many people," he added with a dismissive gesture.

No offense was taken on Lark's part. He felt relieved. Things were complicated enough, he thought ruefully.

"How's little Arican doing?" asked Philip with a smile. He tickled Arican under her white furry chin which was still wet with stew. She chirped and licked at Philip's hand, her bright eyes looking to him fondly.

"She's doing fine. Only, she's really not meant to handle this kind of cold weather," said Lark, gazing down at the ocelot in his arms. He looked around at the sound of footsteps and his expression cringed with annoyance to find Philomena coming over to them. She crinkled her nose at him in return and brushed roughly passed him to her grey stallion.

Lark set his jaw and looked to Philip who smirked and rolled his eyes.

"Did you make sure the dishes are clean?" Philip asked her with a joking grin.

"Yeah, sure, Philip," said Philomena as she tucked the cooking pot and bowls away in her saddlebags.

Philip lifted his eyebrows and sighed. She really was angry. He turned his attention back to Lark

"Spear's saddlebags are empty, Lark, so maybe Arican will be warmer riding in one of them," suggested Philip.

Lark agreed and thanked him. He moved over to Spear, and the bay stallion nudged him and nickered in greeting. Lark patted him on the neck with a small smile. Arican sniffed curiously at the stallion's nose, eyeing him with caution. Spear shook his head and blew in the cub's face. Arican chirped excitedly and stretched out her paw to the stallion.

Philomena lifted a repulsed gaze over Coursio's saddle at Lark as he stuffed his cloak into one of the saddlebags for Arican.

"You are seriously bringing that ocelot thing along?" she asked with disgust. "*Why?*"

Lark snapped a defensive glare on to her. Philip shifted his jaw with dread.

"I'm taking care of her. I don't see why you are complaining," Lark said bluntly, lifting Arican into her bedded seat. The cub sniffed and gurgled with approval as she curled herself inside the saddlebag.

"It's an extra mouth to feed. Why should we let it tag along when we can hardly eat ourselves," Philomena argued pointedly.

"We couldn't eat because we were going through the Ashen Lands and Poacher's Land; and it's not her fault that its winter," said Lark, trying to keep the heat out of his voice.

Philomena sniffed disdainfully. "It's just an annoying pest we can't be distracted by," she grumbled, checking Coursio's girth.

"Oh, lighten up, Philly," grinned Philip, draping his arms across Nimbius' back. "What's so wrong with Arican staying with us? She can't take care of herself. Besides, young ladies usually like something cute and furry to hug now and then," he added.

Philomena gave him a disbelieving stare, and then looked away without out a word, grumbling under her breath.

Philip's grin faded. He glanced over at Lark and squared his shoulders. Lark dipped his head in appreciation for Philip's support, for he hadn't expected it. He closed the flap of the saddlebag with Arican tight enough to keep the warmth in but loose enough for her to have air.

Philip drummed his fingers against the seat of his saddle, his brow wrinkled with disturbance as he considered his cantankerous sister.

"Well, speaking of cold," he said casually, pulling out some folded pieces of buckskin from his saddlebag. "We'll need a little extra protection ourselves. We don't want our faces to freeze off," he said, handing each of his companions a piece of buckskin. The third he kept and tied it at the back of his head, the front part of the cloth widening to cover his nose and mouth. Philomena and Lark did likewise.

The three of them climbed aboard their horses and gathered their reins, a cold breeze blowing their hair and biting at any exposed skin. Looking to one another with their protective masks, they appeared to be associated with a group of bandits about to terrorize the city.

Philip grinned behind the buckskin cloth, the thick smell of leather filling his nose. "Right, let's go," he said, deciding not to joke.

Seven hours and thirty minutes later, they stood atop what would have been a grassy hill had in not been winter. They gazed out upon the land that lay before them, twenty some acres of uneven terrain; a forest of rolling, cascading hills.

Beyond the hilly landscape smoke wafted on the breeze and they could just barely discern a stone wall where a cluster of stone buildings nestled within. A river that shone dully in the evening light snaked behind the city and disappeared into a thick forest that carpeted the ground at the feet of two kingly mountain peaks with snow caps. The mountain range continued to the west with smaller mountains, appearing to be kneeling respectfully to their larger brothers.

Philomena pulled her mask down and her breath misted before her face. "Please tell me that's Ezleon," she said tiredly.

"It is," assured Lark with the ghost of a smile, the innocent ignorance these two showed never seeming to get old. Philomena appeared relieved as she looked to the city, but then a thought occurred to her.

"Should I even ask how faraway Caelum is?" she asked thickly.

"I'm afraid you'll have to look that one up," said Lark.

Philomena grunted, her earlier relief somewhat deflated. The thickening grey clouds that blotted out the sun drew Philip's attention. He stared up at them grudgingly.

"Oh, I hope it doesn't snow," he moaned, his voice muffled through his mask. Looking to the sky, Philomena shared his dread. A grumbling gurgling sound emitted and Arican pocked her nose outside of Spear's saddlebag.

"It's okay, Arican," Lark soothed, touching her reassuringly.
"We'll be there soon," he said. Arican gurgled again and
retreated back in to the warmth of the saddlebag.
"What's wrong with her?" asked Philomena.
Lark gave her a warning stare. "She's hungry," he said.
"We just ate," said Philomena in a complaining tone. The corner
of Lark's mouth twitched irritably.
"*I* know we ate not long ago but I'm starving too." Philip
chipped in. "I agree with Arican. Let's hurry to the city so we
can eat," he said, pushing Nimbius down the hill at a canter.
Philomena rolled her eyes and pulled her mask back in place.
Her and Lark urged their horses forward and followed Philip
towards Ezleon.

37

Before they came within sight of Ezleon's gates, Lark rotated an emphatic, stony expression on Philomena and her sword. Philomena narrowed her eyes at him offensively.

"What?" she demanded. Her buckskin mask covered that arrogant glower of hers Lark knew she was wearing. It made her single smug word a bit more tolerable.

Still, Lark considered her with light abhorrence. "I think you should be reminded that society today is not accustomed to seeing a girl carrying a sword around. Really, I don't believe society has *ever* seen such a thing," he said dryly, looking away from her.

A careless snort of laughter emitted from Philomena. "I don't care if they are accustomed to it. I'm not going in to this city unarmed,"

"You're a walking arsenal," said Lark without looking at her. "What's so bad about losing the sword so you being armed is inconspicuous to Ezleon's sentries?"

Philomena's brows lowered resentfully and her gaze hardened.

"Is Ezleon well kept?" asked Philip on Lark's opposite side.

"If you mean well guarded, yes it is," said Lark without hesitation. "It is the largest city in Staleveer realm, and unfortunately the most fortified in the country other than Caelum. Commander Moth has a strong dominance over his men; they'll do whatever he says, and Moth is not a pleasant man,"

This information settled over Philip like a damp rain. "Not pleasant as in similar to Commander Xavier?"

Lark gave him a small almost pitying glance.

"Worse," said Lark, again without hesitation. Disappointment washed over Philip's features, though he did not allow himself to be pulled down too far. He set his jaw in a firm line and gripped his reins with determination. With much persuasion, he convinced Philomena to tie both of her swords to her saddle to where they were able to be sufficiently covered by her saddlebags and bedroll. This she did with grumbling complaints, which Philip and Lark chose to ignore.

It was getting darker as they climbed and descended three more rolling hills. The thick curtains of grey clouds blotted out the moon and any surfacing stars. Once they ascended the third hill, the walls of Ezleon were suddenly before them on a stretch of flat ground. Rooftops of the clustered stone houses and buildings peaked just above the heights of the stone wall. Smoke spouted from the many chimneys, giving the cool air an ashy scent. Torches blazed along the wall and illuminated the heavy wooden gates. The torchlight reflected in a series of frozen puddles just left of the gates.

As they approached the entrance to the city at a steady walk, they eventually discerned the many sentries patrolling atop the walls, their armor gleaming in the torchlight and clinking with their movements. A pair of sentries stood guard on either side of the gates gripping pikes. Even from this distance, Philip could detect the swords at their hips and the maces in leather loops on their belts.

"Well guarded did you say?" Philip muttered out of the corner of his mouth to Lark.

"You wanted to know," said Lark casually, stroking Arican who sat in the saddle before him looking quite content. Lark glanced with little surprise over at Philomena who gritted her teeth and balled her sword hand into a tight fist, obviously fighting the urge to reach for her favored blade.

"It looks like they can take out an army of angry trolls," said Philip rigidly.

"Trolls?" Lark frowned.

"It looks like they're ready for war," put in Philomena, her voice stern and her fierce gaze locked on the sentries.

"We are at war though aren't we? We just don't realize it yet," Lark said bitterly. Philip looked to him, his brow lowered with regret.

The sentries guarding the gates of Ezleon finally brought attention to the travelers' approach. They signaled to their comrades atop the wall. Voices shouted and equipment clanked in the hustle. Seemingly out of the ground, more armed men came filing out before the gates at a stiff jog, their swords unsheathed.

"Ooh, these guys know how to perform," said Philip with sarcastic admiration.

The sentries of Ezleon turned towards them and locked in to a defensive line, their weapons pointed at them. Arican chirped nervously at the sight, and daintily slipped back in the safety of her saddlebag. Lark watched her curiously, and met Philip's gaze.

"Not a good sign," said Philip with a shake of his head. Lark tilted his head knowingly.

They reached the line of stiffly readied sentries and stopped their horses before the sharp tips of the sentries' swords.

"There is no entrance in to Ezleon!" one of the pike bearers boomed. Philip scrutinized the man. He had a bulky build beneath his armor, and Philip could make out his abnormally crooked nose and the large mole under his right eye beyond the cover of his helmet's visor.

"Yes, but we really need to get inside the city. We're only passing through," said Philip mannerly. His outward politeness made Philomena itch with aggravation.

"Didn't you hear him boy?!" blurted out the other pike bearer, his breath fogging the cold air. "There's no entrance into the city, especially at this time of night. There's a curfew ya' know,"

"Ah, yes. Hard to forget the curfew," Philip grumbled, rubbing the back of his neck and forcing himself to handle the situation with patience.

"And only worshippers of the god Dandis are permitted into Ezleon, ain't that right Tershus?" added the first pike bearer, the one with the mole and crooked nose.

"That's right, Mazkus," agreed Tershus with a nod. He peered up at Philip. "You and your friends don't serve Dandis do ya boy?" he asked, leaning against the staff of his pike.

"No, and proud not too," said Philip with a grin, his brow scrunched curiously.

"Who the hell is Dandis?" Philomena blurted carelessly.

The pike bearers looked to her horror struck and their fellow sentries shifted uneasily. Tershus put a finger to his lips in a hushing gesture. His eyes were wide with fright under his visor. "You don't want to insult the great Dandis, girl. You don't know what your doin'," said Tershus in a scared hushed tone.

"Oh please!" laughed Philomena, astonished by how afraid these grown men were by a few ill words against their Dandis. "This god of yours isn't even real," she said.

The sentries gasped in terror, shuffling nervously.

"Quiet!" hissed Tershus, stepping swiftly towards her with an angry stare. "The great Dandis is real!"

"And he doesn't fancy being insulted," added Mazkus in a timid voice as if afraid of getting in trouble.

"Yes, and he is real," said Tershus in a shaky voice, his eyes flashing. Philomena frowned down at the nervous sentry. Tershus licked his lips and wiped his mouth, hesitating in his speech. "I know this by the ball of fire he sent to destroy my house," he whispered. "Everything was gone,"

Philip and Lark exchanged perturbed glances.

"How do you know it was this Dandis? Anyone could have set fire to your house," said Philomena pointedly.

"I know it was him! The minute I insulted him, I lost

everything," said Tershus, in the same hushed voice. Philomena lifted her eyebrows, considering the superstitious sentry with new repulsion.

"Yes, well we're very sorry to hear that," said Philip unconvincingly. Tershus switched his gaze onto him. "Still, might you be kind enough to open those gates so we can pass?" The other pike bearer, Mazkus, tilted a foreboding look on Philip. "Do we look like we are kind?" he asked sarcastically. Philip's brow scrunched confusedly. He opened his mouth to reply but Mazkus continued. "Did he just imply that we have kindness, Tershus?"

"We are not kind, Mazkus, surely. We are evil," replied Tershus, his nose wrinkling nastily.

"Absolutely malevolent," agreed Mazkus, lifting his chin with deliberate pride.

Philomena glowered at the two sentries with annoyance, yearning to draw her sword on them.

"You may as well turn back the way you came without making a fuss," said Tershus with a shooing gesture. The line of sentries bearing swords pressed forward, ready to use force if necessary. "You are outnumbered after all," the pike bearers chuckled coldly.

"How much?" asked Lark firmly, pushing Spear forward. The sentries tensed.

"Sorry?" Mazkus asked stupidly.

"How much will it cost to enter the city? Spit it out quickly. We have better things to do than talk to you all night," said Lark boldly. Philip and Philomena regarded him with astonishment. Mazkus and Tershus squinted up at Lark like they were still deciphering what he had said. Finally, Tershus signaled the swordsmen to stand down. With a clatter of equipment they obeyed.

"Now we're talking," said Mazkus, grinning wickedly at Lark. Philip and Philomena stared wordlessly, further surprised that the sentries were taking Lark's offer of money.

The pike bearers regarded them further sizing them up, as if they could measure how much gold they carried simply by staring at them.

"Twenty gold pieces ought to cover the passage for you three," Tershus said after a moment, rolling his tongue greedily over his teeth.

"The last time it was only five gold pieces each," said Lark, calculating the price.

"Oh it's still five but not for you," said Tershus pointing a finger at Lark.

Lark narrowed his eyes coldly, silently demanding an answer. Philomena was rather surprised by how dark his expression had become.

"You're a half breed," Mazkus provided carelessly. "Not all the people care to have you around, neither do we," he added with slight disgust.

At this, Philip's expression shadowed and his jaw line tightened. Philomena snapped a glare at the prejudice guards, heated anger bubbling in her as well.

"You vile little-" Philip began to grind out but was cut off by a raised hand by Lark. Philip fell silent, but his eyes still flashed angrily at the guards.

Lark scowled at the men, too angry to say anything, and dug in an inside pocket of his father's coat. He brought out the few gold pieces he had, eight in total the last he had received from Master Finn. The heavy coins were cold in his hand and gleamed dully in the flickering torchlight.

"Change is cruel, hey peasant," grinned Mazkus, snatching the gold coins from Lark's hand. Lark glowered at him, vicious words weighing threateningly on his tongue.

"Change *is* cruel," Philip agreed sincerely having simmered down, averting the pike bearers' attention. "I mean, look at what happened to your face," Philip pointed out, gesturing to Mazkus' crooked nose and ugly mole. Philomena snickered. Mazkus gawked at Philip, his mouth gaping open and his face reddening. Tershus ducked his head to hide an amused grin but he couldn't restrain his laughter. Mazkus swung an infuriated look on his companion.

Philip winked at Lark secretly, and Lark grinned lightly in return. "How many coins did you give them, Lark?"

Tershus and Mazkus glared at him offensively. "What? You don't trust a sentry to tell the truth?" they challenged.

"Not really," said Philip frankly, his bottom lip puckering out in consideration.

"I gave them eight," said Lark, watching the pike bearers.

"Right," said Philip. While Philip rummaged in his saddlebag for his coin pouch Tershus peered curiously at Philomena. He stepped closer to her, and Philomena narrowed her eyes with a fierce warning.

"Don't I know you?" asked Tershus, staring up at Philomena as if he were seeing her for the first time. Lark watched him suspiciously out of the corner of his eye.

"No you don't," said Philomena flatly, her voice cold. Coursio sidestepped uneasily, sensing her building disdain.

"Hmm, I suppose I would remember a girl as pretty as you," said Tershus, now looking to Philomena with a greedy lustfulness. Something red hot bubbled within Lark at his words that he difficulty fought to swallow.

"You are awfully beautiful," continued Tershus. "But you seem to have such a bad temper. Maybe I can . . . help you cool off," he suggested, reaching a hand out to touch her.

Philomena forced a sly smile at him, one that never reached her eyes. She lifted her booted foot and shoved him in the chest before his fingers could reach her. Tershus stumbled backwards, wind-milled his arms in attempt to regain his balance but failed to do so. He yelped and fell into one of the frozen puddles with a crack and a splash. Everyone looked over at him with little surprise.

"I'll show you a bad temper," muttered Philomena, glaring down at Tershus who was spraying water out of his mouth. The pike bearer clambered clumsily in the puddle, his eyes bulging and his dark hair plastered to his forehead beneath his helmet.

Now it was Mazkus' turn to laugh. Suspicion set across Philip's features as he directed an interrogating gaze on Philomena. Philomena shrugged her shoulders carelessly in reply.

"Did ya see that!" spluttered Tershus, pointing accusingly at Philomena. "She's crazy is what she is!" A sentry helped him out of the puddle.

"Next time you should show a little self control and maybe you won't get shoved into a puddle," suggested Lark, his voice somewhat heated.

Tershus stared at him wide eyed, looking pathetic as he stood there dripping wet and patched with mud. Philip switched a furious glare on him now.

"You better not touch my sister. The craziness runs in the family," warned Philip. He handed the twelve coins to Mazkus who was still chuckling.

Tershus gawked at Philip. "She's your sister?" he asked. Philip gave him a knowing look that answered his question well enough.

Tershus ducked his head, his cheeks blushing bashfully. "Oh," he mumbled meekly; yet something in his reply stirred suspicion in Lark that he couldn't explain.

"Right, let them through!" Mazkus called up to the sentries atop the walls. They waved in acknowledgement and disappeared past the top of the wall.

A few seconds later a creaking groaning noise filled the air as the sentries turned the heavy wheel that pulled the double gates apart. The gates slid open scraping against the frozen ground and receding within a designated gap in the stone wall.

Philip and Philomena's features slacked with disappointment, for the gates had only revealed the entrance to a dark tunnel into Ezleon's wall, a void of seemingly endless blackness. They looked uncertainly to the sentries who had cleared the way for them.

"Ugh," Philip started doubtfully, staring into the shadows that yawned before them.

"Thank you," Lark cut in, nudging Spear into the tunnel. Philip and Philomena had no choice but to follow. Tershus directed a smart smirk at Philomena as she passed by. Philomena wrinkled her nose and stuck her tongue out at him in reply. Tershus looked after her in irritable bafflement.

The shadows of the tunnel swallowed them instantly once they entered. Mazkus signaled to the guard atop the wall and the gates began to slide close.

"That's a strange girl that one. Did you see the clothes she wears? And that's her *brother*," muttered Tershus to Mazkus as they watched the gates slide shut.

"She is strange indeed. Do you think they are the ones?" asked Mazkus.

"Who else could it be," said Tershus

"Should we send word to the commander?" asked Mazkus.
Tershus nodded in agreement.

*****

Inside the tunnel, Philip and Philomena were really starting to have strong doubts about their situation. There was no light at all so it was impossible to see or detect anything. It was damp and smelled of soil. The horses bobbed their heads and chomped anxiously at their bits, not too fond of their location either.

"Do you think we are in Ezleon's dungeons?" suggested Philip from the darkness. Somewhere close by Lark replied.

"You've obviously never been to Ezleon before. The gate into the city is just down this way. We just keep going forward. The sentries will open the gate once we reach it."

"You've been here before then?" asked Philip.

"A couple times," said Lark.

"They've always had that stupid passage fee?" grumbled Philomena.

"As far as I know, and it's only for those who don't worship that false god of theirs. The sentries will let you in only if you pay them for the favor. They pocket the money for themselves," explained Lark.

"So, bribery?" said Philomena thickly. The disgust was evident in her voice.

"You haven't seen the worst of it yet," said Lark ruefully, for he knew the siblings had been shielded from the ugly consequences of the depression.

"They are a prejudice group too," Philip spoke thickly from somewhere in the dark. "I'm sure being prejudice has spread to divide and weaken the people," he added.

Lark didn't say anything, but he clenched his teeth trying to forget being treated like a half breed.

Gates suddenly yawned open to their left, startling them and their horses. The gates grated against the ground and vanished within the wall like the first pair. Dim evening light poured into the dark tunnel, making them blink. Somewhat disorientated from their stroll through the unpleasant tunnel, they walked their uneasy horses through the open gates and suddenly the congested maze of stone houses and makeshift shacks of the city lay before them.

The horses' hooves clopped noisily against a stone ramp that gradually descended to the city's streets. Another pair of grim faced armored pike bearers stood guard at either side of the gates. Thankfully they had no reason to converse with them and they rode their horses down the stone ramp to the dirt roads.

The main road they came to stretched horizontally before them with several side roads splitting off it and running vertically in to the depths of Ezleon.

More frozen puddles glistened here and there and icicles clung to the shadowing overhangs of the houses. The city was rather quiet with only a few straggling villagers and workers filtering through the streets. Most of them were dressed poorly with grime smudged on their unsmiling faces and dread filling their dim eyes.

Philip and Philomena took in their surroundings with stunned expressions, not sure what to do next.

A ruffle of wings pulled Lark's gaze skyward and his brow pinched at the sight of the cream colored underbelly of a hawk soaring overhead towards the center of the city. *What is a hawk doing flying at this late hour*, Lark wondered.

"Lark," said Philip, noticing Lark frowning upward. "Is something wrong?"

Lark shook himself bringing his gaze back down to ground level.

"It's nothing," he said, deciding to dismiss what he had seen.

Philip gave him a curious look, not convinced.

"You said you came here to get supplies," Lark reminded, diverting Philip's train of thought. Philip nodded.

"Good luck with that," scoffed Philomena. "The streets are empty. We won't be able to get any food from the market till the morning," she said irritably, sneering at the empty roads grudgingly.

"Who said anything about a market? We can stock up at the local tavern," said Philip grinning happily.

Philomena scowled at him. "You just want to drink an ale and eat right now,"

"That too. Do you know where the tavern is, Lark?" asked Philip, turning expectantly to their companion.

"This way," said Lark, turning Spear to the left. Philip and Philomena followed him. He led them down the main street, Ezleon's stone wall on their left and the line of houses to their right.

They rode to the end of the street where it curved to the right.

The overhangs of the many rooftops jutted out fiercely on the curve with a cluster of icicles that nearly touched the dirt ground. Another line of buildings that appeared to be various shops started against the stone wall as they followed the street towards the north. A lone lamp glowed brightly ahead on one of the cottages. A couple of sentries patrolled this street, strolling along proudly. What appeared to be dirty sacks of grain or maybe flour were sprawled about the fronts of the shops, but as they approached the lone lamp Philomena sucked in a breath as they found that the dirty sacks were really the homeless.

"Oh my god," she whispered, horrified by the sight.

The people were filthy, skinny, and ragged with hardly any clothes to ward off winter's cold. Many of them were elderly, withered and scarred, but some were families with young children, cuddled up against their parents and siblings for warmth. A few were fortunate enough to have a blanket, but they obviously lacked food, water, and shelter.

Philip looked on as they rode by, just as shocked and upset as Philomena. His tightened jaw was a sign he was fighting back his roiling emotions. Lark glanced over pityingly, but he did not hesitate to pass by.

Her very soul shook by the overwhelming sight, Philomena looked to Philip. He could see the fiery determination in her eyes, something he usually did not grapple with but this time he pursed his lips with disagreement. Philomena gawked at him, not having to hear him say that he wasn't going to do anything.

A brittle shout broke out up ahead, drawing their attention. Two homeless elderly men were fighting over a dirty ripped blanket. They tugged and groaned incoherently as they fought over the prize to be won. The sentries barked at them to stop. When the elderly men ignored them, a pair of the sentries rushed over and broke the men apart. The homeless men then turned on the sentries, clawing at them and pulling at their armor. The sentries reeled back and roughly shoved the men away.

The homeless men fell to the ground, too weak to stand back up. One of them groped for the blanket that had started the brawl. The sentry closest to him bent down and ripped the blanket away.

"No, no, please," the old man sobbed groping at the sentry's feet. The sentry sneered in disgust and kicked the homeless man away.

Philomena felt her blood boil as she watched the sentries march away with the confiscated blanket, leaving the homeless man to lay crying into the dirt ground.

"We have to help these people, Philip. We're the ones who can make things better. Just look at what's going on," hissed Philomena. A downcast reluctance was etched into Philip's pinched brow.

"I want to help them as much as you, Philomena. But we have other matters to deal with right now," Philip said gently, his voice hoarse. His own blood was pulsing heatedly to have seen what had just happened. Lark kept his eyes locked on the road ahead, sensing the difficulty of the situation that was growing. Philomena stared at her brother, utterly flabbergasted and deeply angered. "How can you just walk away from these people! They *need* our help,"

"Philomena, the best way for us to help them is to end this depression," said Philip firmly, his jaw set in a hard line. Philomena looked away from him, chewing her lip fumingly. She felt more angry and restless than ever.

38

The road on which the tavern was situated held an entirely different atmosphere than the road of the homeless. While the rest of the city dozed restlessly in the gloomy dark, the tavern created a small speck of light and spirit within its bleakness. A steady stream of villagers and travelers made their way to the appealing tavern, attracted by the smell of good food and the sound of laughter.

Philip, Philomena and Lark were amongst them. They went on foot, having stalled their horses in the travelers' stables. Though not wanting to leave Arican behind, Lark carried her with him in Spear's saddlebags which he now had slung over his shoulder. Following the other rugged people lumbering towards the tavern, the sound of cheery music flowed from the tavern's open door and reached their ears. A wooden sign hung just above the tavern's doorway reading 'The Brimming Barrel.'

Boisterous laughter and shouting was also in abundance. Arican made a disturbed gurgling sound within her saddlebag.

"Quiet, Arican," Lark hushed. He put a hand to the saddlebag, feeling the ocelot cub wriggling around inside.

Philomena turned a disgusted look on him. "Are you seriously bringing that thing inside the tavern? We'll probably get in trouble for it,"

Lark scowled at her. "Since when do you care if you get in to trouble or not?" he said, vividly remembering the chaos they had stirred in Niche.

"He's got a point, Philly," said Philip with a light grin.

Philomena glared at him resentfully. Philip cocked a studying look on her. "You're still mad at me for not helping those people?"

Philomena looked away from him without a word, which was a sufficient enough answer for Philip.

"I'll take that as a yes," said Philip grimly.

A large, square fire pit blazed in the street before the tavern, its warmth radiating to them as they reached the Brimming Barrel's verandah. A hunched over old man sat on the steps beside his handcart of caged animals. The poor creatures howled and whined, chewing at the wooden bars of their cages, their frightened eyes pleading for help.

"Poachers," Lark whispered, gazing distastefully at the old man. Philip lifted his eyebrows. Philomena caught sight of a fairy stuffed in a glass jar amongst the caged animals. The fairy was slumped on the bottom of her prison, her wings drooping and her gold light dim with despair. Philomena felt a pang of sympathy for her.

The old man brightened as they approached the steps. "What say you youngsters?" he croaked, wobbling to his feet with the aid of a crooked walking stick. He wore a sleeveless fur vest that dropped unfashionably on the back of his shoulders and drug on the ground.

Lark, Philip, and Philomena exchanged curious looks. They didn't want to be rude, but they didn't want to trifle with poachers either.

"Would you like a nice new coat for this cold winter?" the old man went on toothlessly, fingering his own fur vest. "Freshly skinned before your eyes, whichever animals you choose,"

Philip's eyes widened. "Ugh, you know . . ." he stuttered. He caught Philomena's eye, and she signaled for him to keep the old man's attention. Philip frowned within, but directed a grin to the old man. "I might just be in need," he said.

The old man hooted delightfully, and answered Philip's questions with vigor. He had his attention completely away from his cart. Philomena went over to the caged animals.

Lark glared fixedly at her. *What are you doing?* He mouthed. Philomena lifted the jar with the fairy. Lark's features lightened, and he inched in front of the cart to hide what she was doing. Glancing around to be sure no one could see, Philomena unsealed the jar and tapped the glass to wake the fairy.

"So how does this work?" Philip asked the old man, still unsure of why he was doing this at all.

"Oh, it's very simple, boy," the old man grinned. "You pick what fur you like and we fashion it into a coat." He looked to his cart and frowned at Lark, clearly unpleased with him standing so close to his merchandise. The corner of Lark's mouth twitched. He hoped the old poacher couldn't see Philomena.

"And what of your friend here?" the old man asked, gesturing to Lark.

"He already has a coat," said Philip with a dismissive gesture.

"Yes, but he also has a fine specimen in that bag of his," the old poacher said, tapping Lark's saddle bag with the end of his walking stick. Arican gave a startled chirp and retreated back into the saddle bag. Lark looked down. He hadn't realized Arican had poked her head out.

"Ocelot, isn't?" the old poacher asked, with an undertone of relish. Philip set his jaw, not liking where this was headed.

"She's just a cub," Lark said guardedly. Behind him, Philomena gritted her teeth in agitation. The fairy wouldn't come out! And the way the conversation was going, they needed to leave. Biting her lip, Philomena upturned the jar and dumped the fairy on to her palm.

"Yes, but she will grow. An ocelot fur is truly a prize, especially now that it is so rare," said the old poacher, his eyes widening with pleasurable thoughts. "Would you be interested in bartering?"

Lark stared at him with disguised disgust. Philip looked like he might punch the old poacher.

"Sorry, but Arican stays with us," Lark said calmly. Just as he said that, Philip glimpsed a shimmering gold orb zip across the road and fly over the rooftops out of sight.

The old man puckered his lips and rubbed his chin, clearly disappointed in Lark's response.

"We should probably leave then," said Philomena, standing at Lark's shoulder. The old poacher frowned at her, wondering where she had come from.

Lark didn't need any more urging. He stepped onto the verandah without another word, his hand tightly clasping the saddlebag with Arican. Philomena followed quickly behind him.

Philip stared after them, rather baffled by their behavior. "Sadly, I don't need a coat, but thanks anyway," he said to the old poacher and hurried after his companions. The old man grumbled upsettingly and slouched on the verandah's steps once more, muttering to himself.

"What the hell was that about?" Philip hissed once he caught up with Lark and Philomena. Lark looked to Philomena obviously saying it was her place to reveal what she'd done. Philip looked expectantly at her.

Philomena clenched her jaw. "I was just admiring his selection," she said with a shrug.

"Of course you were," Philip grumbled, narrowing his eyes suspiciously. He flicked his gaze to Lark. "Did she do something wrong,"

To his surprise, Lark smiled. "Actually, the exact opposite of wrong," he said.

Philip was taken aback by the admiration in his voice, as was Philomena. They didn't speak anymore of the matter. They walked over the threshold of the Brimming Barrel to be bombarded by the roar of yelling and laughing, mixed with the bouncy music produced by the musicians.

Lively drunks filled the tavern, making hearty toasts, telling jokes or sharing stories. They occupied the majority of the round tables and the armchairs that made a half circle before the inviting hearth that crackled with a warm fire.

The smell of bread, bubbling porridge, and alcohol circulated about the room. Dried wax was piled on the wood floor. A chandelier made of antlers hanging above made them aware of an ascended walkway skirting the perimeter of the tavern ten feet off the floor.

A single drunken man stumbled away from his friends, cackling and hiccupping with a goofy grin on his face. He wobbled in front of them, trying to take a swig of ale from his tankard but most of it poured down his front. He let out a loud belch reeking of ale, making Philomena recoil, scrunch her nose and wave her hand before her face.

The drunk laughed, hesitated and his eyes rolled back in his head and he toppled backwards unconscious.

Philomena shook her head in disgust. Philip and Lark looked down at the passed out drunkard with little care.

"We're in a happy place," Philip noted, looking up with a grin. "Shall we?"

Lark took the lead to the bar. Philip made a point to follow closely behind Philomena, for as usual, she was turning several of the men's heads. They went by a group of cackling drunks seated around a table with plates of bread and cheese, and of course tankards of ale. One of the drunks, a greasy haired filthy man with a crooked grin on his face, stretched out a dirt-smeared hand to Philomena as they passed by. Philip grabbed the man's sticky fingers in a crushing grip, making him yelp.

"Didn't your mother teach you to keep your hands to yourself," Philip growled. He shoved the man back. The momentum made the drunkard's chair teeter on two legs. The man's eyes widened. He yelped as his chair gave way and collapsed backwards, its two back legs busting on impact. His friends sitting around the table exploded with laughter, and lifted their tankards of ale to their fallen friend.

This particular commotion was drowned out by the rest of the

noise in the tavern, and Philip was grateful for that. He didn't
need any extra attention drawn to them.

The bar was empty apart from an old man with stringy white hair
dangling before his aged face. He sat hunched over on a stool at
the end of the bar gingerly sipping a bowl of stew, seeming
content to keep to himself. The barkeeper, a husky man of
average height with receding dark hair, hustled busily behind the
bar filling orders that were being shouted to him. Some tavern
girls assisted him, going back and forth carrying tankards of ale
or rum and wooden platters of food.

The barkeeper spotted them and said he'd be right there.
Rotating his gaze around and taking in the various smells, Philip
couldn't help but feel terribly hungry. "How about we have some
supper before we leave?" he suggested, looking to his
companions.

Lark shrugged agreeably, and took a seat at the bar shifting the
saddle bag with Arican on to his lap.

"Do we really have time for that?" asked Philomena in drawling
tone, her arms folded across her chest.

"Of course not," said Philip. "But we don't have time for
anything, so why not? You can't tell me you're not even a little
bit hungry,"

Philomena gaped at him. She opened her mouth to object, but
was cut short when a tavern girl carrying a platter of food
collided in to Philip's side. Philip stumbled half a step. There
was an angry hiss, and a gasp from the tavern girl as a gooey red
substance spewed from her platter of dishes and splattered onto
Philip's face. Lark cringed at the sight.

"Oh my gosh! I'm so sorry!" the tavern girl blurted, hurriedly
setting down her platter of dishes on the nearest table. The two
men sitting there grinned at one another and gleefully helped
themselves to the food they hadn't paid for.

"No, no it's fine," Philip said reassuringly, wiping his face
against his coat sleeve. The flustered tavern girl still scurried

over with a cloth in hand. Philomena glared haughtily at her and flexed her jaw.

"Oh, but you don't understand," the tavern girl said upsettingly. "That was a hissing pepper that just exploded on you,"

"A what?" Philip frowned. Just then he felt his skin prickle and his face burned like it had just burst in to flames. He slammed his eyes shut and chewed at his lip as the white hot torture only grew more intense.

"Do you see?" groaned the tavern girl, her brows knitted. She dabbed at the red sauce on Philip's face. Philip let out a breath and leaned against the bar, enduring the stinging, throbbing heat.

"Come on, Philip. It's just a pepper. It can't be *that* hot," said Philomena laughing. Lark gave her a look that said she was dead wrong.

"Hissing peppers are the second hottest pepper in our world," said the tavern girl, focused on cleaning Philip's face.

"Oh," said Philomena, a little deflated lowering her gaze to the bar.

"They are beneficial when it comes to clearing your sinuses though. But when they are angered they have a tendency to erupt," said Lark, explaining further.

"How can a pepper get angry?" asked Philomena puzzled. Lark shrugged and shifted his saddlebags. So far, Arican hadn't made a sound. The barkeeper came over to them, wiping his hands against his grease smeared apron. When he noticed the red goo from the pepper on Philip's face, he swung an angry gaze on the tavern girl.

"Teshna! Not again!" he shouted.

The tavern girl, Teshna, winced. "I'm sorry, sir," she said weakly, unable to meet her master's fierce gaze. Lark figured he could relate to how she was feeling right now.

"I hope you can forgive this girl's clumsiness, young man," said the barkeeper, turning his attention to Philip. "I assure you, she'll make it up to you," he added heavily, directing a pointed look to

Teshna. Her head dropped and her shoulders slumped submissively.

"There's no need for that," Philip managed, still tolerating the gnawing spice from the hissing pepper. It felt as though it were eating his skin. "No hard feelings," he said hoarsely with a dismissive gesture.

"Nonsense!" the barkeeper barked. "You," He pointed to Teshna. "Get back to work. And you two, don't think you're going to get away without paying for that," he added to the two men munching on the food Teshna had set down. They looked gravely disappointed.

Teshna ducked her head meekly. She left her cloth with Philip, gathered the plates from the table and went back to work. Philip watched her go, feeling guilty.

A sharp whistle from the barkeeper startled all three of them. A dog barked and trotted out from behind the bar in response. He was a wiry haired, copper colored mutt with pointed ears and a wagging tail. He came over to his master. The barkeeper gave him a signal and the dog sat in front of the table and stared at the two men who had helped themselves to what they had hoped would be free food. The men groaned, apparently familiar with the technique.

"Not Otis," one of them moaned.

"Come on, Reis, you know we can't afford to pay for all of that," the other put in.

"Then you shouldn't have eaten eat," the barkeeper, Reis, chided. He turned back to Philip, Philomena, and Lark who were watching curiously. "Otis will make sure they won't leave before paying. He's never let anyone go without making them pay in full," Reis explained, patting the dog fondly.

They looked to the dog with new interest.

"You lot look hungry," said Reis. "How about some porridge? I would offer you a better meal if only our butcher was still in business," he said regretfully.

"As long as it doesn't have one of those hissing peppers in it," Philip grumbled with repulsion, making a mental note never to trust a pepper again.

The barkeeper chuckled. "A man would be daft to ruin a fine porridge with one of those devils," He shifted to leave.

"Why isn't the butcher in business anymore?" Philomena spoke up. The barkeeper turned back to her, regarding her with disbelief.

"That's a naïve question if I ever heard one," he muttered, shaking his head. "All the meat that is ever gotten is given to Caelum and to the armies. It's a delicacy nowadays. Us poor folk can't afford a slab of ribs or beef."

This enlightment sunk Philip and Philomena's mood. Reis pointed to the far end of the bar where a large man wearing a red stained apron was chopping cheese with an oversized cleaver meant for meat. He hacked the cheese with slow strokes, his round face slack with boredom and his eyes staring off into space.

"Look at what this blasted depression is doing to poor ol' Ned," said Reis.

The three looked to the butcher with uncertain pity.

"He hasn't sliced any meat in years," Reis said sadly. A scrawny customer tried to sneak some cheese in Ned's blind spot, but the butcher turned on him and brought down his cleaver aiming for the man's fingers. The man squealed in fright and jerked back, the momentum sending him tumbling on the floor with a loud crash. Ned's cleaver bit deeply in the bar's wooden surface. He pulled it free with a grunt and went back to chopping cheese with the same bored, distracted expression.

"It looks like he has blood stains on his apron," Philip pointed out, squinting at the butcher.

Reis snorted with sardonic laughter. "Ned put those stains there himself last week. It's just some red dye. I guess he was trying to cheer himself up," said Reis, his voice becoming heavy with sadness again.

The three watched him awkwardly, not knowing what to say. Reis noticed them staring and cleared his throat. "I'll go get your porridge," he said, and hustled away.

They didn't speak at all while they waited for their meal. Gazing over at Ned the butcher, they watched him dejectedly chop at the block of cheese, ever so often a tavern girl coming by to collect some. Ned still stared off into space, seeming oblivious to everything around him.

"Here we go," came Reis' voice redirecting their attention. He set three bowls of porridge before them. Some of the thick, creamy contents sloshed over the bowls' rims as he placed them down. The porridge steamed, not the most savory smell but it was a hot meal and free at that. They thanked him. Philip and Philomena sat down gratefully.

"I know I said we'd make up for that incident before," Reis said, gesturing to Philip. "Is there anything else I can get you?"

"Actually, we need some food for our journey. At least enough to last us two weeks," said Philomena taking up her spoon. She was pleased to find nothing resembling a worm or grub floating in the thick broth.

Reis nodded. "Long distance travelers huh? No problem," he said, and hastened back down the bar to attend to other orders.

Philomena looked to Philip who sat next to her. His face was flushed from the effects of the hissing pepper sauce. "Are you alright?" she asked tentatively.

"Fine," said Philip, though his skin burned readily from the pepper.

"You've got sauce in your hair," Philomena laughed. She took Teshna's cloth and tousled Philip's hair that was plastered to his forehead.

"Listen," said Philip seriously once she had finished. "I'm sorry about before, with those poor people. I wish we could help them too, but we just can't afford to right now,"

Philomena looked down, the corner of her mouth twitching regretfully. "I know, I'm sorry too," She lifted her gaze back up to her brother and was glad to see a smile of relief on his features. She hated it when they had disagreements, and was always relieved when they made peace. Sometimes she just couldn't help her quick temper. It was something she wished she could rid herself of.

They turned their attention back to their supper. It wasn't the greatest, but it still filled them. Philip though preferred Lark's cooking. Lark however did not care. He was use to a peasant's porridge.

Otis the dog remained at his post, never taking his eyes off the two men sitting at the table before him. Whenever they attempted to sneak out of their chairs, Otis emitted a deep growl and stood, ready to chase them down. The two men would then sulk heavily back into their chairs, and Otis would sit back down again, his intent eyes glittering. The men even attempted to distract Otis with some cheese, waggling it before the dog's nose and then tossing it away. Otis looked after the cheese, licked his chops, and looked back to the men as if to say, *I think you might be tastier if I could have a bite.*

This comedy was quite amusing to listen to while they ate their dinner.

Ten minutes passed, and Reis returned with four large parcels in his arms. He plopped them on the bar next to Philip and sighed. "That should hold you up for two weeks," he said, patting the parcels confidently.

Philip lifted his eyebrows. "More like two months,"

Reis shrugged. "You'll be hungrier than what you think. Winter's coming in early this year. That's a sign it will be a long, and cold one. Where are you headed anyways? Perhaps somewhere foreign to get away from our deranged king," Reis said his last words with disdain.

Lark glanced at Philomena next to him, and wasn't surprised to see resentment boiling on her face.

"We're headed north, to Lacemore Realm," said Philip, managing to remain passive.

Reis grunted with disagreement. "That's not good. Not only will you be getting closer to that accursed castle but you'll be crossing the mountains and they are beasts to trifle with at this time of year. To add to it, the only feasible mountain pass ends with the border patrol,"

"There's a border patrol?" Philomena asked ignorantly. Reis looked to her in disbelief.

"Young lady, you've obviously been sheltered. The border patrol was put together a year ago. I suppose it's a way for the king to know everyone who's coming in to his realm. He's getting panicky it seems. Anyone who so much as looks like an enemy is detained and sent to Caelum in chains; there's no way around that patrol either. That king is evil," With that, Reis scurried away as if he had frightened himself.

Philip and Philomena looked to one another worriedly and turned expectant looks to Lark. Lark stared back incredulously. "I didn't know about any border patrol," he said, squaring his shoulders innocently.

Philip breathed inwardly. "We'll figure it out later," he said, trying to sound calm but Philomena could tell he was bothered by this new knowledge. It bothered her too. She clenched her jaw, her eyes brimmed with anxiety. It felt like more than just a coincidence that a well maintained border patrol sprung up not long before they escaped Tosh.

Lark fished out a dumpling from his porridge and slipped it to Arican. "I'm sure you two will manage just fine," he said. The siblings looked to him curiously.

"Why do you say it like that?" questioned Philomena suspiciously.

"We made a deal. I'm sure you remember," said Lark, switching a hard gaze on her. Recollection wavered on Philomena's face and the memory disturbed her. So much had happened between the night she had convinced Lark to help to now that she had forgotten his request. She cursed silently.

"What deal?" asked Philip, switching a perplexed look between them. Philomena dropped her gaze to the bar and chewed at her lip regretfully. Philip's confusion wasn't surprising to Lark. Philomena wasn't the kind to share things.

"I agreed that I'd help you to Ezleon, but I'm not tracking across the entire country with you. I've played my part," said Lark in an unyielding voice, his stare unwavering.

"I think I told you why you can't leave us, Lark," said Philomena, using her most convincing voice which irritated Lark.

"Yes, but you agreed that I could leave after I brought you to Ezleon," Lark pointed out.

"You never said anything about *leaving*," said Philomena emphatically.

"You understood the implication," Lark grinded out.

"But I didn't specifically agree that you could leave once we got here," Philomena insisted forcefully.

"So you lied," said Lark accusingly.

"I didn't lie," Philomena stammered. Lark's penetrating gaze made her hesitate. "Alright maybe I lied, but I knew if I hadn't you would have never helped us,"

Lark let out a frustrated breath. "I don't care what you did or why you did it, all I want is to go home,"

"Why do you want to go back there anyway?" asked Philomena, remembering how seemingly miserable of a life Lark had.

"You don't understand obligations. My family is back there and they need my help," Lark said angrily, his gaze blazing.

Philomena set her jaw haughtily. It was obvious Lark had struck a sensitive cord, but Philomena managed to restrain herself.

"I think it's time to get some more rope," she said, her underlining intention quite clear. Lark narrowed his eyes.

"Enough!" Philip cut in, slapping a hand on the bar. He casted an infuriated gaze between them. "You both need to knock it off. It's irritating," he snapped, his nose crinkled.

Lark and Philomena looked away from one another, flushed from their argument. The tension between them still bubbled.

"If Lark wants to leave than that's his choice, Philly," said Philip. Outrage quickly took over Philomena's expression as she switched her gaze to her brother.

"You know why we can't let him go, Philip," Philomena said under her breath. Resentment tugged at Lark when he heard her words. He felt like a criminal who didn't have the luxury of a trial.

Philip considered Philomena's reminder. She was right of course. Once they allowed Lark to leave, he could easily betray them and reveal them to their enemies. But they knew Lark. Perhaps things hadn't turned out the way Philip had hoped, but Lark had still saved his life in Staleon Wood.

"I don't believe Lark will betray us," Philip finally said. "After all, we wouldn't have made it here without his help, and if you agreed with him that he could go on his way after reaching Ezleon than we should honor that word,"

"I didn't agree!" Philomena argued desperately, thoroughly frustrated. But Philip held up his hand for silence. Lark glanced around, feeling a little uneasy.

"An agreement is an agreement," said Philip, leaving no room for arguing. He looked to Lark steadily. "Lark has my trust. He's not our prisoner after all,"

Lark was pleasantly surprised by Philip's unwavering trust, though he could see Philomena was ready to explode.

"This is not what I would do, Philip," she said severely, switching her stony stare from Philip to Lark.

"Luckily, you don't have the final say so, little sister," Philip said evenly, leaning away from the bar and pushing aside his empty bowl.

"I still think you're making a mistake," said Philomena.

"I can't say I'll miss your company," Lark said bluntly.

Philomena sniffed and looked away. The feeling was mutual. Lark glowered at her. He looked to Philip who was grinning.

"A word, Lark," Philip requested, standing. He walked away a pace. Shouldering the saddlebag with Arican, Lark joined him. Philomena watched them go with a scowl.

A clear expression was on Philip's features when Lark reached him. "I wanted to say thanks for helping us more than what you had to. We owe you a great deal," said Philip, his voice filled with gratitude.

Lark shifted, peering at Philip. "You had to tell me this away from your sister?"

"Come on, you know how she is," said Philip with a smirk. Glancing over at Philomena and seeing that annoyed, smug look, Lark had to agree.

"Anyway," continued Philip. "I'm sure we most likely won't cross paths in the near future, not that you'd want that to happen, but if we do succeed in what we are planning, I hope you won't be disappointed. If we do succeed, we'll remember you. Until then, I want you to take Spear,"

Lark looked to him astonished. He opened his mouth to object but Philip raised a hand for him to be quiet.

"I don't want to hear it. You and Arican need Spear more than us. We don't need an extra horse to feed. Besides, it's the least we can do," Philip said, folding his arms. He wore that smart satisfied smile of his that told Lark he was firm in his decision. Lark let out a sigh. He knew he couldn't sway Philip. It was a trait that somehow convinced Lark more every time that he was in fact a prince. "I suppose riding to Niche beats walking all the way back," Lark figured, warming up to the idea.

Philip grinned. "For sure," he said, lifting his eyebrows. He unfolded his arms and offered a hand to Lark. As usual, Lark glanced down at it wearily.

"Take care, Lark," said Philip.

"And you as well," said Lark, taking Philip's hand in a firm grip.

Philomena watched Philip and Lark from where she sat at the bar. Resentment boiled in her like a thick poison. If it were up to her, Lark would have been unconscious, bound, and slung over his horse by now. The risk Philip was taking was infuriating. But Philip always had his way.

The corner of Philomena's mouth twitched. Perhaps she felt a twinge of jealousy too. Ever since Lark had come in to the picture, Philip had treated him almost like a brother. He even valued Lark's opinion over hers. Something roiled inside Philomena. It bubbled and churned unyieldingly, making her thoughts swirl.

A tavern girl passed by, blonde and pretty and Philomena recognized her.

"Hey," said Philomena, slipping off her stool. The tavern girl turned to her. "It's Teshna right?"

Teshna nodded with a smile.

"I need you to keep my brother occupied for a time," said Philomena, her idea falling in to place in her mind.

"Oh," said Teshna her smile fading. She glanced around uncertainly.

"Don't worry, it's nothing you'll get in trouble over," Philomena reassured impatiently. "I just need to deliver something down the road,"

"Oh, ok," said Teshna brightening, her smile returning.

"Anything to make up for what I did earlier,"

"Good," said Philomena, taking up the parcels of food they had ordered for their trip. "Just keep my brother from leaving," she added, pointing Philip out for Teshna.

"I'll do my best," said Teshna, looking to Philip speaking with Lark.

Tucking the parcels under her arm, Philomena slunk by Philip and Lark unnoticed. She weaved around some tables and slipped by a group of men sharing stories. She reached the door and walked out on to the verandah grateful to see that the old poacher was gone.

Descending the steps Philomena headed down the dirt road, smiling to herself at her success. She didn't need Philip to do something she thought needed to be done, or his permission. She was capable enough to accomplish it herself. This thought contented her.

The only thing she failed to notice were two pairs of eyes lurking in the shadows across the road watching her.

39

In the center of Ezleon, Commander Moth sat in his chamber. He leaned comfortably in his chair, his booted feet resting on his desk. In his hands, on which he wore black fingerless gloves, was a small gold statue of a king sitting on a throne with a sheathed sword across his lap. On the statue's base was engraved the name King Leif Leonard.

Commander Moth stared at the gold face of the old king. The likeness was well, as so many people had told him. Moth's striking green eyes seemed to penetrate through the statue, as if searching the very past of Leif's life. His lips puckered pensively, as if musing what it would be like to push the king off his own throne and sit in it himself.

Such thoughts kept Moth in silent meditation with the king's statue. His well tanned complexion glowed in the candlelight. His features were as sharp as a knife's edge. His dusty blonde hair cascaded about his muscular shoulders. He was like a smooth glass mirror, only stained black with no framing to protect one's hands from the razor sharp edges.

Unlike Commander Xavier's dark, bleak chamber, Moth had his well lit and well kept. Although his chamber was bright and clean, Moth's heart was the exact opposite. It was a black gnarled thing where no light could penetrate.

The door to the chambers clinked and swung open on well oiled hinges. Three sergeants filed in, their boots clicking against the wooden floor. Moth flicked a sour look on them, his pleasant musings disturbed. "This better be important," he said coolly.

The middle sergeant grinned around his helmet. "It is,"

"The fugitives are at the Brimming Barrel," said the sergeant to

Moth's left.

At this, Moth's expression brightened. He slipped his feet from his desk and sat forward attentively.

"What of our plan?" Moth asked eagerly, setting down the statue of King Leif.

"According to our lookouts, they have already separated," informed the sergeant on the right.

"Excellent," Moth grinned wickedly, his eyes glimmering as pleasurable thoughts returned to his mind. The three sergeants exchanged perturbed glances. Moth considered them, setting his jaw with building annoyance.

"We were wondering, sir," began the middle sergeant uncertainly. Moth settled an unnerving stare on him. "Who are they exactly?"

"That's no concern of yours at the time," Moth said coldly.

"We are your sergeants, though sir," said the sergeant on the left boldly.

"Correct, you are my sergeants and you shouldn't forget it," Moth said maliciously.

"Yes, but we have a right to know," pursued the ambitious sergeant. Moth lifted his eyebrows at him in an icy warning. The sergeant shifted and glanced about nervously.

"With all due respect, commander sir," cut in the middle sergeant, redirecting Moth's attention. "Everyone is rather curious. We would like to know more,"

"Why are we being ordered not to lethally harm them? It's very unlike you," said the sergeant on the right with a hard edge to his voice. "And why is Captain Avador himself coming to acquire them?"

Moth narrowed his eyes. "You've always been too inquisitive for your own good, Werik," he said in a low voice.

Unlike his comrades, Werik didn't break eye contact with his commander.

Letting out a sigh through his nose, Moth decided to reward him for his fearless persistence. "Captain Avador is required to take them back to Caelum because they have offended our future king. There, they will be punished fittingly."

"If Captain Avador is going through all this trouble just to bring them back to Caelum then they must be important," the middle sergeant mused, rubbing his chin pensively.

"Important?" Moth said, cocking an irritable glare at the man.

"They are the highest level of fugitives in this country. They are *important* to capture and put away for good,"

The sergeant Werik pinched his brow inquisitively. "What have they done to earn such attention?"

Moth swung a hardening stare on him, shifting his jaw. "No more questions," he snapped. "Not all are entitled to know the full truth. What you should know is that what we are doing is a great service for our future king and you should see it as a great honor to provide such a service. Are you satisfied now?"

The three sergeants looked to one another and then back to Moth. They nodded their conceit, but Werik corked his mouth unsatisfactorily.

"Good," said Moth, lifting his chin satisfactorily. "Is everyone ready for the next phase of the plan?"

"We still have to inform them," said the middle sergeant.

This deepened the irritation in Moth's features. "And it took all three of you just to tell me this?" he asked sternly.

The sergeants' eyes widened at the realization of such a mistake and shuffled nervously with anticipation; all but Werik who remained stone-faced with aggravation. Moth shook his head with absolute disgust.

"Go and prepare for our guests," he said emphatically. "Seal all the exits, and post sentries all around the city. Let it be known that if anyone aides them that they will be severely punished. Make sure there is no chance for them to escape before you come to me again,"

The sergeants nodded and eagerly made for the door.

"And remember," said Moth, stopping his men in their tracks. "These two are meant to be taken alive. Under no condition are they to be harmed,"

"We'll remind everyone, commander," assured the middle sergeant.

With that, the three sergeants departed. The door clicked shut in their wake and Moth happily went back to his pleasurable musings. He took up King Leif's statue once more and reclined in his chair. He gazed at the name that glowed on the base of the statue, engraved assertively at the king's feet. The king sat nobly with a regal expression of just on his kind face which sent prickling agitation down Moth's spine. If only he had lived to serve Sullivan Corea, or even Zenroy Corea, he was certain that they would have succeeded in their plans without having to exhaust their male heirs as they had.

But that was long past, Moth reminded himself. What mattered was Salvador had found him, and his loyalty was firm in serving him to avenge his forefathers and gain the throne the Corea name had been promised.

A crooked grin spread across Moth's face. "Time's up, old king," he said to Leif's statue.

40

Philip was sad to see Lark go. He was very helpful when it came to traveling through the woods and surviving in the wild. Yes, he would truly miss the native's son. But Philip wasn't going to force him to stay, even if he hadn't known about the deal Philomena had made with him.

As Philip watched, Lark departed out the tavern's door without a backwards glance. Philip was certain that it would be the last time he saw him. With a sigh, Philip turned back to the bar. Instantly, he realized something was wrong. Philomena wasn't there.

Philip's brow furrowed. He hurried over to the bar where their empty bowls still sat before their abandoned stools. Turning to the boisterous crowd, Philip searched for the familiar face of his sister. Panic swelled in his chest when he didn't see her. His heart thudded against his chest. Reis the barkeeper came up and said something Philip didn't hear. With a frown, Reis swept up their bowls and walked away.

Feeling faint with worry, Philip wracked his brain to figure out where Philomena had gone. Had she been captured by some sergeants he had failed to notice? Or maybe one of the crazed men in here had taken her? The thoughts sent another wave of torturing worry over Philip.

The tavern girl, Teshna, caught sight of his stricken expression and maneuvered around some laughing men to reach him. "Is everything ok?" she asked him.

"Not really," Philip admitted, his eyes still scanning the crowd. "Have you seen my sister?"

"She left a few minutes ago," said Teshna, gesturing to the

tavern's door.

"She *left*? To go where?" asked Philip, exasperated. His sudden flare of anger made Teshna uneasy. But the tavern girl forced a smile.

"I don't know where she went exactly, but she told me to keep you company in her absence," said Teshna, appraising Philip appreciatively.

Philip paid her no mind. He muttered irritably and ran a hand uneasily over his face. *What was Philomena thinking sneaking off by herself,* he thought angrily.

Teshna giggled at his fretfulness. "Don't worry so much. She said had to deliver something down the road and that she'd be back. Until then, I think I still owe you for causing that hissing pepper to explode on you," she said, stepping closer to him. Philip's brow lowered.

"Wait? She's delivering something?" he asked, ignoring Teshna's clear lustfulness.

"The food Reis prepared for you. She took it with her," said Teshna, somewhat frustrated that Philip was disregarding her.

At the mention of food, Philip quickly figured out Philomena's intention. "She's taking the food to the poor," he thought out loud.

"Maybe," Teshna said distractedly, her lip pouting out. Persistent to fulfill her promise, she drew in even closer to Philip. "Until she returns though, I believe we still have each other's company to enjoy," she said, her brown eyes sparkling desirably up into his face.

Philip dragged his attention to her with difficulty. Her hinting words made his skin prickle with annoyance. "Look, I'm not like these other men you find here. I have-"

"Oh, I know you're not just some drunk," laughed Teshna with a luscious smile. She fiddled with his jerkin collar. "You're far too noble for that aren't you?" she whispered, leaning far too close for comfort.

The repulsion Philip felt was enough to gag him. "Alright, knock it off," he said sternly, taking a step back and brushing Teshna's hands away from his chest. The smile Teshna wore quickly faded. "No offense but I'm not in the least bit interested in you. I need to find my sister so why can't you just leave me alone," With that, Philip turned abruptly away and started for the tavern's door. Teshna gaped after him. Feeling the boring stare of Reis from behind the bar, she hurried after Philip.

"Wait! I'm sorry!" said Teshna, catching up to Philip and holding him back by his arm. Philip set his jaw. "I usually don't act like this. I just promised your sister I'd cover for her," she stammered.

"Does it look like I care about how you usually act?" Philip said bluntly, pulling free from her grip and moving away once more. "I don't have time for this and I'm sure you've acted like this before to get the attention of these men," he grumbled over his shoulder.

"No, that's not true! Please, I didn't mean anything against you. At least let me make up for what I did before," Teshna tried desperately, pursuing Philip to the door.

Releasing an aggravated breath, Philip stopped and turned to her to tell her to get lost again. But the nervous desperation squirming on Teshna's features stopped him short. He considered her with a pensive frown. "Are you . . . going to get in trouble if you don't pay me back?"

Teshna hesitated, looking away guiltily. "Maybe," she said. Philip nodded chewing at his lip as his brain quickly untangled the curious situation. "Then in that case, why don't you pack me some more food for my travels. I'll wait here," He took a seat at the empty table beside them.

"Oh, thank you sir! You won't regret it," said Teshna with beaming relief. She hurried away happily.

Leaning back in his chair, Philip fought to appear at ease. He knew the longer he remained in the Brimming Barrel separated from Philomena the more vulnerable they both were. He watched with growing impatience as Teshna busied herself behind the bar. He muttered under his breath as she stopped to chat with a fellow tavern girl. Teshna smiled and laughed as she conversed with her friend which greatly irritated Philip. His insides roared with approval when Reis barked at them both to get back to work. The girls scurried apart. The other girl carried a platter of food out to the crowd and Teshna disappeared into the storage. That was Philip's cue.

Grinning satisfactorily to himself, Philip casually stood and made for the door. He ducked between some drunks playing some sort of tossing game with their tankards and departed the tavern.

*****

Meanwhile, Philomena picked her way between the sleeping homeless, careful not to wake them. She slipped parcels of food to some of them as she passed by. Peering in to their pale, thin faces made her heart ache. What upset her more was she couldn't give food to them all. Only two parcels remained clutched under her arm and she was conflicted on whom to give them to. Every sad sleeping face she gazed upon needed the food. Philomena's chest swelled with anger at the thought of someone who could sentence innocent people to such a hopeless life as this. The name Salvador Corea flashed through her mind. She gritted her teeth, battling to restrain her emotions as she waded through the homeless.

Her eyes fell upon a sleeping family, a mother with two young children nestled on either side of her. Philomena went silently over to them and tucked one of the parcels of food beside her. She took a moment to gaze upon them, and wondered what their story was. The innocent faces of the children reflected hopelessness even in their sleep.

What had led them to live like this, Philomena pondered. Where was the children's father? Was he even alive?

A bitter tasting lump swelled in Philomena's throat as she straightened and turned away. She wished she could do more. She wished she could sweep away this depression and help the people start anew.

The way to do that is to defeat Salvador, a voice in her head said so crystal clear she glanced around to be sure no one was there. She exhaled with aggravation. Even her own conscious seemed to take Philip's side.

Gripping her last parcel, Philomena pushed aside her pestering thoughts. She continued to maneuver quietly about the homeless. Philomena slowed as she neared the end of the line of sleeping homeless and casted her gaze around to find someone to bestow the parcel to. A boy curled on the dirt ground caught her attention. He was just as rugged and filthy as the others, but his locks of curly blonde hair and tanned skin were oddly familiar to her.

Frowning, Philomena went closer to him. She peered down at his sleeping form and with a shock recognized his face.

"Trez?" she murmured under her breath. Her brow knitted. The alley fight she had jumped in to back in Niche to help Lark flashed in her mind. Memories of their summons to Commander Xavier's station flooded her head. She and Lark had been tested by Xavier's lie detecting monster, the durjock, all because Trez had blamed them for starting the fight in the alley.

That same Trez lay at Philomena's feet, sleeping in the dirt like a dog.

Her lingering presence caused Trez to shift in his sleep. His brow wrinkled like he could sense something different about his bleak surroundings. His eyes flashed open and locked on Philomena. Recognition instantly settled over his features.

They stared wordlessly at one another for what seemed like hours. Trez eased himself into a sitting position, his eyes never leaving her. Philomena tensed and groped at her waist. She cursed silently, having forgotten she had no sword. She had left them strapped to her saddle.

Trez narrowed his eyes on her, knowing what she had intended. In a dry voice, Trez spoke. "You've got some nerve coming here, girl,"

41

Hurrying along the streets of Ezleon all alone, Philip felt
dreadfully lost. This frightened him greatly. He couldn't
remember if they had taken a left or a right on to the road with
the Brimming Barrel. He flung his gaze about him, desperately
trying to find some sort of landmark; a house, a puddle in the
road, anything he remembered passing before.

He didn't remember the weird, creaking sign with a wart covered
witch riding her broom hanging over a foreboding black door, or
the home with a bunch of broken flower pots on its window sills.
It was as if the occupants of the home had attempted to bring
some life and color on the bleary street. He definitely didn't
remember the cottage with its roof collapsed inward as if a giant
had stepped on it. Coming closer to the rubble of the cottage,
Philip saw that it looked like it had been burned. The skeletal
timbering was charred black and faintly smelled of ash.

Philip remembered the pike bearer before the gates of Ezleon
had said his home had been destroyed, burned by the malice of
their pagan god, Dandis. Philip wondered if this had been his
home.

Looking away from the burned cottage, Philip felt more helpless
than ever. Here he was wandering stupidly about the city's
streets not knowing where he was while Philomena could be in
actual danger.

Philip ran a hand through his hair, trying to control the huge,
roaring storm of panic that threatened to engulf him. He let out a
frustrated breath. Oh what he'd give to have Lark with him now.
He could at least lead him out of here.

"This is just great," Philip muttered, angry with himself. "In most cases you can at least ask for directions but there's nobody here," he complained with an irritable gesture to the empty street.

The silent homes gave him no reply, but they seemed to stare at him with their dark glass windows. It was kind of unnerving. Philip flexed his jaw, unsure of what to do. Worry for Philomena made his thoughts scramble. He knew what she'd say to him if she were here; *Stop whining to yourself and pull it together before I do it for you.*

The thought made Philip grin. Hearing Philomena's voice in his head helped him focus. During their time in Tosh, Philomena had been his rock. She had reminded him every day that he had a reason to keep going.

As he glanced around, only one plan surfaced clearly. He would have to retrace his steps back to the Brimming Barrel and try again from there to find the street of the homeless.

"I guess that's the best thing to do. I cannot believe I got myself lost," he grumbled to himself. He started back the way he had come. He passed the freaky witch sign, and the cottage with the broken flower pots. He turned left onto a small side road and then right onto another he was sure led back to the Brimming Barrel. Coming half way up the road, something shuffled in the shadows.

Philip froze as he caught movement out of the corner of his eye. He closed his fingers around the hilt of his sword. Every grain in his body was as taut as a bow string.

"What are you doin' round here, boy?" asked a rough voice accompanied with heavy footsteps. Tension rippled through Philip at the sound of the voice. He turned stiffly around to peer up at the stout sergeant two feet taller than himself. The sergeant's bulging chest and huge arms along with his violent features suggested he was better at solving problems physically rather than diplomatically. A sword and mace hung from his belt at his fingertips.

"You look lost, boy, and Commander Moth doesn't like wanderers heavily armed in his city," the bulky sergeant said with a sneer.

Philip didn't know whether it was his desperate situation or the fact that the gigantic sergeant had him outnumbered three to one, but he felt his confidence shrinking. "You call this *one* sword heavily armed? I just carry it so people won't bother me," Philip tried to sound casual, forcing a friendly smile.

The giant sergeant stared at him in disbelief. "So you're not lost?"

"As as matter of fact I am lost," Philip replied, swallowing nervously. The sergeant peered down at him as if he were just realizing how much larger he was than Philip.

"You wouldn't happen to know where the road with all those homeless people live is would you?" asked Philip, unconsciously taking a step back. His feet were screaming run, but the rest of his body was numbed to the spot.

"I'm familiar with it. Are you looking for someone?" the sergeant rumbled.

"Ugh, yeah I am actually," said Philip, his voice guarded. "Would you mind just pointing me in the right direction? I'm in a bit of a hurry,"

The giant sergeant glared with annoyance. "Sure. Turn that way," he said, pointing in a vague direction.

"What way?" frowned Philip, turning to look. As he did, a sensation prickled his spine. Without thinking he flicked his sword out and raised it to block a wooden club that swung out from the shadows. The sergeant wielding the club shoved Philip back with an angry growl.

His adrenaline pumping and his senses working overtime, Philip countered the sergeant's overhead attack, his wrists stinging as he withstood the ferocity of the blow. The sergeant was strong. Crinkling his nose, Philip overpowered the sergeant's club. Their weapons were locked between them now, steel biting wood.

Philip could feel his left arm quivering. His wound still hadn't fully recovered from the native's arrow. He gritted his teeth, sweat beginning to bead his face. He couldn't give in.

The sergeant snickered from behind his helm, and Philip knew he could see weakness. With a new gear of strength, the sergeant hefted his club and slashed Philip's blade away. Philip stumbled back, his sword singing from the clash. The sergeant grinned and stepped forward lifting his club.

Heavy footsteps sounded, and Philip snapped his gaze to the side to see the giant sergeant lumbering towards him with his mace gripped in his shovel sized hands.

Grimacing, Philip sidestepped out of the way of the rampaging sergeant. The sergeant stumbled clumsily, growling in aggravation. He twirled around to face Philip with surprising speed, swinging his mace in the process. Philip ducked, and slashed out his sword at the sergeant's leg. The sergeant howled, and angrily jabbed out with his mace. Philip easily evaded the attack, and slashed the sergeant's mace wielding arm making him howl again.

Finally feeling that he was gaining some ground, Philip forgot the second sergeant. Like a silent shadow stalking its unexpected victim, the club wielding sergeant snuck up behind Philip. His spine prickling again, Philip spun around just in time to see the sergeant's club rushing towards him. The club slammed in to his face with a crushing sound.

Philip's eyes rolled in the back of his head and he crumpled to the ground, his sword clattering next to him.

The giant sergeant managed a snicker despite his stinging cuts. His comrade rested his club against his shoulder and sighed.

"Well, that was less exciting than what I had hoped for,"

"But at least *we* took him down," the giant sergeant pointed out.

"True. The commander will surely reward us handsomely," said the club wielder. He knelt down and retrieved Philip's sword. "Why is Commander Moth making such a fuss over this boy?"

asked the giant sergeant. "He doesn't look like anything special," He nudged Philip roughly with the toe of his boot.

The second sergeant shot a glare at him. "Careful. We were ordered not to batter him up so much,"

The giant sergeant shuffled his feet bashfully and grunted. "You're one to talk, the way you bashed his face in with your club," he mumbled.

"Misjudged the strength of the swing," the other sergeant shrugged carelessly. "Come on, we should get him back to the chambers," The sergeant stood and gestured for his friend to do the honors.

The giant sergeant huffed and rolled up his sleeves. He bent down and gripped Philip's coat. He swung him over his shoulder like a sack of meat. With their prized prey safely secured, the sergeants proceeded down the road.

42

"What are you doing here?" Philomena demanded a hand on her hip. She glared down at Trez. Trez corked his mouth skeptically, as if considering how much truth to reveal to her.

"Isn't that rather obvious?" he said dryly. "The last time you saw me, Commander Xavier said he'd deal with me later," Trez sat up and drew his knees to his chin. He peered at Philomena from underneath his shaggy mane of blonde hair.

"The last time I saw you, you were whimpering on the floor like a girl because you were afraid of the durjock," said Philomena harshly. He wasn't the same pompous Trez Gregus she remembered back in Niche. There was a deep dejection that gripped him now.

Trez shuddered at the memory, and his face flushed with resentful embarrassment. "This is my punishment," he said, gesturing to the poor people around them.

Philomena glanced around. "What? Living in the slums?"

"Commander Xavier stripped me of everything; my standing, my potential, my home, and my family," said Trez grimly.

"Isn't that a little harsh?" asked Philomena.

Trez snorted. "Lying to your commanding officer in these days is unforgivable," He hesitated. "Now I know why,"

"What do you mean?" Philomena drawled uncertainly.

There was that considering gaze again that suggested Trez was weighing out how much more he should say. Glancing around as if fearful of being overheard, he hefted himself to his feet with a sigh.

Philomena tensed, taking a step back and dropping a hand to her knife. Trez dusted himself off and peeled something that resembled a rotten banana peel from his tunic with a crinkle of his nose. Philomena gave him a pitying, disgusted look.

"After you," said Trez with mock courtesy. He motioned her in to the run down cottage before them, its busted door hanging from the bottom hinge, half way open like a black gaping mouth.

"Are you serious?" asked Philomena with thick sarcasm after a glimpse of the cottage.

Trez slumped impatiently. "We cannot talk out here," he hissed. He glanced around them again.

"I don't trust you, Trez," said Philomena with a shake of her head.

"If you want to hear what I have to say then you'll follow me," said Trez with annoyance. He turned away and entered the foreboding cottage without a second glance. The shadows swallowed him up.

Philomena cursed under her breath. *This is probably a stupid idea*, she thought. She grumbled another curse and marched after Trez.

The cottage was even darker than Philomena had anticipated. She cautioned her step as she entered, and slipped her knife from its sheath. She'd forgotten she still carried her last parcel of food. Philip would probably be upset to find that she gave it all away. Aside from the small square of light coming from the open door that highlighted the floorboards, Philomena could make out nothing of her surroundings inside the cottage.

Once her eyes adjusted to the dim light, she could see outlines of a cupboard in the back, and a small table in the center with a lonely chair seated at its head. A shadow moved at her right side. She jumped from a sudden scraping sound. Something sparked, and a tiny yellow light flickered.

"You are certainly the strangest girl I've ever met," said Trez glumly. He set the candle with its dusty holder on the small table. The little light emanated warmly in the poor cottage.

"I sense that's a bad thing," Philomena figured carelessly,

gripping her knife.

"What you are and who you are do not coexist," said Trez, turning a hardened expression to her. Philomena shifted uneasily.

"What's that suppose to mean?"

"You talk like a man, you dress in boy's clothes, and you bested me in a fight," Trez said slowly.

"So," Philomena shrugged, wondering what point Trez was trying to make or if he simply wanted revenge for her beating him in the alley back in Niche.

Trez stared at her solemnly. "I know who you are . . . Princess Philomena," he said quietly.

Philomena started at her name. Trez watched her calmly, not in a way that suggested he'd keep her secret, but in a manner that said he'd fling her over his shoulder and turn her over to her enemies in a heartbeat if it meant gaining back what he'd lost. Philomena had to resist the urge to flee. She swallowed a sudden swell of panic. "Ho-how do you know this?"

"Judging by your reaction it must be true," said Trez, considering her with new interest.

"I asked you a question," Philomena said grindingly, setting her jaw. Trez huffed irritability. "I can force the answer out of you if you like," she added, stepping forward and lifting her knife threateningly.

Trez flashed a sneer at her, revealing some of his old personality. "I'm sure you'd enjoy that," he said scornfully. Running his tongue over his teeth, Trez inhaled a breath and started to explain. "After our meeting with the durjock, I ran away for two days. I was too afraid to face what fate Xavier had in mind for me. I stayed in Staleon Wood till I decided to go back. When I finally returned, one of the sergeants gave me a letter to be delivered by hawk. The letter was from Captain Avador to Commander Moth. It had been a mistake. The sergeant hadn't known that I was no longer in Xavier's favor,"

Philomena listened intently.

"Instead of correcting him, I went along with it and took the letter to be delivered. The letter of course was top priority and extremely secret. I already knew I was going to receive the sack from Xavier, so I ducked in an isolated alley and read the letter. Unfortunately, I am not the most educated, but I know enough to have made out the centerpiece parts. It had revealed that Captain Avador and his company are a posse; a posse to capture you and your brother. It referred to you and your brother as the prince and princess, the heirs we believed to have been dead all these years.

This information was so baffling to me I couldn't believe it at first. I went to Xavier in a daze and received my punishment. I didn't say a word of what I read. I knew that if I did I would have either been imprisoned or killed. I didn't go back to my family either. Instead, I went back to Staleon Wood. The letter still troubled me, and after thinking about it for a time, I filled in the gaps. I figured that if the true heirs had been alive this whole time, the king isn't really insane. Salvador Corea is to inherit the rule of Alamia, so he must have created this depression. Everything we know is a falsehood to cover Salvador's wickedness," Trez chewed out vengefully. The truth that was flooding passed his lips made Philomena shiver fearfully.

Trez fixed his gaze on her. "After that, I came here, and so here I am now talking to the princess who's said to be dead," He looked Philomena up and down.

"And you believe all of that?" Philomena sneered, doing her best not to appear shocked. "I think I've heard enough," She turned on her heel, shooting a glare of repulsion over her shoulder at Trez. She started for the door, but Trez grabbed her by the arm with an iron grip. The parcel slipped from under Philomena's arm and fell to the floor.

"Let go of me, Trez," Philomena snarled dangerously, lifting her knife to his chest. He didn't even flinch.

"You are the princess aren't you? A princess who can fight," said Trez, his eyes filled with conflicted malice. His grip tightened on her arm, and he slowly forced her against the wall. Philomena's nostrils flared and she flexed her jaw. "I fight well enough to beat you," she said sharply. The reminder made Trez snicker amusedly.

"I can't believe that stable boy had the nerve to even look at you," he scoffed, his face coming uncomfortably close to hers.

"His name is Lark, and he has more respect than you can manage with that rock you call a brain," Philomena flared defensively, shoving Trez back and making him stumble. Trez huffed disdainfully, glaring nastily at her.

"That stable boy is a worthless mutt. He's a half breed. His blood is mixed with a filthy Rogue father," Trez spat spitefully. His vicious words made it difficult for Philomena to keep her composure, but she fought the temptation to strangle him.

"As I said Trez, you know no respect, and you'll never know what peace or fairness really means. All you are is a bully," Philomena said coolly. Trez frowned, and rotated his gaze, seeming to have not heard her.

"Where's your brother?" Trez blurted out.

"Why do you care?" Philomena asked with a sneer.

"You should. This city is fortified. Do you see those red flags that have just been raised on the wall?" Trez pointed out the trio of red pointed flags through the cottage's doorway. The flags flapped lazily on three poles atop the wall. "Those mean all exits of the city are sealed. There's no way out,"

"What?" Philomena stammered staring at the red flags and stepping towards the doorway. Fear mounted within her.

"Commander Moth is after you. He's probably under orders from Captain Avador to hold you," said Trez.

Philomena turned brusquely to him, her features glazed with hate-filled anger. "You sent the letter?!" she shouted.

"Of course; I was told to," Trez shrugged in an arrogant manner.

"Why?!" Philomena hollered, her face flushing red. "Why would you do that?! Whose side are you on?!"

Trez glared at her distrustfully. "I'm on no one's side, princess,"

Philomena surged forward and slammed him against the wall. She pressed her knife to him again, this time against his throat. "What else do you know?! Tell me!" she demanded.

No fear or surprise flickered across Trez's face. Not even irritation. Just that smug look that was accustom of him. "I don't know anything else," he said calmly.

"You're lying," Philomena growled through clenched teeth. She pressed her knife even harder.

"Are you worried about your brother?" Trez said icily, a ghost of a grin sneaking across his face. "You should never have left his side, but then again you wouldn't have done him much good against Moth's sergeants. They're killers. They won't let you leave Ezleon. Not unless you're in Avador's custody, or if you're dead,"

Terror clutched Philomena. Philip could already be captured or hurt, or . . . even worse. "Where's Moth's chamber? Tell me now or I swear I'll split you in half for the buzzards,"

"You should kill me," Trez whispered in a strangely tempting voice. "I would if I were you. With everything I know, I could be your worst enemy,"

Philomena's features darkened. It was like Trez wanted to die. "I'm not like you, Trez. Now tell me what I want to know," Philomena demanded, jerking Trez emphatically. Trez swallowed against her knife on his throat.

"If I tell you, Commander Moth will easily trace the leak back to me. I'll surely be killed then," said Trez, his hard stare unwavering.

"Has it ever occurred to you that there are bigger things in the world than yourself? You've already lost everything," said Philomena, her skin prickling with anxiety and adrenaline.

"Not my life," Trez said in a low voice.

"How do you call this living?" Philomena asked bluntly. A grim expression shifted across Trez's face. He was silent for a moment, but then he gave in with an exhaled sigh.

"In the center of the city, in the town square," he said, looking away with a hurt expression. The simple directions sparked hope in Philomena, even though she knew she couldn't trust Trez. With difficulty, she eased her knife against his throat and released her hold on him. Shooting a contemptuous glare at him, she hastened to the door her boots clicking.

"You should know," Trez spoke huskily. Philomena slowed and looked over her shoulder. "It's all a trap," he whispered, his gaze solemnly guarded.

"That doesn't matter anymore," Philomena said, sheathing her knife. Her expression was ablaze with determination and fear. She turned away from Trez and covered the distance between her and the door in three strides. The last parcel of food remained forgotten on the cottage floor. Feeling defeated and vulnerable, Trez slumped against the wall and held his face in his hands. The city was no longer safe for him.

Bursting from the cottage, Philomena flew out on to the street, nearly tripping over the sleeping homeless. She pounded up the street, her breath streaming in white clouds in her wake. Trez's directions to the commander's station should be easy enough to follow. She just had to get to the center of the city as fast as she could. She wondered what she'd do once she got to the commander's station. Just storm in, knock everyone out and get Philip? It wouldn't be that easy. The commander here was organized, and his defenses strong. She alone wouldn't be able to rescue Philip.

Just thinking about it made Philomena fret dangerously. Her confidence ached. She mentally shook herself. She didn't have time to worry. She focused her entire being on reaching Philip. This only worsened her worry.

How could I have been so stupid! She tormented herself. Back in the tavern, she had actually felt angry, even jealous towards

Philip . . . and Lark. How could she have felt such things towards her own brother who had done nothing but look out for her. Philomena bit back the sting of tears.

If they had done anything to him, she would never be able to forgive herself.

Please, forgive me, Philip. A tear streaked down her cheek. Suddenly, something blunt and piercing snagged against her shins. With no time to react, and having been in a full run, she flew forward and hit the ground hard. The breath escaped her lungs in a sharp gasp. The world loomed about her dizzily. Before she could recover, rough hands gripped fistfuls of her overcoat and yanked her to her feet. Philomena clenched her teeth.

The sergeants who restrained her cackled with their success. "Look at what we've caught here, Cupde. A little girl, a helpless little girl," one of them mocked with a chuckle.

"A beautiful girl at that, and with a beautiful knife," the other sergeant, Cupde, leered over Philomena's shoulder. He pulled her knife from its sheath that was hooked to her belt. The pair of them cackled some more.

"And they told us you'd be hard to capture, sweetheart," the first sergeant jibbed. Philomena scrunched her nose angrily, something triggering inside her. Shaking their hold on her, she jabbed one of them in the gut with her elbow. Spinning on her heel, she popped the second sergeant over the ears with cupped hands. The two sergeants toppled over, the first clutching his sore stomach and the other groaning as his ears rang readily. Wasting no time, Philomena raced away, swinging into a narrow alley. She glanced over her shoulder, and saw the two sergeants still sprawled pathetically in the middle of the road. Grinning to herself, Philomena rushed into the alley . . . and slammed right into a third sergeant. An iron grip clasped both of her wrists and held her fast, giving her no chance to draw another knife. The sergeant's dark eyes bore in to her mercilessly.

"We've been expecting you," he said.

Philomena stared back, panting.

"Commander Moth will be most pleased that both of you are in custody," the sergeant said, tugging some twine from his belt. Horror stabbed Philomena like an icy knife. It was true then, they did have Philip as she suspected. For a moment she was speechless in her fear. Anticipation made her imagination run riot over the endless possibilities of what they might have done to him.

"Where's my brother? What have you done to him?" she stuttered, having the audacity to sound threatening even as the sergeant began to bind her hands.

The sergeant lifted his eyebrows incredulously. "You'll see, soon enough,"

"We'll both get out of this, and when we do you'll be wishing you never came to know us," Philomena spat, jerking her hands about to make it difficult for him to wrap the twine around her wrists.

"Frankly, I don't know who you are," the sergeant replied calmly. With a quick twist of the wrist, he twirled the twine about Philomena's hands, astonishing her with his patience. With another flick, he secured her bonds with a final knot, tugging her forward in the process and making her stumble. Philomena couldn't help flushing haughtily.

"And I don't really care to either, so let's go," The sergeant steered her roughly along, leading her back out to the road where his comrades still lay groaning. Once they shambled to their feet, they started for the commander's chamber with watchful eyes on Philomena who staggered between them. As she allowed herself to be willingly lead to whatever sinister fate was in store, it felt like the whole world was collapsing with her underneath it.

43

Ezleon was behind Lark as he rode Spear up their third hill.
Looking back, the city was small and quiet, and bathed in the
soft moonlight and starlight. The sky had been swept clean of
grey clouds to create a clear night. A cloud of chimney smoke
hung above the homes and buildings of the city. The damp cold
of the winter's night made the scenery seem desolate and the city
gloomy. Somewhere down there, Philip and Philomena
remained. *They were probably enjoying themselves in the
Brimming Barrel*, Lark thought ruefully.

Regret was gradually building in Lark's heart, making him
hesitate. It also annoyed him. He couldn't turn back now. He
needed to return to Niche, back to his family. That's where he
belonged. Not on some crazy, wild mission on which there was a
great chance of being killed or worse. He wasn't a knight, or a
hero. He was a stable boy, a farmer's son; a native's son at that.
He had no status for doing something great.

But unfortunately for Lark, his mind kept circling around this
logic to the thought of never seeing Philomena or Philip again.
The thought pained him, and ate away at his heart. Even though
they had pretty much kidnapped him and forced him to help
them, they were the only two people who had ever treated him . .
. equally. They were the closest Lark ever had to friends.

It's crazy is what it is, Lark thought grudgingly.

An agitated chirp came from Arican making Lark stir from his
contemplations. He looked down and saw the cub watching him
from the saddlebag on Spear's side. She peered up at him with
inquisitive eyes. Lark attempted a smile as he fondled the cub
between the ears. She seemed to sense his true feelings.

"I know, Arican," said Lark. He took one last look at Ezleon before nudging Spear forward. Lark wondered what he'd do with Arican when he got back home, and Spear too. His mother would never let him keep an animal in the house, and there was no way he could support Spear at Master Finn's stables. With a dejected sigh, Lark pushed these troubles aside for the time being.

Spear swooshed his tail and started trotting up the hill. Just before they reached the hill's peak, the bay suddenly froze. His ears pricked forward and his nostrils flared.

"What is it, Spear?" asked Lark, putting a hand to the horse's neck. Spear blew his nose and took a few steps back. Crinkling his brow, Lark looked ahead. He couldn't see any obvious thing that could be bothering the horse. Arican gurgled nervously and withdrew deeper into the comforts of her saddlebag. Rather baffled, Lark was unsure of what to do. Then the rumble of approaching hooves reached his ears.

Thinking quickly, Lark swung Spear around and galloped over the hill side. The crest of the hill offered them cover as well as the shadows of the night. The thundering hooves pounded over the peak and stormed by fastly. Spear shook his head and chomped at his bit with agitation as the vibrations of the other horses' passing rippled through him. Lark scratched his withers and whispered soothingly to the horse.

Ignoring his own agitation, Lark gently touched Spear's sides. They inched forward till Lark was able to peer around the grassy hillside. A group of ten riders were descending the hill in quite a hurry. The occasional glint of moonlight reflected off their equipment, and Lark could see the feather shafts of arrows sticking out of their quivers. Long bows were slung over their shoulders. They appeared to be natives.

A suspicion stirred in Lark. Only one commander was out there that he knew of that led native soldiers. He dug in the saddlebag that Arican wasn't in, knowing that Philip hadn't had the chance to collect his few belongings that were in there. His hand clasped about the cool brass telescope. He brought it out and lifted it to one eye.

Peering through the device, Lark saw the native soldiers. He moved his line of vision along until he found their commander at the head. A jet black stallion carried him, and he wore matching black garments. His black hair whipped about his shoulders, and his fierce gaze was enough to break the magnifier in the telescope.

A tremor of fear rippled through Lark as he lowered the telescope, for he recognized the rider in black. It was Avador, no mistake about it.

How had they reached Ezleon so fast? Lark thought. Tucking away the telescope, Lark watched the company descend the hill then start climbing the next. They galloped over the hill's peak, and one by one disappeared to the other side. Once the last native soldier rode over the hill out of sight, Lark breathed with relief. Tension though still gripped him. He was well aware Avador was headed to Ezleon after Philip and Philomena. An outside force seemed to be propelling Lark to do something about it.

A chirp sounded, and Arican climbed in the saddle before him. Lark stroked her, still staring off in the direction Avador and his company had gone. The gears in his mind began to creak and whirr noisily. He knew the reason for Avador's pursuit to the city, but why Avador had gotten here so fast still perturbed him. Oddly, the image of the hawk Lark had seen just as they had entered the city flashed in his mind's eye. He knew it had been a messenger hawk sent from the guards' watch tower. It couldn't have been a coincidence.

Lark's brow furrowed. Assuming that it wasn't a coincidence, the hawk must have been carrying a message to the commander of Ezleon; a message that told him of Philip and Philomena's entrance into the city. If that were true, than Commander Moth would have been forewarned of their approach, and ordered to hold them.

The pieces of the puzzle started to fall in to place quickly now. If anyone would have forewarned Commander Moth it was Avador. That's why he had gotten here so fast. Avador knew that once he had lost them in Staleon, his safety net was Commander Moth, so he had headed straight for Ezleon. All he had to do now was collect Philip and Philomena from Commander Moth and be on his merry way to Caelum.

This frightening realization made Lark's head spin. Gazing passed the hill tops to Ezleon, Lark felt drawn back to the city. But looking over his shoulder, he remembered that his family needed him also. Still, even though he hated to admit it, he couldn't bear the thought of leaving Philip and Philomena to the fate Avador had in store for them.

Arican chirped again, peering up at him expectantly. Spear sidestepped and arched his neck anxiously.

"If all of that is true," Lark said aloud, his expression glazed pensively. "Avador is going through a lot of effort to capture them," Another realization clicked to him. "They were telling the truth. They really are the prince and princess,"

His own words sent a jolt through him that propelled him in to action. "Alright, let's go,"

He nudged Spear and the bay obliged, breaking in to a gallop as they descended the hill. Lark chose a path that veered slightly off the main road to avoid coming right behind Avador. He kept a hold of Arican so she wouldn't plummet from the saddle.

Feeling somewhat out of place in his choice, Lark wondered how he'd accomplish rescuing the prince and princess all on his own. A tug pulled at his chest as he remembered Niche. He hoped his family would forgive him for turning his back on his one chance of returning home. Unworthy or not though, Lark felt certain he had made the right decision. After all, since the cheery young man and the cantankerous girl he knew were in fact the true heirs

of the kingdom, there wouldn't be much of a future for his
family if he didn't save Philip and Philomena.

With a flare of determination, Lark urged Spear faster, laying
low over the horse's neck. He had to reach Philip and Philomena
before Avador.

Lark just hoped he could find a way to do that.

44

The blue towers of Caelum rose against a stormy sky before Philip. The massive dark clouds sparked with lightning. Pilascus Harbor rippled beneath him.

It was all so vivid, Philip would have thought it was really happening, but he knew it was a dream. He couldn't fly after all, and he was soaring over the harbor. Still, the sight of his home gave him a thrill of happiness.

The image was raw and his movements clear. He was desperately trying to reach Caelum, but something heavy was slowing him down. More lighting crackled, and suddenly the castle was burning. The glow of the fire reflected in the water. Terror choked Philip, and he thought he would suffocate.

A voice came from before him, though he couldn't perceive anyone on the shoreline. It sounded like Avador's voice. *You're too late, prince. You're family and home is ruined, and so is your country. You only have yourself to blame,* said the voice.

Nooo! Philip screamed. He writhed as something ice cold washed over him. His eyes flew open. Panting and his pulse racing, Philip glanced around. He frowned as he found himself on his knees in a neat, well lit room that was unfamiliar too him. His whole head ached, but he couldn't remember why. A thick fog distorted his memory. Sweat rolled off him, making him shiver.

He didn't know why he was on his knees, or why the sergeants standing around were staring at him, but he felt relieved. His home hadn't really burned to the ground, and he hadn't really heard Avador's spooky voice.

He sighed inwardly. Wait . . . sergeants?

Philip took a better look around, and his small glimmer of relief sank. Something itchy and strenuous rubbed against his wrists. Looking up, Philip realized he was bound by thick ropes that were hooked to chains dropping from the rafters. Memory began to rush back to him. He remembered trying to find Philomena and getting lost in the process. Then the sergeants found him, and that's when they bashed his face with a club. After that, Philip couldn't remember anything.

Another wave of uncontrollable shivering came over him. He stared solemnly at the stone floor. His head throbbed achingly, making it difficult to think. Frankly, Philip didn't want to think. He was too tired. He felt like an old garment worn so thin it was on the verge of crumbling apart.

Footsteps echoed towards him. "Are you with us now, boy," said a voice.

Philip strained to lift his gaze. A sergeant stood over him, his dark eyes piercing from behind his helm. He wore armor far greater than the sergeants from Niche. Durable, fit, well made and consistent with the Stalveerian design with Ezleon's emblem of a stag stamped below the neckline of the breastplate.

"Do you even know why you are here?" asked the sergeant when Philip did not reply. The other sergeants in the chamber perked up, and listened intently.

"You sound like you don't even know yourself," Philip managed huskily. He tried to swallow but his throat was too dry.

The sergeant clenched his jaw, his eyes roiling. "Commander Moth has never gone through so much trouble to capture a fugitive alive. Why are you so important?"

Philip shrugged as best he could being bound. "I've never met your Commander Moth, or stepped foot in this city till tonight. Why I'm so important to you I cannot say,"

"Who are you?" the sergeant asked, his eyes narrowing. Philip ducked his head emitting a rattling cough, feeling suddenly taciturn. Nausea made everything swirl and seem faraway.

A second sergeant stepped in to the scene. "Give us an answer, boy. What is your name?" he demanded belligerently. His sharp voice penetrated Philip and made him feel queasy.

"Werik," the first sergeant warned. "He's not all that well,"

"He won't be at all once I'm through with him. Your name, boy," said Werik.

"What is my name to you?" Philip croaked, straining to peer up at the sergeants. Werik gritted his teeth moodily. The other sergeants tensed.

The first sergeant clenched his hands uneasily. "Why don't you make yourself useful and fetch the boy some water, before he faints from thirst," he said, turning his back on Philip.

His expression suddenly darkened, Werik scrunched his nose and pulled a knife. The first sergeant looked to him with anticipation.

"I'll give him some water, after he tells us who he is," Werik growled, gripping his knife's hilt.

"Stop, Werik," the first sergeant demanded, gripping his comrade's forearm. "We are under orders not to harm him,"

"I'll gut him with a dull knife," Werik snarled, defiantly shaking off his comrade's grasp.

"I am lieutenant here, you oblige by me. I'm commanding you to leave him be," the first sergeant growled, stepping between Werik and Philip. A few other sergeants came forward, their hands at their weapons.

Werik snapped an enraged glare at the lieutenant. "Don't you want to know the truth, Kaiden? You know there is something more to this capture than a simple crime,"

"That is not our place to know," said Kaiden, though his taut expression betrayed him. Philip struggled to listen, but his aching head was making everything hazy.

"Isn't it?" said Werik. "For years we've done Moth's bidding. We tore Ezleon apart for him. Should we be treated like mindless children who only know how to obey orders?"

Kaiden's expression flickered, heavily weighing out Werik's words. For a moment, Werik thought he would side with his reasoning, but the small hint of rebellion quickly faded from Kaiden's eyes. The lieutenant took in a breath to speak.

"Stay away from the prisoner, Werik. I don't want any trouble," Kaiden said stonily. He started to walk away.

"Coward," Werik lashed, glaring at his lieutenant's back.

Kaiden froze. There was a ripple of hushed disapproval amongst the sergeants.

"That's why Moth made you his second in command. When it comes to thinking on your own, you just don't have the guts," Werik spat aggressively. He gripped his knife and moved to Philip kneeling at his feet.

Kaiden turned just in time to find Werik seize a fistful of Philip's hair. It all happened in a matter of seconds. Werik yanked Philip's head back so his face was upturned to his own. Philip opened his eyes blearily, and saw Werik looming over him. The vengeful sergeant raised his knife, his eyes glittering murderously.

"Werik!! Put that knife away!" Kaiden boomed. A hand flew to his sword as he stormed forward. There were several ringing, slithering sounds as his comrades behind him drew their own weapons.

Their movement had a stinging effect. His nose crinkling in an irritated manner, Werik pressed his knife to Philip's throat. His mind sluggish and his strength sapped, Philip could only react with a wrinkle of his brow.

Kaiden and the sergeants stiffened in their actions.

"Come closer I dare you," Werik hissed at them. He flicked his eyes to his knife at Philip's throat. The message was all too clear. There was a tense tightening in Kaiden's chest. "This won't accomplish anything. Put the knife away now and nothing will befall you," said Kaiden.

"Aren't you tired of taking orders, lieutenant," said Werik, sneering at Kaiden. "What of all you, comrades? Aren't you tired of bidding by Moth?"

"That is what we signed on for," a sergeant said pointedly.

Werik glared with annoyance at his comrade's simple viewpoint. He turned his attention to Philip once more. "What of it, boy?" he growled, shaking Philip roughly. "Will you give us your name if only to save yourself?"

Fighting back a wave of nausea, Philip met Werik's eyes. He looked away pointedly, his nostrils flared.

"No?" Werik guessed, flexing his jaw impatiently. He tightened his grip on his knife. The blade drifted to Philip's shoulder, and Werik jabbed the point into him.

"How about now?" Werik jeered.

Philip grimaced, growling as the knife penetrated through his clothes to his skin. Slowly, Werik drug the knife down over his collar bone, cutting cloth and skin, leaving a trail of blood in its wake.

"You better speak, boy, before my blade reaches your heart," Werik muttered, bringing his face inches from Philip's. Kaiden and the sergeants gaped in alarm.

Pain twisted Philip's features, but he did not utter a significant groan of agony, nor allow himself to think of giving in to Werik's terms. As the hateful sergeant's knife inched closer to his heart, it felt as though a hoard of wasps were stinging him over and over again. Sweat began to drip from his paling face, and his breath came in stabbing gasps.

As if surfacing from a pool of deep water, Kaiden shook himself out of his shock. "ENOUGH! LET HIM GO!" he roared.

The sergeants surged forward, their swords raised.

Werik bared his teeth at them and snapped his knife back, ready to stab Philip's racing heart. The door to the chambers banged open, emitting a tall blonde man, his face tight with rage. In one fluent movement, he raised his own knife and threw.

WHOOSH! The knife sliced the air with a flash of silver and made a sudden stop, burying its blade deep in to Werik's chest. Werik sucked in one last breath, then his eyes glazed with emptiness and he crumpled over. His knife clattered to the floor at Philip's feet. Philip glanced around confusedly, his sluggish mind taking its time to process what had happened. The long cut Werik delivered to him gnawed stingingly.

Stunned by the speed of events, the rest of the sergeants turned wide-eyed shaken expressions to the blonde man in the doorway. The blonde man closed the chamber's door and strode over to the fallen Werik. With a careless grunt he nudged the lifeless body with the toe of his boot.

"Don't stand there and gawk," the blonde man said flatly to the staring sergeants. "Someone tend to the prisoner, and start digging a grave for this man,"

"Yes, Commander Moth," the sergeants murmured. The name perked Philip's attention. He lifted a weary stare to the commander standing before him.

The sergeants started about their orders, some going off to fetch water and medicine, and the rest moving to carry their fallen comrade from the chamber. Kaiden sheathed his sword and stepped over to Moth, looking a little nervous.

"My apologies, commander," Kaiden said sheepishly. "He took advantage of our trust,"

"I never liked him," Moth grumbled, his sharp eyes following the sergeants carrying Werik's body through the doorway. He looked back to his lieutenant. "At least now you know what befalls those who are disloyal to me,"

His cold voice put a chill in Kaiden. "At least the prisoner was saved," he said.

"No thanks to you," Moth muttered, shooting a demeaning glare at Kaiden before walking to his desk on the far side of the room. Kaiden's gaze darted around the chamber, not knowing which way to go.

Some of the sergeants returned with water, cloth bandages, and a small round jar. They went over to Philip and went about cleaning and bandaging his wound. This they did with negligent hands and without undoing his bonds.

Though their tending was rough and without care, Philip was grateful. The white salve they scooped from the jar cooled the sting, and the thick bandages kept his ripped tunic and coat from rubbing the cut.

Moth regarded Philip with burning intrigue from his seat behind his desk. He stroked his smooth chin with his forefinger absently. He watched Philip carefully, noting that the boy didn't flinch, or give in to the smallest wince as his sergeants bandaged him.

"I hope you can forgive that little escapade," Moth said to Philip with mocking kindness. He stood, his chair scraping like mean claws against the stone floor making Philip shudder within. Philip lifted a weary glare.

"You're Commander Moth," Philip breathed, the pain in his chest lingering. Each breath he took made the fresh wound burn nastily.

Moth spread his arms as he neared Philip. "Commander Moth, overseer of Ezleon, and leader of Staleveer's first defenses for Lord Leif," he introduced, sounding fond of his titles.

His presentation gave Philip a headache.

"I've never trifled with you before. This capture isn't personal is it?" Philip ventured, his heavy conscious slowly untangling the connections.

Moth regarded him expectantly, his thin eyebrows lifted.

"You have orders from Avador," Philip murmured, his brow knitted with concentration.

"Exactly," Moth grinned with vague pleasure. He paced slowly before Philip, lacing his hands before him. A sword with a wicked pommel wrapped in black leather was sheathed at his side. "We received orders by hawk of your coming, and we were told to hold you until Avador can collect you," said Moth.

The muffled disturbance of what sounded like a pack of dogs tearing each other apart for a scrap of meat came from outside. Kaiden frowned over his shoulder as growling, thrashing sounds gradually grew louder. He walked over to the door to see what was going on.

Moth's thin mouth twitched with a grin, not at all surprised by the noise. Anticipation bubbled in Philip and twisted his gut in to uncomfortable knots.

"Now, I believe in following orders," Moth went on casually. "But . . . I also believe in extracting my own enjoyment,"

The door to the chamber burst open before Kaiden dared to open it. Three sergeants stumbled in with a small, thrashing, kicking figure between them. Kaiden hurried to help.

"LET ME GO YOU SONS OF ROACHES! I'LL TAKE YOU ONE BY ONE!" roared a girl's voice.

Moth looked over appearing partially annoyed. Philip's raspy breath caught short and his heart lifted with joy. He knew that enraged voice anywhere.

"Philomena!!" he called.

"PHILIP!" she hollered back, still giving the sergeants the most difficult time she could. She thrashed and lunged and growled. She kicked out and slammed Kaiden in the gut with her boot. The lieutenant stumbled back clutching at his sore stomach, his expression awash in pain. The other three sergeants struggled to contain her.

Relief swelled in Philip. *Thank god, she's safe and angrier than ever*, he thought.

Philomena continued to resist, her eyes ablaze with fury. The sergeants' wrestling with her wore beat red faces, hating every moment of their embarrassment.

For a thrilling few seconds, Philomena thought she had a chance of breaking free. She yanked loose of the sergeant on her right, and head slammed the one behind her leaving only the one on her left whose confidence was shriveling quickly away.

Moth exhaled and rolled his eyes. He strolled over to them like he hadn't a care in the world, but Philip could see the strength and confidence in his stride. Moth wasn't one to be underestimated.

Moth's cold impassive stare lingered on Philomena.

"What are *you* looking at?" Philomena snapped snootily. Philip laughed within and shook his head. Philomena never knew when to hold her tongue when she got angry.

A smile tugged at Moth's mouth that never reached his eyes.

"Act more like a lady, girl, and you and your brother might get out of here without being killed first," he said.

His slithering voice gave a daunting effect to Philomena's resistance. He grabbed her roughly by the arm and dragged her over to Philip. The sergeants took a moment to regain their composure, relieved that their commander had taken over.

"Come over here and have your happy little reunion so we can move along with our plans," Moth grumbled, shoving Philomena to the ground before Philip.

Philip snarled at Moth, anger growing in the pit of his stomach like a bed of red hot coals.

Shuffling in to a sitting position, Philomena raised a look of dread to her brother. When her eyes washed over her brother's bruised, battered face she had to suck back a chocking sob. Emotions of relief, dismay, and rage flashed over her face. Philip's brow knitted with concern.

"Philip, I-I'm so sorry," Philomena stuttered, her voice cracking. "It's all my fault,"

"Hey, don't worry about it. We'll figure this out," Philip whispered as comfortingly as his hoarse voice could manage.

"What have they done to you?" Philomena said through gritted teeth, her eyes scanning his bruised face.

"I can't look that bad," Philip tried a smile. Philomena shook her head.

Before they could exchange anymore words, Moth gestured to

his sergeants. "That's enough," he said flatly.

The sergeants stepped forward, bent over and jerked Philomena to her feet. They dragged her a considerable space away, enough for her to see Philip but not close enough for them to converse quietly. Philomena fought against them even more vigorously than before, throwing in curses and calling them names.

Philip tugged at his own bonds. Fiery pain shot through his shoulder and chest as he did so, his fresh wound stinging venomously. But he didn't care; he just wanted to get out of there.

Moth strolled over to him once more, studying him as if he were a piece of meat hanging in the butcher's and he was wagering on whether to buy it or not.

"As I was saying," he said. "I like having my own enjoyment from my orders. No one really knows who you are, so I've arranged something quite special for you,"

To the side, Philomena growled like a caged animal as the sergeants pinned her against the stone wall. They pulled out a ring of keys and secured her into shackles cemented in the stone. The cold iron clicked soundly around her wrists and ankles, holding her fast.

"What do you mean *special*?" Philip sneered at Moth, his teeth meshed. He clenched his fists, his rising abrasiveness making his breath sharp.

Kaiden came over, looking like he had just swallowed a sour grape. He rubbed his still sore stomach. "Sorry, to interrupt, Commander, but are we keeping to our arranged plans?"

"Yes," Moth said with light annoyance. "Start the summons. Wake everyone, and order them to the town square."

The lieutenant gave a loyal bow, backed away and departed with the rest of the sergeants. The door slammed in their wake, leaving Philip and Philomena alone with Moth. Philip frowned confusedly. *What did Moth mean by summons?* Philip wondered. His reaction to their movements made Moth relish with satisfaction. "Curious now, boy?"

Philomena made a frustrated gurgling sound. "Ugh! Why don't you stop trying to play mind games and spit it out already!"

"Aren't you lively," Moth chuckled amusedly. He directed a cool smile to Philip. "You ought to be proud of her. She's brave, for a girl,"

He turned and walked leisurely over to his desk, obviously enjoying the moment. He picked up a pipe from his desk and faced them again. His calm, sauntering manner was beginning to wear on Philomena's patience. They watched Moth as he pinched some dried leaf material from a jar and stuffed it into his pipe to smoke.

"To be frank with the pair of you," Moth said, lighting his pipe and puffing a cloud of smoke. "We've known of your arrival for quite some time. Avador gave me orders as you already know, and he should be here shortly. I'm the only one here who knows why such a troubling fuss has been stirred up for you,"

Philomena stared stunned. "You mean . . . you *know*?"

Moth shrugged, sucking on his pipe and blowing more smoke. "You think such information could be kept a secret from everyone?"

Irritable defensiveness swelled in Philomena. Their so called secret was not only held on the unfaithful tongue of the infuriating Trez Gregus, but now with the slick Commander Moth? It was just plain unfair. They weren't ready to expose their true identities to the world yet.

Glancing over at Philip, Philomena noticed he didn't seem too surprised, but he did look angry.

"Such important individuals as yourselves must be handled accordingly. You could be the destruction of everything Lord Salvador has thus achieved, making you a deadly threat. Especially you," Moth pointed to Philip with his pipe. He spoke so casually, they could have been discussing plans for a merry dinner.

"So, as a faithful follower of Salvador and the future he promises, I see myself obliged to tend to the threat you have created for him,"

"Would you just get on with it," Philomena snapped.

Moth leaned lazily against his desk. "Outside that door is a stage that stands before the expanse of the town square. In thirty minutes or so, you will walk out there with me in front of the entire city. I will then expose you as a dangerous fraud who believes he is something he is not; a conspiracy theorist who is the greatest threat to our future of salvation. Do not think they won't believe me. They have no reason to ignore a claim such as this,"

Moth's words seeped in the air like black, venomous vapor. Philip felt like the air in his lungs was being sucked out. Even Philomena was subdued by the commander's bold declaration.

"Why just me?" Philip asked hoarsely, forcing himself to sound undeterred. "Why not both of us?"

Moth's eyes were suddenly drained with any playfulness. They iced over like pools of merciless malice. "The future of your sister has not yet been revealed. You are the main course of tonight's entertainment, Prince Philip Stilwell,"

The sound of his full name gave Philip a chill down his spine, but not knowing what horrid fate waited Philomena frightened him even more.

"If you don't cooperate with my plan, the one who will feel the sting of my blade is her," said Moth, his eyes shifting to Philomena. Philomena glared back, but now there was a shade of fear in her that Moth easily detected.

"She is my guarantee of your cooperation, so she stays in here, safe and sound." said Moth. Philip let his gaze drop to the ground, his mind whirring with anxiety. What was he going to do?

He heard Moth's footsteps come towards him.

"Just remember this, prince," Moth spoke and Philip looked to him. "You are nothing more than fresh meat readied to be tossed to hungry wolves," Moth blew smoke in to Philip's face with a satisfied snicker, and Philip knew hope for escape was dim.

Please God, Philip prayed in silent desperateness, *if You can hear me now help us get out of here. Even if it means that I must sacrifice myself. Just keep my sister safe. Please.*

Moth chuckled and turned away, humming cheerfully to himself as he smoked his pipe.

Please God . . .

45

"Are you really serious?" Lark grumbled, his breath fogging on the biting cold air. He lay on his stomach on the peak of the last hill before Ezleon, peering through Philip's telescope. Arican gurgled playfully next to him. She poked her head over the hill top with curious eyes. Lark pulled her back down, tossing some grass at her to play with. The cub chirped excitedly and snatched at the loose grass. Lark shook his head and went back to his investigating.

Through the telescope, Lark could see sergeants fiercely patrolling the walls and the three red flags that signaled that the gates were locked flapping lazily. No mere traveler or villager would be able to make a great enough excuse to convince the sergeants to open the gates now.

Moments ago, Lark had witnessed Avador and his men file in to the gaping black entrance of the city. Amongst the native soldiers, Lark had spotted Philip and Philomena's uncle, Balin, along with another rugged looking man who was obviously a captive as well. Lark remembered Philip mentioning something about a knight who had helped them back in Niche. The second captive must be that knight, Lark reckoned.

The sentries guarding the entrance of Ezleon had given Avador no gripe about his passage. The company was in the city within seconds of their arrival at the gate. The main entrance was the only apparent way back in to the city.

Cursing, Lark slunk back behind the crest of the hill. He hurried down the uneven ground, locking Philip's telescope back into its compact form. Arican scrambled at his heels, pouncing at a stick. Spear waited for them at the bottom of the hill. The bay lifted his head as Lark came near chewing a mouthful of grass around his bridal's bit. Lark patted his nose and stowed away the telescope in the saddlebag.

Frowning pensively, Lark folded his arms and chewed at his lip, his brow pinching. He knelt down and broke off a piece of the stick Arican was chewing on.

Maybe if I draw it out, I can figure a way to get in, Lark thought hopefully. With one end of the stick, he drew an outline of Ezleon's hexagon shaped wall in a patch of dirt, the moon providing enough light for him to see. He added the watch towers as spots on each corner.

The only possible blind spot, or more correctly phrased, the only possible minute of luck Lark could perceive was climbing one of the watch towers themselves. There was just the small problem of getting to the tower unseen. Of course there was also the predicament of scaling the tower without any rope or aide to climb it.

Glancing over at Spear, Lark realized that he wouldn't be able to bring him along if he were to climb one of the towers. He couldn't leave him either. Now that he thought of it, he would have to get Philip and Philomena's horses, and if they were to escape quickly, the horses would have to be tacked and ready in a place that was easy to get to. How on earth was he going to do that?

Frustration having mounded to the size of a mountain, Lark tossed away the stick he had been drawing with. Arican chased after it, her tail twitching excitedly.

"This is the worst rescue mission ever," Lark groaned aloud. He rubbed his face tiredly, feeling weary. The aggravation of just trying to help Philip and Philomena was enough to drive him back on the road home.

Lark mentally kicked himself. *No, that's not going to happen*, he thought determinedly.

He had decided to come back and help them. He wasn't going to give up just because the mission was near to the impossible. Willing himself to think positive, Lark rose to his feet. He had to accomplish what he came to do, even if it meant making a few more sacrifices. If he was going to get in to the city, the only way in was as he had figured: to climb one of the towers.

He pulled the saddlebags from Spear's back. The bay turned a curious look on him, as if asking what he was doing. Lark looked to the horse he had become fond of.

"Sorry, Spear," said Lark, pursing his lips regretfully. He could carry Arican up the tower, but there was no way Spear would be able to come. He had to let the horse free. The idea put a bitter lump in his throat.

"Maybe you can meet me on the other side, huh?" His voice cracked with emotion. He stroked the horse's neck. Spear nickered, and rubbed his head against Lark's chest.

Gritting his teeth to keep back the tears he felt, Lark realized had never come to care about any other living thing besides his family till he had been with Philip and Philomena. Now, he felt the pain of letting go of something he cared for.

Swallowing hard, Lark unbuckled Spear's girth and pulled the saddle off, dropping it on the ground. He slipped the bridal over Spear's head. Spear dropped the bit from his mouth, and then looked to Lark uncertainly.

Lark tossed away the bridal, and it caught in a clump of dry grass. "Go on, boy. It's okay."

He pushed gently on Spear's shoulder, telling him to go. Spear took a few uncertain steps forward. He stopped for a moment, shook his mane, and then bolted away, galloping over the hills.

Watching the stallion fly over the land under the starry sky, Lark felt a thrill of joy for him despite the feeling of loss. It must feel good to be free.

Turning away, Lark shouldered the saddlebags and whistled for Arican. The ocelot came trotting over. Then a small, long legged nocturnal bird scurried out from a burrow letting out a high pitched tweet. Chirping excitedly, Arican chased after it, pouncing over the side of the hill.

"Arican!" Lark hissed upsettingly. Growling with frustration, Lark hurried after her. He followed her down the hillside, muttering to himself and wondering if things ever went as planned.

The little cub bounded after the tweeting bird until it scurried into another burrow. Sticking her nose into the burrow, Arican seemed rather disappointed.

Lark snatched her up before she could spot something else to chase.

"We've got to work on your obedience," Lark muttered, scratching the mischievous cub under the chin. Arican chirped and stretched a paw out to him, gazing at him with big yellow eyes.

Lark shook his head and slipped her in to the saddlebag. All Arican wanted to do was play, completely unaware of anything serious. He shouldered the saddlebags with a sigh.

Walking along the hill's face, Lark tripped over something he had failed to notice. Lark regained his balance and frowned over his shoulder. A rock? No, it hadn't felt like one.

He knelt to the ground and felt around until his hand came to something smooth and curved, with a gap between it and the ground. A handle?

Lark's frown deepened. He ran his hand from the handle along the ground next to it, and found that it wasn't the ground at all. Sure, a thin layer of dirt was there along with clumps of grass growing here and there, but Lark could feel carved wood beneath it all. Arican wiggled in her saddlebag against his shoulder, and emitted a gurgling chirp, wondering why he had stopped.

"Just hang on," Lark murmured to her, his brow pinched with curiosity as he stared at the handle.

Deciding there was no harm in it, Lark gave the handle a tug. The force pulled it and the wood it was attached to, shifting the ground and outlining the rest of the object. It was rectangle in shape and faced skyward at a forty degree angle. It was a door. Lark sat back and stared at the thing, pondering on why a door would be built in to the side of a hill in an area of little significance.

Suddenly, the door creaked making Lark jump.

The ground that lived on the door shifted as the door groaned open on crusty hinges. Crumbs of dirt showered down from the door, and a clump of dry yellow grass fell at Lark's feet. Lark took a few steps back with a stricken expression.

In the open doorway before him stood a raggedy man with dreadlocks reaching passed his shoulders and a wispy mustache that dangled on either side of his slim face. He was smeared with dirt from head to toe, and he squinted in the moonlight like he had lived underground his whole life.

The man directed a lopsided grin at Lark, shading his eyes with his hand as if it were a clear sunny day. "Lookin' for something, lad?" he asked with a friendly voice.

Lark stared wide-eyed too stunned to talk. He felt Arican shift in the saddlebag.

When Lark remained standing there gaping at him, the man sniffed from the cold and shrugged his thin shoulders dismissively. His eyes roamed about, bored of looking at Lark though Lark's staring at him didn't seem to be a bother. The man took in the view of the outside world with wonder, but also with an edge of repulsion.

Then his gaze fell upon the clump of grass that had fallen off the door still at Lark's feet. The man's eyes popped open and he let out a strangled gasping yelp that made Lark jump.

"No!" the man cried rushing out of his tunnel. Tiny shells and bits of pebbles dangling from his leather overcoat by short lengths of string jangled with his sudden burst of speed. He fell to his knees before the clump of grass as though it were a dying friend of his. He reared his grief stricken face to Lark.

"Wha- what happened? How?" the man choked, looking to his clump of grass and then back to Lark.

"Di- did you do this?" the man asked accusingly, gesturing shakily to the grass.

"No," Lark managed nervously, unconsciously taking a few weary steps backwards. "It just fell off when you opened the door,"

The strange underground man let out a sob, his bottom lip protruding and his chin quivering with emotion. Lark wondered when the flow of tears would start.

"It's just an old clump of grass," Lark tried. "These hills are full of them and so is your door,"

Instantly, Lark regretted his feeble attempt to cheer the man up. The man lifted a twisted expression of grief and bitterness.

"Just? Just a clump of grass?" the man spoke in a shaky, barely discernible tone. He shambled to his feet, eyes still fixed on Lark.

"Lad, every blade of grass counts. What happens when there's hardly any left? One clump of grass could make all the difference. You can't just turn away and let everything fall apart," he said.

Lark lifted his eyebrows. The man turned away, looking wounded. He knelt down and gently cradled the disheveled clump of grass in his arms as though he were handling a newborn child. He carried it over to his door, whispering encouraging words to it as he went about replanting it.

Lark regarded him frightfully. This man must have been living underground his entire life without association with any other people besides his own conscious. Lark had never met someone so wildly passionate over his foliage.

Finishing tending to his beloved grass, the man turned back to Lark with a beaming grin. He dusted his grimy hands together with a satisfied air.

"So, do you have a tunnel around here too?" the man asked.

"Ugh, no," Lark said slowly, his brow creasing.

"Oh, well, I guess you just don't know how to make one," said the man naively, bobbing his head in agreement with his own words.

"Yeah, yeah I suppose that's the reason," Lark replied, quite perplexed and not for the first time wondering how long the man had lived underground. Yet his neutral approach only encouraged the man.

"Not everyone can dig tunnels like I can," the man went on, putting a fond hand to the side of his tunnel's opening. "You see, my pa taught me how, never knew my ma. But pa taught me how to dig the soil and mold it to my liking. He showed me how to make tunnels, stairs, shoots, and even doors. But the doors have to be made from wood though, not dirt. The dirt just can't do that,"

As the man spoke, his entire face glazed over with a gleeful sort of pride. Lark let out an impatient breath, and rubbed the back of his head itchingly. He pondered the possibility of edging silently away while the man spoke, yet he didn't want to be rude.

But his friends were in trouble! He had to help them. He couldn't stand around and listen to some weird mole man and his obsession with underground dwellings.

"Look!!" Lark blurted. The man snapped a confused frown on him. "I don't mean to be rude but I don't have time to hear this,"

"Easy, lad. I was just getting to the part with my secret passages in to Ezleon," the man said with an undertone of annoyance.

"What?" Lark stammered, his impatience stopping short. "You have secret tunnels opening in to Ezleon?"

The man nodded proudly. "Five in fact; one goes to the Brimming Barrel's cellar, another goes to a baker's, then one goes to my pa's old house-"

"Alright, I got it!" Lark interrupted rudely.

"No need to be snappy, lad," the man said, somewhat deflated.

"Sorry," Lark grimaced, trying to restrain his growing irritation.

The man puckered his lips and squared his shoulders childishly, hurt by Lark's brunt words. Lark shifted uncertainly.

"I know I'm being blunt, but is there any chance you could get me in to Ezleon?"

The man considered him. "I wouldn't mind giving an abrasive fellow such as yourself passage, but my conscious won't allow me to do so without pay,"

"Pay?" said Lark, his hope diminishing.

"Yes, pay," the man said coming toward Lark. "You know, what you use those small round disks of silver and gold for. I'm sort of the doorkeeper of these tunnels and they don't work for free," he added as if he were speaking to someone ignorant.

"I don't have any money," said Lark glumly.

"No pay, no play. Goodbye," the man, or doorkeeper, said briefly. He turned on his heel for his tunnel.

"Wait!" Lark exclaimed, grabbing the door to keep the doorkeeper from closing it. The doorkeeper rotated an intolerable scowl on him. "I don't have any money, but I have other things. Can't we come to some sort of agreement?" Lark tried fervently.

The doorkeeper pursed his lips and contorted his features with deep contemplation. "I guess it wouldn't hurt to see what you have," He came back out of his tunnel and gestured for Lark to show him what he had for barter.

Eagerly, Lark brought his saddlebags forward and turned the one upside down so its contents spilled on the ground. Roused by the sudden movement, Arican poked her head out from the other saddlebag.

The doorkeeper looked to her frightfully, taking a few steps back. "What's that? A small man eating bear?" he asked nervously.

"She's an ocelot. She won't hurt you," Lark reassured, swallowing his resurfacing impatience. He motioned towards the few items that he had emptied from his one saddlebag. "Please, pick whatever you want,"

Corking his mouth uncertainly and giving Arican a weary glance, the doorkeeper knelt down and rummaged through the stuff. He instantly picked out Philip's telescope. Lark winced, hoping Philip wouldn't be mad at him for giving it away. Mumbling quietly to himself, the doorkeeper passed on Lark's flint and steel kit and his half filled canteen, though he happily relieved Lark of his parcel of food.

"You mind? I'm a little short," the doorkeeper said bashfully, lifting the parcel. Lark gestured dismissively. He could easily find food on his own.

The doorkeeper took up his chosen treasures and dropped Lark's remaining things back in to his saddlebag. Then something caught his attention and his eyes lit up. "What's in the secret compartment?"

"What secret compartment?" Lark asked confused.

"Right there," said the doorkeeper, pointing to the saddlebag Arican was in.

"The ocelot is in there," said Lark.

"Maybe she takes up the top part, but not the bottom part here," said the doorkeeper. He lifted a dirt smeared hand to Arican's saddlebag and flipped back a flap of leather that Lark hadn't noticed before. The flap of leather had covered a crease to an opening that went around the saddlebag, tied to the top compartment by a leather cord.

Stunned, Lark undid the cord and the secret compartment fell open, hanging off the other by well concealed leather hinges. Unconsciously, both Lark and the doorkeeper leaned forward to peer inside. Arican gurgled, perceiving them curiously.

The secret compartment wasn't deep, but was still shadowed by the night. At the bottom, they could just barely make out what looked like a tightly rolled leaf of parchment. But it was what was next to the small scroll that caught their eye.

It was something round, the size of a compass, and gold. It shone dully in the dim light, and Lark could see that there was some sort of engraving etched on to it that looked like the face of an owl.

The doorkeeper stared wide-eyed over Lark's shoulder at the shiny trinket. Lark did his best not to recoil from the reeking smell of mud and sewage that wafted thickly off him.

"For that shiny bobble I'll dig you a tunnel to Castle Caelum itself," the doorkeeper whispered mistily.

Lark frowned at him and noted the dreamy expression that had washed over his face.

The offer was tempting, but Lark sensed that the intriguing object wasn't his to giveaway. He faintly recalled in the back of his mind Philomena and Philip having lost something or other that was from the knight who had helped them before. This could be what they were missing.

"Sorry," Lark said abruptly, closing the secret compartment. The doorkeeper snapped out of his mesmerized state and glowered upsettingly at Lark. "But this particular item I'm afraid is not for barter,"

The doorkeeper pouted and huffed. Lark paid no mind. He tied the compartment shut and covered its crease with the leather flap. In its inconspicuous state, Lark would have never guessed the compartment was there. He glanced over at the whining doorkeeper, wondering how he had noticed it so easily. Then he remembered he was in a hurry, and shook himself out of his thoughts.

"Look, I really need to get in to Ezleon. The things you chose should be enough to cover my passage. I really need to help some friends of mine," Lark said earnestly.

"I guess," the doorkeeper muttered, chewing at a nail and corking his mouth thoughtfully. He switched a suspicious frown on Lark. "Why the hurry anyway, lad? Are your friends in some sort of trouble?"

"No," Lark lied.

The doorkeeper pursed his lips and regarded Lark. Then he said with a sigh, "I suppose there's no harm in leading you in," He started for his open tunnel. Lark followed, than stopped abruptly when the doorkeeper turned on him with a hand held up.

"Get some ale to me before you leave the city?" he requested hopefully.

"Fine," said Lark. The doorkeeper beamed happily, and made a wide welcoming gesture for Lark to follow him.

Fifteen minutes later they were traveling through the tunnels beneath the city. Lark gladly allowed the doorkeeper to navigate even though being behind him meant he got a good whiff of the terrible smell that radiated off the man.

The doorkeeper walked briskly enough to content Lark, humming a merry song as he went, the trinkets hanging from his coat jingling with his movements. He munched on shelled peanuts, popping two or three nuts in his mouth at a time still in the shells, making loud crushing noises as he chewed. Tinkering with the telescope he had chosen as part of his payment, he blew the peanut shells from his mouth as he did. The empty crumpled shells shot to the side and hit the tunnel wall.

Lark averted his gaze, shaking his head slightly. Even though the obsessive earth loving doorkeeper lacked manners, his tunnel was to Lark's surprise the exact opposite. It was warm and well lit by the occasional torch. Lark had expected mold, rats, dripping water, and that damp wet smell that drifts off bare soil. But it was tidy, and in a way homey.

Horded treasures of odds and ends, bottles and shiny instruments, were piled here and there; most likely passage payments from past travelers. The tunnel was basically packed earth, but in places stone and bits of brick paved the floor and sides. Frequently, they'd pass a thick timber column that helped support the ceiling.

"You know, I feel rather rude," the doorkeeper spoke around the peanuts he was chewing.

Lark stared at the man's back, the perturbing tone the doorkeeper used making him fearful that the man might exclaim he had taken a wrong turn or had forgotten that the tunnel really didn't go under Ezleon.

"Would you like a peanut?" the doorkeeper asked, half turning as he thrust a ruddy old pouch filled with peanuts to Lark.

"No," said Lark, exhaling gruffly. The doorkeeper shrugged, facing forward once more and spitting peanut shells.

"Are you sure this passage is safe?" Lark questioned at the doorkeeper's shoulder. "The sergeants don't know about these tunnels?"

"Lad, you're looking at the man who helped dig these tunnels. Trust me, none of Ezleon knows about them. Well, except for my vagabond friend, Stephen, but you know," the doorkeeper said, squaring his shoulders carelessly.

Setting his jaw with annoyance, Lark followed the doorkeeper down a small flight of rugged, stairs made out of dirt. Arican ventured a peek out of her saddlebag, glancing inquisitively around at the tunnel. Lark scratched her cheek reassuringly and she slid back inside.

"I'm Barlow, by the way. Forgot to mention that, silly me," the doorkeeper, Barlow, chuckled. He scooped out some more peanuts and tucked away his new telescope in the folds of his overcoat.

"That's fine," Lark muttered.

"How 'bout you?" Barlow asked.

"Lark," said Lark distractedly.

Barlow snorted with laughter. "Isn't that some sort of bird?"

"So," Lark grumbled.

"Why'd your parents name you for a bird?" Barlow asked, still laughing and nearly choking on a stray peanut shell.

Lark glowered defensively. "Why'd your parents name you Barlow?" he bristled emphatically.

"Good one, lad. I can't say I know," said Barlow, grinning over at Lark and not at all perturbed. He swung his gaze back around, and started to hum to himself again.

Lark inhaled a deep breath, scrunching his nose in a light snicker. Under normal circumstances, an individual like Barlow wouldn't get under his skin so much, but the urgency of his task was breathing down his neck and making his tolerance very low. They continued through the tunnel for another five minutes without saying a word. Barlow kept up his jaunty tune. When they passed a side tunnel that forked off to the east, Lark began to feel a little uncertain.

"Are we almost there?" he asked.

"That all depends on where you want to be," the doorkeeper replied. "We're already beneath the city. That branching tunnel we just passed leads to my pa's old place. I'm sure you don't want to go there, unless you have an aptitude for dead insects in jars,"

A thought came to Lark. "Can you get me close to the stables?"

"I can get you *in* the stables, lad," said Barlow matter-of-factly.

"Really?" asked Lark.

"Certainly," Barlow beamed. "I have a secret passage that opens into the stables. Never knew why I made it, guess I just wasn't paying attention to where I was digging. But hey, at least its proving its worth today right?" he grinned, winking at Lark.

"Yeah," Lark agreed, pleasantly surprised.

Another few minutes, and Barlow turned off to the right into a branching tunnel. Lark followed more eagerly now. The branching tunnel was smaller and darker with only one torch flickering in the center. The firelight danced about the tunnel, and illuminated the door that was at the end.

"To the stables as you requested, good sir," said Barlow with a bow when they stopped before the door.

"Thanks," Lark said gratefully, reaching out for the brass door latch. But Barlow lifted a hand to stop him.

"Oh, I should add before you leave that there's no coming back this way once you do. You see, I designed the doors so that they can only be opened from the inside. So if you want back in here, well, you're pretty much out of luck unless you knock really, really loudly and I happen to hear it," Barlow explained, squaring his shoulders and spreading his hands apologetically. The corner of Lark's mouth twitched nervously and he gripped the reassuring hilt of his sword. "Great, I'll remember that," he said, his throat dry.

Barlow beamed a crooked grin at him and clapped him on the shoulder. "It was nice walking with you,"

Gathering himself up, Lark reached out for the door latch once more and lifted it. A square of dim light poured into the tunnel. Peeking around the door to be sure it was the stables he was going in to which was confirmed by the sight of straw and a baffled looking horse, Lark thanked Barlow once more and stepped through the doorway. The doorkeeper whispered 'good luck' to him, and then closed the door with a soft thud, or so he thought. Lark caught the edge of the door with the toe of his boot just before it could click shut entirely and materialize into the wall of the stables.

He pulled out a couple arrows from his quiver and jammed them in the door, arrow tip first. The door would appear closed enough so as not to alert Barlow or anyone else for that matter. Lark hoped Barlow wouldn't mind. He covered the arrow shafts with some straw so no one could see them.

The tunnel door had let Lark out in to one of the stable's stalls. The horse in it snorted nervously and regarded Lark with fright from his sudden appearance. Lark calmed him by speaking soothingly and stretching a hand out to the startled animal. The horse bobbed his head and stepped wearily, but allowed Lark to wade through the dense bedding of straw to stroke his smooth shoulder.

A pang of regret bit at Lark as he patted the horse. He was reminded of Spear, and he missed the gorgeous steed already.

But he knew he had done the right thing. Spear probably wouldn't have liked traveling through Barlow's tunnels anyway. Looking back, Lark couldn't even make out the door even though he had ensured he could use the passage to escape. It was perfectly blended with the stall's timbering.

Remembering why he was there, Lark gave the horse one last friendly stroke, and tentatively walked around him. He peered out over the stall door. No one was there.

Frowning curiously as he opened the stall door and closed it behind him, Lark wondered why no one was around. No stable hands, no night guard, not even a late arriving traveler.

Deciding it might just be luck, Lark swiftly tackled the next part of his plan; he had to find Philip and Philomena's horses, saddle them and hopefully not be caught doing so. He had to have them ready if they were to escape.

After all, time wasn't on his side.

46

Nearly forty minutes later, everything was quiet in Moth's chambers. Philip remained dangling from his chains, kneeling on the cold stone floor. His head lolled to the side, his eyes closed. His breathing was deep as though he was sleeping, but he was far too uneasy for such rest. Though his eyes were shut, he could feel Moth's stare lingering on him.

Moth watched Philip from his desk, his chin cupped in his hand and a finger tapping thoughtfully against his cheek. Besides from him and his two captives, his chamber was empty. The sergeants were still out in the city, waking the residents as Moth had requested.

A steady *thonk thonk thonk* sounded as Philomena bumped her head repeatedly against the wall she was shackled to. Her eyes lingered to the shadowy ceiling and her features were slack with boredom.

Moth ceased his finger tapping and darted his narrowed eyes to her, clearly annoyed. His nostrils flared as he watched her.

The door then swung open letting in a sergeant and a cold gust of air that made the lit candles flicker. Philip shivered, opened his eyes and looked to the sergeant.

"Commander Moth, sir, Kaiden wishes to see you," the sergeant announced.

With a sigh, Moth pushed his chair back and rose to his feet. He met Philip's eyes with a cold knowing look. His strange eye contact unsettled Philip.

Moth and the sergeant walked out, closing the door behind them. Philomena let out a sigh having ceased her head pounding.

"What kind of commander leaves his captives unguarded?" she

drawled huskily.

"The over confident kind," Philip replied, pulling himself to his feet with a painful groan. Despite the fact that the sergeants had tended to the deep cut Werik had inflicted to his shoulder it still throbbed sorely and stung with the tiniest of movement.

Philip craned his gaze upward, studying the chain and hook that held his rope bonds suspended. The hook appeared to be a meat hook. On a hunch, Philip started to work his ropes back and forth, rubbing them against the hook's curve in hopes it was sharp enough to cut.

Philomena watched, chewing at her lip anxiously.

After a few minutes of trying with no success, Philip stopped, cursing under his breath and panting from the effort.

Disappointed, Philomena let her head fall back against the wall. The shackles were starting to dig uncomfortably in to her wrists and ankles.

But Philip wasn't ready to give up quite yet. Reaching out, he gripped his rope bonds at arm's length and heaved himself up. White hot pain that nearly blinded him shot through his shoulder as he began to climb. Philomena gawked at him.

"Philip, what are you doing?" she asked.

"Can't talk right now," Philip grunted. Clenching his teeth, he ignored the pain and concentrated his energy into reaching the hook. It was only three feet away . . . now two and a half.

Sweat beaded Philip's face as he climbed closer and closer to the hook. His fresh wound felt like it was spreading, splitting more of his flesh as he stretched out his arm.

Coming only half a foot away, Philip finally grasped the hook. He pulled himself further so he was face level with it and felt a surge of triumph.

"Hurry! Moth could come back any minute!" Philomena hissed urgently, glancing to the chamber's back door.

Philip's burst of optimism was shortly checked by her reminder and he quickly set to work on untangling the ropes wrapped and knotted about the hook.

Philomena watched anxiously from below, saying a silent prayer. A few minutes passed and there was a shuffling at the door sending jolts of panic rocketing through them. They waited for Commander Moth to stroll in but the door remained close. Philomena released the breath she had unconsciously been holding in, and lifted her gaze to Philip.

He was on the last infuriating knot, his brow furrowed and the tip of his tongue sticking out between his teeth. Delivering a good tug, the knot came free and the ropes slithered off the hook.

"Yes!" Philip whooped, dropping to the ground and landing agilely.

"Shhh!" Philomena snapped. "Do you want to let every sergeant in Ezleon know that you have something to be happy about?"

"Oh, but we do have something to be happy about, little sister," Philip grinned. He slipped the ropes from his wrists and let them fall to the ground.

"Why do you have to be so goofy?" asked Philomena, exasperated.

"Well, ask yourself if I weren't so goofy, what would you do?" asked Philip, coming over to her still grinning. Philomena huffed and shook her head incredulously.

"Oh, this could be a problem," said Philip, lifting his eyebrows at the shackles that locked Philomena to the stone wall.

"It definitely is. You didn't think your plan all the way through," Philomena snipped grumpily, her glare smoldering.

"I can see that," Philip shot back defensively. Philomena groaned. "Just calm down, I'll try to get you out," he assured her. Grasping one of the shackles that secured Philomena's wrists, Philip tugged on the steel putting every grain of strength he had in to it. But it was to no avail. His wounded shoulder was already weakened from his climb up the ropes. Rotating his gaze around the chamber, his eyes fell on their confiscated weapons laying on Moth's desk. He snatched one of their long, double edged knives and hurried back to Philomena. Wedging the blade between Philomena's wrist and the shackle, he slid it close to the bolts that nailed it to the wall and tried to use the knife as a lever. Again, Philip failed. He retracted the knife, growling with frustration. He stuffed the knife in his belt and fingered the keyhole on the shackle. He needed the key, there was no other way.

"It's no use. You're wasting time," said Philomena.

"Do you remember who has the key?" Philip asked, sweat drooling down his face despite the cold temperature.

"Does it matter?" Philomena retorted fiercely. Philip's features darkened suspiciously. "You're free. Leave me behind," she demanded harshly.

"No, absolutely not. That is not an option," Philip countered, cutting the air with an end-of-discussion gesture. Philomena could see the straight faced determination settling over him.

"They won't hurt me. It's you that their focused on, and it's my fault that you are here. So please, go!" Philomena pleaded urgently.

But Philip was shaking his head and grinding his teeth defiantly. "I made a promise to take care of you, and I can't bear the idea of leaving you here," he said.

"Please, you can't end up in Avador's custody. Now leave!" Philomena hissed.

Philip drew breath to argue, but before either of them could convince the other they heard footsteps at the back door. Their eyes snapped to one another, fear clutching them. The latch to the door began to lift.

Seeing no other option, Philip dashed to Moth's desk and vaulted over it sending a fiery stab of pain up his shoulder. Wincing, he ducked low behind the desk, clutching at his sore wound. He heard the door creak open.

Still clamped to the wall, Philomena's heart drummed against her chest resisting the impulse to call out to her brother. Moth stepped in, a cold breeze billowing his hair about his shoulders and unsettling the lit candles. His cold sharp eyes narrowed on Philomena, his uncanny nature instantly sensing something wrong. He closed the door behind him and strode over to her, waggling his fingers at his sides as if loosening them for battle. Philomena sucked in a breath, trying her best to relax her features but she couldn't mask her fear. The whole dreadful situation made her tremble inside.

"So," Moth spoke casually, his voice seeming to echo. "Where is he?" he asked, stopping before Philomena.

No response passed Philomena's lips. She couldn't steal her gaze away from Moth's. This man unnerved her, and she didn't like it. He didn't have to see Philip's empty bonds sprawled on the floor a space away to know he was missing.

Moth lifted his chin in a deliberate manner, sensing Philomena's working thoughts. A confident grin played at the corners of his mouth.

"I see why the men have been whispering about you in such eager interest," said Moth, his voice just above a whisper and flowing like water.

Great, he's playing mind games, Philomena thought grudgingly. She could just make out the wicked, playful glint in his eyes. A rampage of panic pounded inside her, making it difficult to keep her attention focused on the smug commander, but it was all that she could do to keep her eyes from darting to the desk where Philip crouched unseen.

"They realize that your brother is more of an important prize then you to be delivered to Avador. So they have been wondering what will become of you if Avador doesn't take you along with him," Moth went on calmly, seeming not to be concerned over Philip's absence.

"Avador needs my capture as much as my brother's," Philomena smirked sneeringly.

"Does he?" Moth suggested, his eyebrows lifting. "He

emphasized on the prince's capture but not on yours. Perhaps he doesn't care to go through the trouble. You are just a girl after all,"

Irritable offense bubbled in Philomena's chest. "A girl who took down two of your men," she reminded meanly.

A few meters away, Philip edged around Moth's desk silent as a ripple over calm water. His mouth was dry and his palms were sweaty. He peered around the desk, checking to see where Moth was.

"And yet you still ended up here," Moth said, tilting his head knowingly. Philomena flushed with resent. "Let's say if I'm right, well you'll be stuck here all alone, with just us men to keep you company,"

Philomena's features darkened maliciously at Moth's far too obvious remark. The crafty commander cocked an indignant smirk on her, his eyes glittering.

"Think about it, princess. If Avador leaves you here I am not entitled to protect you and neither is anyone else in this city. You won't be a warrior princess anymore, just a prisoner in my custody," Moth stepped closer and lifted a hand to brush aside a strand of hair from Philomena's face. His finger that brushed her cheek was nearly as cold as his stare, and made her skin tingle uncomfortably. The infuriation boiling in Philomena made her breath shorten.

"The men simply won't be able to resist," said Moth, spreading his hands in a mocking helpless manner.

That was the final straw. The rage that had stirred in Philip from listening to Moth simply burst sending him flying out from his cover with an enraged snarl. He rammed in to Moth's side and they went sprawling. Philomena let out an involuntary gasp. Moth groaned, his head having smacked the stone floor. Philip scrambled to regain himself. He sat on top of Moth his face flushed with fury, and brought back his fist hammering it against Moth's jaw. He switched fists and snapped Moth's head the other way, and so continued the beating.

Philomena looked on, her mouth slightly a gap at the sight, conflicted between satisfaction that Philip was knocking Moth senseless and fear to see the rage her brother was capable of. After all this time, she had never seen Philip so horrifying.

After the eighth or ninth punch from Philip, Moth somehow stirred from semi-consciousness. Bellowing with fury, Moth blocked Philip's oncoming blow and slammed a fist against his wounded shoulder.

Philip stumbled away from Moth clutching his shoulder and growling from the searing pain that ripped through his wound. Moth rose and stepped swiftly forward throwing a blow against Philip's jaw. Philip staggered back some more, shaking his head. He turned, his muscles tensed to return the favor, but froze when he felt Moth's blade poking him in the gut.

Moth smirked pleasurably, blood trailing from the corner of his mouth. Philip itched with contempt.

"Excellent attempt, prince, but your temper betrayed you," said Moth.

Bitter self loathing tortured Philip. He stared smolderingly at Moth, flexing his jaw regretfully as he stood at the mercy of Moth's sword. The disappointment Philomena felt nearly reduced her to sobbing.

Lieutenant Kaiden and his comrades chose that moment to enter the chambers. They stopped short in their purposeful stride when they caught sight of the scene before them. Several of the sergeants gawked at Philip free of his bonds with Moth's sword pointed at him and reached for their own weapons.

"Commander, what is-" Kaiden stuttered, his gaze switching between Moth and Philip.

"What is it, lieutenant?" Moth interrupted abruptly, not taking his attention off of Philip. His moody tone made the sergeants flinch.

"Everyone has assembled outside, sir. They're waiting for you,"

Kaiden informed with a twinge of uncertainty.

Philip and Philomena became aware of a hum of muffled voices coming from outside the chambers. The sound was dreading to them.

"Good," said Moth. "Escort this prisoner out on the platform," he ordered.

Sergeants seemed to materialize on either side of Philip. He winced from their rough grip, clenching his teeth against the throbbing pain coursing through his shoulder.

"No need to bind him," said Moth, sheathing his sword. The sergeants looked to him curiously and Moth directed a cold smile to Philip. "He's not going anywhere," he added and casted a pointed look Philomena's way.

The certainty in Moth's tone made Philip resentful, but he knew he was right. Without Philomena safely at his side, Philip wasn't going to try a thing.

"Have some men watch the other prisoner," Moth said to Kaiden before turning brusquely on his heel, leading the way to the chamber door. Kaiden obliged, calling a pair of the sergeants to guard Philomena. The remaining sergeants filed out behind their commander.

Before the sergeants could pull him away, Philip locked eyes with his sister. They each saw the other's fear and desperation, and longing to find something reassuring to say to the other but there were no words that were capable of doing so.

The sergeants tore Philip away, leading him to the open door. Philomena could hear a throng of cheering voices greeting Moth and the sergeants. The sergeants escorting Philip were the last to step on to the plate-form outside. One of the remaining sergeants closed the door behind them.

As Philip was cut off from her sight, panic welled in Philomena and she couldn't stop herself from tugging at the steel clamps that held her, choking on sobs of despair.

Out on the stage like plate-form that jutted out from the front of Moth's chambers, the sergeants spread out to the sides, allowing their commander to take center stage. Some hurried down some steps to level ground to help their comrades control the crowd. Philip stumbled as the sergeants drug him roughly along, keeping him close to Moth. He gave a sideways glance out to the town square and was shocked to see it brimming with shouting villagers waving crazily to Moth. The loud buzz of noises was overwhelming and made Philip's head ache. He caught sight of a giant statue at the right side of the chamber building towering against the night sky. Torchlight flickered and glowed over the crowd.

Moth strode leisurely forward, spreading his arms and beaming as he soaked in the cheers of the people.

Typical, Philip thought sniffing disdainfully to himself and watching Moth with a sneering glower. Moth was the keeper of Ezleon, the most important man in the city, apparently the icon to her people and obviously adored by them. They even respected his cronies.

But how? Philip wondered with frustration. How could they look up to a man like Moth when he was the reason for the city's slow depletion?

"Please, please settle down!" Moth called to the people with admiration, his smile still present. Philip wanted so much to punch him again.

The crowd's overpowering cheers gradually ebbed to a quiet hum.

"I'm so sorry to have woken you and forced you out into the cold," Moth apologized, his gaze sweeping the audience. To the side, Kaiden rolled his eyes.

"But I thought the pressing matter that arose this night should be known to you all immediately. This young man here, though he looks like an innocent traveler, is a criminal," Moth announced. He motioned to the sergeants restraining Philip. They released their grip on Philip and shoved him towards their commander. Philip stumbled and Moth caught him by his coat collar.

"Now, I know we've had some rough spells, but how many times have I lied to you?" asked Moth, spreading his free hand and circling his gaze over the vast sea of villagers. There was a hearty murmur of agreement from them and several nodding heads.

"So I stand before you this night to expose this criminal," Moth went on, thrusting Philip roughly forward. Philip grimaced as several eyes were directed on him.

"Who is a fraud, a conspiracy theorist and the greatest enemy to our future king," Moth finished dramatically.

Gasps emitted, and shouts of outrage and defiance echoed out. Moth's lips twitched pleasurably as he allowed the shouting to turn in to an uproar, the gullible crowd instantly believing his words.

Philip closed his eyes grimly and hung his head in hopelessness.

47

Avador and his company made their way through the silent streets of Ezleon, sitting tensely in their saddles and glancing nervously along the dark empty roads. Their captives, Balin and K'smet rode in the middle, battered and weary.

They followed the booming sound that bounced off the houses and down the roads. As they approached the town square, the sound untangled to be recognized as a voice and soon it became audible enough to discern words.

"- was surprised too!" a single voice called out. "How could someone be so hostile to try to ruin our precious future with the Corea family leading us? But believe me when I say that this young man is twisted inside. He is sick in the mind if you will,"

A pandemonium of hostile shouts lifted on the air, obviously originating from a great number of mouths. The company hesitated as they listened. Avador exchanged a confused frown with Night Hawk riding at his flank before urging his horse in to a trot towards the uproar. The others followed him through a narrow alley created by large looming stone homes. The company members singled out to fit through.

When Avador reached the other end, he stopped short at the sight of a mass of townspeople gathered before a crude stage. Torchlight ebbed from the square, and casted mean shadows with the movements and angry gestures of the crowd. Sergeants patrolled the perimeter, armed with triangular shields and pikes. They gripped their weapons at the ready, sensing that their commander was creating a mob.

"What is this?" Night Hawk questioned, peering passed his captain's shoulder.

"I don't know," Avador grumbled shaking his head. His heated gaze roamed over the crowd, his own temper beginning to rumble in the pit of his stomach.

"And why? Why does he want to do this?" the voice they had heard before thundered over the mob.

Avador darted his attention to the stage, and narrowed in on the two individuals in the center. His expression darkened instantly. "Oh," said Night Hawk knowingly, recognizing the speaker and his prisoner. "Looks like Commander Moth is enjoying himself again,"

"He's no commander," Avador retorted disdainfully, his gaze fuming as he stared at Moth and Philip. "He's just the kind of man my father chooses as a mercenary,"

"I'll tell you why! The poor boy believes he is something that he's not! He thinks he's a prince! He thinks he's your long lost heir! THE SON OF KING PAUL STILWELL!" Moth bellowed. The crowd went wild with bafflement and infuriation. Sharp curses were directed to Philip, as well as odd pieces of rubble thrown from the townspeople.

Remaining in the shadows of the alley, Avador's temper surged as he watched Philip fling himself at Moth only to be held back by several sergeants. The disorderly group on stage was clearly struggling to keep Philip back, and they sprawled at their commander's feet. Moth was shouting and giving sharp gestures. Avador shook his head in disgust. He had seen enough. "I'm tempted to put this man out of his misery," he grumbled.

"That would not go well with your father," Night Hawk reminded heavily, with a hinting joke. Avador swung his gaze over his shoulder at his second in command. He eyed him for a moment before looking ahead once more.

"Tell Fall Leaf and Swift Deer to keep the prisoners back. The rest of us will go have a chat with the commander," Avador ordered, flexing his jaw and gripping his reins. Night Hawk passed the order along. Avador's black stallion shifted anxiously beneath him. Avador stroked his neck reassuringly. A minute later, Night Hawk reported back.

"Weapons out," Avador said, and there was a slither of steel as he and his men unsheathed their swords and knives.

Being sure they were ready, Avador tapped his heel against his horse's side and led the plunge in to the jeering, boisterous sea of villagers. A sergeant stepped in their path, shield arm high and his pike leveled at Avador.

"I'm sorry, but I cannot permit you to distur-" the sergeant began, but Avador cut him off.

"No one needs to give me permission to do anything. Now either stand aside or be trodden under our horses," Avador said bluntly. He gave the sergeant no time to ponder, and urged his horse forward again, bumping the sergeant with his stallion's shoulder. The sergeant stumbled backwards in to the crowd receiving mean glares in return.

Encouraging his horse into an easy trot, Avador parted the angry villagers. His company filed behind him, and as they wedged their way through, the villagers began to take notice and were craning their heads towards the new arrivals.

Once Avador reached the stage, the crowd had quieted and now hummed with curious whispering. On stage, Moth stared, his features having gone slack with perturbed annoyance. His sergeants had finally untangled themselves. They stood panting, several of them holding on to Philip who glowered hatefully at Moth.

"Captain Avador, what a surprise," Moth greeted, forcing a smile. The significant name caused a wave of excited whispers to ripple through the crowd and many casted admiring looks Avador's way.

"How much of a surprise could it have been since I was expected here," said Avador, swinging down from his saddle and stepping on to the stage. Night Hawk reached over and grabbed the reins of his horse.

Avador walked over to Moth, fixing him with a glare of disapproval and detest. Moth watched him closely, his lip curling with contempt.

Avador halted a few feet away from Moth. He looked to the sergeants, then to Philip, and then back to Moth. "What the hell are you doing?" he demanded, the question drawn out.

The crowd was deathly silent now, clinging to Avador's every word. Lieutenant Kaiden and his fellow sergeants were taken aback, and glanced uncertainly at one another.

"I ordered you to hold the two suspects till I arrived to collect them and take them back to Caelum, not announce them to the city," Avador lashed harshly, his brows lowered over his dark eyes like threatening storm clouds.

"Oh come now, Captain Avador," Moth laughed coolly, placing a firm grip on Avador's shoulder. "There's no real harm in what I've done. I've merely exposed the truth of this . . . filth to the people," he added, raising his voice so everyone could hear.

A hearty ripple of appreciative agreement went through the crowd. Philip snarled and tried again to lunge at Moth, but the sergeants held him firmly.

Moth snickered at Avador, his eyes glinting with a mean playfulness. Avador smacked Moth's hand from his shoulder, making Night Hawk smirk with satisfaction.

"You have no authority or right to expose him as anything to anyone. He's a prisoner who belongs to my father," Avador grinded out.

"I'm doing a service for you father by eliminating his greatest enemies," Moth cut in, spreading his arms innocently.

"Did you not hear me?" Avador snapped, stepping in to Moth's face. "You have no authority to do so. Now before your little gathering here becomes a killing mob, my company and I will take custody of both the captives and leave Ezleon at once," Avador beckoned Night Hawk and the others on to the stage. Spreading his hands submissively with a mocking expression as though he had just been struck, Moth stepped back.

"Whatever you say, *captain*," he said emphatically, sneering at Avador. Then he turned to the crowd of baffled onlookers. "My apologies, my fellow citizens, but Captain Avador is taking away the prisoner to be tried at Caelum,"

Several groans and outbursts of disappointment rose up.

"Why can't he be tried here?" called out a villager.

Avador hesitated, frowning sidelong at Moth. "My father, Lord Salvador, will be the one to decide his fate," he explained to the people.

"But why? If we know he's an enemy, than we know what to do with him!" the villager yelled, and several chorused his confidence. Avador set his jaw, beyond aggravation.

Moth stepped forward with a grin. "What Captain Avador is trying to say is that we are not capable of handling such an important prisoner as this,"

Angry remarks rose and rude gestures were directed to Avador and his company. Silver Stream and Night Hawk, having taken Philip away from the sergeants, glanced around uncertainly as hostility in the crowd increased. The disturbed villagers were protesting vengefully now.

"We know how to deal with scum!" one shouted.

"He's a traitor!"

"There's no need for a trial!"

Seeing what was happening, Avador turned angrily on to Moth.

"You best get this under control before I-" he started, but Moth interrupted him, shoving him aside and making him flush red.

"So, good people of Ezleon, what is it that we do with enemies and traitors?!" the commander boomed.

"We behead them!" yelled a villager, thrusting a wooden staff above his head.

"We kill them!" another pitched in. The rest chorused enthusiastically, pounding their fists in the air.

Their threatening shouts echoed in Philip's head, making

everything swim sickly. Most of his energy had already been spent, and Silver Stream and Night Hawk were supporting most of his weight.

Avador gawked at the mob in disbelief. Fury for Moth burned dangerously in his chest and he turned a heated stare on the commander who smirked happily. The mob started to chant, shifting forward and trying to swarm passed the sergeants and Avador's company to get closer to the stage.

"KILL HIM! KILL HIM!"

*****

The murderous cries and chants of the mob easily soaked through the chamber walls. Philomena stared at the dark ceiling above, her heart thudding frightfully as she listened. Mental images of what the crazed citizens might be doing to Philip tortured her from within. Tears brimmed her eyes at the thought of the images actually happening, and the realization of Philip possibly being killed made her choke on her own breath.

She couldn't take it anymore. The chanting was unbearable. She sucked in a shaky breath and leveled her gaze to the sergeants sitting at a table across from Moth's desk. She watched them swigging their ale and playing some sort of board game with dice.

A glint of candle light reflected dully on the ring of keys that hung on the belt of the sergeant closest to her. She was certain that one of those keys would open her shackles. Determination settled over her, and Philomena decided she'd take matters in to her own hands.

Wriggling her wrists against the resilient steel clamps, she grimaced in concentration. The steel rubbed meanly against her raw skin. Her right hand wedged in the shackle. Keeping close watch on the sergeants, she finally maneuvered her hand free. A red mark left by the shackle circled her wrist. She flexed her wrist and fingers delightfully. There was nothing stopping her now.

Time for the second step, she thought.

Philomena worked her tunic and coat sleeve down her forearm, and then pushed her hand back through the shackle. A scraping of wood on stone made her start, and she glanced up to see one of the sergeants standing. He took the empty jug from the table and walked away, passing through the doorway in to the storage. His comrade remained.

Philomena tugged at her wrist, being sure that she could get it through easily enough. She grinned to herself to feel that she could. Without her coat sleeve encumbering her, it was much easier to pull free of the shackle. She now directed her attention to the sergeant still sitting at the table, his back to her.

"Hey, excuse me sergeant sir," she said, trying to sound helpless and defeated.

The sergeant lifted his head and turned in his chair. He gave her a suspiciously quizzical stare from behind his helmet. Philomena hesitated on purpose, and made her bottom lip quiver.

"I know I'm not supposed to talk, but the window above me is letting in a terrible draft. Is there any way you could close it for me?" she requested, her voice fragile.

The sergeant rolled his tongue over his teeth in consideration. He stared at her, then up to the cracked window above her.

"Yeah, I guess there's no harm in that," he decided, clearing his throat.

"Oh, thank you," Philomena breathed with relief.

The sergeant went over to her, bringing his chair along. He placed it in front of her, and gave her a pointed look before stepping on to it. As he reached to close the window, Philomena slipped her hand through the shackle. With dainty care, she liberated the ring of keys from his belt that was just below eye level to her. She stuffed the keys in her trouser's pocket, careful not to let them jangle and put her hand back in the shackle just as the sergeant climbed down.

"There," he said simply.

"Thanks, that's much better," she replied gratefully. The sergeant nodded acknowledgement and carried his chair back to the table.

Much better indeed, Philomena thought happily.

48

It wasn't hard to figure out where Philip and Philomena were. Since Lark knew that Avador was involved, he figured they would be in Commander Moth's chambers about now or at least somewhere in that area. Inaudible chanting that ebbed against the night came from the town square, reassuring him that he was most likely right. The dreary sound made it clear that nearly the whole city was there, and Lark was sure all of Moth's sergeants were present. It was an intimidating thought, but Lark decided he'd deal with the problem once it arose.

He galloped along the road, riding Philip's stallion, Nimbius and leading Philomena's horse at his side. The rhythmic pounding of their hooves calmed Lark's tension. Keeping a sharp eye on the line of buildings and houses, no one appeared to be jumping out at his obvious passing through; just another reassurance that everyone was in the square. If there was anyone in the still homes Lark was passing, they were women and children bunkered to keep from the possible chaos. Not even so much as a lonely beggar scuffled in the back roads.

The hairs on the back of Lark's neck stood on end, unnerved by the vacant streets and the continuous chanting from ahead that was growing louder. Lark steered the horses in to a narrow back road, just wide enough for the two stallions to trot abreast.

Not entirely familiar with Ezleon, Lark remembered enough to navigate a faster route to the town's center. He had been in the city once before with Master Finn to sell yearlings. It hadn't been an enjoyable trip.

Easing Nimbius to a walk, Lark peered out from the back road, searching for any sign of patrolling sentries. But just as the road before, it was absent of any late night strollers. Lark road out on to the street his gaze roaming about wearily. Firelight from hanging lamps and torches danced along the road setting it with a sleepy glow. This was where the higher society resided, Lark figured. He could tell by the large, well maintained stone homes and the fine verandahs that nearly each one had.

But Lark didn't care so much for the wealthy housings as the chanting he had been hearing for some time cleared in to recognizable words.

"KILL HIM! KILL HIM! KILL HIM!"

The morose reciting blew a chill down Lark's spine.

Instinctively, he knew who the many voices were referring too. Crossing the street, Lark pulled gently on the reins and Nimbius and Coursio stopped before one of the verandahs. He slipped down from Nimbius, and pulled the reins over both of the horses' heads, securing them to the verandah's railing.

"I'll be back with them," Lark promised quietly, patting the horses' on their necks.

He unslung his bow from Nimbius' saddle and strapped it over his chest. Unbuckling the saddlebag, Lark peered in on Arican who blinked her wide yellow eyes at him.

"You stay here and keep quiet," Lark whispered to her. She gurgled, and he buckled the saddlebag closed. He hated to leave her behind, but he figured he shouldn't be laden down with an ocelot cub in a saddlebag. At least staying with the horses would keep her out of any immediate danger, and judging by the deranged chanting Lark guessed there was plenty of that.

Sucking in a steadying breath, Lark started down the narrow passage that opened before him. The shadows of the two homes that loomed on either side engulfed him.

On the other end of the passage, Lark could see the glow of torchlight, and the shifting mangled shadows of many people. Their chanting and the terrible threats they added in between filled his ears. His stomach churned nervously and his throat grew dry. Stepping to the left, Lark pressed his back to the stone wall as he slid to the passage's opening.

Every muscle in his body taut, Lark peeked around the house's corner. His eyes widened at the sight of the jeering mob that swelled in the town square. Sergeants fully armed were attempting to gain control over the hostile crowd, but their orders and threats were drowned out. Avador's company members still on their horses were helping to patrol the perimeter, but even they were having trouble.

A huge statue of a past queen stood to the chamber building's right, glaring down at the chaos in the square. Lark doubted a statue could show emotion, but this one appeared disapproving of the turmoil.

Lark's gaze traveled from the statue and beyond the mob where he found Moth and Avador shouting and gesturing at one another and the crazed townspeople who swarmed at the foot of the stage. The sergeants on stage were keeping them back at spear point.

Lark searched the stage with narrowed eyes and finally spotted Philip held between two natives. Even from Lark's point of view, he could see that Philip was battered and hurt but he could also see the scornful contempt grinding in every line of his body. Philip was furious.

Looking further along the stage, Lark failed to find Philomena. She wasn't there.

If Philip is angry and he's doing nothing about it than Philomena must still be in Moth's chambers, Lark figured. Knowing what he had to do, Lark crept out from the narrow passage's cover. He glanced at the three or four sergeants manning the back of the mob. They were swamped with their task at hand, and weren't thinking of looking around for outsiders.

Lark moved around the thundering mob towards Moth's chambers. It was easy enough. No one so much as caught a glimpse of him as he snuck stealthily by the stage and alongside the chambers.

As Lark hurried by, one of the townspeople ripped the spear from a sergeant's hands and lunged at the stage crazily. The mob roared encouragement and pushed forward. The villager managed to pull himself half way on the stage before Moth shoved him in the chest with his boot sending him reeling backwards in to the crowd. There was a wave of disapproving remarks that rose from the townspeople.

Lark hoped Moth and Avador could control the mob just a little longer. If they didn't, Philip was in for a world of trouble.

Hurrying along the chamber wall, Lark slowed to crane his gaze skyward and found a window. It was small, nearly eight feet off the ground, and its shutters were closed. It might be accessible, Lark thought doubtfully. If he went around the building he could just use the front door. No one would suspect that an enemy would just charge through the front door, though if he used the window he might be able to avoid confronting anyone. All he needed to do was get in, get Philomena, and get out to save Philip.

It was hard to think and strategize with pulsing shouts and cries from the mob behind him.

"Hey!" shouted an angry voice.

Lark started, swinging around and drawing his sword. He grimaced when he saw a sergeant standing before him.

In the next instant, the sergeant was pulling a horn from his belt and lifting it to his lips. Cursing, Lark flipped his sword and surged forward. A mournful howl bellowed from the horn echoing against the night. Lark smashed his sword pommel in the man's face, cutting off the howl. The sergeant reeled and his knees buckled, and he crumpled to the ground next to his fallen horn

*****

"Someone's here!" a sergeant on stage shouted over the roar of the mob.

"Yes, thank you, we are not deaf," Moth growled irritably, having heard the sound of the horn. "Go take some men and find out what's going on,"

The sergeant nodded eagerly and hurried off stage, calling two comrades to join him. They jogged down the short flight of stairs leading to ground level. Avador watched from where he stood at the edge of the stage with a spear gripped in his hands to fend off the mob.

Lieutenant Kaiden moved to leave also but Moth held up a hand to stop him.

"You stay here," Moth demanded. Kaiden stepped back, and instead went to assist the spearmen with keeping the mob at bay.

"What's happening?" Avador questioned, stepping toward Moth.

"A horn sounded. We may have company," said Moth. He directed a sneer at Philip who remained detained between Silver Stream and Night Hawk.

*****

Three sergeants rounded the corner. They spotted Lark and charged, drawing swords. One threw a mace that Lark evaded. Pulling his bow free and knocking an arrow, he drew, sighted and released at the charging sergeants. The arrow whistled through the air, and stopped with a meaty smack in one of the sergeant's thigh.

The sergeant gave a sharp cry and tumbled, clutching his bloody leg. His comrades didn't even stop. They kept coming. Lark drew a second arrow and let it fly. The sergeants had started a weaving maneuver in attempt to throw him off course, and Lark's arrow glanced harmlessly off one of their breast plates with a ringing *clank*!

Bellowing battle cries, they closed in on Lark. His heart pounding audibly in his throat, Lark dropped his bow and reached for his sword. The first sergeant tried a jab to Lark's chest which he barely deflected. Their swords slid apart with a teeth jarring hiss. Twirling his blade, the sergeant attacked again, driving Lark back.

Lark's ears buzzed with the repeated clashing of steel. The sergeant's sword flashed in and out, over and under in quick attacks. All Lark could do was shift to block his blade keeping it from beheading him. His spine prickled with an eerie sensation, and without thinking Lark dropped to the ground as his opponent swung for an overhead cut. Lark's hair stirred as the blade whooshed over him only to slash the second sergeant who had snuck behind hoping to catch Lark in the back.

Simultaneously, the second sergeant's sword crashed against the side of his comrade's helmet knocking him sideway's in to the stone wall. The sergeant stumbled back, tried to keep his balance but still crumpled over.

The other sergeant was doubled over on his hands and knees, his comrade's sword having sliced through a leather part of his armor.

Panting and feeling a little shaky, Lark sheathed his sword and recovered his bow. Composing himself, he broke in to a run towards the wall and stepped on the disorientated sergeant shoving him face first in to the dirt. Lark leapt from the man's back for the chamber wall, grabbing for a crevice between the stones. Groaning softly, he heaved himself up reaching out for the next crevice, and started to climb for the window above him. The cold stone was rough even for Lark's callused hands, but he ignored it and kept climbing, finding hand holds and foot holds. Below, the sergeant rolled over moaning dirt covering his whole face and front. He attempted to struggle to his feet but failed. His comrades also remained where they lay, unconscious or nursing their wounds.

Muttering under his breath, knowing his cover was blown as it was; Lark grasped the window's ledge. He had to quicken the pace, for once one of the sergeants managed to get word to Moth escaping would prove to be much more difficult.

Tensing his muscles, Lark swung his leg up and over. There was a crashing sound as his knee and boot bashed open the shutters. Lark moved with the momentum and rolled over the ledge, dropping in to the chamber building.

He didn't have a second to take a breath. He was instantly greeted by a roaring sergeant and his mace. The sergeant threw and the mace spiraled through the air aimed for Lark's head. Lark's eyes widened and he fell to the ground. There was a crushing sound, and then a clatter as the mace fell beside Lark. Glancing up, Lark glimpsed the small crater the mace had dented in to the stone wall.

A slither of steel on leather sliced the air accompanied with quick footsteps. Looking around, Lark saw the sergeant, a snarl twisting his features and his sword raised for a deadly blow as he charged towards him. Lark scrambled to his feet to meet his attacker. His breath shortened as he fumbled for his sword. Then things happened fast.

A small figure plunged seemingly out of nowhere in to the sergeant's side knocking him off balance. The sergeant regained his footing and turned vengefully to his new opponent. The figure brandished a sword, and the fight was on. Swing, block, jab, and parry.

Lark watched, stunned, as the figure reeled backwards, the sergeant's blade passing only inches from her chest. *Her?*

Yes, it was a girl, Lark realized. Immediately, he knew who it was.

The sergeant slashed away her sword and it clattered to the floor. Lark started forward, ready to help but she didn't need it. She snaked her arm around the sergeant's and twirled to the side, disarming him. The sergeant growled in furry and swung wildly after her. She cart wheeled toward him and caught him in the face with her boot, making him stumble back and trip. His head snapped against the side of a table and he slumped unconscious. Lark hurried over sheathing his sword, and feeling relieved as he looked down at the knocked out man. He looked to the girl who had probably saved him from a terrible beating. She was bending over to retrieve her sword, and now that the fight was over and she wasn't a blur of motion Lark could see her clearly. She straightened and faced him, her clothes torn and dirty and her face smeared with grime.

Lark's stomach lurched and his heart skipped a beat.

"Are you alright, Philomena?" he asked, stepping a pace toward her.

Philomena did not answer, but regarded him, looking him up and down with a new light in her eyes as if she were seeing him for the first time. "You came back," she said softly.

Lark nodded, shifting uneasily. "Look, I know you're not too fond of me but I-"

Philomena didn't allow him to finish. She tackled him with a hug, causing him to stagger back a step.

Quite startled by her behavior, Lark gaped his mouth open as if to say something but couldn't. He went to embrace her back, but thought better of it and stood there awkwardly. She smelt of leather and soil which was somehow pleasant.

After a moment, her sudden show of affection ended almost as soon as it began. She stepped back, customarily shoving him away as she did. She brushed the loose hair from her flushed face, and cleared her throat bashfully. Lark stared at her with a baffled expression.

"Did they drug you or something while I was gone?" he asked, stunned. Philomena flashed a warning glare at him.

"Why'd you come back? I thought you had to go home," she demanded, a little flustered.

"I did, and I was, but I realized you were telling the truth about everything," Lark replied, stepping forward and explaining with earnest.

Philomena perceived him curiously.

"You really are the prince and princess of Alamia. I believe you now, so I came back to help," he added.

Corking her mouth in consideration, Philomena eyed Lark with something like disbelief. Lark stared back steadily, waiting for a response. The muffled shouting of the mob outside and the sergeants trying to control it penetrated disturbingly through the stone walls.

"I know you're probably trying to figure out if I'm double crossing you or lying in some way but there really isn't time for it," Lark told her bluntly, lifting his eyebrows sarcastically.

"That's true," Philomena agreed her mouth a tight line. She sized him up again. "Just so you know, if you are double crossing us-"

"You'll skin me alive," Lark cut in. "Yeah, I think I know that by now,"

Philomena nodded satisfactorily. Her features softened a touch.

"And if you aren't lying, and we get caught and thrown in Moth's dungeon you'll be punished just as severely. You don't have to do this,"

"This was my decision. I'll live with the consequences, good or bad," said Lark. There was no detectable trace of regret in his voice which put most of Philomena's doubts to rest.

"So, how are just you and me going to fend off this angry mob, Moth *and* Avador, to rescue Philip before they torture him to death?" Philomena asked levelly.

Her posture was tense with anticipation which Lark understood. He still marveled at how calm she could remain. Most girls would be a whimpering, tearful mess.

Lark circled his gaze about the chamber, trying to conjure some way they could separate Philip from his captors. He remembered the statue overlooking the square and the idea hit him. It was crazy and could kill them in the process but if they didn't do something they were going to be killed anyway.

"I might have an idea," said Lark eagerly. He glanced around.

"We need rope,"

Philomena pointed to Philip's bonds that were still sprawled on the floor, but Lark declined it with a negative gesture. It wasn't enough.

"Storage closet then," said Philomena.

They hurried to a side door and it creaked open. A lit lamp hanging in the back amidst the dusty shelves and cabinets flickered in greeting. Lark took two coils of rope from a hook shouldering the one and handing the second to Philomena. She considered it curiously.

"You need this much? What are you planning on doing?" she questioned with puzzlement.

"I'll tell you as we go," said Lark. He could feel his adrenaline racing again as they made for the chamber's back door. They stepped over the still unconscious sergeant.

"Should we really be using a door?" asked Philomena.

"Doesn't matter, they already know I'm here," Lark figured, remembering the horn the sergeant had blown before and the sergeants he had fought just outside the window.

"Perfect," Philomena grumbled as they hurried out the door.

49

Disgruntled shouts and jeers continued to come wave after wave from the mob that was beginning to lose its patience and its temper. There was no longer a united chant. They wanted Philip, and they wanted him dead. They hefted staffs, axes and other peasantry weapons over their heads. Even some of the women present were enthralled and joined in the ruckus.

"This is getting out of control!" Kaiden hollered over the ear pounding noise.

"Our men will keep them at bay," Moth replied carelessly, sweeping his gaze over the sea of townspeople. The corner of his mouth upturned satisfactorily at the chaos he had created.

"With all due respect, but I believe we need to move the prisoner to a safer location before he gets killed," Kaiden said firmly, glancing out at the many weapons the mob wielded.

Moth turned a threatening glare on him, his jaw set in a hard line. "Are you questioning my orders, lieutenant?" he asked dangerously.

Kaiden held his ground with difficulty, feeling himself shiver inside. Before he could respond, a metallic clang sounded and a hammer sailed end over end before them and clattered against the wooden planks. They looked to the side and saw Avador standing in front of Philip his sword drawn.

"Thanks, I really owe you one," Philip said sarcastically. He had regained some of his former strength, though he remained relatively compliant between Night Hawk and Silver Stream. Avador eyed him for a moment before switching his gaze to Kaiden and Moth.

"We cannot keep him here, Moth. It's too dangerous," he said, keeping in front of Philip. "At this rate he'll end up looking like a pincushion. I need him alive,"

"And where do you suggest scurrying him off to?" Moth rounded on Avador shoving Kaiden aside.

Avador opened his mouth to reply but was cut off by a shouting sergeant. Turning to the stage's flight of steps, they saw two men pounding on to the stage with wildly fretful expressions. Moth's brow pinched irritably, his sharp eyes noticing the blood stain on the one man's side and a terrible dent in the other's helmet.

"Commander!" they shouted, coming to Moth and panting for breath. "The chamber has been breached!"

"By who? How many are there?" Moth demanded.

The sergeant with the dented helmet answered after ducking to let an ax thrown from the mob sail overhead. "One, sir,"

"ONE! You let *one* man get passed you when there were *three* of you?!" Moth bellowed his face flushing. The sergeants shuffled nervously, glancing sideways at one another.

"He got inside?" Avador cut in. Moth stomped a pace away, shaking his head and fuming with disgust.

"Yes, through the window," said the sergeant with the slash on his side.

"Did he have a bow?" Avador asked his thoughts clearly working.

The sergeants nodded. "He shot Edwin. We sent him to the infirmary and told Mascus to circle the chambers. We believe he managed to get to the other prisoner,"

"And this intruder, did he appear to be native?" Avador pressed. Glancing at one another, the sergeants shrugged. "He could have been. He had black hair, though his skin wasn't very dark,"

"And he had a scar under his right eye," the other sergeant added.

At this, Avador's eyes darkened with recognition. He looked to Philip who was smirking happily.

"I believe we both know who that is, captain," Philip grinned.

*****

On the right side of the chamber building, Lark and Philomena were dragging the sergeants they had just knocked out in to the cover of the armory which was a dark shed built in to the side of the chambers. They lugged the unconscious men by the arms and pulled them alongside their three other comrades sprawled between the racks of weaponry and armor. The dim moonlight reflected off swords, axes, and various parts of armor. Philomena rotated an appreciative gaze around at the supple supply of weaponry. She went over to a rack of swords and quickly picked out three, the blades making a dull slither against their wooden stands.

"What are you doing?" Lark demanded his voice low. His breath clouded the cold air.

"Restocking my weapons supply. I left our other knives back in Moth's chambers," Philomena replied quietly, moving to the back of the shed where the shadows nearly engulfed her.

Lark waited anxiously at the entrance, his gaze constantly darting out to the road in expectation of more sergeants appearing and charging after them. He heard Philomena clicking her tongue thoughtfully as if she were shopping on a sunny market day.

"Philomena! We don't have time for this!" Lark hissed urgently, about ready to burst with impatience.

"I know that," said Philomena, coming forward again and stepping over the sprawled sergeants. In her hands she gripped a longbow of Stalveerian design crafted from oak, and a quiver of arrows with grey shafts.

"Do you even know how to handle that bow?" Lark questioned with a skeptical gesture.

"No, but I know you're a pretty good shot," Philomena said, a challenge in her eyes. "See what you can do with a real bow," She handed him the bow and quiver.

Just as when Philip had been given him his sword, Lark saw the beautiful craftsmanship, but felt the quiet deadliness in the bow's strength. He shouldered the quiver and bow without a word, a steely look set in his features.

"Let's get to that statue," he said, retrieving the rope they had dropped during the fight. Philomena took up her coil and followed, their pace set at a swift jog in the shadow of the chamber building. They came to a halt just before the chamber's corner, pressing their backs against the wall.

Sweeping an attentive gaze around to be sure no one had spotted them; they cut across the road at an angle. They reached the statue and slipped in its shadow, scurrying behind its massive form. The statue's base was nearly as tall as they were. In the front, Lark had noticed the name 'Queen Adelaide' etched deeply in the stone. Philomena kept a keen look out while Lark uncoiled the rope.

"Now what are we doing?" Philomena asked, staring across the road at the maddened mob that was getting louder and louder. A sergeant attempting to control the perimeter of the crowd tried shoving some of the townspeople. Turning an angry glare on him, a burly townsman shoved him in return and he fell on his backside.

From the looks of it, Moth and his men were far too busy dealing with the mob to send out more men after them. They needed all the help they could get.

"You're going to keep a look out, and I'm going to tie this rope around the statue," Lark informed, knotting the two lengths of rope together. Philomena craned her gaze back, peering up at the statue. It was easily twenty feet tall.

"Exactly why are we doing this?" she asked confused.

"Feed me the rope," said Lark, shoving the rope in to her hands and gripping the other end. He hauled himself on top of the base and started climbing.

Philomena huffed irritably. "I wish you'd talk more," she mumbled, but she did as he asked feeding the rope from the coil as he went and making sure it didn't snag or tangle. She kept her gaze continuously sweeping around, alert for any enemy. On the outside, she maintained a calm composure, but on the inside Philomena fought to control a writhing panic that threatened to drive her mad.

Lark swarmed up the statue, easily finding good handholds and footholds in the rounded folds of the queen's gown. Climbing over the arch that made the statue's backside, Lark stopped at the half point. He called down to Philomena for more slack. Hauling on the rope, he wrapped it a few times around the midsection of the statue. This he did carefully so as not to lose his grip, for the queen was not only twenty feet tall but also four feet wide.

There was one scary moment when Lark reached over to grab the rope from the front and his boot slipped. He caught himself by grabbing the queen's long sleeve, his breath shortening frightfully. The ground loomed far below, making Lark's mind swim dizzily.

Philomena winced, and made a cautioning gesture. Lark nodded and took a moment to compose himself, taking a few steadying breaths before continuing his task.

Adjusting his actions to be more tentative, Lark successfully retrieved the rope from the front and brought it around. He tied the rope off, double knotting it and making sure it was secure. Satisfied, Lark quickly climbed down. His feet touched the base and he swung over the edge, dropping nimbly down next to Philomena.

"What now?" Philomena asked.

"Under the stage," said Lark, grabbing the rest of the rope. He pulled his sword out as he went readying himself in case of an encounter with irritable sergeants.

"Why?" Philomena blurted with a confounded gesture. She hurried after him anyway, doing as he did and arming herself. The rope raced after them. Philomena flicked her sharp eyes around as they moved speedily to the stage. No one on the stage spotted them. Philomena caught a glimpse of Philip, battered and angry, and a fleeting fearful joy gripped her.

A warning from Lark forced her to tear her gaze from her brother, and she was suddenly face to face with a sergeant. The man swung his blade, making her duck. Lark rushed in. He grabbed the man's sword and twirled him around into the corner of the chamber building. The man's helmet clonked against the stone edge and his nose crunched, trailing lines of blood from his nostrils. His eyes rolled in the back of his head and he fell over.

"Thanks," Philomena breathed. Lark nodded acknowledgement. He handed her the rope and drug the unconscious sergeant under the cover of the stage. Philomena followed, glancing around. Thankfully, no one else saw them.

Accepting the rope back, Lark made his way further under the stage with Philomena keeping pace beside him. Footfalls and various clanking sounds echoed through the timber from above. The noise from the mob was like a vicious churning ocean. They hurriedly picked their way over and around the hefty support beams, traveling a quarter of the way under the stage before the rope went taut nearly jerking Lark off his feet. Panting, Lark glanced around and went back a pace. He looped the rope over a horizontal support beam.

"You know, an explanation would be great right about now," said Philomena with a welcoming gesture for him to oblige. Lark shot an annoyed glare at her.

"It's like a pulley system," he said hurriedly, the roaring of the mob jarring his nerves. "Even though the object at the other end is heavy it still may be moved with less effort. Now will you help me pull,"

Philomena's eyes grew wide and the bubbling pit of panic in her gut instantly began seeping at the notion. "Are you serious?! You want to bring down that statue! What? So we'll be squashed to save us the trouble of being tortured by Moth and Avador?!"

"Do you have any better ideas?!" Lark yelled back.

"You have completely lost it! Yes, let's bring down the enormous statue that will flatten my brother before he can dive out of the way!" Philomena went on sarcastically with sharp, irritable gestures.

"Philomena! Shut up!" Lark snapped. His tone made Philomena stop short, and she stared stunned.

"Have you looked out there? It's literally two of us against an army to save your brother!" Lark added harshly, waving an arm at the wild mob of townspeople visible through the forest of support beams.

Philomena shifted, her features conceding but still unsure. "It's just . . . it's a big risk we're taken here, Lark,"

Lark could see the anticipation and the fear. What if Philip can't get out of the way? What if he's taken before they can get to him? What if they get hurt? What if innocent people get killed because of them? What if?

"I know," he said in a gentler tone. Philomena looked to him.

"But we both know if that statue doesn't kill us than Avador certainly will if he catches us now. Please, just trust me,"

Several emotions surfaced on Philomena's features. She gazed up at the planks of the stage, knowing Philip was there depending on them. She looked back to Lark and wavered.

"Alright," she breathed.

Lark nodded, relieved and turned to face the beam that the rope trailed over. Philomena stepped in place behind him and gripped the bristly rope.

"Not too much pressure, we want it to come down slowly," Lark advised.

"Yes, because they always come down like that," Philomena snipped.

Lark smirked to himself.

"Ready," he said and together they leaned back. The rope went tight, tensing against the support beams. The statue at the other end was an unmovable weight.

"I think we need more hands for this," Philomena grunted from behind.

"No," Lark grinded determinedly. Sweat was already starting to drip from his face. "We can do this. Try stepping backwards," Their muscles were already burning. Attempting to step backwards was like trying to walk through half dried mud. The statue wasn't budging.

"Come on, Philomena!" Lark growled over his shoulder, his breath coming in gasps. "You're the strongest girl I know and you can't pull this statue down?!"

She replied with a grunt and a muttered curse. The skin on her palms was peeling off against the rough rope.

"PULL!"

Gathering their strength in every straining muscle they took two steps back. Lark felt the statue on the other end move, and encouraged Philomena.

Above on stage, Avador and some of Moth's men stood in front of Philip serving as a human shield against the many axes, staffs, and other crude weapons flung from the mob. A frying pan bounced off one of the sergeant's swords with a loud clang. Those on the ground attempting to force the resilient mob back were in danger of being beaten to a pulp or trampled, except for Avador's remaining men still on their horses. Just when Avador thought the mob was going to engulf the stage, a loud shout drew their attention.

"The statue! The statue's falling!"

"It's coming down on us!" another screamed.

Moth, Avador and everyone else on the stage turned puzzled looks that way. Just as the townsman had warned, the giant statue of Queen Adelaide was tilting over. A terrible stone on stone grinding filled the square instantly setting panic in the crowd.

"Oh great," said Philip, gaping up at the statue. He saw the way it was falling and he knew it was aimed for the stage.

The mob no longer wanted to suffocate the stage; they were scrambling desperately to get away from it now, their hatred for Philip forgotten. Frightened yells and panicked screams rose as the townspeople ran for their lives. They pushed, shoved, and trampled one another to be the first out of the square. The sergeants joined them, some even leaping from the stage to get clear of the falling statue.

"GET BACK HERE!" Moth roared after his fleeing sergeants. "Cut the rope! The rope on the statue! Cut it NOW!" Avador yelled desperately. But no one listened, and no one was willing to approach the falling statue.

The statue groaned. Time was up. Avador flung his gaze to Night Hawk and Silver Stream. "GET OFF!"

Silver Stream and Night Hawk scrambled to obey, dragging Philip between them. Avador followed, swinging his gaze around at the statue that seemed to be hovering on the edge of its base.

"Come on, Moth, before we get crushed!!" Avador hollered to the commander.

"If anyone's going to get crushed it's going to be HIM!" shouted Moth. He grabbed the scruff of Philip's coat and yanked him out from between Silver Stream and Night Hawk before they could react. They turned back on Moth. The commander had a knife pressed to Philip's throat.

"What are you doing?!" Avador shouted.

Looming just above them, Queen Adelaide's statue groaned again and the base crumbled under her weight, making the ground tremble. Kaiden and his few comrades forgot about being brave. They dropped from the stage and ran.

Moth grinned wickedly as the twenty foot Queen Adelaide began its descent, increasing in speed. He met Avador's gaze and in the next instant flung Philip in the path of the falling statue. Philip slammed hard against the wood planks, sending a blinding pain in his bad shoulder and knocking the wind out of him.

Avador swept past Moth to pull Philip out of harm's way, but Moth intervened, grabbing him from behind. Night Hawk and Silver Stream jumped to their captain's aide.

Below, Lark and Philomena shot out from under the stage and rushed around it. They searched desperately for Philip. Queen Adelaide's head hit the chamber building, crumbling the wall and sending loosened stone flying and rolling. Part of the stage collapsed beneath it with a loud crunch. Splinters flew.

"Oh god," Philomena murmured, her expression frantic, a hand covering her mouth. She couldn't see Philip through the tears that blurred her vision.

"There!" Lark yelled, pointing to the middle of the stage where Moth, Avador, Silver Stream and Night Hawk were grappling. They ran, rushing past Avador's remaining company and sprung on the stage. The trembling that vibrated through the splintering boards underneath their boots was unnerving. Queen Adelaide's head was rushing towards them like a stone battering ram ready to crush them.

"Philip!!!" Philomena cried, spotting him still sprawled semi-conscious on the cracking planks. The shadow of Queen Adelaide suddenly blanketed him. When they reached him, the statue was just above their heads. Cracking wood and crushing stone filled their ears. Philomena's eyes bulged at the sight, and she knew they'd be squashed. But Lark pulled Philip to his feet, draping Philip's arm over his shoulder. Philomena grabbed his other arm, and they ran towards the falling statue. They lost their footing and slid down the collapsing stage.

Then, darkness engulfed them.

Still fighting, Avador and Moth seemed to forget their danger. Queen Adelaide's head rammed in to the stage, shaving the chamber wall and sending more stone crumbling down. They stumbled from the final shuddering tremor and fell over one another on the remaining quarter of the stage. The cracking and splintering suddenly stopped, and the queen's head rested on the ground in a bed of broken wood and stone.

A cloud of dust wafted on the air. The surviving part of the stage drooped on its fragmented end, missing several beams underneath.

Moth, Avador, Silver Stream and Night Hawk clambered to their feet in a daze.

Moth swung his gaze around. "The prisoner!" he shouted.

Avador straightened and smashed a fist against Moth's jaw, and followed it with another left hook. The commander tumbled backwards in to Night Hawk. The native soldier shoved the limp commander away with a disgusted look and let him fall.

"Don't let him go anywhere," Avador commanded. Night Hawk and Silver Stream nodded.

Avador turned and signaled for Bright Sky to bring his horse over. They came galloping over. Avador leapt in to his saddle from the stage and accepted his reins from Bright Sky. He swung his horse around and led the company out of the square past the wreckage and the fallen statue, the hooves of their horses clopping loudly against the cobblestone.

Underneath the fallen statue in the small crevice where it had not made contact with the ground, Lark and Philomena struggled to their feet surprised to find themselves alive with just a few bruises and scratches. Philip rolled over coughing, now fully conscious.

"Philip, are you alright?" Philomena asked, kneeling beside him.

"Hard to say," Philip replied thickly.

Philomena helped him to his feet, and after checking to be sure he was alright, hugged him. He embraced her in return, though grimaced as a wave of pain washed over his shoulder.

"Ow," he muttered.

"Sorry," Philomena said sheepishly, untangling herself from him, but she still smiled with overwhelming relief.

Philip shook his head dismissively, smiling in return. When he noticed Lark, his grin widened through the mask of stone dust covering his face.

"I knew you'd come back," he said, swaying on his feet.

"We can talk later, but right now we have to get of here," Lark said urgently, brushing the wooden splinters off his shoulders.

"How? Aren't you forgetting that the entire city is locked down," Philomena reminded.

"I know a way out," said Lark.

"Just lead the way, Lark," said Philip, still swaying.

"I'm not arguing with you two, so let's just go," Philomena grumbled. She stepped over to help Philip but he assured her he could make it on his own. He happily accepted two of the swords Philomena had confiscated from Ezleon's armory and strapped the belts about his waist.

They moved to the triangular opening the statue had left and stopped short at the sound of approaching hooves. Avador and his company galloped by, stirring more clouds of dust.

"We'll never be able to outrun them on foot," Philip said quietly.

"We don't have to, not all the way at least. I have the horses at the end of that alley there," Lark informed, pointing across the square

"Then what?" Philomena questioned.

"We head for the stables," Lark replied.

"So we can hide in the straw," Philomena said sarcastically, her eyes blazing at Lark.

Lark's brow wrinkled at her tone and he turned a scowl on her. He noticed the way she was keeping close to Philip, as though fearful he might disappear. He swallowed his annoyance.

"Just follow me," he said levelly. He ducked out from under the statue and checked for any possible threats. Seeing the square was empty besides the native soldiers standing on the last of the stage next to a still form, Lark motioned for Philip and Philomena to come out.

Leading the way along the outskirts of the square so they wouldn't be spotted, Lark found the alley which he had come through earlier. He peered down it cautiously, found it empty, and proceeded up its narrow path. Philip and Philomena stayed close, swords drawn. Philomena kept a lookout for threats from the roofs above while Philip kept watch from behind. Everything was quiet.

At the end of the alley, their horses lifted their heads at their approach. Lark breathed an inward sigh of relief, having been fretful that someone might have found them and taken them. Nimbius and Coursio greeted them. Philomena patted Nimbius, then went over to Coursio and hugged his neck. The grey stallion bobbed his head happily.

"Only two?" Philip looked questioningly to Lark. "Where's Spear?"

"I'll explain later," Lark said firmly, glancing nervously down the road where he could see a few townspeople scurrying in and out of the alleys. Most likely they were from the mob and were finding their way back to the comforts of their homes.

Philip pursed his lips, but said nothing and checked Nimbius' girth. Philomena pulled a cloak out from their saddle bags and handed it to him, advising him to wear it with the hood up to prevent anyone from recognizing him.

Lark unbuckled his saddlebags that he had draped across Nimbius' back, and peered inside. Arican blinked up at him and gurgled a soft greeting. Lark stuck his hand in and stroked her between the ears, reassuring her it wouldn't be long till they were safe. At least he hoped that would be so.

A few shouts wafted on the air from down the road, making their nerves tense anxiously. Lark swallowed, gave Arican one last pat and buckled her saddlebag closed once more. Philomena swung up in to her saddle, and Lark did likewise with Nimbius.

What about me?" Philip asked, spreading his arms in a questioning manner. His face was shadowed by the deep cowl of his cloak.

"You're riding with Philomena," Lark said gathering Nimbius' reins.

"Why don't you ride with Philomena?" Philip suggested, folding his arms. Philomena shot a mean glare at him.

"No, I'm not the one they're after and I'm not the one hurt," Lark said flatly.

Disappointed, Philip unfolded his arms and climbed on board Coursio behind Philomena, wincing slightly from the action. They started off, trotting in to the cover of the alley across from them.

"He is *my* horse you know," Philip added, looking pointedly over at Lark.

"I have no intention of keeping him," Lark reassured matter-of-factly. Philip corked his mouth in consideration.

Two or three townspeople ran by the alley's entrance and they instinctively halted their horses. The men raced by without a glance down the dark alley, gripping staffs and pitchforks and communicating noisily as they went.

"They're looking for us," Philomena noted grudgingly after the townsmen's voices ebbed away.

"Luckily for us they're searching in a rather obvious manner. We'll hear them before they can spot us," Philip said behind her with a smirk.

"Avador will not be as stupid and neither will his men," Lark put in.

"That's true," Philip admitted, his mouth twisting with displeasure. After a minute of silence, they nudged their horses onward.

"Remember, we have to get to the stables," Lark reminded them quietly as they continued up the narrow alleyway.

"Right, so we can hide in the straw," Philip grinned teasingly. Philomena snickered. Lark glared sidelong at the pair of them. Philip gave an apologetic gesture, but Lark could still see the grin in the shadow of his hood. Lark shook his head.

"Let's just try to be quiet," he said, switching his gaze ahead of them as they neared the alley's opening. "They don't know where we are," he added.

They looked out to the road, being sure it was empty, and then moved along silently, keeping to the shadows.

50

As inconspicuous as they tried to be, they couldn't avoid Avador and the angry mob members forever. Once everything had settled after Queen Adelaide's statue took a tumble, the mob had re-grouped and were flocking nearly every street, assisting Avador in his search. They seemed angrier than before, and more dangerous due to their suddenly organized minds.

Philip, Philomena and Lark thought their nerves would burst in to flames. They were in another side street, a filthy winding one where it appeared several townspeople disposed of any trash. The place reeked of rot and sewage. Their horses' hooves clopped in a stream of murky water that trickled down the middle of the alley. A stray cat shot out of the rubble and scampered away, startling their horses.

Despite the occasional shouting from their search party, they kept at an easy pace, walking silently up the smelly side street. Lark glanced over his shoulder at his companions and noticed Philomena holding her nose against the stench and Philip's cheeks bulging out around his cloak's cowl as he held his breath. Lark looked ahead once more, not bothering to do either. He was accustomed to dealing with the occasional odor.

They reached the side street's opening and fresh air poured in from the main road against the reeking smell. Glancing out, Lark could see a few townspeople searching further up the road, but none close by enough to notice them. They exited the side street, and Lark could hear Philip take in a refreshing gulp of air.

"What a stench," Philomena complained under her breath.

The stables were in view, just a five meter walk across the street. They started toward it, and after covering less than a meter heard heavy footsteps running in their direction from the side street they had just left.

"Take cover," Philip hissed, grabbing the reins from Philomena and wheeling Coursio into a nearby shack. Lark followed, ducking his head as he rode in behind them. A black sheet, torn and ripped on the end fell in their wake over the entrance serving as a curtain.

They kept silent as they listened to the approaching footsteps grow louder, their heads bowed over their horses' necks to keep from hitting the shack's ceiling. A minute later, a group of men were hurrying by, equipment clicking purposefully. They glimpsed them through the small gap the curtain left.

"You look further down this stretch, we'll look 'round here," a gruff voice spoke.

"Right, let's find 'em!" another replied. More footsteps and a portion of the group broke off to search down the road. The remaining men stuck around. They could hear them shuffling noisily about, poking in neighboring shacks and cottages. Perspiration beaded on the three's faces despite the wintry chill. It would only be a matter of time. They were pressed in the corner of the shack side by side with no room to move and no way of escape.

A shadow leaked beneath the curtain. Philip slipped down from behind Philomena before they could stop him.

"Philip!" Philomena hissed, but Philip shushed her and wedged between the two horses. He moved silently over to the curtain and pressed himself against the wall. Flicking his gaze to Philomena and Lark, he signaled for them to be still. Lark wrapped his fingers around his sword hilt anyway.

Looking back to the curtain, Philip could see the boots of the man approaching the shack beneath the torn cloth. The man slid a hand inside and yanked the curtain back as he entered. The curtain fell back in place with a soft rustle as the man swung his narrowed gaze around the shack's interior. He wore no armor and was obviously a townsman.

Philip sucked in a readying breath.

The townsman's gaze fell upon Philomena and Lark and his eyes popped. Lark winced and involuntarily put a hushing finger to his lips. The townsman's jaw dropped and he sucked in a breath to shout.

Philip lunged forward and wrapped his arms around the man's neck, clasping his hand over the man's mouth. The man struggled, his eyes bulging and his voice muffled. After a moment though, the man fell unconscious under Philip's grip. Snickering happily, Philip dragged the man by his arms to the back of the shack and hid him behind some small barrels. Lark and Philomena watched, somewhat stunned.

"Someone's coming," Lark whispered calmly, his eyes peeled on the entrance. They snapped their gazes forward and glimpsed another approaching townsman.

"Lark, above you!" Philip whispered sharply, hurrying back over to them and pointing to the ceiling.

Half expecting to find a crazed mob member there, Lark lifted his gaze upward and his eyes lit up when he saw what Philip had noticed. Another curtain rolled tightly and tied to a beam of the ceiling. Lark raised a hand and pulled on the leather ties. The dark curtain dropped to the ground hiding them from sight just as Philip clambered behind Philomena once more.

The second townsman yanked back the entrance's curtain and swung a searching gaze about the shack. He stepped inside and stood in the shack's center, darting his gaze around.

The shack was a tidy little studio where the local candle maker worked. Jars and various tools were stored neatly on the tables lining the sides. Already made candles hung from the ceiling. A fire pit with a spit over its bed of ashes was in the back near a work bench covered with dried drips of wax.

Seeing nothing unusual, the townsman turned to leave, but then his eyes befell the curtain in the back. He froze and stared at the black cloth suspiciously.

Behind the curtain, the three exchanged glances, their hands gripping their weapons. It was quiet for a drawn out moment, broken by a voice from outside the shack that startled them.

"Virgil! Anything in the candle maker's?" a man asked.

"Nothing," the man, Virgil, said from inside the shack.

"Where's Harris?" the other man asked.

"Don't know, but he's not in here," Virgil replied.

Lark, Philip and Philomena held their breath as they listened. They picked up the sound of shuffling feet, then the rustle of cloth and the townsman, Virgil, was gone. The group of searchers was moving on up the road, but they were still close by.

Philomena exhaled irritably. "For the love of a half witted mutt," she muttered, exasperated. Lark and Philip turned perplexed glances on her.

"They're going to find us anyway so why don't we just make a break for it," she said with an insistent gesture.

"We can't!" Lark hissed. "We have to get to the stables unseen. Once we're in that tunnel, they won't be able to find us,"

"Then wake me when there's no one out there to spot us," Philomena replied grudgingly. Lark shook his head and glared at the dark curtain that hid them.

"We need a distraction," Philip said quietly.

"Like what? I didn't see any other giant statue we could push over did you?" Philomena questioned, glancing sidelong at him over her shoulder.

Scrunching his brow, Philip glanced around for inspiration, rubbing his chin pensively. His expression lifted when his eyes fell on an open crate situated in the opposite corner near the barrels that hid the unconscious townsman.

Several bottles were laying in the crate, cushioned by shredded parchment.

"I think I have just the thing," Philip said. He slid carefully down from Coursio once more.

Philomena and Lark watched him eagerly. Philip stepped over to the crate, glancing wearily at the shack's opening, and lifted one of the bottles for them to see. It was ale. Philomena and Lark considered it doubtfully.

"Either you're saying we lure them away with their favorite drink or we get ourselves wasted so being captured will hurt less," Philomena said.

"Hear me out," Philip said, hesitating when the sound of galloping horses went by and then faded. He went over to them back behind the cover of the curtain and then continued more quietly. "Remember the fire pit near the Brimming Barrel? If we throw this bottle of ale in there still sealed it will create an explosion. That will surely create a fascinating distraction for our friends out there don't you think?" Philip grinned excitedly. The way his eyes glittered and the way he lifted the bottle so the ale sloshed, he looked more like a boy about to play a rude prank instead of a prince needing to escape.

"So . . . you want to throw that bottle of ale in to the fire pit," Philomena said slowly, her brow furrowed skeptically.

"It will work. I've seen it happen before," Philip insisted confidently. "The explosion will give us just enough time to slip in to the stables unseen,"

"If you believe it will work then it's worth a try," said Lark, cocking a silencing stare on Philomena. "Who's going to throw it in?"

"I will, it's my idea," said Philip.

"No you won't," Philomena cut in. She slipped down from Coursio.

"But-" Philip tried.

"I don't want to hear your lame excuses. I almost lost you back there and I'm not going to let that happen ever again if I can help it," Philomena persisted firmly.

Inhaling reluctantly and gripping the ale bottle, Philip switched his gaze to Lark for his opinion. Lark shrugged impassively. "This is your decision not mine," he said evenly. Philip let out a submitting breath and looked back to his sister, his gaze suddenly becoming steely.

"You promise me that you'll come back," he said sternly, pointing the bottle at her.

"One way or another, I promise," Philomena said, taking the bottle from him. He pursed his lips worriedly and hugged her. Watching them, Lark realized how much they depended on one another.

"I'll meet you in the stables," said Philomena, stepping back. Philip nodded, and she was off, brushing past the curtain and slipping out of the shack quiet as a hunter. Chewing at his lip, Philip hoped he wouldn't regret his decision later.

"She'll be fine," Lark reassured softly.

"Yeah," Philip agreed, turning to him.

"Could you hand me a bottle of that ale?" Lark asked, gesturing to the crate.

"Why? Are you thirsty?" Philip smirked jokingly.

Lark shook his head negatively. "Its payment," he said.

Philip frowned confusedly. "You know, I'm not going to ask," He retrieved a second bottle of ale, hoping the candle maker wouldn't be too angry, and brought it to Lark.

*****

Further down the road, Philomena slithered along in the shadows keeping low to the ground with a hand hovering at her sword and the other clutching the ale bottle. She kept to the line of shacks belonging to the local craft masters. The further she progressed, the more townsmen she saw. A few sergeants were amongst them, along with one of Avador's men.

"Check these stalls here, and be thorough," the native ordered, pointing to the market stalls across the road.

"We've looked there already," complained a townsman.

"And you'll look again until we find them," the native retorted firmly.

Slinking behind some tall baskets, Philomena glimpsed the rugged native astride his flashing pinto stallion. The feathers tied in his black hair rustled with a light breeze. He turned his gaze her way, and his dark eyes nearly froze her in place. He seemed to see right through the baskets keeping Philomena from sight. After a moment, he swung down from his saddle and started over to her.

Pulse racing, Philomena darted further in the shack. A table draped with a long white linen displaying smaller baskets was in the center. Philomena ducked under it, the linen falling in her wake just as the native came to the line of baskets to peer inside. He scanned the shack slowly without moving and without uttering a sound. Though Philomena couldn't hear him, she felt his penetrating gaze when it fell on the table she was crammed under. She held her breath, her eyes wide. She just hoped that the native's keen senses wouldn't be able to discern the sound of her pounding heart.

"We might have found something over here!" one of the townsmen called. There was a light shuffle, and then the sound of footsteps walking away. The native had left. Philomena exhaled, rather enthralled by the native's uncanny sixth sense yet just as relieved that he could still make mistakes.

She waited for a minute and then slid out from under the table. The ale sloshed noisily in its bottle as she moved to the next shack, making her wince. She glanced over and saw the search party tearing through the market stalls across the street. One of them tossed a small table that shattered to pieces. Philomena grimaced, realizing they were getting irritable.

Sneaking along three more shacks, she halted, pressing her back against a barrel and crouching low. The Brimming Barrel was across from her, and the fire pit blazed in the center. All she had to do now was throw the bottle in to the fire. Only a couple of chatting mob members drinking coffee stood in her way.

"We've looked all over," moaned one of them.

"They just disappeared," said another.

"They're in here somewhere. We just haven't found where that somewhere is yet. Let's keep looking. They deserve the punishment we have in store for them," murmured a determined one.

They threw the dregs of their coffee in the fire and moved on. Philomena kept concealed behind the barrel, listening to them rummage through the nearby shacks and market stalls. After counting out a minute, she peered around the barrel. No one was near the fire pit. *How easy could it get*, she thought.

Something rustled behind her, and before she could turn around a pair of strong hands grabbed her and drug her out from behind the barrel. The man cackled merrily as she growled and resisted defiantly. He pulled her in to the light of the fire pit, several of his fellow men lifting curious gazes their way.

"Look what I've found here, lads!" the man called, yanking Philomena to her feet. "One of the escapees we've been looking for so desperately," he added.

The men whooped gleefully, some coming over and pounding their triumphant friend on the back approvingly. Philomena tried to shake free of her captor's grip, but he was a large man who towered several feet above her. She was like a tiny fly caught in a massive spider web.

"Moth and Avador will surely reward you handsomely for this, Smug," a smiling townsman said to Philomena's captor.

"And I'll gladly accept his gold," Smug beamed. "I can put a new roof on me home and buy some fancy drink perhaps, or even a few steak dinners somewhere foreign,"

The men cheered in agreement, rejoicing for their friend. A loose crowd of them had gathered about Smug and Philomena. The native Philomena had seen before strode forward pushing his way through with a serious look. Philomena's throat went dry at the sight of him.

"Looks like she may have started you off on that drink there, Smug," spoke up a townsman. He gestured to the ale bottle still in Philomena's hands. "Look at what she's holding,"

"Well, what do ya know! There is a Creator after all," Smug laughed.

He reached for the bottle, but Philomena jerked it away, her jaw set and her eyes angry. There were some awed 'oohs' emitted from Smug's friends. Smug grunted upsettingly.

"You best hand me that bottle, little lady. You have no need for it," said Smug, holding out his hand for the ale. Philomena glared at him, and her eyes darted to the native who was on the verge of intervening. This was her only chance.

"You want this bottle so badly? Then go and get it!" Philomena tossed the ale bottle away. It sailed end over end and tumbled in to the teeth of the flames flaring from the fire pit.

"You wench!" Smug wailed, slapping Philomena against the cheek with the back of his hand. She fell backwards from the force, and when she hit the ground there was an ear shattering explosion and a roar of flames.

Philomena rolled and covered her face against the ground as the fire shot high in to the air, spurting wildly.

Confused shouting rose. Insane screaming suddenly started and lifting her face from the ground, Philomena caught sight of Smug running down the road, his coat blazing with fire and a trail of smoke trailing in his wake.

Shoving herself off the ground, Philomena found that most of the townsmen had fled in fear. The smell of burning wood wafted to her, and she found the Brimming Barrel's verandah was in flames, as well as several market stalls and shacks. Smoke thickened the air, and the heat of the fire grew intensely.

Having no opposition to stop her, Philomena started running back down the road, lifting her arms over her head and turning her face away as she passed the snarling fire pit. The tower of flames still spurted angrily.

Sergeants and a few brave townsmen rushed by her without a backwards glance, shouting and carrying buckets of water. The fire sizzled defiantly when they threw the water on it.

Philomena ran on, not bothering to conceal herself in the shadows of the shacks. She could feel the heat of the fire on her back and knew it was spreading. More townsmen ran by her. A mule pulling a wagon rattled by filled with barrels of water. Its driver smacked the mule urgently making the animal wail frightfully.

Philomena felt a twinge of guilt to see the destruction and panic she had caused, but she pushed the feeling away. When all was well again, she'd make it up to the people of Ezleon.

A thrill of relief rushed through her when she reached the candle maker's and found that it was empty. Philip and Lark were in the stables waiting for her. The plan had worked. She turned to the stables, but all of a sudden Avador stepped before her as if morphing from the city's gloom. No sword or weapon was in his hands and he appeared to be alone. Frankly, Avador looked exhausted through the serious expression he wore.

Philomena recovered quickly from the shock of his sudden appearance.

"You and your brother really are a pain in my ass," said Avador, flexing his jaw haughtily. The comment made Philomena feel glad. She fixed him with a scornful glare.

"I'm not going to tell you where they are," she said.

"Did I ask?" Avador questioned moodily. He stepped toward her slowly, his dark eyes staring steadily at her.

"Then step aside," Philomena said threateningly. She pulled her sword out and pointed it at his chest.

Avador looked at it with little interest and lifted his gaze to her underneath lowered brows. "As much fun as it would be, I cannot do that. My father wants you alive in one piece. He has special intentions for you,"

This information made Philomena shudder. To know Salvador had a certain interest in her for what she could not imagine. But she had no time to ponder over it now. Flicking her sword, she feigned an attack to the right and spun to the left. She flipped her sword around and jabbed Avador hard in the gut with the pommel. His air was forced out in a gasp, and he doubled over, clutching his stomach.

Philomena raced for the stables. It didn't take long for Avador to recover and come charging after her. He caught up to her, just a pace behind her. Philomena yanked the stable door open, her spine prickling with Avador's presence so close. He lunged for her and she slammed the door in his face. Bellowing in rage, Avador rammed the door with a shattering blow.

On the other side, Philomena staggered against his sheer strength. Recovering, she pressed her back against the door once more. The door shuttered again under Avador's shoulder.

"Gosh, does he do anything else besides train," Philomena muttered, a little breathless.

"Philomena!" Philip called, rushing over to her from an open stall. He carried a hammer. Lark followed with a board in his hands.

"It's Avador," Philomena told them.

They slid the board across the door. Philip handed Lark the hammer and dug some nails from his pocket. The door shuddered, and they heard Avador growling loudly on the other side. Philip and Philomena held the board in place while Lark pounded the nails. The nails bit in to the wood and held fast. Lark moved to the opposite side and they gave him room. Two more nails and the board held, absorbing Avador's resilience. Lark threw aside the hammer and they ran up the aisle.

"Did the plan work?" Philip asked.

"It did most of the way anyway, but Avador was waiting," Philomena replied, out of breath.

"Ah, it figures," Philip grumbled.

They turned into an open stall where their horses were waiting. Philomena casted a curious frown at a grey horse standing in the aisle way with no tether or halter, munching on some hay.

"Hurry, Philomena!" Philip urged. Philomena looked to him and he motioned her impatiently towards Coursio. She hurried in to the stall and swung in to the saddle. Philip climbed behind her. Kneeling amongst the straw near the back wall, Lark pushed aside the thick bedding and found the arrows he had jammed in to the secret door earlier.

Wedging his fingers in to the crevice, Lark tugged the door open and stowed his arrows in his quiver.

"Inside quickly," he said, gesturing Philomena forward. She obeyed, riding Coursio in to the dark tunnel. Lark lead Nimbius behind them, hearing Avador's persistent pounding against the stable door.

Lark pulled the door closed, shutting them inside the tunnel. It took a moment for his eyesight to adjust. When it did he lowered the door's latch and it clicked satisfactorily. Lark let out a breath of relief. They were in the tunnel, safe.

Looking ahead he could make out Philip and Philomena aboard Coursio. Next to him, Nimbius nudged him seeming a little uneasy. Lark stroked the stallion soothingly.

"It is quite dark in here," said Philip. His voice seemed unnaturally loud in the quiet tunnel.

"How do we know which way to go?" Philomena asked.

"It's fine, just go forward. We'll reach the main tunnel." Lark reassured. He climbed on to Nimbius and gathered the reins, still stroking him and whispering comfortingly. His head nearly touched the tunnel's ceiling.

Philomena rode onward carefully, going slow. Soon the tunnel widened, and flickering torch light greeted them in to the main tunnel. The horses relaxed beneath them, feeling more secure in the wider better lit tunnel. Philip and Philomena gazed around curiously.

"This is pretty cool," said Philip, nodding approvingly.

Philomena lifted her eyebrows skeptically.

Arican gurgled and wiggled in her saddlebag. Lark reached back and unbuckled the leather flap. The cub stuck her head out and sniffed the air. She looked to Lark and gurgled again. She was hungry, Lark could tell.

"You'll have to wait," Lark told her, feeling guilty.

"Don't say that to her, Lark," Philip said chidingly, noticing Arican. He rummaged in Coursio's saddlebags and produced a couple dried strips of meat. He offered them to Lark. "You can't let her go hungry, she's waited patiently," he said with a grin. Lark accepted them with a reluctant twitch of the mouth. "I'll pay you back," he said, giving the dried meat to Arican who took it hungrily and retreated in to the saddlebag once more.

Philip laughed. "No worries! You just rescued us," he said gratefully.

"How did you get in here?!!" hollered a voice making them all jump.

Looking ahead, Lark recognized Barlow the doorkeeper. He was wide eyed with fury.

Philip and Philomena regarded him with matching bewilderment. Barlow stomped over to them, the beads and shells on his coat swinging madly.

"Sorry, Barlow, but I kept the door open. It's closed now," said Lark, shifting uneasily in his saddle.

The doorkeeper crinkled his nose as though he smelt something foul. "I didn't give you permission to come tramping back in here with your uninvited friends and the hairy beasts that are carrying you!" he fumed.

Philip cleared his throat uncomfortably, and Lark noticed Philomena's hand lingering over her sword.

"And did you even consider that some nosy idiot might find the door you kept open and come waltzing in to my secret labyrinth! The place is probably crawling with them like a roach nest! It's all ruined!" Barlow went on, his anger choking with emotion on his last words. He gazed around watery eyed, looking as though he might burst in to tears.

Philip pursed his lips perplexed and looked sidelong to Lark. Lark shook his head and stuck his hand in his saddlebag. He brought out the bottle of ale Philip had given to him earlier and tossed it to Barlow. The doorkeeper fumbled, almost dropping it. He frowned at the bottle and his face instantly lifted.

"Ale!" he exclaimed delightedly.

"You requested a bottle," Lark reminded. "But I hope you'll consider it as payment to lead us passed Ezleon's northern walls."

Barlow opened his mouth to protest, the area above his nose pinched smartly.

"We did bring it all this way to deliver it to you," Lark put in before he could speak.

Considering the bottle for a moment, and puckering out his bottom lip thoughtfully, Barlow lifted a grin to them. "I suppose you did. Very well, I'll lead the way for you. It will spit you out right at Ember River. And the payment . . ."

"We already paid," Philomena drawled, staring at the doorkeeper steadily, her jaw set in annoyance.

"Oh! Right you are! Very sorry, I'm rather forgetful half the time, most of the time really. Being alone down here I guess I don't have to remember anything, that is accept which way is which and to empty the sewage pales," Barlow babbled with a naïve grin, tapping his head with his forefinger.

Philomena gave him a disgusted look. Philip spluttered with laughter, doing his best to restrain it and hide his grin behind Philomena's shoulder.

"We're in a bit of a hurry, Barlow," Lark urged awkwardly.

"Yes, yes as you were before," Barlow sighed tiredly. He turned away and started up the tunnel, waving them along. "Follow me then," he said.

Lark and Philomena nudged their horses onward. Barlow uncorked his prized ale and took a gulp, some of it splashing on the ground. He smacked his lips and sighed with pleasure, then dug in to his grimy pouch tied at his belt.

"Anybody want a peanut?" he asked.

51

By the time Avador busted in to the stables, his prey was nowhere to be seen. A startled grey horse flinched at his violent entry and cantered free out the door. Avador made no move to catch him.

The young captain strode in to the quiet stables, his eyes roaming about and his fingers hovering over his sword hilt. After standing there for a moment, he took his time to search every nook and cranny the stables offered. He searched the loft, and peered in every stall. Coming to an empty stall where the grey stallion must have been, Avador gazed in. A minute passed and he shook himself, realizing there was nothing there but straw. He moved on down the line of stalls.

Searching for over half an hour, Avador finally came to the conclusion that the prince and princess had escaped along with their half-rogue friend. Avador stormed back to the stable door, furious beyond belief. He angrily kicked aside the broken board that had held the door shut. The horse stalled closest to the entry way bobbed his head nervously as if to ask Avador why he was so angry.

Night Hawk and Bright Sky came rushing in, their faces flushed and perturbed.

"We can't find them," Night Hawk reported reluctantly.

"That's because they're not here," said Avador crossly. Night Hawk and Bright Sky stared at him curiously.

"How could they have gotten out?" Bright Sky demanded.

"It doesn't matter how. The point is that they did," Avador snapped, annoyed by the query. "You are wasting time asking questions. Gather the others and get some provisions. We're leaving in an hour,"

Avador brushed past them and they turned to watch him go.
"What about the prisoners?" Night Hawk asked after him.
"Leave them with Lieutenant Kaiden. We travel light," said
Avador without looking back. He stormed out of the stables.

*****

The morning was already rising coolly against the sky, making
Ember River sparkle gold. The water murmured and bubbled
over a bed of smooth rocks, some dark and some light that
sparkled brilliantly with the tiniest ray of sun. A haze of smoke
was curtained over Ezleon, and the smell of burnt wood tainted
the crisp air.

Beyond the stone bridge that arched over the Ember River and in
to the beginnings of the Twin Peak Forest, Philip, Philomena and
Lark stood just in the cover of the trees. They huddled atop their
horses, hungry and exhausted from the exciting night.

Gazing back at the city they knew their enemies were stirring.
"We have to keep going before we can rest," Lark told them,
feeling utterly drained. Philomena yawned at the idea of more
traveling.

They steered their horses further in to the forest, riding side by
side. Philip was nearly asleep, sitting behind Philomena. His
eyelids drooped wearily. Philomena glanced over her shoulder at
him from time to time, looking a little worried, but she knew he
needed rest after the ordeal he had gone through.

Arican chirped and tentatively climbed in to the saddle with
Lark. She yawned and blinked in the morning light. Lark stroked
her thick, patterned fur.

"It was quite a night," Philip murmured tiredly. They looked to
him and he grinned. "I reckon I don't ever want to visit that city
again, at least not with Moth still in charge,"

"Moth is an unpleasant person," Lark agreed mildly, looking
ahead.

Philomena snorted. "Unpleasant is an understatement. If it weren't for you helping us we would have been stuck in his chambers," she said derisively. Lark shrugged lightly.

"That reminds me," said Philip, looking to his friend with curious expectation. "Why did you come back?"

Lark looked around at him and saw that Philomena was waiting for his response as well. He hesitated, unsure of how to put his thoughts in to words.

"You two . . . are the craziest people I've ever met," he finally said. They stared at him with lowered brows and perplexed frowns.

"You're resilient, you're strong, you're honest, and you could probably pound anyone in to the ground if you had to. And even though you literally kidnapped me and forced me to help you," Lark said these words with some heat, but then his voice softened as he continued. "You are the only people I can truly call friends. I knew you were in trouble, and I'm sure if you knew I was in trouble you'd come and help me," He looked to them and saw that they were smiling, even Philomena. He shrugged uncomfortably.

"I believe you. Everything you've claimed to be, I realize that it's the truth," Lark finished frankly.

"Well, I'm glad we finally won you over," said Philip, beaming. He leaned toward Philomena and whispered, "Our brain washing technique really works,"

They all laughed, feeling the bond growing stronger between them. Philomena looked to Lark, a question lingering in her mind.

"I suppose though, you want to go home now?" she asked. Lark thought he heard a twinge of reluctance in her voice, but her expression was an impassive mask. He considered her question for a moment, knowing they were watching him.

"No," he finally said, shaking his head. Philip's grin widened. "I'm not going back towards Ezleon. They're all rather angry right now, I imagine. Besides, there's no way you two could survive in this forest without me,"

"No way at all," Philip agreed, clapping Lark on the shoulder. Philomena still looked doubtful, maybe even concerned.

"But you wanted to go home, Lark. It's going to be dangerous where we're going, and it's a long journey to Caelum. Do you even realize how long of a journey this will be?" Philomena pointed out critically. Philip frowned at her and poked her upsettingly in the ribs.

"Fifteen days," said Lark. "Caelum is fifteen days away, even more depending on the weather. What you're planning on doing will take another month maybe, and that depends on the situation Salvador has brewed for us. I won't get back home till the end of spring," There was a hint of thought in his voice as the notion of not returning to his family for another three months or so sunk in.

Philip considered him now with a pang of guilt. "You can always change your mind," he said gently.

"No," said Lark, shaking his head. "I'm helping you. I'm with you both to the end,"

Philip nodded, still appearing guilty. The decision felt right to Lark though. Ending the depression would help everyone. It would restore peace and balance even if he were to lose his life trying Lark knew his purpose was to help them accomplish defeating Salvador. He shook himself out of his ponderings.

"Anyways, as someone once told me, the right thing to do is not always our choice, it's given to us so we must choose," he said, turning a remembering look to Philomena. She blushed faintly under his gaze and looked away.

They continued onward up the winding trail in to the Twin Peak. The path began to dip and rise with the rolling land. They ducked under a low growing tree.

"I can't wait to stop so we can eat. I'm starving," said Philip, rubbing his growling stomach.

"You're always hungry," Philomena told him.

"Escaping from Ezleon really took it out of me. I'm famished," Philip insisted firmly. His stomach growled some more.

"Speaking of our escape, how'd you know about that trick with the ale bottle? Have you exploded one before?" Philomena asked.

"Nah," Philip said with a dismissive gesture. "I've seen it done before when we were in Tosh. One night there were a bunch of crazy young guards down in the courtyard all drunk. They started throwing the ale in to the fire and one of them wound up tossing a sealed bottle in there. Scared themselves half to death. It was hilarious," Philip chuckled at the memory.

"But Toshinians don't drink," Lark pointed out.

"Like I said they were crazy, and they put on quite a show. Their captain was furious. He came running out in his night gown," Philip laughed, and Philomena joined in. Lark shook his head and grinned at the mental picture Philip's description had formed.

"Hey, isn't that Spear?" Philomena suddenly asked. She pointed to the right and Lark and Philip followed the line of her gaze. A bay horse was picking his way through the trees and brush. A white marking in the shape of a diamond shone brilliantly on his forehead. His head lifted and his ears perked at the sight of them. He whinnied a greeting and trotted over to join them. Lark stared in disbelief a thrill of happiness was welling inside him.

"I hope you ride bareback," said Philip, drawing Lark's attention.

"We won't run you over if you fall," Philomena assured.

Lark couldn't help but smile.

Acknowledgements

I want to first express my deepest gratitude to my parents, Gary and Theresa, who have supported and encouraged me this whole time. Thanks to God for giving me such wonderful gifts in this world and to my special guardian Angel who I know is always looking out for me. Thanks to my brother, Nathan, who is the greatest big brother a sister could ask for. Thanks to all of my family who have never given up on me. Thanks to Resa Reid and the wonderful team at Printwell for helping make my book cover possible. Thanks to all of my friends who have always believed in this story. Thank you everyone for your love and support!

The story continues!

Find out if Philip, Philomena, and Lark succeed in their
sequel:

Nature's Prince

And

The Conquest of Caelum